W9-DHH-402

Welcome to the intensely emotional world of
USA TODAY bestselling author

Margaret Way

in her thrilling new duet

The Langdon Dynasty

*A family torn apart by betrayal,
brought together by love*

In book one, follow Dev Langdon on his mission
to succeed his father as the Cattle King of Kooraki
Station and win back the heart of his childhood
sweetheart, Mel.

The Cattle King's Bride
April 2012

In book two, read Ava Langdon's story of ignited
passion and love reawakening when she meets an
exotic and dangerously sexy Argentinian rancher.

Argentinian in the Outback
May 2012

A few moments later she felt without seeing when Varo came to stand directly at her shoulder. He was greeted warmly by everyone, but it was Ava he had come for.

"I hope you realize, Ava, as I am the captain of the winning team, you owe me a dance. Several, in fact," he said, with his captivating smile.

"Of course, Varo."

She turned to him, her eyes ablaze in her face, brilliant as jewels. Inside she might feel pale with shock, but outside she was all color—the golden mane of her hair, dazzling eyes, softly blushed cheeks, lovely deep pink mouth. She was determined now to play her part, her only wish to get through the night with grace.

For all he hadn't been completely honest with her, Juan-Varo de Montalvo would never leave her memory—even when he disappeared to the other side of the world.

MARGARET WAY

Argentinian in the Outback

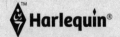

Harlequin®

TORONTO NEW YORK LONDON
AMSTERDAM PARIS SYDNEY HAMBURG
STOCKHOLM ATHENS TOKYO MILAN MADRID
PRAGUE WARSAW BUDAPEST AUCKLAND

If you purchased this book without a cover you should be aware
that this book is stolen property. It was reported as "unsold and
destroyed" to the publisher, and neither the author nor the
publisher has received any payment for this "stripped book."

ISBN-13: 978-0-373-17805-6

ARGENTINIAN IN THE OUTBACK

First North American Publication 2012

Copyright © 2012 by Harlequin Books S.A.

The publisher acknowledges the copyright holder
of the individual works as follows:

ARGENTINIAN IN THE OUTBACK
Copyright © 2012 by Margaret Way, Pty., Ltd

CATTLE RANCHER, SECRET SON
Copyright © 2008 by Margaret Way, Pty., Ltd

Recycling programs
for this product may
not exist in your area.

All rights reserved. Except for use in any review, the reproduction or
utilization of this work in whole or in part in any form by any electronic,
mechanical or other means, now known or hereafter invented, including
xerography, photocopying and recording, or in any information storage
or retrieval system, is forbidden without the written permission of the
publisher, Harlequin Enterprises Limited, 225 Duncan Mill Road,
Don Mills, Ontario, Canada M3B 3K9.

This is a work of fiction. Names, characters, places and incidents are
either the product of the author's imagination or are used fictitiously, and
any resemblance to actual persons, living or dead, business establishments,
events or locales is entirely coincidental.

This edition published by arrangement with Harlequin Books S.A.

For questions and comments about the quality of this book
please contact us at Customer_eCare@Harlequin.ca.

® and TM are trademarks of the publisher. Trademarks indicated with
® are registered in the United States Patent and Trademark Office, the
Canadian Trade Marks Office and in other countries.

www.Harlequin.com

Printed in U.S.A.

Margaret Way, a definite Leo, was born and raised in the subtropical river city of Brisbane, capital of Queensland, Australia, the Sunshine State. A conservatorium-trained pianist, teacher, accompanist and vocal coach, she found that her musical career came to an unexpected end when she took up writing—initially as a fun thing to do. She currently lives in a harborside apartment at beautiful Raby Bay, a thirty-minute drive from the state capital. She loves dining *al fresco* on her plant-filled balcony overlooking a translucent-green marina filled with all manner of pleasure craft—from motor cruisers costing millions of dollars and big, graceful yachts with carved masts standing tall against the cloudless blue sky, to little bay runabouts. No one and nothing is in a mad rush, and she finds the laid-back village atmosphere very conducive to her writing. With well over one hundred books to her credit, she still believes her best is yet to come.

Books by Margaret Way

THE CATTLE KING'S BRIDE *(The Langdon Dynasty)*
MASTER OF THE OUTBACK
IN THE AUSTRALIAN BILLIONAIRE'S ARMS
HER OUTBACK COMMANDER
AUSTRALIA'S MAVERICK MILLIONAIRE

Other titles by this author available in ebook format.

ARGENTINIAN IN THE OUTBACK

Margaret Way

CHAPTER ONE

THE French doors of her bedroom were open to the cooling breeze, so Ava was able to witness the exact moment the station Jeep bearing their Argentine guest swept through the tall wrought-iron gates that guarded the main compound. The tyres of the vehicle threw up sprays of loose gravel, the noise scattering the brilliantly coloured parrots and lorikeets that were feeding on the beautiful Orange Flame Grevilleas and the prolific White Plumed species with their masses of creamy white perfumed flowers nearby.

As she watched from the shelter of a filmy curtain the Jeep made a broad half-circle around the playing fountain before coming to a halt at the foot of the short flight of stone steps that led to Kooraki's homestead.

Juan-Varo de Montalvo had arrived.

She didn't know why, but she felt *excited*. What else but excitement was causing that flutter in her throat? It had been a long time since she had felt like that. But why had these emotions come bubbling up out of nowhere? They weren't exactly what one could call appropriate. She had nothing to get excited about. Nothing at all.

Abruptly sobered, she turned back into the room to check her appearance in the pierglass mirror. She had dressed simply: a cream silk shirt tucked into cigarette-slim beige trousers. Around her waist she had slung a wide tan leather belt that showed off her narrow waist. She had debated what to do with her hair in the heat, but at the last moment had left it long and loose, waving over her shoulders. Her blonde hair was one of her best features.

Cast adrift in the middle of her beautifully furnished bedroom, she found herself making a helpless little gesture indicative of she didn't know what. She had greeted countless visitors to Kooraki over the years. Why go into a spin now? Three successive inward breaths calmed her. She had read the helpful hint somewhere and, in need of it, formed the habit. It *did* work. Time to go downstairs now and greet their honoured guest.

Out in the hallway, lined on both sides with gilt-framed paintings, she walked so quietly towards the head of the staircase she might have been striving to steal a march on their guest. Ava could hear resonant male voices, one a little deeper, darker than the other, with a slight but fascinating accent. So they were already inside the house. She wasn't sure why she did it but, like a child, she took a quick peek— seeing while remaining unseen—over the elegant wrought-iron lace of the balustrade down into the Great Hall.

It was then she saw the man who was to turn her whole life upside down. A moment she was destined never to forget. He was in animated conversation with her brother, Dev, both of them standing directly beneath the central chandelier with all its glittering, singing crystal drops. Their body language was proof they liked and respected each other, if one accepted the theory that the distance one maintained between oneself and another said a great deal about their relationship. To Ava's mind these two were *simpatico*.

Both young men were stunningly handsome. Some inches over six feet, both were wide through the shoulders, lean-hipped, with hard-muscled thighs and long, long legs. As might be expected of top-class polo players, both possessed superb physiques. The blond young man was her brother, James Devereaux Langdon, Master of Kooraki following the death of their grandfather Gregory Langdon, cattle king and national icon; the other was his foil, his Argentine friend and wedding guest. Juan-Varo de Montalvo had flown in a scant fifteen or so minutes before, on a charter flight from Longreach, the nearest domestic terminal to the Langdon desert stronghold—a vast cattle station bordered to the west and north-west by the mighty Simpson, the world's third-largest desert.

In colouring, the two were polarised. Dev's thick hair was a gleaming blond, like her own. Both of them had the Langdon family's aquamarine eyes. De Montalvo's hair was as black and glossy as a crow's wing. He had the traditional Hispanic's lustrous dark eyes, and his skin was tanned to a polished deep bronze. He was very much a man of a different land and culture. It showed in his manner, his voice, his gesticulations—the constant movement of his hands and shoulders, even the flick of his head. Just looking down at him caused a stunning surge of heat in her chest that dived low down into her body, pretty much like swallowing a mouthful of neat whisky.

There was far too much excitement in her reaction, even if it was strictly involuntary. She was a woman who had to defend her inner fortress which she had privately named Emotional Limbo. Why not? She was a woman in the throes of acrimonious divorce proceedings with her husband Luke Selwyn who had turned nasty, even threatening.

She had long reached the conclusion that Luke was a born narcissist, with the narcissist's exaggerated sense of his own importance. This unfortunate characteristic had been fostered from birth by his doting mother, who loved him above all else. Monica Selwyn, however, had pulled away from her daughter-in-law. Ava was the woman who had taken her son from her. The pretence that she had been liked had been at times more than Ava could bear.

When she'd told Luke long months ago she was leaving him and filing for divorce he had flown into a terrible rage. She would have feared him, only she had tremendous back-up and support from just being a Langdon. Luke was no match for her brother. Why, then, had she married him? She had thought she loved him, however imperfectly. Ava knew she couldn't go on with her life without asking herself fundamental questions.

In retrospect she realised she had been Luke's trophy bride—a Langdon with all that entailed. Her leaving him, and in doing so rejecting him, had caused Luke and his establishment family tremendous loss of face. That was the truth of the matter. *Loss of face.* She hadn't broken Luke's heart, just trampled his colossal pride. But wasn't that a potentially dangerous thing for any woman to do to a vain man?

Luke would mend. She was prepared to bet her fortune on that. Whereas she now had a sad picture of herself as a psychologically damaged woman.

Maybe everyone was damaged—only it came down to a question of degree? Some would say one couldn't *be* damaged unless one allowed it, furthermore *believed* it. Unfortunately she had. She felt she was a coward in some ways: afraid of so many things. Afraid to trust. Afraid to stand her ground. Afraid to reach out. Almost afraid to move on. That hurt. For all her lauded beauty, at her core was painfully low self-esteem. Her skin was too thin. She knew it. Pain could reach her too easily.

Ava had lived most of her life feeling utterly powerless: the *granddaughter*, not the all-important *grandson* of a national icon. In her world it was *sons* who were greatly to be prized. But surely that was history? Women through the ages had been expected to make as good a marriage as possible, to honour and obey her husband and bear him children. In some privileged cases for the continuation of the family dynasty.

She didn't give a darn about dynasty. Yet she had found enough courage—perhaps courage was the wrong word and *defiance* was much better—to fly in the face of her authoritarian grandfather's wishes. He had despised Luke and warned her off him. So had Dev, who'd only had her happiness and wellbeing at heart. She had ignored both of them—to her cost—she had got it badly wrong. Proof of her poor judgement.

It would take her some time before she was able to pick herself up and walk back into mainstream life. She had so many doubts about herself and her strength. Many, many women would understand that. It was a common pattern among besieged women trying so hard to do the right thing, with their efforts totally disregarded or held in contempt by their partners. She sometimes wondered if genuine equality between the sexes would ever happen. Women were still receiving horrific treatment at the hands of men all over the world. Unbearable to think that might remain the status quo.

To be truthful—and she believed she was—she had to own up to the fact she had never been passionate about Luke, or indeed any man. Certainly not the way Amelia was passionate about Dev. That *was* love—once in a lifetime love. In Ava's eyes, one had to be incredibly blessed to find it. Ava was an heiress, but she knew better than anyone that although money could buy just about anything it couldn't buy *love*. Her marriage, she acknowledged with a sense of shame, had been an escape route from her dysfunctional family—most particularly her late grandfather.

Her grandfather's death, however, had brought about swift changes. All for the better. Dev now headed up

Langdon Enterprises, of which Kooraki, one of the nation's leading cattle stations and beef producers, was but an arm; their estranged parents were back together—something that filled her and Dev with joy; and Sarina Norton, Kooraki's housekeeper for many years and her grandfather's not-so-secret mistress, had taken herself off to enjoy *la dolce vita* in Italy, the country of her birth.

And last but not least Sarina's daughter—the long-suffering Amelia—was putting the seal on her life-long unbreakable bond with Dev by getting married to him. Ava had long thought of Dev and Amelia as twin stars, circling a celestial field, never far apart. Now at last they were coming together, after delaying the wedding for some months as a mark of respect for Gregory Langdon's passing.

She now had the honour and privilege of being Amelia's chief bridesmaid—one of three. Together the lives of Dev and Amelia had gained their ultimate purpose. They would have children—beautiful children. Mel was strong. Ava had always been stunned by Mel's strength. Beside Mel she was very conscious of her own frailty. Despite the fact that all her own hopes had vanished like a morning mist she couldn't be happier for them. Dev was gaining a beautiful, clever wife who would be a great asset to the family business enterprises, her parents were gaining a daughter-in-law, and she was gaining the sister she had longed for.

Triumphs all round for the Langdon family. The past had to make way for a bright future. There had to be a meaning, a purpose, a *truth* to life. So far it seemed to Ava she had struggled through her existence. How she longed to take wing! She had suffered through the bad times—surely things could only get better?

From her vantage point it was plain to see their visitor projected the somewhat to be feared "dominant male" aura. Man controlled the world. Man was the rightful inheritor of the earth. In a lucid flash of insight she realised she didn't much like men. Her grandfather had been a terrifying man. But at the end of the day what did all that power and money matter? Both were false idols. Strangely, the dominant-male image didn't bother her in her adored brother. Dev had *heart*. But it put her on her guard against men like Juan-Varo de Montalvo. He looked every inch of his six-three—the quintessential macho male. It surrounded him like a force field. Such men were dangerous to emotionally fragile women wishing to lead a quiet life. In her case, she came with baggage too heavy to handle.

De Montalvo, she had learned from Dev, was the only son and heir of one of the richest land-owners in Argentina—Vicente de Montalvo. His mother was the American heiress Caroline Bradfield, who had eloped with Vicente at the age of eighteen against her parents' violently expressed disapproval. Not that Vicente had been all that much older—twenty-three.

The story had made quite a splash at the time. They must have been passionately in love and remained so, Ava thought with approval and a touch of envy. They were still together. And Dev had told her the bitter family feuding was mercifully long over.

Why wouldn't it be? Who would reject a grandson like Juan-Varo de Montalvo, who made an instant formidable impact. He had the kind of features romance novelists invariably labelled "chiselled". That provoked a faint smile—but, really, what other word could one use? He was wearing a casual outfit, much like Dev. Jeans, blue-and-white open-necked cotton shirt, sleeves rolled up, high polished boots. Yet he still managed to look…the word *patrician* sprang to mind. That high-mettled demeanour was inbred—a certain arrogance handed down through generations of a *hidalgo* family.

Dev had told her the Varo side of the family had its own coat of arms, and de Montalvo's bearing *was* very much that of the prideful Old World aristocrat. His stance was quite different from Dev's New World elegant-but-relaxed posture, Dev's self-assured nonchalance. Only as de Montalvo began moving around the Great Hall with striking suppleness a picture abruptly flashed into her mind. It was of a jaguar on the prowl. Didn't jaguars roam the Argentinian *pampas*? She wasn't exactly sure, but she would check it out. The man was dazzlingly exotic. He spoke perfect English. Why *wouldn't* he speak perfect English? He had an American mother. He would be a highly educated man, a cultured world-traveller.

High time now for her to go downstairs to greet him. She put a welcoming smile on her face. Dev would be expecting it.

The wedding was in a fortnight's time. The bride-to-be, Amelia, was still in Sydney, where she was finishing off work for her merchant bank. Dev was planning on flying there to collect her and their parents and some other Devereaux guests. That meant Ava would be playing hostess to Juan-Varo de Montalvo for a short time.

The season was shaping up to be absolutely brilliant for the great day: the sky was so glorious a blue she often had the fancy she was being drawn up into its density. Despite that, they were all praying the Channel Country wouldn't be hit by one of its spectacular electrical storms that blew up out of nowhere and yet for the most part brought not a drop of rain. For once rain wasn't needed after Queensland's Great Flood—a natural disaster that had had a silver lining. After long, long punishing years of drought, the Outback was now in splendid, near unprecedented condition.

Kooraki was a place of extraordinary wild beauty, with every waterhole, creek, billabong and lagoon brimming with life-giving water that brought an influx of waterbirds in their tens of thousands. So the station was in prime condition—the perfect site for the marriage between her brother and her dear friend Amelia.

Guests were coming from all over the country, and Juan-Varo de Montalvo was, in fact, the first overseas visitor to arrive. In his honour Dev had arranged a polo match and a post-polo party for the coming weekend. Invitations had gone out, generating huge interest. Most Outback communities, with their love of horses, were polo-mad. De Montalvo would captain one team, Dev the other. The two men had forged their friendship on the polo field. Dev had even visited the de Montalvo *estancia*—a huge ranch that ran Black Angus cattle, located not all that far from the town of Córdoba. So here were two polo-playing cattlemen who had every reason to relate to each other.

How Juan-Varo de Montalvo would relate to *her* was an entirely different matter. As she moved, her heart picked up a beat a second. Sometimes the purely physical got the better of the mind. She consoled herself with that thought.

Both men looked up as Ava began her descent of the curving staircase, one slender hand trailing over the gleaming mahogany banister. Ava, herself, had the oddest sensation she was walking on air. Her blood was racing. She felt in no way comfortable, let alone possessed of her usual poise. How could feelings run so far ahead of the rational mind?

"Ah, here's Ava," Dev announced with brotherly pride.

Dev's eyes were on his sister and not on Juan-Varo de Montalvo, whose dark regard was also fixed on the very fair young woman who was making her way so gracefully to them. He had known in advance she was beautiful. Dev had boasted many times that he had a beautiful sister. But the reality far exceeded his expectations. He was used to beautiful women. He was a man who loved women, having grown up surrounded by them—doting grandmothers, aunts, female cousins. He adored his mother. He had three beautiful sisters—one older, very happily married with a small son, his godchild, and two younger, with legions of admirers—but something about this young woman sent a jolt of electricity shafting through his body.

He could see beneath the grace, the serene air and the poise that she was oddly *vulnerable*. The vulnerability seemed inexplicable in a woman who looked like an angel and had grown up as she had, with every material advantage. Dev had told him about her failed marriage. Maybe she saw it as a humiliation? A fall from grace? Maybe she was guilty of heedlessly breaking a heart—or worse, inflicting deliberate pain? He had been brought up to frown on divorce. He had lived with two people—his mother and father—who had made a wonderful life together and lived side by side in great harmony.

She had to tilt her head to look up at him. There was a curiously *sad* look in her jewel-like eyes, the same dazzling aquamarine as her brother's. She had flawless skin, with the luminescence of a pearl. Few women could claim a face so incandescent.

It was in all probability a symptom of jet lag, but he felt a distinct low-pitched hum in his ears. Her smile, lovely and effortlessly alluring, seemed to conceal secrets. He had a certainty it was she who had ended her marriage. A cruel thing for an angel to do. One would expect such coldness only of a young and imperious goddess, who would only be loved for as long as it suited her.

Ava released a caught breath. "Welcome to Kooraki, Señor de Montalvo," she said with a welcome return of her practised poise. Heat was coming off the Argentine's aura. It was enveloping her. "It's a pleasure to have you here." It was necessary to go through the social graces even when she was *en garde* and taking great pains not to show it.

"Varo, please," he returned, taking her outstretched hand. His grip was gentle enough not to crush her slender fingers, but firm enough not to let her escape. "It's a great pleasure to be here. I thought it impossible you could be as beautiful as Dev has often described, but now I find you are even more so."

She felt the wave of colour rise to her cheeks but quickly recovered, giving him a slightly ironic look, as though judging and rejecting the sincerity of his words. "Please—you mustn't pander to my vanity," she returned lightly. She couldn't remember the last time a man had caused her to flush. She didn't like the enigmatic half-smile playing around his handsome mouth either. The expression in his dark eyes with their fringe of coal-black lashes was fathoms deep. She was angry with herself for even noticing.

"I had no such thought," he responded suavely, somehow establishing his male authority.

"Then, thank you."

There was strength behind his light grip on her. As a conductor for transmitting energy, his touch put her into such a charged state it caused an unprecedented flare of sexual hostility. It was as though he was taking something from her that she didn't want to give.

The warning voice in her head struck up again. *You have to protect yourself from this man, Ava. He could burn down all your defences.*

That she already knew.

"I find myself fascinated with Kooraki," de Montalvo was saying, including Dev in his flashing white smile. "It is much like one's own private kingdom. The Outback setting is quite extraordinary."

"From colonial times every man of ambition and means came to regard his homestead as the equivalent of the Englishman's country manor," Dev told him. "Most of the historic homesteads were built on memories of home—which was in the main the British Isles."

"Whereas our style of architecture was naturally influenced by Spain."

Dev turned his head to his sister. "As I told you, Estancia de Villaflores, Varo's home, is a superb example."

"We have much to be proud of, don't we?" de Montalvo said, with some gravitas.

"Much to be grateful for."

"Indeed we do." Brother and sister spoke as one.

Ava was finding de Montalvo's sonorous voice, with its deep dark register, making her feel weak at the knees. She was susceptible to voices. Voice and physical aura were undeniably sensual. Here was a man's man, who at the same time was very much a *woman's* man.

He was dangerous, all right.

Get ensnared at your peril.

They exchanged a few more pleasant remarks before Dev said, "I'm sure you'd like to be shown your room, Varo. That was a very long trip, getting here. Ava will show you upstairs. I hope you like what we've prepared for you. After lunch we'll take the Jeep for a quick tour of the outbuildings and a look at some of the herd. An overview, if you like. We have roughly half a million acres, so we'll be staying fairly close in for today."

"I'm looking forward to it," de Montalvo returned, with a sincere enthusiasm that made brother and sister feel flattered.

"Your luggage is already in your room, Varo," Ava told him, aware she was struggling with the man's magnetism. "One of the staff will have brought it up by now, taking the back entrance." Although de Montalvo had travelled a very long way indeed, he showed no signs whatever of fatigue or the usual jet lag. In fact he exuded a blazing energy.

"So no one is wasting time?" De Montalvo took a small step nearer Ava. An inch or two above average height, Ava felt strangely doll-like. "Please lead on, Ava," he invited. "I am all attention."

That made Dev laugh. "I have a few things to attend to, Varo," he called as his sister and his guest moved towards the grand staircase. "I'll see you at lunch."

"Hasta luego!" De Montalvo waved an elegant hand.

Ava had imagined that as she ascended the staircase she would marshal her defences. Now, only moments later, those defences were imploding around her. She had the sense that her life had speeded up, entered the fast lane. She had met many high-powered people in her life—none more so than her grandfather, who hadn't possessed a shining aura. Neither did Montalvo. It was dark-sided, too complex. It wasn't any comfort to realise she had been shocked out of her safe haven. Worse yet to think she might be shorn of protection.

How could any man do that in a split second? The impact had been as swift and precise as a bolt of lightning. Maybe it was because she wasn't used to exotic men? Nor the way he looked at her—as if he issued an outright challenge to her womanhood. Man, that great force of nature, totally irresistible if he so chose.

The thought angered her. Perhaps it was borne of her sexual timidity? Luke had early on in their marriage formed the habit of calling her frigid. She now had an acute fear that if she weren't very careful she might rise to de Montalvo's lure. He was no Luke. He was an entirely different species. Yet in some bizarre way he seemed familiar to her. Only he was a stranger—a stranger well aware of his own power.

As he walked beside her, with his tantalising lithe grace, glowing sparks might have been shooting off his powerful lean body. Certainly *something* was making her feel hot beneath her light clothing. She who had been told countless times she always appeared as cool as a lily. That wasn't the case now. She felt almost *wild*, when she'd had no intention let alone any experience of being any such thing. To her extreme consternation her entire body had become a mass of leaping responses. If those responses broke the surface it would be the ultimate humiliation.

His guest suite was in the right wing. It had been made ready by the household staff. Up until their grandfather's death the post of housekeeper had been held by Sarina Norton, Amelia's mother. Sarina had been most handsomely rewarded by Gregory Langdon for "services rendered". No one wanted to go there…

The door lay open. Varo waved a gallant arm, indicating she should enter first. Ava had the unsettling feeling she had to hold on to something. Maybe the back of a chair? The magnetic pull he had on her was so strong. How on earth was she going to cope when Dev flew off to Sydney? She was astonished at how challenging she found the prospect. What woman reared to a life of privilege couldn't handle entertaining a guest? She was a woman who had not only been married but was in the process of divorce—she being the one who had initiated the action. Didn't that qualify her as a woman of the world?

Or perhaps one could interpret it as the action of a woman who didn't hesitate to inflict pain and injury? Perhaps de Montalvo had already decided against her? His family of Spanish origin was probably Roman Catholic, but divorce couldn't be as big a no-no now as it had been in the time of Katherine of Aragon, Henry VIII's deposed, albeit lawfully wedded, wife. Not that taking Katherine's place had done Anne Boleyn much good.

Ava put the tension that was coiling tighter and tighter inside her down to an attack of nerves. It was all so unreal.

The guest room that had been chosen for de Montalvo was a grand room—and not only in terms of space and the high scrolled ceilings that were a feature of Kooraki's homestead. The headboard of the king-sized bed, the bed skirt and the big cushions were in a metallic grey silk, with pristine white bed-coverings and pillows. Above the bed hung a large gold-framed landscape by a renowned English-Australian colonial artist. Mahogany chests to each side of the bed held lamps covered in a parchment silk the same colour as the walls. A nineteenth century English secretary, cabinet and comfortable chair held pride of place in one corner of the room. The rest of the space was taken up by a gilded Louis XVI-style sofa covered in black velvet with a matching ottoman. All in all, a great place to stay, with the added plus of a deep walk-in wardrobe and an *en suite* bathroom.

He said something in Spanish that seemed to make sense to her even though she didn't know the language. Quite obviously he was pleased. She did have passable French. She was better with Italian, and she even had some Japanese—although, she acknowledged ruefully, keeping up with languages made it necessary to speak them every day. She even knew a little Greek from a fairly long stint in Athens the year after leaving university.

De Montalvo turned back from surveying the landscaped garden. "I'll be most happy and comfortable here, Ava," he assured her. "I'm sure this will be a trip never to be forgotten."

She almost burst out that she felt the same. Of course she did not. She meant to keep her feelings to herself. "I'll leave you in peace, then, Varo," she said. "Come downstairs whenever you like. Lunch will be served at one. Dev will be back by then."

"Gracias," he said.

Those brilliant dark eyes were looking at her again. Looking *at* her. *Through* her. She turned slowly for the door, saying over a graceful shoulder, *"Nuestra casa es su casa."*

His laugh was low in his throat. "You make a fine attempt. Your accent is good. I hope to teach you many more Spanish phrases before I leave."

Ava dared to face him. "Excellent," she said, her tone a cool parry.

CHAPTER TWO

THEY set out after breakfast the next day, the horses picking their way through knee-high grasses with little indigo-blue wildflowers swimming across the waving green expanses. Dev had flown to Sydney at first light, leaving them alone except for the household staff. She would have de Montalvo's company for a full day and a night and several hours of the following day before Dev, Amelia and co were due to fly back. So, all in all, around thirty hours for her to struggle against de Montalvo's powerful sexual aura.

For someone of her age, marital status and background Ava was beginning to feel as though she had been wandering through life with her eyes closed. Now they were open and almost frighteningly perceptive. Everyone had the experience of meeting someone in life who raised the hackles or had an abrasive effect. Their Argentine visitor exerted a force of quite another order. He had *roped* her, in cattleman's terms—or she had that illusion.

Dinner the previous evening had gone off very well. In fact it had been a beautiful little welcoming party. They'd eaten in the informal dining room, which was far more suitable and intimate than the grand formal dining room only used for special occasions. She'd had the table set with fine china, sterling silver flatware, and exquisite Bohemian crystal glasses taken from one the of numerous cabinets holding such treasures. From the garden she had picked a spray of exquisite yellow orchids, their blooms no bigger than paper daisies, and arranged them to take central pride of place. Two tall Georgian silver candlesticks had thrown a flattering light, finding their reflection in the crystal glasses.

The menu she'd chosen had been simple but delicious: white asparagus in hollandaise, a fish course, the superb barramundi instead of the usual beef, accompanied by the fine wines Dev had had brought up from the handsomely stocked cellar. Dessert had been a light and lovely passion-fruit trifle. She hadn't gone for overkill.

Both Dev and his guest were great *raconteurs*, very well travelled, very well read, and shared similar interests. Even dreams. She hadn't sat back like a wallflower either. Contrary to her fluttery feelings as she had been dressing—she had gone to a surprising amount of trouble—she had found it remarkably easy to keep her end up, becoming more fluent by the moment. Her own stories had flowed, with Dev's encouragement.

At best Luke had wanted her to sit quietly and look beautiful—his sole requirements of her outside the bedroom. He had never wanted her to shine. De Montalvo, stunning man that he was, with all his eloquent little foreign gestures, had sat back studying her with that sexy half-smile hovering around his handsome mouth. Admiring—or mocking in the manner of a man who was seeing exactly what he had expected to see? A blonde young woman in a long silk-jersey dress the exact colour of her eyes, aquamarine earrings swinging from her ears, glittering in the candlelight.

She was already a little afraid of de Montalvo's half-smile. Yet by the end of the evening she had felt they spoke the same language. It couldn't have been a stranger sensation.

Above them a flight of the budgerigar endemic to Outback Australia zoomed overhead, leaving an impressive trail of emerald and sulphur yellow like a V-shaped bolt of silk. De Montalvo studied the indigenous little birds with great interest. "Amazing how they make that formation," he said, tipping his head back to follow the squadron's approach into the trees on the far side of the chain of billabongs. "It's like an aeronautical display. I know Australia has long been known as the Land of the Parrot. Already I see why. Those beautiful parrots in the gardens—the smaller ones—are lorikeets, flashing colour. And the noisy ones with the pearly-grey backs and the rose-pink heads and underparts—what are they?"

"Galahs." Ava smiled. "It's the aboriginal name for the bird. It's also a name for a silly, dim-witted person. You'll hear it a lot around the stockyards, especially in relation to the jackeroos. Some, although they're very keen, aren't cut out for the life. They're given a trial period, and then, if they can't find a place in the cattle world, they go back home to find alternative work. Even so they regard the experience as the adventure of a lifetime."

"I understand that," he said, straightening his head. "Who wouldn't enjoy such freedom? Such vast open spaces virtually uninhabited by man? Our *gauchos* want only that life. It's a hard life, but the compensations are immense. Kooraki is a world away from my home in Argentina," he mused, studying Ava as though the sight of her gave him great pleasure. "There is that same flatness of the landscape. Quechua Indians named our flatness *pampa*—much like your vast plains. But at home we do not know such extreme isolation at this. There are roads fanning out everywhere from the *estancia*, and the grounds surrounding the house—designed many decades ago and established by one of our finest landscape designers—are more like a huge botanical garden. Here it is pure *wilderness*. Beautiful in the sense of not ever having been conquered by man. The colours are indescribable. Fiery red earth, all those desert ochres mixed in beneath dazzling blue skies. Tell me, is the silvery blue shimmer the mirage that is dancing before our eyes?"

"It is," Ava confirmed. "The mirage brought many an early explorer to his grave. To go in search of an inland sea of prehistory and find only great parallel waves of red sand! It was tragic. They even took little boats like dinghies along."

"So your Kooraki has a certain mysticism to it not only associated with its antiquity?"

"We think so." There was pride in her voice. "It's the oldest continent on earth after all." Ava shifted her long heavy blonde plait off her nape. It was damp from the heat and the exertion of a fantastically liberating gallop with a splendid horseman who had let her win—if only just. "You do know we don't call our cattle stations *ranches*, like Americans? We've kept with the British *station*. Our stations are the biggest in the world. Anna Creek in the Northern Territory spreads over six million acres."

"So we're talking thirty thousand square kilometres plus?" he calculated swiftly.

"Thirty-four thousand, if we're going to be precise. Alexandria Station, also in the Territory, is slightly smaller. Victoria Downs Station used to be *huge*."

He smiled at the comparatives. "The biggest ranches in the U.S. are around the three thousand square kilometres mark, so you're talking ten times that size. Argentine *estancias* are nowhere in that league either. Although earlier in the year a million-acre *estancia* in north-west Argentina was on sale, with enormous potential for agriculture—even eco-power possibilities. Argentina—our beautiful cosmopolitan capital Buenos Aires—was built on *beef*, as Australia's

fortunes were built on the sheep's back—isn't that so?" He
cast her a long glance.

"I can't argue with that. Langdon Enterprises own both
cattle and sheep stations. Two of our sheep stations produce
the finest quality merino wool, mainly for the Japanese market. Did Dev tell you that?"

"I believe he did. Dev now has a great many responsibilities following your grandfather's death?"

"He has indeed," she agreed gravely, "but he's up to it.
He was born to it."

It was her turn to study the finely chiselled profile de
Montalvo presented to her. He wasn't wearing the Outback's
ubiquitous akubra, but the startlingly sexy headgear of the
Argentine *gaucho*: black, flat-topped, with a broad stiff
brim that cast his elegant features into shadow. To be so
aware of him sexually was one heck of a thing, but she
strove to maintain a serene dignity, at the same time avoiding too many of those brilliant, assessing glances.

"Your father was not in the mould of a cattleman?" he
asked gently.

Ava looked away over the shimmering terrain that
had miraculously turned into an oasis in the Land of the
Spinifex. The wake of the Queensland Great Flood had
swept right across the Channel Country and into the very
Red Centre of the continent.

"That jumped a generation to Dev. He was groomed from
boyhood for the top. There was always great pressure on
him, but he could handle it. Handle my grandfather as well.
The rest of us weren't so fortunate. My father is much happier now that he has handed over the reins. My grandfather,
Gregory Langdon, was a man who could terrify people. He
was very hard on all of us. Dad never did go along with or
indeed fit into the crown-prince thing, but he was a very

dutiful son and pleasing his father was desperately important to him."

"And you?"

Ava tilted her chin an inch or so. "How can I say this? I'm
chiefly remembered for defying my grandfather to marry
my husband. Neither my grandfather nor Dev approved of
him. It soon appeared they were right. You probably know
I'm separated from my husband, in the process of getting
a divorce?"

Varo turned his handsome head sideways to look at her.
Even in the great flood of light her pearly skin was flawless. "I'm sorry." Was he? He only knew he definitely didn't
want her to be married.

"Don't be," she responded, more curtly than she'd intended. He would probably think her callous in the extreme.

He glimpsed the flash of anger in her remarkable eyes.
Obviously she longed to be free of this husband she surely
once had loved. What had gone so badly wrong?

"I too tried very hard to please my grandfather," she
offered in a more restrained tone. "I never did succeed—
but then my grandfather had the ingrained idea that women
are of inferior status."

"Surely not!" He thought how his mother and sisters
would react to that idea.

"I'm afraid so. He often said so—and he *meant* it. Women
have no real business sense, much less the ability to be
effective in the so-called 'real' world. Read for that a *man's*
world—although a cattle kingdom *is* a man's world it's so
tough. Women are best served by devoting their time to
making a good marriage—which translates into landing a
good catch. Certainly a good deal of time, effort and money
went into me."

"This has led to bitterness?" He had read much about
the ruthless autocratic patriarch Gregory Langdon.

Ava judged the sincerity of his question. She was aware he was watching her closely. "Do I seem bitter to you?" She turned her sparkling gaze on him.

"Bitter, no. Unhappy, yes."

"Ah…a clarification?" she mocked.

"You deny it?" He made one of his little gestures. "Your husband is not putting up a fight to keep you?" Such a woman came along once in a lifetime, he thought. For good or bad.

Ava didn't answer. They had turned onto a well-trodden track that led along miles of billabongs, creeks and water-holes that had now become deep lagoons surrounded on all sides by wide sandy beaches. The blaze of sunlight worked magic on the waters, turning them into jewel colours. Some glittered a dark emerald, others an amazing sapphire-blue, taking colour from the cloudless sky, and a few glinted pure silver through the framework of the trees.

"One tends to become unhappy when dealing with a divorce," Ava answered after a while. "My marriage is over. I will not return to it, no matter what. Dev at least has found great happiness." She shifted the conversation from her. "He and Amelia are twin souls. You'll like Amelia. She's very beautiful and very clever. She holds down quite a high-flying job at one of our leading merchant banks. She'll be a great asset to Langdon Enterprises. Mercifully my grand-father didn't pass on his mindset to Dev."

"Dev is a man of today. He will be familiar with very successful women. But what do *you* plan to do with your-self after your divorce comes through?"

She could have cried out with frustration. Instead she spoke with disconcerting coolness. "You are really inter-ested?"

"Of course." His tone easily surpassed hers for hauteur. She knew she had to answer on the spot. Their eyes were locked. Neither one of them seemed willing to break contact. They could have been on some collision course. "Well, I don't know as yet, Varo," she said. "I might be unequal to the huge task Dev has taken on, but I want to contribute in any way I can."

"Then of course you will." A pause. "You will marry again."

It wasn't a question but a statement. "That's a given, is it? You see it as my only possible course?" she challenged.

He reached out a long arm and gently touched her delicate shoulder, leaving a searing sense of heat. It was as though his hand had touched her bare skin.

"Permit me to say you are very much on the defensive, Ava. You know perfectly well I do not." The sonorous voice had hardened slightly. "Dev will surely offer you a place on the board of your family company?"

"If I want a place, yes," she acknowledged.

He gave her another long, dark probing look. "So you are not really the businesswoman?"

She shook her head. "I have to admit it, no. But I have a sizeable chunk of equity in Langdon Enterprises. Eventually I will take my place."

"You should. There would be something terribly wrong if you didn't. You want children?"

She answered that question with one of her own. "Do you?"

He gave her his fascinating, enigmatic half-smile. "Marriage first, then children. The correct sequence."

"Used to be," she pointed out with more than a touch of irony. "Times have changed, Varo."

"Not in *my* family," he said, with emphasis. "I do what is expected of me, but I make my own choices."

"You have a certain woman in mind?"

It would be remarkable if he didn't. She had the certainty

this dynamic man had a dozen dazzling women vying for his attention.

"Not at the moment, no," he told her with nonchalance. "I enjoy the company of women. I would never be without women in my life."

"But no one as yet to arouse passion?" She was amazed she had even asked the question, and aware she was moving into dangerous territory.

Her enquiring look appeared to him both innocent and seductive at one and the same time. Did she know it? This wasn't your usual *femme fatale*. There was something about her that made a man want to protect her. Possibly that was a big mistake. One her husband had made?

"I don't think I said that," he countered after a moment. "Who knows? I may have already succumbed to *your* undoubted charms, Ava."

She raised a white hand to wave a winged insect away—or perhaps to dismiss his remark as utterly frivolous. "It would do you no good, Varo. I'm still a married woman. And I suspect you might be something of a legend back in Argentina."

"Perdón—perdonare!" he exclaimed. "Surely you mean as a *polo player*?" He pinned her gaze.

Both of them knew she had meant as a *lover*. "I'm looking forward to seeing you in action at the weekend." She declined to answer, feeling hot colour in her cheeks. "It should be a thrilling match. We're all polo-mad out here."

"As at home. Polo is the most exciting game in the world."

"And possibly the most dangerous," she tacked on. "Dev has taken a few spectacular spills in his time."

He answered with an elegant shrug of one shoulder. "As have I. That is part of it. You are an accomplished rider," he commented, his eyes on her slender body, sitting so straight but easy in the saddle. Such slenderness lent her a deceptive fragility, contradicted by the firmness with which she handled her spirited bright chestnut mare.

"I should be." Ava's smile became strained as memories flooded in. "My grandfather threw me up on a horse when I was just a little kid—around four. I remember my mother was beside herself with fright. She thought I would be hurt. He took no notice of her. Mercifully I took to riding like a duck to water. A saving grace in the eyes of my grandfather. As a woman, all that was expected of me was to look good and produce more heirs for the continuation of the Devereaux-Langdon dynasty. At least I was judged capable of expanding the numbers, if not the fortune. A man does that. I expect in his own way so does Dev. Every man wants a son to succeed him, and a daughter to love and cherish, to make him proud. I suppose you know my grandfather left me a fortune? I don't have to spend one day working if I choose not to."

"Why work at anything when one can spend a lifetime having a good time?" he asked on a satirical note.

"Something like that. Only I *need* to contribute."

"I'm sure you shall. You need time to re-set your course in life. All things are possible if one has a firm belief in oneself. Belief in oneself sets us free."

"It's easier to dream about being free than to accomplish it," she said, watching two blue cranes, the Australian brolgas, getting set to land on the sandy banks of one of the lagoons.

"You thought perhaps marriage would set you free?" he shot back.

"I'm wondering if you want my life story, Varo?" Her eyes sparkled brightly, as if tears weren't all that far away.

"Not if you're in no hurry to tell me," he returned gently, then broke off, his head set in a listening position. "You hear that?"

They reined in their horses. "Yes." Her ears too were registering the sound of pounding hooves.

Her mare began to skip and dance beneath her. In the way of horses, the mare was scenting some kind of danger. De Montalvo quietened his big bay gelding with a few words in Spanish which the gelding appeared to understand, because it ceased its skittering. Both riders were now holding still, their eyes trained on the open savannah that fanned out for miles behind them.

In the next moment they had their answer. Runaway horse and hapless rider, partially obscured by the desert oaks dotted here and there, suddenly burst into full view.

De Montalvo broke the fraught silence. "He's in trouble," he said tersely.

"It's a workhorse." Ava recognised that fact immediately, although she couldn't identify the rider. He was crouched well down over his horse's back, clinging desperately to the flowing black mane. Feet were out of the stirrups; the reins were flailing about uselessly. "It's most likely one of our jackeroos," she told him with anxiety.

"And he's heading right for that belt of trees," De Montalvo's expression was grim. "If he can't pull up he's finished. *Terminado!*" He pulled the big bay's head around as he spoke.

The area that lay dead ahead of the station hand's mad gallop was heavily wooded, dense with clumps of ironwood, flowering whitewoods and coolabahs that stood like sentinels guarding the billabong Ava knew was behind them. The petrified rider was in deep trouble, but hanging on for dear life. He would either be flung off in a tumble of broken bones or stay on the horse's back, only to steer at speed into thick overhanging branches. This surely meant a broken neck.

"Stay here," de Montalvo commanded.

It was an order, but oddly she didn't feel jarred by it. There was too much urgency in the situation.

She sat the mare obediently while de Montalvo urged the powerful bay gelding into a gallop. Nothing Zephyr liked better than to gallop, Ava thought with a sense of relief. Nothing Zephr liked better than to catch and then overtake another horse. That was the thoroughbred in him.

The unfortunate man had long since lost his hat. Now Ava recognised the red hair. It was that Bluey lad—a jackeroo. She couldn't remember his surname. But it was painfully clear he was no horseman. One could only wonder what had spooked his horse. A sand goanna, quite harmless but capable of giving a nervous horse a fright? Goannas liked to pick their mark too, racing alongside horse and rider as though making an attempt to climb the horse's sleek sides. A few cracks of the whip would have settled the matter, frightening the reptile off. But now the young jackeroo was heading full pelt for disaster.

Ava held up a hand to shield her eyes from the blazing sun. Little stick figures thrown up by the mirage had joined the chase, their legs running through the heated air. She felt incredibly apprehensive. Señor de Montalvo was their guest. He was a magnificent rider, but what he was attempting held potential danger for him if he persisted with the wild chase. If he were injured… If he were injured… She found herself praying without moving her dry lips.

Varo had been obliged to come at the other horse from an oblique angle. She watched in some awe as he began to close in on the tearaway station horse that most likely had started life as a wild brumby. Even in a panic the workhorse couldn't match the gelding for speed. Now the two were racing neck and neck. The finish line could only be the wall of trees—which could prove to be as deadly as a concrete jungle.

Ava's breath caught in her throat. She saw Varo lean side-ways out of his saddle, one hand gripping his reins and the pommel, the other lunging out and down for the runaway's reins. A contest quickly developed. Ava felt terribly shaken, not knowing what to expect. She found herself gripping her own horse's sides and crying out, "Whoa, boy, whoa!" even though she was far from the action. She could see Varo's powerful gelding abruptly change its long stride. He reined back extremely hard while the gelding's gleaming muscles bunched beneath its rider. Both horses were acting now in a very similar fashion. Only a splendid horseman had taken charge of them, bringing them under tight control.

The mad flight had slowed to a leg-jarring stop. Red dust flew in a circling cloud, earth mixed up with pulped grasses and wildflowers. "Thank God!" Ava breathed. She felt bad enough. Bluey was probably dying of fright. What of Varo? What an introduction to their world!

The headlong flight was over. She had a feeling Bluey wasn't going to hold on to his job. She was sure she had heard of another occasion when Bluey had acted less than sensibly. At least he was all right. That was the important thing. There had been a few tragic stories on Kooraki. None more memorable than the death in a stampede of Mike Norton, Sarina Norton's husband but not, as it was later revealed, Amelia's actual father. Sarina Norton was one beautiful but malevolent woman, loyal to no one outside herself.

Ava headed off towards the two riders who had sought the shade to dismount. Her mare's flying hooves disturbed a group of kangaroos dozing under one of the big river gums. They began to bound along with her.

It was an odd couple she found. Bluey, hardly more than a madcap boy, was shivering and shaking, white as a sheet beneath the orange mantling of freckles on his face. Varo showed no sign whatsoever of the recent drama, except for a slick of sweat across his high cheekbones and the tousling of his thick coal-black hair. Even now she had to blink at the powerful magnetism of his aura.

He came forward as she dismounted, holding the mare's reins. They exchanged a measured, silent look. "All's well that ends well, as the saying goes." He used his expressive voice to droll effect. Far from being angry in any way, he was remarkably cool, as though stopping runaway horses and riders was a lesson he had learned long ago.

Ava was not cool. He was their guest. "What in blue blazes was *that* exhibition all about?" she demanded of the hapless jackeroo. She watched in evident amazement as the jackeroo attempted a grin.

"I reckon I oughta stick to motorbikes."

"I've seen you before, haven't I?" Ava asked with a frown.

"Yes, miss." The jackeroo sketched a wobbly bow. "I'm Bluey. This gentleman here did a great job of saving me life. I'd have broken a leg, for sure."

"You'd have broken a great deal more than that," Varo pointed out, this time making no attempt to hide the note of reproof.

"It was a mongrel goanna." Bluey made a wild gesture with his skinny arms. "About six feet long."

"Nonsense!" Ava shook her head. "It was probably a sand goanna, half that size. You must have alarmed it."

"Well, it rushed me anyway," Bluey mumbled, implying anyone would have reacted the same way. "Sprang up from under a tree. I thought it was a damned log, beggin' your pardon."

"Some log!" It was all Ava could do not to tell Bluey off. "You could have frightened it off with a few flicks of the whip."

"Couldn't think fast enough," Bluey confessed, looking incredibly hot and dirty.

The expression on Juan-Varo de Montalvo's handsome face conveyed what he thought of the jackeroo's explanation. "You're all right to mount your horse again?" he addressed the boy with clipped authority in his voice.

"Poor old Elvis." Bluey shook his copper head. "The black mane, yah know? I thought his heart would burst."

"The black mane?" Varo's expression lightened. He even laughed. "I see."

Ava was finding it difficult to keep her eyes off him. He looked immensely strong and capable, unfazed by near disaster. His polished skin glowed. The lock of hair that had fallen forward onto his tanned forehead gave him a very dashing, rakish look. He wore his hair fairly long, so it curled above the collar of his shirt. She tried not to think how incredibly sexy he was. She needed no such distraction.

As they paused in the shade small birds that had been hidden in the safety of the tall grasses burst into the air, rising only a few feet before the predatory hawks made their lightning dives. Panicked birds were caught up, others managed to plummet back into the thick grass. This was part of nature. As a girl Ava had always called out to the small birds, in an effort to save them from the marauding hawks, but it had been an exercise in futility.

"What were you doing on your own anyway, Bluey? You should have been with the men."

Bluey tensed. "Headin' for the Six Mile," he said evasively. "You're not gunna tell the boss, are you?" he asked, as though they shared a fearful secret.

Varo glanced at Ava, who was clearly upset, her eyes sparkling. He decided to intervene. "Get back on your horse. I assume the red hair justifies the nickname! We'll ride with you to the house. You'll need something for those skinned hands."

"A wash up wouldn't hurt either," Ava managed after a moment. "Think you'll be more alert next time a goanna makes a run for your horse?"

"I'll practise a lot with me whip," Bluey promised, some colour coming back into his blanched cheeks. "I hope I didn't spoil your day?"

"Spoil our day?" Ava's voice rose. "It would have been horrible if anything had happened, Bluey. Thank God Varo was with me. I doubt *I* could have caught you, let alone have the strength to bring the horses under control."

"Sorry, miss," Bluey responded, though he didn't look all that troubled. "I could never learn to ride like *you*." Bluey looked to the man who had saved him from certain injury or worse.

"You can say that again!" Ava responded with sarcasm.

"Thanks a lot, mate." Bluey leaked earnest admiration from every pore.

Varo made a dismissive gesture. "M-a-t-e!" He drew the word out on his tongue.

"Well, that's *one* version of it." Ava had to smile. Did the man have any idea what a fascinating instrument his voice was? "Well, come on, Bluey," she said, giving the jackeroo a sharp look. "Get back up on your horse."

Bluey shook himself to attention. "Dunno who got the bigger fright—me or Elvis." He produced a daft grin.

As they rode back to the homestead Ava couldn't help wondering if Bluey would ever make it as a station hand. His derring-do could prove a danger to others. From fright and alarm he had gone now to questioning his hero about life on the Argentine pampas, confiding that everyone— "I mean everyone!"—would be turning up to see him play polo at the weekend. "You got one helluva lot of strength inside you," Bluey told the South American visitor with great admiration.

"Just as well. It was a titanic struggle," Ava said, resisting the impulse to call Bluey the derogatory *galah*. "Common sense goes a long way. If I find you've used up eight lives…?" She paused significantly.

"Please don't tell the boss, miss," Bluey begged. "One more sin and he'll kick me out."

"And there goes your big adventure." Ava shrugged, thinking admonition might well fall on deaf ears. "It could be later than you think, Bluey. Now, let's get you cleaned up."

CHAPTER THREE

WHEN they arrived back at the homestead, Varo sent the jackeroo off to the first-aid room.

"Let me have a word with this young man." He inclined his head towards Ava.

"You think you can talk some sense into him?" she asked sceptically. "I remember now—he once put Amelia in danger with one of his ill-conceived stunts."

"I think I can make him see sense," he answered with quiet authority. "He knows there's a strong possibility he will be sent home if Dev hears about this."

"Maybe we should tell Dev?" she suggested with utter seriousness. "In rescuing Bluey you put yourself at considerable risk."

"One doesn't think of that at such a time." He dismissed the risk factor, looking deeply into her eyes.

"All right," she consented, trying not to appear flustered. "I'll see to lunch. This afternoon I thought I might show you the hill country. It's not all low-rise on Kooraki. The hills reach a fair height. A good climb, anyway—and there's so much to see. Aboriginal rock paintings. And there really *was* an inland sea—but we're talking pre-history. There are drawings of crocodiles on the rock walls. X-ray depictions of fish. We even have a waterfall of sorts at the moment. It plunges downhill into the rock pool beneath it. Not even a trickle in the Dry, of course."

She knew the rock pool would be a great place for a dip. The waters were fairly deep, and crystal-clear, but Juan-Varo de Montalvo made her feel far too aware of herself as a woman to risk donning a bathing suit.

"We will ride there?" he asked, already filled with fascination for the fabled Outback.

She shook her blonde head. "We'll take the Jeep. I'll even let you drive." She gave him a quick smile which he thought as alluring as any water nymph. "There's no wrong side of the road."

"Gracias, Señora," His black eyes glittered as he acknowledged her marital status.

It was quite a job to keep her expression composed. Infatuation was the last thing she had seen coming.

From the passenger window Ava eyed the Wetlands, home to thousands upon thousands of waterbirds. The vast expanse of water had joined up with the lignum swamps to the extent one didn't know where the lignum swamps ended and the Wetlands started up.

"In times of drought this great expanse of water will dry up," she told Varo, who drove like he did everything else. With absolute skill and confidence. "The parched surface becomes crisscrossed by cracks and the footprints of the wildlife—kangaroos, emus, camels, wild pigs, snakes, or any human walking across the dry ochre sand."

"Camels I *have* to see," he said, giving her a quick sidelong smile.

"You will," she promised. "The Afghan traders brought them in the early days. 1840, to be precise. They thrived here. We even export them to Arab countries. They're part of the landscape now, but they can be very destructive. Not as much as hoofed animals, however. Their feet are adapted for deserts. They have soft pads, but they eat everything in sight, depleting the food supply for our indigenous species. They're very dangerous too, when the male goes on heat."

"The *male?*" One black eyebrow shot up.

"Bizarre, but true. At the last count there were over a million feral camels scattered over the desert areas of the Territory, Western Australian, South Australia and Queensland's desert fringe. The introduced water buffalo of the Territory do tremendous damage to the environment and the ecosystem. Even our dingoes were introduced."

"But I thought they were native Australian animals?" He glanced back at her. She had taken her beautiful hair out of its plait. Now it was sliding over her shoulders and down her back in shining, deep sensuous waves. She had changed for lunch, as had he. Now she was wearing a blue T-shirt with a silver designer logo on the front. The clingy fabric drew his eyes to the delicate shape of her high breasts.

"They've been here for thousands of years," she was saying, snapping him back to attention, "but they came from South East Asia originally, where they must have been domestic dogs. Over the four or five thousand years they've been here, they've established themselves in the wilds. They're our number-one predator. They can attack, even kill—especially if the victim is small, like a child."

"One doesn't like to think of that," he said gravely. "What about sheep? Mature cattle would be able to fend them off, surely?" He was frowning slightly.

"Not the calves. The alpha male is especially dangerous. So is the alpha female. They hunt in packs. We don't have the Great Wall of China, but we do have the longest man-made fence in the world."

He was quick to reply. "I have heard of the famous Dingo Fence."

"We'll take you to see Kooraki's section of it before you go home," she offered.

Even thinking of his departure gave her a distinct wrench. That only added to her sense of unreality. Who could expect to be so susceptible in such a very short time? She had to be aware her sense of trepidation was spiced with undeniable excitement. She only hoped he wasn't witness to it.

"The Dingo Fence is close to six thousand kilometres long," she carried on, her tone rather clipped. "It was shortened from well over eight thousand kilometres in 1980 because of the high repair costs. Six feet of wire mesh with steel and timber posts. It's a never-ending job maintaining it, but it protects over twenty-six million hectares of sheep and cattle grazing country. You're in trouble big-time if you forget to shut a gate."

"Who would know out here?" He waved a hand at the empty miles that ran for as far as the eye could see.

"You'd be surprised. Everyone keeps an eye out. Everyone knows if there are tourists or strangers in the area. Cattle-and-sheep men would never be guilty of such an offence."

He could see the jagged shape of the hills off to the northwest, their broken peaks and domes silhouetted against the cobalt-blue sky. The furnace-red of the earth made a wonderful contrast to the cloudless blue sky and the amazingly green trees and vegetation. The most beautiful tree he had seen along their route Ava had told him was the Outback's iconic Ghost Gum. It was easy to understand why. The tall upright tree with pendulous dark green leaves had a smooth, near blindingly white trunk and branches that made it glow in the sunlight. Even the distant hills were changing colour from brown to an orange that deepened into the red of the earth.

"You can stop here," Ava said as they arrived near the foot of a tumbling white waterfall.

Once out of the Jeep they could hear the loud murmur of the waters and their splash into the circular pool. A surprising amount of water was falling into it.

Varo moved closer, looking down into the depths. The silvered mirror-like surface threw back his own reflection. That too of the beautiful blonde Ava, who stood at his shoulder like an ethereal vision.

"It's so hot. A swim would be most welcome." He turned to her, the movement of his wide shoulders causing a flutter of air to cross the pool and form ripples.

"Bathing suits optional?" The coolness of her voice was intended not to give her inner turmoil away.

"You don't think it the duty of a good hostess to—"

"Varo, I know you're teasing," she protested, looking up into his brilliant mocking eyes.

"Even if you're really tempted?" He seemed to be towering over her. "The water is crystal-clear." He bent to dip a hand into it. "And so refreshingly cool."

"Varo, I'm getting a little nervous around you," Ava murmured.

He straightened. "You are *very* safe with me."

"I know that," she said hurriedly. "You also know what I mean. If you want a swim we have many lagoons. Dev, Amelia and I spend countless hours swimming in our favourite lagoon, the Half-Moon. The most gorgeous water lilies on the station grow there—the sacred blue lotus. They decorate the perimeter, along with all the water reeds. The lagoon is very deep in the middle. One day you can swim there. Maybe have a picnic."

"With you?" He fixed his dark eyes on her.

"Maybe," she said, half turning away.

"Maravillosa!" He had an instant vision of her, naked

as a water nymph, her long golden hair cascading over her shoulders, her beautiful skin with the lustre of a pearl.

Ava, for her part, was glad of her gift for composure—even if it was being giving an almighty workout. She pointed upwards, a pulse beating in her throat. "There's a big cave up there that goes so far back into the hills I used to be terrified I would get lost if I ventured too far. See, Varo?" She glanced at him, only to find him looking at her. "It's the one partially camouflaged by those feathery sprays of acacia. You'll have to duck your head at the entrance, but the interior at the central point is over two metres high."

"The roof has never caved in on anyone?" he asked, beginning to stare upwards.

Ava gave a little shudder. "Never. But I didn't dare to venture into the cave's recesses like Dev. Even Mel was scared. We have a famous mystery novel called *Picnic at Hanging Rock,* written by Joan Lindsay. It was made into a film way back in the 1970s. It tells the story of the disappearance of several schoolgirls and their teacher during a picnic at Hanging Rock on St Valentine's Day. The book is in our library at home. I've read and re-read it. It's a haunting tale. The missing party was never found."

"You think you will disappear as well?" he asked in teasing fashion.

"Wait until you're inside the cave," she replied, her composure regained.

"You think I'll get cold feet?"

"Laugh all you like." She gave him a sparkling look that was like a brief taunt. "I've known visitors to our great desert monuments, the aboriginal sacred sites Uluru and Kata Tjuta, come away stunned by the atmosphere. Why, some find the Valley of the Winds at Kata Tjuta very scary—especially when the winds are blowing. It's another world."

"One I intend to visit." He put out his elegant tanned hand. "Let me help you."

His wonderfully expressive voice sounded so tender her heart shook. She had no recourse but to put her hand in his, feeling his long fingers close around hers. She had known from the start nothing was going to be *normal* with this man. The suppressed excitement, the assault on her senses was way out of her experience. She had not dreamed of anything like this.

Together they climbed. A rock wallaby, startled by the approach of two figures, bounded back down the steep slope, making short work of reaching the bottom. Once when Ava's foothold slipped Vero gathered her close, wrapping one arm around her. She gave an involuntary little cry. She knew it wasn't fright. It was something far more dangerous that had her catching her breath.

At that height the rumbling of the waterfall was much louder. Big splashes fell over them—not enough to soak on such a hot day, but having a wonderful effect. Ava found herself taking droplets of cold water into her dry mouth. She wondered if this was how Amelia felt with Dev. There was a palpable ache inside her. It was sexual.

Gradually the footholds became narrower, but she turned her feet sideways just as she had done as a child. Varo might have been an experienced rock climber for all the trouble *he* was having. For all she knew he might have made an attempt on Mount Everest at one time. His own majestic Andes were close by his *estancia*, with a splendour rivalling the Himalayas.

In a final burst they reached the top, both of them turning to stare down at the infinite plains that spread out to the horizon. Not a single cloud broke up the dazzling peacock-blue of the sky.

"This is magic!" Varo exclaimed. "Superb!"

He still kept an arm around her. Maybe he had forgotten?

"And there's much more to see." She broke contact, restless and madly energetic. She might have caught fire from him. "Keep your head down until I tell you to lift it," she warned, preparing to enter the cave first.

In their shared childhood she, Dev and Amelia had always brought torches so they could explore inside. On a fairly recent climb she and Dev had left a lantern behind. When lit, it threw a very satisfactory light over the interior.

Varo reached out to pull away the curtain of vines that wreathed the neck of the cave.

"It's dark inside," she said over her shoulder. "Don't forget to keep your head down."

He nodded. He had no need to be told. In actual fact he had kept right behind her, to catch her should she slip on all the loose pebbles as fine as gravel.

Then the plunge into the tunnel!

It wasn't as dark as he'd expected. Although no ray of blazing sunshine pierced the cave, it still managed to cast a luminescence. He was able to judge the moment to stand erect. He saw her kneeling on the ground near one wall of the great tunnel, then there was suddenly light. Golden light that lit the cave and danced over the sandstone walls.

Varo stood mesmerised, his eyes tracking the images of the primitive art gallery. Even Ava, who had been inside the cave many times, stood rapt. More than anything she wanted their guest to be stirred and fascinated by what he saw. Varo moved closer to inspect one smooth, clean wall of the great cavern. It was dominated by a highly stylised drawing of a great serpent—a python—executed in chalky white with dark bands encircling the body and a black neck and head. The powerful reptile wound its sinuous body around two sides of the cave, its head high on the rock ceiling.

Evidently the great serpent was an important, even sacred creature from the aboriginal Dreamtime. Human figures with white circled eyes were represented only in stick-like form. The female forms with pendulous breasts. There were animals—kangaroos, emus—trees, and flocks of birds radiating over the walls, but what was most incredible, just as Ava had told him, was an outstanding drawing of a *crocodile*. It was surrounded by what could only be tropical palms. Fish too were represented, and what appeared to be turtles. Human handprints acted like a giant frame.

He turned back to Ava, who was watching his expression and trying to gauge his reaction. "This has to be a significant site!" he exclaimed. "Quite extraordinary."

"It is," she confirmed, "but very few people get to see it. It's not a sacred site, but it has to be protected. That's *our* job."

"Then I'm honoured. Thank you for bringing me here." He resumed his tour of the gallery, taking his time. As he walked he talked about the Inca civilisation of Peru, and the culture that had been shattered by the cruel and bloody Spanish Conquest. "Ancient temples and tombs were pillaged by the Conquisadors. Gold and silver booty to enrich the coffers of the Spanish Crown. In return Catholicism was forced on them."

"Your family is Catholic?"

He shrugged without answering.

"I've often wanted to visit South America," she said. "Especially since Dev came home filled with the marvels of your world. You were the one who took him to Machu Picchu?"

"Ah, yes—the secret cloud-shrouded ceremonial city of ancient Peru. That vast empire included the north-west of Argentina. Machu Picchu is one of the must-see places one should visit before one dies, Ava. Anyway, when you come to Argentina it will be my privilege to show you all we can offer." He turned suddenly, bending his dark head so he could whisper softly in her ear. "I'll even teach you how to dance the tango."

"Of which you are a master?" She felt the flush rise to her face.

"Of course."

It was so quiet inside the cave it was almost as though they were in some ancient cathedral, cut off from the rest of the world.

Varo was looking at the tunnel that led off the main cavern and went as far as anyone knew back deep into the eroded hills. It appeared as if he were debating whether it was wise to explore it.

"*No,* Varo!" she found herself exclaiming. "No one has ever mapped any of the passageways. No one even knows if there are exits. You're not Indiana Jones."

He turned back. The brilliant dark glance that swept over her was amused. "Maybe not. But I have been in some very scary places—including the South Pole. You're frightened I might want to explore in there?"

"I'm frightened I might lose you," she said.

"That won't ever happen."

It was said so gently, yet Ava thought she would remember his expression for as long as she lived. "We *must* go," she implored. "Back into the sunlight."

"We've only just arrived. You realise this would probably lead to a whole cave system?"

"The hill country is honeycombed with them," she admitted. "But even Dev backed off after he had gone a good distance. In some places there's only crawling space. I have to tell you I'm a bit claustrophobic." She wrapped her arms around herself as though she were cold.

He remained quite still, not making any move towards

her. "There's no reason to be frightened, Ava," he assured her, his voice pitched low.

"I'm not frightened. I'm more *worried*."

He gave her a slight and dangerous smile. "That you'll find yourself lost?" Now he made a move towards her, extending his hand to lift her face to him. "You fight the attraction?"

It was so strangely quiet she could hear her blood whooshing through her veins. "What attraction?" Unnerved, she tried to deny the obvious.

"*Our* attraction," he said. "You think it inevitable I might want to kiss you?"

"Don't, Varo," she whispered, shaking her head. This man could mesmerise her.

"One moment in time," he coaxed. "It occurs to me you are suffering in some way."

"I've had years of it." She hadn't intended to say it, but she had.

"Then you need a new start."

Just like that.

The note in his voice sent her head spinning. She felt herself sway towards him even before he gathered her into his arms in a way no man had gathered her to him before. She couldn't move away. She didn't want to move away. Why she was allowing this she didn't want to understand. She should feel daunted. Their instant connection was near incomprehensible. Yet every last little thing about him was proving an intoxicant. Even the cool air inside the cave was aromatic with the scents of the wild bush.

"I love that mouth of yours," he muttered, his handsome head poised over hers. "A man might only dream of kissing it." He touched her lower lip with the pad of one finger, effectively opening up her mouth to him.

That ignited such a response inside her she feared her

heart might stop. She was desperate for this, but all the while she felt deeply perturbed. From here on she was in his power. Yet she didn't push away, or ask him to stop. She knew he would if she did. Only right at that moment she knew this was what she wanted. She *had* to have it before she let go.

He was kissing her, tasting her, cupping her face with strong but exquisitely gentle hands. He kissed her not once but over and over, each time more fully, more deeply. A thousand brilliant stars were bursting behind her closed eyelids. Her hands had come up to clutch at his shirt, bunching it, her long nails maybe even hurting him if they pierced the fine cotton. This was longing, *desire*, on a grand scale, and the sensation was worth anything. She was far, far more vulnerable than she could ever have imagined. A near stranger had taken her captive when her husband had never succeeded in even pushing her to a climax.

He didn't stop. Perhaps he couldn't. If so, neither could she. She was utterly bewitched. He would have already identified that. He understood the power of the flesh would be too great. Ava felt as though her bones were dissolving, her flesh melting, yet the delta of her body felt oddly *heavy*. One of his hands was hard at her arched back. The other swept over her breast. Her nipples were standing erect with the height of arousal that was in her. His every action, so masterful, demolished all coherent thought. She felt in another moment they would sink onto their knees before falling back on the sand. Neither of them stopping. Neither of them prepared to try.

You've got to fight out of this delirium.

Her inner voice was crying out to her, desperate for her to listen. This could turn out to be a bitter, very traumatic mistake.

Make yourself care. No matter what you feel, this could come back to haunt you.

Her eyes flew open, coming slowly into focus, though she still felt bound to him.

For an instant Varo felt profoundly disorientated. Then he realised it was her soft moan that had forced him back to reality, back to control. He hadn't been able to get enough of her. The pressure on him had been unrelenting. Never in his life had he wanted a woman more. Locked in his arms, she'd seemed to him to be the very image of man's one great desire. But it was all so very complicated. This beautiful woman was still married—however unhappily. She was the much loved sister of his friend. He was a guest on Kooraki.

He told himself all this as he fought down the tumult inside him. Without thinking he raised a hand to brush her tumbling cascade of golden hair away from her face and over her shoulders. "There's no point in denying attraction, Ava," he said quietly. "Your life is complicated at the moment, but I can't think kissing you was a mistake."

"A woman is to be enjoyed?" she asked, brittle-voiced. Her tone was far sharper and more cynical than she'd intended.

There was a hush before he answered. "Do not demean the moment, Ava. Come, let's go back into the light."

She caught his arm as he started to turn away. "Forgive me, Varo. I didn't mean that the way it came out. I'd given up feeling—" She broke off.

"Did you love your husband at all?" He stared down into her eyes.

"If you had asked me back then I would have claimed I did."

"But he loved you? He continues to love you?"

The air around them seemed to be trembling. "Leave it there, Varo," she advised. "You know nothing about it."

His dark, handsome features tautened. "I know you want an escape."

"What else should I do?" she burst out with too much emotion. "Come on, tell me. Stay in a loveless marriage?"

"On *your* side," he pointed out.

"So judgemental?" Now there was an immeasurable distance between them. She might have known. "With your strict moral code I'm shocked you resorted to kissing me. Me—a married woman!"

He shrugged a wide shoulder. "Maybe I've been possessed, enchanted, bewitched…whatever. Temptation clings to you like a diaphanous veil. You're a very beautiful woman, Ava. Surely there have been other men in your life?"

"Irrelevant!" she said, with a downward chop of her hand. "Let's think of this as a summer storm. Over as quickly as it began."

Except it wasn't over. They both knew that.

CHAPTER FOUR

Ava spent a sleepless night. Never for a moment could she get Juan-Varo de Montalvo out of her mind. He might have been sleeping alongside her, so palpable was his aura. The power he had over her had arisen on its own. She hadn't invited it. Her conscience was clear on that point. Neither had she planned it.

It was some comfort to realise he too had surrendered to the massive force that had reached out for them and held them fast. The electrical charge that flowed between them was mutual. What had happened—and really were stolen kisses so illicit?—had caught him up too. He had not persisted when he heard her involuntary little moans. He had swiftly drawn back, only to brush back the wild mane of hair that had tumbled all around her face, with golden skeins clinging to the skin of his face and his neck.

But, *oh!* She had never known a kiss could make one's heart rise like a lark. It had been so unbelievable to take wing. She thought she would always be able to recall that weightless feeling, the shooting stars behind her eyes. Why hadn't Luke kissed her like that?

He didn't know how. He simply wasn't capable.

Yet she had been faithful to him. She wasn't the sort of woman who indulged in meaningless flings. Until now. If one could call rapturous kisses infidelity. For the first time all thoughts of Luke blurred. It was the past. Luke would move on.

Or so she believed.

Dev flew in around noon, with his bride-to-be Amelia and their parents, Erik and Elizabeth, for so long estranged, now back together again, and looking happy and wonderfully fit after a trip to beautiful Tasmania. There were three other passengers, all Devereaux relatives, including her cousin Karen.

Karen's parents were supremely self-assured people, partners in a blue chip law firm, and Karen too was a very confident, good-looking young woman, but remarkably exacting—almost driven, to Ava's mind. Two years older than Ava, she had always adopted a patronising attitude towards her younger Langdon cousin. There was plenty of money in the family. Like her, Karen had no need to work, but Karen was in fact a successful interior designer of the minimalist style. Whenever she stayed at Kooraki she had a habit of mooching around the handsomely decorated rooms—so many collectors in the family—as though she'd like to clear the lot out and start again.

Surely that would be like obliterating the past? In any case Kooraki was the Langdon stronghold. She remembered her grandfather referring to Karen as "that very unpleasant girl."

Thank God for Amelia, Ava thought as she hugged her. Amelia was a kindred spirit—the sister she'd never had and now would.

Karen locked on to Juan-Varo de Montalvo the instant her startled dark eyes fell on him. If expressions were anything to go on their Argentine guest had come as an enormous surprise. Indeed, her mouth fell half open as if in shock. Ava even thought she heard a gasp.

How fantastic was this!

They were all assembled in the Great Hall, with Dev making introductions.

Varo had no difficulty in recognising what qualities his friend Dev saw in his bride-to-be. Not only was Amelia beautiful in the Italianate fashion—large, lustrous dark eyes, lovely olive skin and wonderful thick dark hair—her manner would always draw people to her. As far as he was concerned she suited Dev perfectly. The Devereaux relatives, however, were quite different from the warm and friendly Langdons. They acted as though they owned the earth, their manner, to Varo's mind, almost ridiculously regal. Same with the daughter, Karen.

She was much too thin for her height, but graceful, with a long elegant neck, good bones, long almond-shaped brown eyes, and glossy dark hair cut in a bob with a deep fringe to draw attention to her unusual eyes. She was dressed from head to toe in black. Skin-tight black jeans, black T-shirt with a white logo, black high-heeled boots. She stood staring at him with such intensity she might have been testing to see if he were real.

All three Devereauxes, he thought, were surprisingly *arrogant*. He had to use that word—but on the basis of what? Having money and a position in society appeared to be an end in itself. Dev, his beautiful Amelia and of course Ava displayed no such characteristic, and they were the ones with the *real* money and a fantastic ancestral home.

Ava had the job of escorting her relatives upstairs. Her mother and father headed off to their old suite of rooms. Natalie Devereaux nodded her approval of the guest room with its adjoining *en suite* bathroom. Mercifully it would do. Karen stalked ahead to her room, just down the hallway, turning on Ava the minute they were inside the door.

"Why on earth didn't you tell me that man was going to be here?" she demanded, her brown gaze snapping so sharply it could drill holes.

Ava took her time to answer. "That man?" she queried gently.

"De Montalvo," Karen said with a frown. "Oh, for God's sake, Ava, don't play silly games. He's *gorgeous*!"

"Much too *masculine* for gorgeous, don't you think?"

Karen ignored her cousin as though her opinions were of little importance. "I've never seen such a stunning-looking man. And that voice! God, it nearly melted my bones. He is no doubt rich?" She shot Ava another piercing look. "Any Argentine of that class means rich."

"Varo's *parents* are rich," Ava offered mildly. She didn't add that Varo's mother was an American heiress.

"How long has he been here?" Karen continued her interrogation in an accusatory voice.

"Why do you ask?" Ava took a moment to push a beautifully scented pale apricot rose further into its copper bowl. Pal Joey, she recognised.

"Well, you will have been *alone* here, wouldn't you? With Dev in Sydney?" Karen opened her narrow eyes wide.

Ava's smile was amused. "I promise you, Karen, we didn't indulge in wild sex."

"As though you could!" said Karen, and threw her a pitying look. "You still have that virginal look, Ava. You must know that. How's the divorce going, by the way?"

Ava allowed herself a sigh. Karen never had been a sympathetic person. In fact Karen had given her rather a bad time of it when they were both at boarding school. It was Amelia who had always come to her rescue—like a protective big sister.

"Luke has been...*difficult*," she confessed. She didn't

mention the threatening letters and e-mails. "He believes it's my clear duty to go back to him."

"Well, he's a lovely man!" Karen said, on a wave of disapproval.

That hurt. Was Karen deliberately trying to hurt her? "What would you know about it?" Ava countered. "All he ever did was butter you up." The more over the top the compliment, the more Karen had swallowed it.

"He never *did*!" Karen protested, clearly outraged.

"The compliments were so thick you could eat them," Ava said. It suddenly struck her that Karen would have made a far more suitable bride for Luke than ever she had. "Maybe it's better if we don't talk about Luke."

"Especially as he's not here to defend himself," Karen huffed. "No, let's talk about Juan-Varo de Montalvo." Karen took a seat on the antique chest at the end of the four-poster bed. "He's not married? If he were his wife would have been invited."

"Of course. No, he's not married—but I would think he has legions of adoring admirers."

"South American women *are* very beautiful," Karen said, nibbling hard on her lower lip. "Where have you got him?" She fastened her eyes on her cousin.

"Got him?" Ava was rather enjoying acting dumb.

Karen shook her head so vigorously her thick fringe lifted off her smooth forehead. "Okay, you're having a little joke. Which one of the guest rooms is his?"

"You plan to drop in on him?" Ava lifted a delicate brow.

Karen leaned back on her hands. "No need. Are you sure *you* know what you're doing, cousin?"

"Meaning?" Ava's tone took on a surprising briskness.

"Maybe you should take care?" Karen cautioned. "Luke wouldn't like to hear you were alone in Kooraki with the sexiest man on earth."

"Is this a way of threatening me?" Ava held herself very still. "You plan to tell him?" Her years of tolerating Karen appeared abruptly over.

Karen must have grasped that fact—if not in its entirety. "Don't get me wrong, Ava. I've tried to keep a cousinly eye on you all our lives. I'm a real softie that way."

"What a pity I never realised that," Ava said, making a decision to leave before Karen upset her further. That was her style. "I'll leave you to unpack. Lunch at one."

Karen rose languidly to her feet, her legs as long and thin as a crane's. "When is he leaving?" she called.

Ava turned about. "Whenever he wants. He's most welcome to stay. He's our guest, Karen. He's come a long way."

Karen wasn't finished with her questions. "But after the wedding?" She moved abruptly towards Ava. "After Dev leaves on his honeymoon?"

"Dev won't be going on his own," Ava reminded her, not holding back on the sarcasm.

Karen scowled. "Does she *know* how lucky she is to get him—what with that mother of hers?"

Her cousin was on dangerous ground. "I'm astonished you haven't got the message, Karen," Ava said. "Dev is madly in love with Amelia. He's loved her since childhood. If I were you I wouldn't bring up the subject of Sarina Norton. In a very short time Amelia will be mistress of Kooraki."

"Never liked Amelia," Karen muttered.

"I well remember. She always did get the better of you. So heed my warning. Amelia and her mother are off limits."

Karen, a confident horsewoman, threw up her hands as though to quieten a fractious horse. "Yo, cousin!" she cried. "Yo! We're *family*. Surely we can have a private chat?"

"Certainly. Only you must remember Amelia is family too. I'm absolutely delighted to have her as a sister."

Karen quickly mustered some common sense. "She'll make a beautiful bride," she admitted, trying not to show her long-standing jealousy of the luscious Amelia. "I can see that. I'd let you see my own outfit, only it's going to be a big surprise. I had thought Amelia would ask me to be one of her bridesmaids. I mean we *did* go to school together."

Sometimes the clever Karen could be remarkably obtuse. "Be glad you were invited," Ava said, waggling her fingers. "See you soon."

"Can't wait for the polo match!" Karen called, a lift in her voice. "I have another outfit planned."

"Bet it cost plenty." Karen hardly wore the same outfit twice.

"Around a thousand bucks," she answered casually.

Ava closed the door after her. So Karen was going to spend her time trying to capture Varo's attention? At least she was a free agent, and she could be charming when she chose to be.

There was no reason to think Varo wouldn't respond. What she and Varo had shared had been a kind of enchantment—a surrender to an overpowering sexual desire. There were different words for it. Love was a long, long way from that.

The days flew, with everyone in high good spirits. Karen seemed to be laughing from dawn to dusk, changing several times a day, and all the while skipping around with Dev and Varo, as enthusiastic as a teenager, accompanying them on all their tours of the station. Or as many times as Dev allowed, being well aware where his cousin's interests lay.

"She's got it bad!" Amelia breathed softly in Ava's ear as Karen hurried out through the front door to join the men.

"She told me she thinks Varo is as magnificent as a black panther." Amelia paused a moment. "Actually, he *is*." She pulled a comical face. "A paragon of masculinity!"

They both laughed.

"It seems to me that if his eye is anywhere it's on *you*, Ava," Amelia continued shrewdly.

"Varo enjoys women," Ava said, glad her long hair was partially obscuring her expression. "Anyway I can't look at anyone—even someone who puts Karen in mind of a black panther—until my divorce is final."

"I wouldn't be *too* scrupulous," Amelia advised. "Luke doesn't deserve it."

"I know. He wants me back."

"Of course he does!" Amelia exclaimed, no admirer of Ava's weak, excessively vain husband. "You're a prize. He's stupid enough to think once he has you back again he can continue to control you."

"That's not going to happen." Ava sounded very firm. "It's just taking a while for it to sink in."

"He contacted me, you know," Amelia confessed after a considered moment.

"What? Just recently?" Ava struggled not to show her anger.

"Before we came away. He's a desperate man. We spotted him at a reception. He says he loves you. He adores you. If this divorce goes through it will destroy him."

"What did you say?"

"Exactly what you'd expect. I told him it was over. Dev and I think he was one lousy husband. Not worthy of you. It's his colossal pride that's hurt, Ava."

"No one knows that better than I," Ava murmured, checking a pang of regret for what might have been. "Let's go for a swim," she suggested.

"Good idea!" Amelia swiftly agreed. She stood up, glowing with health and energy. A woman on the eve of marrying her one true love. "Half-Moon?"

Karen usually spent time in the homestead's swimming pool, doing endless laps up and down. No matter how thin she was Karen thought she could be thinner. It was impossible to change her mindset.

"Half-Moon it is."

In the heat they took one of the station vehicles to the lagoon, where the silvery-blue heatwaves were throwing up their fascinating illusions. They might have been lost in the mirage.

Amelia parked at the top of the slope leading down to their favourite lagoon. She was wearing a black nylon-Spandex one-piece that fitted her beautiful body with its hourglass curves like a glove. Ava had chosen one of the four bikinis she kept in her closet. Spandex top and bottom, its colours were a mix of ocean hues—cobalt, emerald and aquamarine.

They raced across the sand, leaving their things in a heap and moving to the water's edge. As always the perimeter was decorated with exquisite blue lotus lilies.

Amelia turned with a smile. "All right, let's get it over!" she challenged.

Both knew the water would offer a shock of cold in the golden heat of the day. With a cheer Amelia waded into the shallows that quickly fell away to the deep, but Ava, always fleet of foot, beat her into a dive. It sent up glittering arcs of spray that fell back into the lagoon. Ava was actually the better swimmer of the two, but built for speed not stamina.

After their invigorating swim they padded back up onto the pale ochre sand, patting themselves dry before spreading out their towels. They had moved back so all their faces and bodies received of the sunshine was a dappled light through the overhang of trees. Amelia, with her olive skin, tanned easily, but she wasn't after a tan for her wedding day. And Ava had always had to protect her "lily-white" skin. As Amelia's chief bridesmaid she wanted to look her best.

As they lay there, eyes closed, they discussed all aspects of the big day. Dev and Amelia were to honeymoon in some of the great cities of the world—London, Paris, Rome— before jetting off to the U.S.A. New York first, then San Francisco, before returning home. Two months in all. It wasn't either one's first time in any of those cities, but this time they would be together as man and wife.

"It will be so *exciting*!" Amelia breathed, suddenly pulling herself up to lean on one elbow and looking back over her shoulder. "Looks like we're having visitors."

Her beautiful face was vivid with delight. Amelia and Dev were every inch and for all time passionate about each other.

Ava sat up very quickly her heart giving a rhythmic jolt as she turned her head in the same direction.

"Look—it's Dev and Varo." Amelia sprang, laughing, to her feet. She looked gloriously happy. "Karen too." A dryness entered her tone.

Ava, however, was pierced by embarrassment. Always comfortable in a swimsuit—she was very slender without being bone-thin like Karen—she suddenly felt a strange panic that Varo's eyes would be on her. She didn't want that. She wanted to keep calm. She knew she was being foolish, but there it was. She could hardly reach for the sarong she had draped around her hips. That would be too obvious a cover-up. Instead she waved a hand as Amelia moved to greet the new arrivals.

She stood up, paused a moment, then headed back into the water as if wanting to cool off on this steamy hot day. Maybe they would be gone before she emerged? She knew she was acting like an overly shy and modest schoolgirl, but she felt incredibly self-aware around Varo. She was actually shivering a little in reaction. She had so little experience of the powerfully sexual. Luke had never been a turn-on, she fully realised.

When she came up, blinking the lagoon water out of her eyes and off her lashes, she saw with a kind of dismay the party of riders were stripping off, obviously intent on cooling off in the crystal-clear water.

"Oh, my God!" Her breath whistled between her teeth. They were coming in.

Dev and Varo had stripped to dark-coloured swimming briefs. Karen had exposed her ultra-thin body in a postbox-red one-piece with a halter neck. She stood at the water's edge, squealing at the cold as she put a toe in. She didn't even bend to splash her face. No preliminaries to accustom herself to the cold water. Both men charged past her like young gods, diving in unison into the water. Amelia was still at the water's edge, perhaps saying a few coaxing words to Karen, who now had her long arms criss-crossed over her body. Ava began to wonder if her cousin would come in at all.

There was a flat rock platform on the other side of the lagoon. It overhung the emerald-green waters by two or three feet. As children they had often used it as a diving board. She, Dev and Amelia had often sat there to sunbake and be alone. Now she struck out for the platform, proposing to sit there for a short time while the others took their refreshing dip. Dev always had pressing things to do. She would wait it out.

Amelia had joined Dev now, continuing the little rituals of childhood, diving under the water and chasing after each other like a pair of dolphins. Karen had evidently decided the water was too cold for her liking. She had retreated to the shade of the trees, keeping a keen eye on them all. Especially Varo.

He was a born athlete. Ava *knew* he was going to swim over to her. She knew for sure.

He did, his teeth flashing white in his handsome dark face, his skin pearled with drops of water.

"So, I always suspected you were half-mermaid," he mocked. "All you need is a circlet of sparkling crystals and emeralds around your blonde head. You need nothing else. Not even the covering of a swimsuit, however brief." With one lithe movement he hauled himself onto the platform. A trained gymnast couldn't have done it better. "You took one look at me and swam away," he accused her. "You should have been swimming *towards* me, don't you think?"

Now his lustrous dark eyes settled on her, touching every part of her body: Her long wet hair, drying out in the warm air, over one shoulder and down her back, her face, her throat, her breasts, taut midriff, slender legs. All was exposed to his eyes.

"Ava," he said, very gently.

She managed a soft reply. "Yes?"

"Nothing. I'm just saying your name."

She loved the way he said it. Unlike anyone else. There was that tension again. The high, humming *thrum* of sexual energy. He had a superb body, evenly tanned, no betraying untanned skin below his waist above the line of his black swimming trunks. The sun had hit everywhere. He was bronze all over. Totally unselfconscious. Unlike her.

"It is very clear to me, Ava, that you are avoiding me." There was a glinting sardonic look in the depths of his dark eyes.

He shocked her by leaning over to brush her bare shoulder with his mouth, licking up the few remaining sparkling droplets and taking them into his mouth.

"Varo!" She tried to move, her little cry blending with the call of a bird.

"You fear someone is watching?" he asked. "Dev and his beautiful Amelia are totally engrossed in each other, as it should be. It is only your cousin who has the binoculars trained on us."

"Surely not?"

"A joke," he teased. "Though I am quite sure if she had a pair handy we would be in her sights." His voice took on an amused note. "She is very jealous of you, is she not?"

Ava turned her head all the way to him, her expression one of actual disbelief. "Of course she isn't."

His look seemed to say he knew more about her than she would ever know herself. "I think she *is*. Why are you so nervous of me? It's perfectly natural for a man and a woman to sit and talk like this."

"I talk a lot easier when I'm wearing clothes," she confessed on a wry note.

He kept looking at her. "I want to touch you." His voice was low, so emotive he might have been exulting in his own desires. "I want to make love to you. I want to press kisses all over your body. I want to kiss you where you have never been kissed before." His hand moved so that his fingers closed over hers.

She felt a sharp, knife-like thrust deep in her womb, leaving a dull ache. "Why are we going with this, Varo?" she whispered, even with no one to hear.

"Isn't it obvious to you?" His fingers tightened. Very firm. He wasn't going to let her get away. "You have enchanted me."

She could barely answer. "I have made it clear I'm still married."

"You will soon have your freedom. That's what you want, isn't it?" He didn't tell her that her cousin, Karen, had sought to convince him Ava could have been the inspiration for *La Belle Dame sans Merci*. The memory of her words flooded back without prompt.

"Ava might look like vanilla ice cream, but I assure you she has another side," Karen had told him. "We call it the Langdon syndrome. They're tough people, the Langdons. Her husband, Luke, is a lovely man. He idolises her. Puts her on a pedestal. Such a terrible shame, but Ava didn't care to inhabit the role of wife. At least not for long."

Ava now turned to him, her eyes huge. "I shouldn't stay here."

"No," he murmured, his eyes lingering on her. "Your beautiful skin might get burned."

"I haven't *your* olive skin," she said defensively.

He lifted a hand to stroke the side of her neck. "Yours is as lustrous as a pearl. *'Full beautiful'* you are, Ava." He began to quote softly, dark and honey-tongued, "*'Her hair was long, her foot was light, and her eyes were wild.'*"

In truth he was the one doing the seducing, Ava thought. "I love Keats," she said on a surprised note. "Fancy your knowing that poem."

He shrugged. "A famous English poet, a famous poem. *La Belle Dame sans Merci.*"

"And I brought it to mind?" Was that how he saw her? Cool to cold? A little cruel?

He didn't answer. He fell back into the water and held up his arms. "Come here to me."

Little thrills of excitement were travelling the length of her spine. Yet she hesitated, aware Karen could see them. She was a cautious person, not at all adventurous, but it seemed her whole life was changing.

"Come," he repeated.

Her breath shook, but there nothing else she could do but allow herself to fall blindly into his outstretched arms.

They went under together. Down…down…into shimmering crystal depths shot through with rays from the sun. Varo held her body locked to his, as though she would never get away. His mouth pressed down with great ardour over hers. Surely this only happened in dreams? It was simply… *magic*.

But he was in need of more…a man held in captivity by an enchanting woman.

His hand had a life of its own. It plunged into her tiny bikini top, taking the weight of her delicate breast, the pleasure boundless. They were locked together so long Ava thought they might drown. She couldn't seem to care. Somehow this was not real. The moment was timeless. Locked together in the cool silvery-green depths yet burning with passion. This was a secret place of great beauty, the waters like silk against the skin. Best of all, they were far, far away from prying eyes.

They were moving to another stage. It was like a dreaming. They were weighted under water but not conscious of it. Only Varo, his strong arm locked around her, broke the idyll. They shot to the surface, faces turned up to the sky, both gasping for air. Dev and Amelia were lazily stroking their way back to them. Karen was standing right at the shoreline, one arm waving frantically, as though signalling to Ava and Varo to get out.

Ava knew she was in for a good talking-to. Karen hadn't been jealous of her before now. Her cousin had always acted like someone of elevated status—far superior to the younger Ava. She realised Karen had spent a lot of time trying to put her down, deflating any tendency towards a burgeoning self-confidence. Karen would be full of admonitions and she might even talk to Luke. Get in touch with him. Ava wouldn't put it past her. Karen was on Luke's side. She had no loyalty to Ava. She had to remember that. Karen could cause trouble.

Karen waited her moment until they were back at the homestead.

The men, Dev and Varo, refreshed, had returned to the Six Mile, where a thousand head of cattle were being yarded in advance of the road trains that were scheduled to arrive the following day.

Ava had taken a quick shower, washing the lagoon water out of her hair before changing into fresh clothes. She and Amelia planned on continuing their discussions with Nula Morris, the new housekeeper. Nula was a part aboriginal woman married to one of their best stockmen. Amelia's mother, the by now notorious Sarina Norton, had trained Nula as well as the rest of the domestic staff. She had done an extremely good job of it. No one could deny that.

Food and drink had to be planned for the coming polo weekend, and for the buffet at the party on Saturday night. For those who stayed on until Sunday, either camping out or finding a place in the station dorms, there would be a lavish Sunday brunch. All in all, the first big test for Nula—although she would have lots of help. The wedding reception, of course, would be fully catered.

Inevitably, Karen showed up at her door, charging past her. She spun to drill Ava with an accusatory look. Small wonder Amelia had long since christened Karen "The Snoop."

"You're spending a lot of time with Varo," she burst out, not beating about the bush.

Ava didn't hotly deny the allegation. Instead she said, very quietly, "Forgive me, but is that any of your business?" She was determined to hold on to her composure.

"Of course it is," her cousin hissed. "I've been looking out for you since we were kids. I never thought you capable of wayward impulses, Ava, but it seems you are. I believe I have the right as your cousin to point out that you've got your feet planted on the slippery slope." She stared at Ava intently, the pupils of her dark eyes black and huge.

"Which slope would that be?"

"Don't evade the issue, Ava."

"What? My wayward tendencies? You never stop, do you?" Ava sighed. "You have to show me you're far wiser, far more sophisticated than I. For years you were the superior schoolgirl. Now you're the experienced woman of the world. So far *you're* the one who has been chasing after our guest, Karen. We've all noticed."

Karen's face turned red. "Maybe a little," she confessed, trying to make light of it. "But *fun* is all it is," she maintained vigorously. "A bit of a release from my tight work schedule in the city. In any case, I'm a free agent. I have no commitment to anyone. Unlike *you*."

"And you can't help feeling a bit jealous?"

"Yo!" Karen did her extraordinary reining-in gesture. "Don't be so ridiculous! It has never occurred to me to be jealous of you, Ava. *Protective* is the word. We're cousins. Family. Right now you must be feeling very vulnerable. Don't think I can't see how easy it would be for you to fall for someone like Varo. Those dark eyes…the way he looks at a woman like she's the most desirable woman in the world. The smile. The charisma. It's all South American macho stuff. That's the way they are. Let me tell you, Varo is used to making conquests."

"I'm sure of it," Ava returned. "I can't think why you're working yourself up to such a state. Varo hasn't stolen my heart."

"Then *what*?" Karen demanded to know. "I'm a remarkably good judge and I'd say he has."

"I don't know if you're a good judge or not, but you're

remarkably interfering," Ava said. "You are my cousin, but you're also a guest here. I really don't need any lectures."

"Why take it like that?" Karen issued a protest. "Amelia has always carried on scandalously, so *she* won't advise you."

Ava's eyes sparkled dangerously. "I'd take that back, if I were you."

"Okay, okay—but Amelia is not you. Surely you recognise that? She's a very sensual woman. You're the Snow Maiden."

"I haven't been a maiden for years now, Karen. And I've told you before not to discuss or criticise Amelia or her mother. I consider Amelia my champion in all things. Not you."

"Well, then, make a fatal mistake!" Karen exclaimed, angry and affronted.

"Another one, you mean? You've shown far more loyalty to my husband than you've ever done to me."

"Why shouldn't I turn to Luke? He's my friend. He's a good man, Ava, and you've deliberately cast him aside. So much for your marriage vows. Luke loves you. Only now you've got all that money you want to be free."

Ava started walking to the door. "Maybe it's best if you leave now, Karen. You'd make a terrible marriage guidance counsellor. No one on the outside can see inside a marriage. If Luke considers himself unhappy, he made *me* unhappy for most of our married life. Like you, he took pleasure in putting me down, eroding my self-confidence."

Karen shook her glossy head. "I never remember him doing that. I strenuously deny it in my case. You're too thin-skinned, Ava. You take offence too easily. I didn't mean to upset you, but certain things have to be said. You know nothing about Juan-Varo de Montalvo beyond the fact he's Argentine, stunningly handsome, of good family and a splendid polo player. You're very beautiful, in your quiet way. It's nothing to him to start up a flirtation, even an affair. Ask him about the young woman he's left behind."

Ava couldn't ignore the stab of apprehension. "You know about such a woman?"

"I don't *know*," Karen replied in her familiar arrogant tone, "but I suspect it from a few things he's let drop. Think about it, Ava. He's nearly thirty years of age. His family will be expecting him to choose a bride soon. He wants a family. It's *time*. I wonder you haven't thought of all this. He's simply playing you for all it's worth."

"It's a wonder you haven't kept notes," Ava said, maintaining her cool. "Strange, I didn't think Varo had had the time, with you fussing over him, but thank you for your concern. If that's what it *is*. I would appreciate it if you kept all your insights to yourself for the rest of your stay. We Langdons want nothing to spoil this happy time. I could be mistaken—if so I'm sorry—but I think you're out to upset me."

Karen stalked to the door, her dark head held high. "I've simply told you what you need to know," she said sanctimoniously.

"You'll stay in touch with Luke?" Ava asked.

"Are you suggesting I don't?" Karen threw up her chin aggressively. "I'm not taking sides in this. I care for you both."

Ava ignored that spurious claim. "I'm sure he knows you're here. You both think you're in the perfect position to keep tabs on me."

"I'll forget you said that, Ava."

Ava took little heed of the tone of deep hurt.

"Better if you *remember* it," she replied.

CHAPTER FIVE

THE polo day was as brilliant as promised.

There was a great stir of excitement from the crowd as the Red Team, captained by James Devereaux Langdon, and the Blue Team, captained by the visiting Argentine Juan-Varo de Montalvo, cantered onto the field to wave upon wave of applause. Horses were part of Outback life, so it was no surprise polo was a great attraction, drawing crowds over long distances even by Outback standards. Polo was the fastest game in the world, and it had the seductive element of danger.

"Oh, isn't this *exciting*?" Moira O'Farrell, a very pretty redhead and a polo regular, threw back her head, rejoicing in the fact.

Four men to a team, all of them were tall, with great physiques and good-looking to boot, but all female eyes were on the Argentine. He was so *exotic*, so *out there*. Dev Langdon was taken, after all. No use looking to him. All these guys were seriously sexy. All at this point of time bachelors. That was of profound interest and concern. The polo "groupies" were among the most involved spectators. Would it be so amazing if one of them caught the eye of the devastatingly handsome Argentine? Not difficult to see oneself as mistress of some fabulously romantic *estancia* on the *pampas*.

Not to mention the high life in Buenos Aires, home of the
dead-sexy tango.

In the main it had fallen to Ava to organise the weekend's
events. Never one to sing her own praises—Ava was modest
about her abilities—she actually had exceptional organisa-
tional skills. As her mother Elizabeth told her, with loving
pride, "Far better than mine, my darling!"

Multi-coloured bunting decorated the grounds, aflutter in
the light cooling breeze. Prominent amid the fluttering little
flags was the Argentine, pale blue and white—Argentina
was the polo capital of the world, a Mecca for top players—
and the red, white and blue of Australia, a polo-playing nation. The polo field itself was a good three hundred yards
in length and more than half that distance in width. Today,
after concentrated maintenance, it was a near unprecedented
velvety green. The going had to be just right for the game.
Too hard would jar the legs of the polo ponies. Too soft
would slow down the action.

Several of the players on the polo circuit had travelled
overland with their string of ponies—though *ponies* was a
traditional term. The polo ponies of today were full-sized
horses, either thoroughbreds or thoroughbred crosses, their
legs protected by polo wraps from below the knee to the
fetlock. Long manes were roached, tails braided. Nothing
could be allowed to snag the rider's mallet. The taller the
horse, the longer the mallet. Both Dev and Varo were six-
footers-plus.

Amelia was wearing a polka-dotted navy and white shirt,
with chinos in bright red accentuating her long legs. There
was no doubting which team Amelia was barracking for.
Ava had found herself choosing a pale blue silk shirt to go
with her white lightweight cotton jeans. No coincidence
that her outfit bore the colours of the flag of Argentina.
Karen wore dazzling white. Karen was always given to

block colours. All black, all white, or all neutral beige. Once she had claimed she was channelling Coco Chanel. With some success, Ava had often thought. The tall, super-thin Karen always looked elegant. Today for the afternoon match she wore a collarless white shirt tucked into very narrow-legged white jeans with high heeled wedges on her feet. As a concession she had quite dashingly tied a blue silk scarf patterned in sun-yellow around her throat.

Behind her designer sunglasses Karen's dark eyes gleamed. She thought she was on to something. It wouldn't take her long to find the answers. She sat with the family— Erik and Elizabeth Langdon, Ava and Amelia the bride-to-be, and her own parents, who were giving the distinct impression they weren't all that keen on sport in general, and were apprehensive of such a dangerous sport as polo. For all they knew a charging player could lose control of his pony and plough into the area where they were sitting.

"You've done a great job, kiddo." Amelia complimented her friend and chief bridesmaid with real enthusiasm.

"I'm happy with it." Ava was watching Varo riding the bay gelding Caesar for the first chukka. The horse's hide had been lovingly burnished until it gleamed in the sunlight. Rider and polo pony looked magnificent. Out of the corner of her eye she saw Karen wave to Varo, as if he was her champion in a medieval joust. Ava transferred her gaze to her adored brother, who lifted a hand to them, then laughed as Amelia jumped to her feet waving a red bandana. Both young women laughed back in response. It was going to be a great day.

Ava had had the tall collapsible goalposts freshly painted in the colours of the two teams. Even the big white marquees that had been set up for food and drink had been decorated with the teams' colours. Adjacent picket fences had received a fresh coat of white paint.

The periods of play had already been decided. Six chukkas, each the traditional seven minutes long. Dev and Varo would only be playing two ponies, both well-trained Kooraki throughbred crosses. They had the right temperament, and proven speed, stamina and manoeuverability skills. Dev was used to all four ponies, and Varo had taken a hour or two to familiarise himself with his mounts' abilities.

Two members of Dev's team had brought along half a dozen good polo ponies between them, the idea being they could switch a tired pony for a fresh one between chukkas. Ava knew all the players. She had seen them play many times before, so she knew they were highly competitive. Dev's team, all from Outback properties, weren't going to let the Argentine's team win.

They were aiming high.

The best player on a team was usually the number three—the tactical leader and the most powerful hitter. Dev and Varo both wore a large white number three on the back of their coloured shirts, worn over the traditional fitted white breeches and glossy black riding boots. All players wore helmets with a chin strap. This was a dangerous game, with powerful young men wielding hardwood mallets.

"That's one sexy outfit!" Moira was really on a roll. She made the excited comment to the amusement of those around her.

It was a very friendly crowd, with lots of exchanges between spectators. Not that Moira wasn't spot on. Polo always attracted women who just happened to fancy the players more than the game.

It soon became evident that the number three players—the captains, the high-handicap players, hard-hitting, hard-riding, with an impressive armoury of strokes—were the best on the field. Neither was giving any quarter. In fact it was obvious to all the game's fans that the arrival of the dashing Argentine was proving a great stimulus to players and spectators alike.

It was a hard-played, hard-drawn contest, but in the end only one team could win. During the third chukka Tom McKinnon, number one on Dev's team, took a fall while covering the opposition number four. Tom swiftly and gamely remounted, but the Blue Team had gained the advantage. It was Varo who hit a magnificent winning goal that near stupefied the crowd so quickly and unexpectedly had it happened.

The Blue Team won, with good-natured cheers soaring to the cobalt-blue heavens.

It had been a wonderful match. The best for a very long time.

"Let's face it. The Argentine lifted the game. The captains were matched, but the others weren't in the same class."

It was Ava who was to present the cup to the captain of the winning team. Up close to Varo, she was perilously conscious of his sizzling energy, the sheer force of his sexual attraction that blazed like a brand. Indeed, to the crowd she looked like a beautiful and delicate porcelain figurine before him.

"Congratulations, Varo," she said sweetly, though the nerves in her body were leaping wildly. "That was a very exciting match."

"Gracias, señora," he said, silken suave, but with that mocking glint in his eyes. "I thoroughly enjoyed it." Bending his dark head, his hair as high-sheened as a bird's wing, he kissed one of her cheeks, and then the other,

breathing into her ear, "You look as cool as a camellia, *mi hermosa*."

She knew her cheeks pinkened but she moved back smilingly to present him with the silver cup. It was no everyday sort of thing, and one he would be happy to take back to Argentina.

Fresh waves of applause broke out. The crowd had melted for the Argentine. He had such animal magnetism—like some wonderful exotic big cat. Everyone was basking in his physical exhilaration.

Dev joined them now, his hair as golden as Varo's was raven-black. He threw an arm around his friend's shoulder. "My team will make a comeback," he joked. "That was a great game, Varo. You inspired us all."

Not to be left out, Amelia made a move up to them. Dev caught her around the waist, his aquamarine eyes sparkling with health and vigour. Brother and sister side by side could have been twins, which had been remarked on since childhood.

"Let's get ourselves a cold drink," Dev said, and started to move off to a marquee.

Karen bit her lip hard. She wasn't going to be denied her moment. She followed them and caught Varo's arm firmly, causing him to swing about. "May I add my congratulations, Varo?" She brushed his cheek with her hand. "That was a splendid match," she told him with warm enthusiasm, tugging at her blue and yellow silk scarf with its Argentine flag colours.

Varo responded gallantly. "Thank you so much, Karen. I enjoyed it too."

"I'm sure every woman in the crowd was urging you on," Karen said archly. "I know Ava was." She transferred a pointed gaze to her cousin.

"Well, *partly*," Ava responded lightly. "I wanted Dev's

team to win at the same time. But as we all know there can only be one winner."

"And winner takes all!" Karen's tone was decidedly provocative.

"Why did we ever invite that woman?" Amelia asked Ava later.

"Beats me," Ava responded. "We're from different galaxies. But she's family. It doesn't always mean families are nice."

"She always was a pain in the neck," said Mel, giving Ava a hug. "Don't let her bug you. Obviously she's trying to. Jealous, I'd say."

Ava gave a little grimace. "You're the second person who's told me recently Karen is jealous of me."

"So are you convinced?" Mel asked with a quirked brow.

"Getting there," Ava admitted with a laugh.

"I bet it was Varo who made the comment," Mel said very softly in Ava's ear.

"In a word, *yes*." Ava blushed.

Mel's lustrous dark eyes were fixed on her friend's face. "Both of you are playing it ultra cool, but it's not hard to see the attraction. It pulses around you. I'm sure you're aware Karen is keeping you under observation? To report to Luke, I wonder?"

Ava felt a hot prickling sensation all over her body. "There's nothing to report," she said huskily.

"You deserve to be happy, Ava," Mel said with the greatest affection. "Don't turn your back on your chances."

And so they came to the night of the party.

Ava knew she had far more in the way of formal evening-wear than most women. God knew she had attended any number of grand and boring balls, parties, fundraisers and other functions. She counted herself most fortunate in lots of ways. Not all. Luke had once sent her back upstairs to change one of her gowns because he had considered it not stunning enough. In actual fact it had been a designer outfit, purchased when she and her mother had been in Paris, the City of Light. It just went to prove Luke knew nothing about style and *haute couture*.

For tonight's party she chose the same full-length gown. Her mother had insisted on buying it for her because of its masterly cut and glorious colour. She knew Mel had a beautiful gold full-length gown, with bare shoulders and a richly embroidered top. Karen would be channelling Chanel again. Probably slinky black. Karen was forever quoting the infamous Wallis Simpson remark, "A woman can't be too rich or too thin." The other women guests would have brought something to dazzle. Every woman loved to dress up, and there weren't all that many occasions. When one arose they made the most of it.

Ava debated whether to pull her hair back or leave it loose. Men loved long hair. In her experience they considered it an unparalleled look for a woman. In the end she decided to go with movement. She did a little teasing to her thick gleaming locks, and even she thought the end result was very glamorous. It was party-time, after all. The satin gown in a lovely shade of purple hugged every curve, every line of her body. The bodice, ruched from below the bust, was held up by a shoestring halter with a long scarf-like pleat falling down the centre of the gown. Right now Ava felt as attractive as she could get.

For her twenty-first birthday her parents had given her a white-gold sapphire and diamond necklace, with matching sapphire and diamond drop earrings.

She realised what was happening. She was making herself as beautiful as possible for *one* man. Even thinking it brought out a rosy blush. Juan-Varo de Montalvo had had an enormous impact on her from the moment her eyes fell on him. Now she knew all about his powerful charm.

Turning about, she addressed her glowing reflection. "You've changed, Ava. You're almost a dual personality."

Cool, calm Ava and the woman who turned to flame in a near stranger's arms. A man, moreover, from another land.

For all she had lived life as a married woman, she had never felt remotely like this. She had never been in this intensely emotional state or felt such feverish excitement. And she was taking a huge gamble. One she might never win.

"It isn't like you at all," she told herself. "But it's magic!"

And how was it going to end? There were always consequences to actions.

On one side euphoria. On the other a certain trepidation which she sought to subdue but couldn't. She really knew very little about Varo. She could be playing with fire and she had always thought of herself as governed by cool logic. Falling madly in love was madness in its way. And she had a past. Some men didn't like a woman to have a past. Not to marry, anyway. Was it conceivable Varo could be regarding her in some way other than she believed? There was passion on both sides. Neither could deny that. But she would die of shame if he was only thinking of her in terms of a wild affair. How did she really know if he didn't have someone waiting for him at home? Now, *that* was logical. A man like Varo—a man of strong passions—surely would have a special woman tucked away. Karen had hinted at it. But Karen was not to be trusted. Karen only wanted to hurt her.

Momentarily her heart sank. Then she made the effort to throw off any negative feelings. She was like a woman who had been buried alive. Now she was going to enjoy herself. Enjoy life. She had been unhappy for such a long time. That had to change. She had to work at making her life change.

She wanted to be a stronger woman than she had ever been. It seemed to her this man who had come into her life, Juan-Varo de Montalvo, was helping her be just that. Her anxieties dissolved.

A few minutes later, looking supremely beautiful and composed, she made her way down the rear staircase to the kitchen, greeting Nula and her helpers with a warm smile. "Everything going okay?"

"All under control!" Nula assured her.

"Great!"

"You look absolutely beautiful!"

Nula spoke for all of them, charmed and delighted. Miss Ava, such a lovely, friendly person, had never been treated the way she should have been. The Old Man, Gregory Langdon, had been a genuine tyrant. Everyone on the station, family and employees alike, had taken a good deal of punishment from him. Miss Ava's husband—from the viewpoint of the staff, at least—wasn't half good enough for her. Good riddance, they all thought, now they knew Miss Ava was well into the process of divorcing him. She deserved and hopefully would find a far better man.

The party had already started. Music was playing through the house. All the exterior lights, and the lighting around the pool, the pool house and the landscaped gardens, were turned on, transforming the whole area into a fairyland. Couples were dancing in the Great Hall and out on the rear terrace. She had a good view of Dev, with his beautiful Amelia clasped in his arms. Her heart shook with love and gratitude. Everything at long last had turned out so splendidly for them. These were two individuals who had been made for each other. Wasn't that a source of wonder? Everything was so much better with Mel around. She found herself rejoicing that in one week's time Mel would become her sister-in-law—the sister she'd never had.

The instant she spotted the fabulous Argentine momentarily alone Moira O'Farrell broke away from her group, crossing the room swiftly to speak to him while she had the chance. Ava's cousin, the pretentious Karen Devereaux—so terribly hard-edged, wearing a very stylish black jersey dress—had actually unbent sufficiently to tell her Juan-Varo de Montalvo had picked *her*, Moira, out of the crowd.

"It's your wonderful red hair, darling," Karen had pointed out in a voice that hid insincerity. She really disliked red hair.

So he *had* noticed her! Moira had the sensation she was awakening to a dream. The Argentine was *gorgeous*, and Karen had let drop that he came from a fabulously wealthy family. Not only that, he was unattached. She didn't know if she believed that was true or not. How could such a man be unattached?

Well used to the ways of women, especially women dead set on chasing him, Varo was soon alerted to the redhead's intentions. She was very pretty, her small neat head a mass of silky curls, and she was wearing a lovely spring-green dress, but all he could think of was Ava and when she was going to appear.

The intensity of the feelings he had for his friend's sister was threatening to overwhelm him. He was always gentle with women, and tender too, he supposed, but he had never experienced such a potentially dangerous passion. He wanted her. Very, very badly. He had not been prepared for her. He wasn't one to fool around, treating women with a callous hand.

He had no idea where these feelings were going. Ava

was still married. He could not stay in Australia, despite the country's great appeal to him, the people, the way of life. He had to go home. He was his father's heir. He and his father had great plans. He might be able to grow to love Australia, especially the vast Outback, but a woman like Ava would be extremely unhappy away from her homeland. That was if her feelings even came remotely close to his own.

At the moment it was a dilemma. All of it. He cared too terribly much.

The redhead raced up to him, her face full of animation and, it had to be said, invitation. "Please, Varo, I'd love to dance—wouldn't you?"

She was so sweet, so openly flirtatious, he couldn't help but smile back at her. Very gallantly he took her arm, leading her out onto the terrace where everyone was in a rather *loving* dance mode.

"Fabulous party, Ava," one of the male guests said as she passed him. "You look glorious!"

Ava didn't reply, but she smiled and blew him a kiss. Invitations to join different groups were called to her as she made her way from the Great Hall into the living room, wondering all the while if Varo was out on the terrace. He was so tall, so much a stand-out figure, she would have spotted him easily had he been inside the house.

Easier still to spot him on the terrace. He was dancing with Moira O'Farrell. Moira's pretty face was uplifted to him, her expression one of almost delirious excitement.

Ava found herself standing perfectly still, her heart rocked by an unfamiliar pang of jealousy laced with an irrational sense of betrayal. Surely Varo could dance with whomever he pleased? He couldn't help being so devastatingly attractive to women. He appeared to be staring down into Moira's melting blue eyes. There was very little space

between their bodies, although in height they were mis-
matched. Varo's raven head was bent to hear what Moira
was saying. Ava saw him smile—that beautiful white flash
that lit up his polished bronze complexion. He would draw
any woman and compel her to follow him.

Unnerved, inhaling quickly, breasts steeply rising, Ava
turned back into the living room. She was caught by a
sudden fear that Varo might be toying with her. Then she
reminded herself she had always suffered from a lack of
confidence.

About time you took trust as a maxim.

Some time later, someone suddenly and very precipi-
tately bumped into her.

"Oh, for heaven's sake. I'm sorry, Ava." It was Moira
O'Farrell doing the apologising.

From looking radiant, Moira now looked hectically
flushed and, yes, distressed. What on earth had happened
to cause such a change?

"That's okay, Moira," Ava said companionably. "You
look like you're leaving?" She was half joking, half serious. She put out a steadying hand. Moira was a guest.

"No, no. I'm having a marvellous time," Moira's protest
had a touch of mild hysteria. "Look, I shouldn't say this, but
that bitch of a cousin of yours, Karen Devereaux—" Moira
broke off as though she'd suddenly realised to whom she
was speaking.

"Whatever has she said to upset you?" Ava asked, staring into Moira's face. She took Moira's slender arm, moving them away to a relatively quiet corner.

"It was unforgivable, really." Always chirpy, Moira now
looked both downcast and angry.

"Sure you're not being over-sensitive?" Ava questioned.

"She's nothing like you!" Moira shook her head so vigorously her curls bounced. "I always thought she was a bit on the vicious side."

"*Tell* me, Moira," Ava insisted.

Moira's face contorted into a grimace. "She tried to make a fool of me. You'd better ask her."

"I'm asking *you*, Moira. I prefer to speak to you." Ava spoke firmly.

"All right!" Moira made her decision. "She told me Varo had picked me out of the crowd. Her very words. *Picked me out of the crowd.* The implication was he fancied me. Like a fool I believed her. Men *do* fancy me, as I expect you know. But obviously she was having a good laugh at my expense. I practically forced Varo to dance with me. Don't get me wrong. He's a great guy—a perfect gentleman, lovely manners, and a *super* dancer. Stupid me, pressing myself against him… I could die. But it seems he has a girl back home. Of course he would, wouldn't he? A drop-dead gorgeous guy like that. Oh, God, I feel such a fool." A sound like a hot rush of self-loathing escaped her.

"Why would you?" Ava tried hard to sound understanding. Indeed she *was*. But her own fearful thoughts were spinning out of control.

"Oh, Ava, I was so *obvious*," Moira wailed. "I was flirting with him for all I was worth."

Ava gathered herself. Her voice, miraculously, sounded nice and normal. "Nothing much wrong with that, Moira. If you look around, everyone is playing the flirting game. It's a party. Cheer up." There seemed little else she could say.

Varo has someone back home. He's admitted it. Moira wouldn't lie.

"I've never told you this before," said Moira, "but that smug cousin of yours is very jealous of you. I've wanted to tell you for a long time now. You're so lovely too." Moira's eyes were suddenly brimming with tears. "Just you be careful of her."

Ava lent forward and spontaneously kissed Moira's flushed cheek. "Come on, Moira. So Varo has a love interest at home? You can easily find one right here. Blink the tears away and go enjoy yourself. That's an order."

Moira lifted her head with smiling gratitude. "Thanks, Ava. You're an angel."

They parted company with Moira looking brighter. Ava, however, had to take her usual three calming breaths. She tried hard to hold on to some steadying memory. Surely her mother had once said, "You're always good in a crisis, Ava."

She had to cling to that.

Varo, promised to someone else, had got in over his head. So had she. It had all happened so fast. The effects had been mesmerising.

Ava moved to join Dev and Amelia's group. "You look ravishing, Ava!" Dev's tone spoke volumes of pride, while Amelia's expression showed her shared pleasure. "I have two beautiful women in my life."

Dev hugged Amelia to him. Plainly the two of them were enjoying themselves immensely. What she had to do now was not spoil things.

Plant a smile on your face.

A few moments later she felt without seeing that Varo had come to stand directly at her shoulder. He was greeted warmly by everyone, but it was Ava he had come for.

"I hope you realise, Ava, that as the captain of the winning team I am owed a dance by you. Several, in fact," he said, with his captivating smile.

She knew their guests were waiting for her response. And Mel, sharp as a tack, was watching her rather closely.

"Of course, Varo." She turned to him, her eyes ablaze in her face, brilliant as jewels.

Inside she might feel pale with shock, but outside she was all colour—the golden mane of hair, dazzling eyes, softly blushed cheeks, lovely deep pink mouth. She was determined now to play her part, her only wish to get through the night with grace. For all he hadn't been completely honest with her, Juan-Varo de Montalvo would never leave her memory, even when he disappeared to the other side of the world.

Varo took charge, as was his way. He clasped her hand in his, entwining his long fingers with hers, then led her away. Shaken, sobered, incredibly Ava felt *desire* course through her. Where had all this sensuality come from? These wildly extravagant reactions that touched every sensitive spot in her being and body? She had never experienced those feelings before. They had been drawn out of her by this man who had stolen her heart. There was just no fighting it. The connection was too strong.

Oh, God, she thought prayerfully. *Oh, God!* Her head was telling her what to do. Her body was ignoring the dictates of her mind. She had imagined him making love to her. Not a day had gone by when she hadn't fantasised about it. She felt possessed by him. Drawn like a moth to the flame. The huge problem was she couldn't seem to turn away from the flame, though she knew it could devour her.

"Wait," he murmured, steering her to the far corner of the loggia, just as she had known he would. In the light-dappled shadows he slowly turned her into his arms, his brilliant gaze questing. "What is troubling you, Ava?"

The sound of his name on her lips was like the softest swish of air. Yet pressure was expanding in her. *Be brave. Tell him.*

"Nothing." To her surprise her voice sounded normal. Or normal enough.

"Do you think I don't know you by now?"

The honeyed tenderness was almost her undoing. "But you don't *know* me, Varo. I don't know *you*."

He gave a soft laugh. "That is not quite correct." He took her into his arms as though the sole purpose for their coming to the far end of the terrace was to find a relatively quiet area to dance. "This is not the ideal moment to sort it out," he said humorously. "Too many people. Too many glowing lights. I cannot embrace you, or kiss your lovely mouth. I can only tell you I want you desperately." His full attention was focused on her. "You look incredibly beautiful." His arms tightened around her, guiding her in slow, sensual, graceful movements. *"Exquisito."*

What should she do? Their bodies were touching. She *couldn't* break away. Her muscles seemed to be locked. All she could do was stare into his dynamic dark face, wondering how she could live her life without him. It was quite frightening that she should think this way. But passion *was* frightening in its way.

He was wearing a white dinner jacket that served to emphasise his darkly tanned olive skin. It had to have been tailored for him because it fitted his wide shoulders like a glove. "Are you trying to woo me, Varo?" she asked, gripped by her undeniably erotic reaction. But this man *was* erotic. She had grasped that from the moment she had first laid eyes on him.

He was sensitive to her as well, because he had picked up on her mood. "Ava," he sighed over her head. "Ava. You want me to *win* you? Is that it?"

She placed a staying hand on his chest, feeling his heart beating strongly beneath the pristine white dress shirt. "You can't do that, of course," she said with a flare of spirit. "You have to return home soon."

"What *should* I do?" he countered swiftly, as though daring her. "Not for us coffee and conversation. Tell me, please, Ava."

It was a demand couched in exquisite gentleness. She struggled to find an answer but she was encased within his arms, her own heart beating as fast as a wild bird confined to a cage. "Is this all part of the adventure, Varo?"

The tenderness had alchemised to anger. Abruptly he pulled back, his handsome features tautening. "An adventure? What adventure?" A vertical line formed between his black brows. "I should stop your mouth with my own. Only I want to hear about these feelings that are plaguing you. You think me insincere? A social playboy?" He looked passionately affronted at the very idea. "I've fallen in love with you, Ava. Love is a force. The most powerful force on earth. I didn't expect any of this. I was not prepared. But we made an instant connection. You cannot deny it. Except, of course, as you say I don't really *know* you. However, you've allowed me to believe you are seriously affected as well. Or are you a witch?"

"I am *not* a witch," she said with adamance.

It was clear to her she had challenged his pride. He didn't like it. The deep dark emotions that were growing between them were as threatening as any storm. How long could they continue this fraught sensual dance before people began to notice?

Her face was turned up to his. She drew closer. "What about the woman you've left behind?" she accused. "The girlfriend? You told me your attentions were not engaged. Was that a lie?" Abruptly she recognised the fact she was madly jealous of the unknown young woman who no doubt would be stunningly beautiful. There would be strong approval from both families as well. That was the way it was done.

"Woman?" he rasped, as though she were completely stupid. "My God, is *that* it?"

"Of course that's *it*." Her supple body had gone rigid. The careless arrogance of his tone!

He wasn't going to let her go. He retained one of her hands as he stepped down a few steps into the garden and beyond to the radiant moonlight. He went first, compelling her to follow him into the scented darkness.

"Varo, what are you doing?" Her voice shook in alarm. "Where are we going?"

"Do not worry," he said. "Everything will be fine." He kept to the softly lit pathway, mindful of her evening shoes and her lovely long skirt.

She could smell gardenias. All kinds of beautiful blossoming flowers, native and exotic, and the scent of freshly clipped grass. "Varo!" she repeated breathlessly. If she had learned anything about herself it was that she couldn't resist him.

As they moved off the path into the deep shadows of the trees he caught her around the waist. "Who have you been speaking to?" he demanded. "Don't tell me. Sweet little Moira?"

She made no attempt to deny it. The brief conversation she had had with Moira had made her suffer. "You told her you had a special someone waiting for you at home." It was plain accusation.

"Maybe I was simply trying to get a message across?" he countered, his arm tightening around her as he drew her body, arched away from him, in close. "I'm not married. Who else to protect me but the woman I left behind?"

"Whose name is…?" The sad joke was on her!

"There *is* no one, Ava," he said very gently. Although

she knew he wouldn't forgive her if she continued to doubt him. "Just part of my ploy so pretty little Moira wouldn't waste her time," he explained. "If you raise your head a little I can kiss your cheek. You have such beautiful skin. A perfect camellia comes into my mind. Sadly I can't kiss your mouth as I want, because you can't return to the house *sin carmin*. Your hawk-eyed cousin Karen would be so upset."

Why hadn't she figured it all out for herself? The idea of Varo confiding in Moira had affected her so badly she had made a quantum leap. "It was Karen who played a trick on Moira," she confided abruptly. Her whole body was under siege at his touch. "She told Moira you had picked her out of the crowd."

He tilted her head back so he could run his mouth down her cheek, over her delicate jawbone to the column of her throat. "I would say your cousin is a woman full of tricks." His mouth was warm against her skin. "*Peligrosa*. Teacherous. Poor Moira was deliberately led astray. But one wonders why…?"

"Karen wants to see what will happen, Varo."

"Destino," he said, his hand sliding down over her breast with unparalleled sensuality.

She shuddered, on the brink of surrender. "We have to go back inside." It was imperative for her to take action before the pressure became too great.

"Soon. I need this badly." He sounded as if he was in pain.

Ava bit her lip hard, so a moan wouldn't escape her. The spell was at work again, holding them captive.

"Varo!" She forced her eyes open, her hand closing over his at her breast.

"I know… I know…" A sigh was on his lips. He lifted his head, his deep voice slightly slurred.

"I can't be sure," she told him in agitation, "but I think

there's someone moving beneath the trees." The trees were strung with countless tiny twinkling white lights, but there were dark spots.

Varo turned his head, his eyes trying to pierce the dappled dark. "A female puma, perhaps?" he mocked. "Why not acknowledge her?" There was more than a hint of derision in his tone. His resonant, fascinatingly accented voice lifted, carrying on the breeze. "We're over here, Karen," he called. "Feel free to join us. Ava is showing me the most wonderful night-blooming *cereus*."

He was quick witted—and he obviously knew the plant, native to Mexico. Because the cactus with its enormous breathtakingly beautiful creamy cups brimming with golden stamens was twined around a tree not a few feet away from them.

Silence.

"Perhaps I was mistaken?" Ava whispered, her whole body aquiver.

"Give it a minute." His voice was low in her ear. "Ah, the stalker shows herself!"

The ultra-thin figure of Karen, well camouflaged in her black gown, now appeared on the path, all but stomping towards them. "Oh, there you are!" she cried out in an artlessly playful voice that would have fooled no one. "I needed a break from all the noise. I expect you did too."

"What *is* this woman's problem?" Varo, still with his head bent, was murmuring in Ava's ear.

"I think she hates me." Karen was acting more like the enemy than her family.

"She will have to get to you through *me*." All of a sudden Varo sounded very cold and hard.

"I don't remember any night-blooming *cereus*," Karen was remarking caustically, looking dubiously around her.

"Ah, but Ava is far more knowledgeable." Varo spoke

with charming mockery. "You are standing midway between it and us."

"Oh, the cactus, you mean?" Karen's tone reduced the
stunning beauty of the night-blooming *cereus* to that of a
paper daisy.

"Breathtaking," Varo exclaimed, turning his raven head
to Ava. "But I think it's high time for us to return to the
party, don't you, Ava? *Muchas gracias* for showing me such
beauty. Such a mystery why it only blooms at night."

CHAPTER SIX

THERE were not enough days in the following week. They flew by on the wings of mounting excitement. Nothing like a wedding to bring the thrill of joy. Although the great day had been organised down to the last little detail, there still remained things to do.

Amelia had been dropping weight with all the excitement; consequently her beautiful bridal gown needed adjustments.

Amelia's mother, Sarina, had been invited purely as a gesture, everyone knowing full well that Sarina was too busy living the good life in Tuscany.

Ava's husband, Luke Selwyn, had not been invited at all. He and Ava were divorcing, after all, and the split was far from amicable. Luke Selwyn made no bones about wanting Ava back, although he had told Ava many times he wasn't happy with her. There had always been something she wasn't getting quite right. But he *wanted* her. No mistaking that. And she *was* the Langdon heiress.

The homestead, with its twelve bedrooms extended from the original ten, all fitted with an *en suite* bathroom, was full up. So too was the accommodation at the men's quarters, the dormitories, and all the various bungalows— including the one-teacher schoolhouse—that sat like satellites around the main compound.

People streamed through the house, carrying all sorts of boxes for all purposes. A huge consignment of glorious flowers had been flown in from Sydney, along with a renowned floral designer and his team. Top musicians had arrived. Food and drink and a team of caterers were to be flown in first thing Saturday morning.

The ceremony, in the lovely tranquillity of the garden, was to take place at four p.m., after the heat of the day had abated. Vows would be exchanged beneath an eighteenth-century gazebo with carved stone pillars and a delicate white cupola. Great urns nearby had been filled with white cymbidium orchids that had been flown in from Thailand. No expense had been spared. This was a once-in-a-lifetime event—a marriage that was destined to endure.

Dev's best man and his two grooms had arrived in the best man's private Cessna. Amelia's other bridesmaids arrived on Friday. A rehearsal was to take place in the late afternoon.

The reception was to be held in the Great Hall, a large multi-purpose building separate from the house. A celebration barbecue had been organised for Kooraki's staff. It was scheduled to begin at the same time as the main reception. This was a splendid occasion, affecting everyone on the station.

Amelia had bypassed the traditional structured duchesse satin style for a much lighter look perfect for a hot early summer's afternoon. The bride and her three bridesmaids were to wear the same exquisitely hand embroidered chiffon over full-length silk slips. Amelia had chosen for her bridesmaids the soft colours of one of her favourite flowers, the hydrangea. Amelia's own gown, ivory-white, was lightly embroidered with tiny pearls and sparkling beads to within some six or seven inches from the hem, where the embroidery burst into large silver leaves that gleamed like a work of art.

Ava was to wear not the blue of the hydrangea but another colour that suited her beautifully: an exquisite mauve. The other bridesmaids, Lisa and Ashleigh, would be wearing hydrangea-blue and pink. Slender arms were to be left bare. Instead of a veil Amelia would be wearing a floral diadem to encircle her dark head. So too would her bridesmaids. All would wear their long hair loose and flowing. Each bridesmaid's heart-shaped posy would feature one of the flowers in the bride's white bouquet, whether rose, peony, butterfly orchid, hydrangea or lily.

It had been a close collaboration, with input from each bridesmaid as to colours and styles. It was a great good fortune all were tall and slim with long flowing hair. Amelia did not want a *grand* wedding, as such. She wanted a lovely summer's day fantasy. A romantic wedding above all.

Amelia's room was crowded with her bridesmaids, the dresser and hairdresser and Elizabeth, Dev and Ava's mother. Even Karen had found her way in, standing near the open French doors, studying them all with a strange expression—never pleasure or excitement—on her tight-skinned face. She had chosen to wear a black and white outfit, extremely smart, but Ava thought it would have been nicer had she worn a colour.

The instant before Ava stepped into the corridor after the others Karen caught her arm. "Surely you're thinking of someone outside yourself today?" she asked in a steely voice.

Ava turned around, resolving to keep her temper. "Please don't upset me, Karen. It would be entirely the wrong day. What *is* your problem with me, anyway? You've always had one."

"I've had a purpose," said Karen, "to look out for you. And I place a lot of importance on marriage vows." She lowered her voice as Amelia looked back over her shoulder to check on them.

"Wait until *you* get there, Karen," Ava said. "How old are you now?"

Karen's expression became slightly pinched. "I've had any number of offers, Ava. I'm taking my time. I don't intend to make a mistake, like you. And you *are* making a mistake. Luke loves you. He wants you back. Hard to understand why, when you've treated him so badly."

The unfairness of it all!

Ava shook her cousin's hand off just as Amelia moved back to them, a slight frown on her beautiful face.

"Tell me you're not trying to upset Ava?" She stepped right up to Karen, so Karen had to fall back a step or two.

Just like in their schooldays, Ava thought. Mel stepping in to protect her.

"Mel, everything's okay," she said, ever the peacemaker.

But Mel, of Italian descent, had a volcanic temper when aroused.

"Let's say I was trying to talk sense to Ava." Karen adopted a self-righteous pose. "I happen to care about her. She *is* my cousin. I care about Luke too. He's suffering."

"Suffering?" Mel exploded. "Are you serious? Luke Selwyn is your classic narcissist. And a womaniser. As if you didn't know. If you like him so much, Karen, he'll be available in the not so distant future. Look him up. Offer comfort. But, for now, keep out of Ava's affairs. She is *not* your concern. And another thing! How dare you cause upset on *my* wedding day?" Mel's delicate nostrils flared. "Honestly, Karen, you're so stupid you don't even know you're stupid. Here's a word of warning from the bride: *behave.*"

Karen visibly deflated. Amelia had always had that effect on her—that was why she hated her. She gave a strangled laugh. "I can assure you, Amelia, I'll do the best I can."

"Be sure you do," said Amelia with a sharp nod.

"You look wonderful, by the way."

"Thank you so much, Karen," Mel said ironically. "Come along, Ava. This is one bride who isn't going to be late for her wedding."

At four o'clock, in a haze of emotion, the wedding ceremony took place. Bride and groom exchanged vows beneath the shelter of the white wrought-iron lace of a cupola decorated with white flowers and satin ribbons. Amelia stood in her exquisite bridal gown, sewn all over with sparkling crystals, staring up into her beloved Dev's eyes.

It was an ageless ritual but incredibly moving. Ava, ethereal in her mauve bridesmaid's gown, bowed her blonde diadem-encircled head in prayer, the inevitable tears rising to her eyes.

God bless and protect you all the days of your lives. God grant you beautiful children to love and raise to the highest possible level of happiness, confidence and morality.

Dev and Amelia were strong people. They had endured years of conflict—as had she. Only she had been the one who had been openly frightened of her grandfather but desperately anxious to win his approval. Her father had had the same experience, but those days were gone. Life had become more complicated, but in a way very much simpler. They were all working towards the same goal: personal fulfilment within a secure family environment. Dev had his adored wife. She had a sister. Their parents, reunited, had their eyes set on the future. And, needless to say—grandchildren to love and very likely spoil.

The ceremony over, the newly married couple yielded

completely to the bridal kiss. Emotion spread across the garden area. Women guests happily dabbed tears from their eyes, irresistibly reminded of *their* wedding day.

"The happiest day!" Elizabeth Langdon, looking lovely in a short blue silk shift with a matching lace jacket and a filmy blue picture hat whispered to her daughter, "Your perfect day is yet to come, my darling."

Hope that had glimmered, brightened, strengthened by Ava's wildly blossoming emotions, turned as insubstantial as gauze.

In the reception hall white-linen-draped buffet tables were laden with a succulent gastronomic feast: hams, turkeys, chicken dishes—hot and cold—roast duck and lamb, all manner of scrumptious seafood, whole Tasmanian salmons—cold and smoked—reef fish, lobsters, prawns, sea scallops, mussels and oysters, salads galore...

Good-looking young waiters were almost pirouetting, pouring champagne, white wine, red, and the popular rosé. There was also a well-stocked bar for anything stronger, and gallons of icy cold fruit juices and soft drinks.

There was a separate table groaning under the weight of desserts: apricot, peach, banana, mango, berries, citrus cakes and tarts, coconut cakes, and the all-time favourite chocolate desserts. No one would go away feeling hungry. This was a *serious* banquet the like of which was seldom seen.

From the upstairs gallery in the homestead Amelia, now mistress of Kooraki, threw her exquisite grandiflora bouquet: white roses, luxurious white peonies with the faintest flush of pink, gardenia *"magnifica,"* a perfect velvety white, a single large head of white hydrangea and a small cluster of butterfly orchids. She threw it directly towards her chief bridesmaid. Such was her accuracy, Ava had no option but to catch it.

Karen, who was behind Ava, leaned forward to whisper, "I seem to remember you've *already* been given in wedlock."

Nothing, it seemed, could stop Karen. It was a wonder she didn't shout it from the top of her lungs. She wasn't a woman of great subtlety. Even so, Ava found it hard not to remember that fact too. She had ignored all good advice. For once she had made her own decision. Well, it had cost her.

But her grandfather had left her financially set for life. Probably he had never trusted her to determine her own future. Even now she had fallen madly in love with a man who would soon return to his own country, his own life. She had thrown herself wide open to him. They couldn't go backwards. They could only go forward. Varo was only seeing what he wanted to see. Varo wanted her. She knew that. Fate had put her in his path. But Varo had other people to think of. His family in Argentina. They would have important concerns and plans for their only son. In her wildest dreams she didn't think they would accept a divorced woman. Their son could have *anyone*! Any beautiful young woman in their circle. Not a woman from another place. One who couldn't even speak Spanish.

Had Varo's American mother been fluent in Spanish when she'd run off with her Argentine husband? In all likelihood she hadn't been, but neither of them had cared.

By seven o'clock the newlyweds had left to fly to Sydney. The following morning they would board a fight to Singapore, staying at Raffles for a few days before heading off for London, their first European port of all.

This was the signal for the party to step up a gear. No

one wanted the wonderful day to end. It was all so exciting, with everyone so friendly. The older guests retired to the house for long in-depth conversations; the under forties were dead set on having a good time.

There was a great deal of laughter, flirting and, it had to be said, drinking. And dancing to a great band that became more and more high-powered as the night went on was on everyone's agenda. The band members were enjoying themselves every bit as much as the guests. They'd been well fed, and they hadn't gone short on liquid refreshments. No one was counting.

Varo pushed his chair back towards the shelter of a lush golden cane in a splendid blue and white Chinese jardinière. He had been enjoying more than his fair share of female attention, and now he was thankful to be on his own for the moment—free to watch Ava make her way down the staircase with her signature flowing grace, a romantic fantasy in her lovely softest mauve dress. She had removed the silver diadem she had worn around her head for the ceremony. It had suited her perfectly, enhancing the ethereal look. He had loved the idea of the diadem for a headdress. It had been set here and there along its length with tiny real roses nestled into little sprays of sparkling crystals.

Dev had given each bridesmaid a necklace to match her gown. Varo imagined they would treasure it: hand-made pendants featuring large diamond-set gemstones hanging from delicate white gold chains. Ava's gemstone was an amethyst, Lisa's a pink sapphire, Ashleigh's a blue topaz. They had all looked beautiful, with their long flowing hair and filmy summer dresses. He had danced several times with both Lisa and Ashleigh. Now he was waiting for Ava, who was proving as elusive as a woodland nymph.

As he looked towards the staircase he felt a sudden chill

that had him turning in his chair. It couldn't be. But it was. Cousin Karen had appeared again.

"Hi, there!"

She pulled up a chair close to him, crossing her long legs. She was looking very elegant in her black and white gown, but he found himself feeling astonishingly hostile to her. This rarely happened to him—especially with a woman. But there it was!

"Well, that went off extremely well, didn't it?" Karen had prepared a big smile, and was speaking in an enthusiastic kind of voice that didn't fool him one bit. "Slightly odd, Amelia throwing her bouquet to Ava," she slid in, her dark eyes hooded.

"You expected Amelia to throw it to *you*?" he asked suavely.

"No, no!" she protested laughingly. "Lord knows *I'm* in no hurry to marry. I simply meant Ava is already married. Divorce may be streamlined here in Australia—one year and one day of separation. Why the extra day?" she trilled. "But it has to *be* that before an application can be filed in the court. A hearing date can take a couple of months. You may not know this, but that separation date hasn't yet been reached."

"Why are you telling me this?" Varo asked, successfully staring her down. He really wanted to get away from this woman as he would want to get away from a snake.

She made a sound like a strangled giggle. "Go figure! I thought you and Ava were on the verge of having an affair?"

He recognised malevolence when he encountered it. "You think this, do you? Or do you fear it? And would it be *your* business either way?" His voice he kept low, but his black eyes took on a brilliant diamond-like glitter.

Karen could see he was angry. He really was a magnificent man. "Well, I've made it my business because I care about Ava, Varo," she insisted—not for the first time. "And Luke. As I've told you, he worships her."

"Apparently she missed that," he said, with heavy irony.

"Oh, no!" Karen shook her shiny dark bob that was groomed to racehorse perfection. "It was apparent to everyone who knew them or met them. Luke adores her. She's his perfect princess."

"So it's all Ava's fault? Is that it?"

Karen sighed, holding up one of her manicured hands to avoid his penetrating eyes. "Fault? No, I never said fault. But Ava is a fragile creature. She always has been."

"Perhaps she needs a *real* man and not your Luke?" Varo suggested smoothly. He rose to his impressive six-three, a stunningly handsome man, and stared down at Ava's poisonous cousin. "Would it clarify anything in your mind if I said you cannot hide your jealousy of Ava? I suspect it has always been there. She's so beautiful, and I have noted she takes into account *everyone's* feelings. I would say before her own."

Karen appeared genuinely shocked by his action. She too rose to her feet, colour flagging her high cheekbones. "It's much too soon for you to make an assessment, Varo. I'm only trying to prevent a huge mistake."

"And you would be desolate if your little plan came awry?" he challenged. "I think this is all a deliberate attempt at sabotage, Ms Devereaux. Now, if you will excuse me, I plan to dance with Ava."

Karen shook her head sadly. "My conscience is clear. I've done my level best."

"I would say you have. Only it's your motivation that is being questioned. Rest assured, Ms Devereaux, we can handle this ourselves."

Karen blushed and turned away, a white-hot fury moving through her. She would get even with Ava if it was the last thing she did. She was already going along that road, blind to anything else. She didn't really know or understand *why*, but she had always wanted to rob her cousin in some way. She especially wanted to rob her of any chance she might have with the arrogant, supremely macho Argentine. To think she had half fancied him too! He had certainly got her adrenaline going for a while. Now she hated him. Few men intimidated her. Juan-Varo de Montalvo did.

Varo drained a vodka before he went in search of the elusive Ava, who had disappeared. Eventually he found her out on the terrace, dancing with one of the polo-players, a longtime family friend and, as he correctly guessed, a long-time admirer of Ava.

He tapped the polo-player's shoulder, his name having sprung to mind. "May I cut in, Jeff?" he asked lightly. "Ava has promised me my quota of dances."

Jeff didn't look the least put out. "You're saying I've had mine?" He laughed, lingeringly releasing Ava. "Indeed, I have."

"Muchas gracias!" Varo smiled at the other man, who smiled back. Varo then took Ava very smoothly into his arms, their feet immediately fitting the soft, slow romantic beat. "You see me. You disappear again," he chided gently.

She tilted her face to him, caught up in the same physical exhilaration, the sense of *belonging.* "I saw Karen pull up a chair beside you. I didn't like to interrupt."

He gave an exaggerated groan. "Please *do* if there is ever a next time."

His arresting face was all high cheekbones, striking planes and angles in the shadowy golden light. "What was she saying this time?" she asked.

His voice dropped to a low, confiding whisper. "You don't want to know." He gathered her in close, feeling his hunger for her tighten into the now familiar near-painful knots of tension. He only had so much strength to resist such magical allure.

"Possibly what Karen should do is train to become a private investigator," Ava said thoughtfully.

"I promise you she'd be good at it." He laughed.

"So what *did* she say?" Ava persisted, very glad her cousin was going home the following day.

"Same old thing." Varo shrugged. "Your husband wants you back." He hesitated a moment, then said, "Could you tell me how long it is since you've been separated from him?"

They seemed to be dancing alone. Other couples had drifted away. "Ah, now, I'm ninety-nine point nine percent sure Karen told you."

His tone was taut. "I don't listen to Karen. I listen to *you*."

"Why talk about it on a day like today?" She sighed, swaying like a feather in his arms.

"Why refuse when it is something that is important to me?" he countered, steering her into the light so he could capture her exact expression.

Ava realised his intention. "Luke and I are two months short of the mandatory separation time, Varo," she said. "Which is exactly as Karen must have told you: one year and one day. The day after my solicitor will file my application in the court. Luke no longer has a hold on me, Varo. My marriage is over."

"You think the court will look favourably on your application for divorce?" They had stopped dancing, but he was holding her in place.

"Why not?" she fired, her beautiful eyes ablaze. "My solicitor—he's a top man—has assured me it will."

"Your husband may throw difficulties in your way," Varo said. She felt so soft, so silken, so fluid in his arms she might have been naked beneath her exquisite sheer dress. "Perhaps you will be told to provide more information?"

The music had stopped. Now it started up again. Of all things, the famous Bolero. It was being played by the band with a compulsive up beat and a strong tango rhythm. Instinctively their interlocked bodies reacted. Along the length of the terrace other couples devoted themselves to their own form of the tango, while trying to keep within the spirit of the dance. Certainly the embrace was high on their list, with strong body connections, heads and faces touching.

"I know I have to be careful," Ava said, her voice unsteady. "I think we both know Karen will be reporting to Luke the minute she gets back home. If she hasn't done so already. I have come to the sad conclusion there's nothing my cousin wouldn't do to hurt me."

His body was finding it impossible not to move into the dance he knew so intimately. What woman could he desire more than Ava? When he was with her he felt somehow complete.

"When does she leave?" he asked rather curtly beneath his breath.

"Midday tomorrow."

He held her in a formal open embrace, gauging her knowledge of the dance. She followed him in total communication, arching her upper body away in the "ballroom" style of tango she would have been taught. She would know the famous dance had originated in Buenos Aires, but she didn't as yet know the striking difference between the Argentine tango and the positions and steps she had learned.

Only he would show her...

Ava felt rapt, carried along by sensation and responding perfectly to his signals. "You're such a beautiful dancer, Varo," she breathed, in a trance of pleasure.

"So are you. But your style is a little…formal. Let me show you." He moved her in close. Her breasts were against his chest, but there was a space between their hips. "Relax now. Relax totally," he said hypnotically. "Follow where I lead. Argentine tango continually changes. It is very improvisational. Emotion is extremely important. We have that, do we not?"

She felt desperately moved by his words. Did he *mean* them? Or was he giving way to infatuation? She was still so unsure of herself. Karen's planned intervention hadn't helped. They were dancing around the perimeter of the broad spacious terrace. The rhythm in his body, the musicality, seemed sublime. She had never known anything approaching it. It lifted her own dance skills, which she had been told many times were exceptional. But not like *this*. This was a communion of bodies…of souls…

No one cut across them. Everyone was now sticking to their own "lane", casting frequent glances at Varo and Ava and what they were doing. It might have been a master class, with a group of advanced students following the master's lead.

After a while—though Ava was scarcely aware of it, so caught up was she in the dance—the other couples cleared the terrace until it resembled a stage. The tango was the most passionate, the most exciting dance of them all. And here it was being so beautifully, so thrillingly performed on this wondrous day of days.

The wave upon wave of applause was sincere. Couples surrounded them, clapping and chanting, *"Bravo!"*

"That was the best example of the tango I've ever seen," exclaimed a flushed-faced Moira O'Farrell—no mean dancer herself. "I had no idea you were such a terrific dancer, Ava. So *sexy!*"

"This is the day to kick over the traces," her partner supplied.

In fact Ava had surprised them all—almost transfigured from the lovely, serene Ava they knew. She had packed so much *passion* into the famous dance it had been startling to those who knew her. Of course the Argentine was a past master. And the right partner was of tremendous importance. But neither had in any way been consciously showing off. It had passed way beyond that. It had appeared more like one glorious, even blatant, seduction.

The party broke up about three o'clock. The band had ceased playing an hour before that. Time to catch a few hours' sleep before the lavish brunch that was being served from eight o'clock onwards.

All the older guests had long since turned in. Finally the last stragglers went in search of their accommodation. Ava felt it her duty to remain at the party until the very end. Her mother and father had gone off on the crest of a wave, some time before one a.m., declaring themselves thrilled everything had gone so well.

"You don't see a lot of Karen, do you, darling?" her mother had asked, after kissing her goodnight.

"Not really." Ava had kept her smile.

"Good. I never liked that girl. She's rather unpleasant. For once I agree with your late grandfather. He never liked her either. You've got your own life, darling. She has hers. Hate to say it, but I don't trust her." Elizabeth's fine eyes had met those of her daughter's. "Be on your guard," she'd warned.

Ava went around the ground floor turning off all the main lights but leaving on a few lamps. There was no one around now. Oddly enough she didn't feel in the least tired.

She felt wired. It was a kind of refined torture—wanting someone desperately, having to keep oneself apart.

Varo had raised the point of the period of separation. Her application was a few months off being filed. She had an enemy in the house. In her cousin. Luke, for whatever reason, did seem intent on getting her back. Control was natural to men. Maybe even the *best* of men. She could pay a heavy price for allowing herself to have become so involved with Varo.

God, it's worth it!

She took the rear staircase to the upper floor, moving cautiously so as not to make any noise. Now, why did she do that? Was she deliberately playing with fire? Was she out of control? She could see Varo had not gone to bed, although they had said their formal goodnights thirty minutes ago. His bedroom was still illuminated. A shaft of light was raying under the door. She stood in the corridor, staring down the length of it. Wall sconces remained on, shedding a soft light.

All was silence. All was utterly still. The house slept.

She moved on soundless feet towards Varo's door, as if it was some forbidden rite. Her long chiffon skirt softly swished around her ankles. Her heart was beating in a frantic, unnatural way. She tossed her long hair over her shoulder, although golden strands clung to her heated cheeks.

What are you doing?

Her inner voice spoke up so sharply she backed away from the door, feeling a surge of panic.

You're not divorced from Luke yet.

Even so, she stood glued to the spot.

If I'm punished, I deserve it.

Astonishingly, as if he had a super sixth sense, Varo's door came open and his strong arm drew her swiftly inside as if she were a puppet on a string. Tingles started up all over her body...exquisite...probing. She began to flush from head to toe, as though molten liquid was being poured into her. She felt radiant, intoxicated, fearful.

"Varo, what are you doing?" Even her voice sounded afraid.

"Waiting for you. What else?" His dark eyes glittered as they rested on her. Her long blonde hair floated sinuously around her lovely camellia-skinned face, framing it. He could clearly see the pulse beating in the hollow at the base of her neck. That excited him. Her sparkling eyes were huge. Such emotion, such appeal was in them, it only served to inflame his passion.

"Dear Lord," she whispered. "This is *madness*!"

Madness. The word seemed to echo around the room, bouncing gently off the walls.

"Far better than doing nothing," he returned tautly, drawing her into his warm, close embrace. "Let me tell you about my mother and father when they were young. They surrendered to madness too—only they called it *love*."

Words of protest kept coming and going inside her head, but she didn't utter a one. She knew full well she was doing something dangerous. She knew she should be careful. But she wasn't a thinking woman in his arms. She lifted her face to him like a flower to the sun in the sky for its blessing. Tenderly he began to trace the contours of her mouth with a padded finger.

The sensation that poured into her made her shudder. She took his finger into her mouth, her tongue caressing it.

"Don't be afraid," he said.

"Varo, I am. Technically I'm still married." Her voice was strained, full of intensity.

His answer was a mix of hard authority and deep emotion. "It's not you and Luke any more. It's you and me."

"But *how*? You will go away soon. You could forget all

about me. You might say you'll call me, e-mail me—God knows I'd spend my time checking—but once you get home things will be different. Family affairs will keep you very busy. You said you and your father had big plans." She knew she might be left with nothing but a broken heart.

Except he said, very simply, "We wait a while."

Was she to agree to that? Why could she not find her voice? Of course she *had* to wait. Even without Luke's throwing up difficulties, and if her application was successful, the decree nisi would only become final one month and one day from the date of the divorce order. She still didn't know how soon her application would come before the court. What she did know was that she and Varo had reached the point of no return. She had confirmed that by hovering outside his door. He with his finely tuned sensibilities had known she would come to him. He had been waiting as though it were her decision.

Wasn't that your objective? her inner voice questioned sharply.

Yearning rose in her body as his mouth came down across her hair, her forehead, her nose, her cheek. She tipped her head back so he could kiss her throat, before he came back to settle on her receptive open mouth. No feigning of emotion with Varo. No pretence. No mechanical movements. No sense of a deep inner loneliness, lying beneath a man unfulfilled. Varo had lit up every last little part of her with passion. Pure passion. How often did one meet a man with whom one was in perfect accord?

She stood quietly while he removed her beautiful glimmering dress with extreme care, leaving her body covered by the mauve silk slip. Her light, slender limbs had turned heavy, as if she wanted to lie down. He must have known, because he lifted her high in his arms before placing her very gently on the turned-back bed.

"I would not harm you for the world, Ava," he murmured. His lustrous eyes burned. "I only want to love you a little. Give you pleasure. I will wait for you. For the right time. Have no fear. You have only to tell me to stop if you fear I go too far. I want making love to you to be so *natural*." His eyes on her were very brilliant, very tender.

Her whole body was drowning in sensation. She closed her eyes, feeling the heat of her sex but knowing this time was not to be their ultimate encounter. There were demands to be met. "Everything is natural with you," she whispered, as he kissed her inner wrist with its white translucence and faint tracery of blue veins.

"As it should be," he said softly, bending his head to kiss her gently, so gently, cupping her face with his hands.

All he knew was his desire, but he had made a vow not to seduce her into giving herself. The depth of feeling he had for her, the tenderness, the sense of protectiveness, was as potent as it was astounding. He broke contact with her mouth, controlling the fever. His eyes followed his hands. He drew them, imperceptibly trembling, down over the length of her, the indentation of her narrow waist, her hips, her thighs, her long slender legs. He didn't realise it but he was murmuring in Spanish.

"You are a revelation to me."

Such beauty!

He was inhaling the fragrance that rose from her body, his sex hardening, but that was something he could not control. Lovemaking without penetration could be an enormous stress on a man's body, but the lovemaking still retained many elements of rapture.

Convulsively Ava moved, so he could lie more comfortably beside her on the bed. These were Varo's hands on her, kissing, stroking through the silk of the light bra and wisteria-coloured silk slip that covered her. Oddly, it

seemed incredibly erotic. At some point she felt the cool
breeze hit her naked breasts. Her senses were flooded with
the warmth and the clean male scent of him. Lovemaking
with Varo was an extraordinary bewitching ritual. She could
hear little whimpering sounds. They were issuing from her
own lips. All there was was her desire for him; his desire
for her. She kept her eyes tightly closed, lost in a world of
exquisite sensation.

At one point she found herself gripping his strong naked
back in an effusion of heat and light, desperate to give him
as much pleasure as he was giving her. He had thrown
off his shirt long ago. They were both turning and twisting, bodies interlocking, totally absorbed the one in the
other, their bodies imploring, wanting consummation. Varo
wanted to know the whole of her, her glorious white flesh.
She was allowing it. He was finding it near impossible to
hold off the brilliant, overpowering rush of blind sex. Her
beautiful body had already dissolved beneath his hands.
He knew, like him, she could barely withstand the flood of
sensation.

His steely resolve was under threat. She was his. Those
inciting little exhalations! They were like a torch held
against his skin.

With a deep groan, his handsome face near tortured, he
began to breathe deeply, mustering control. Then he very
gently began to ease her bra and her silk slip back onto her
delicate white shoulders, kissing one and then the other.

"Ava, I have to stop," he muttered.

She opened her jewelled eyes to him. "I know." She put
up a caressing hand to stroke his handsome chiselled face,
moving her hand to clasp his nape, damp from his rising
temperature. Their lovemaking, however curtailed, had
been agony and ecstasy both. A rapture too extravagant to

describe. She had to marvel, and then bless Varo's capacity for control. She had been lost, adrift in a sea of sensation.

He fell back on the bed beside her, staring up at the orante plaster rose in the ceiling. "I knew it would be you," he murmured, almost to himself. "I knew it in that very first moment."

"As did I." Ava's response came from the depths of her heart.

That was the great mystery of it all. Destiny at work. Only the heart, once given, could never be recalled.

Ava knew beyond all question that she had given hers.

CHAPTER SEVEN

THE first thing Luke Selwyn did when he got up that morning, after yet another anger-racked night, was check his e-mail. He was hoping for some communication from Karen. Karen was a good sort—a loyal pal. He should have married someone like Karen, only she was totally lacking in sex appeal. *That* his poor Ava had in abundance. The joke was she didn't know it.

He was absolutely furious—his parents were too—that they hadn't been invited to Langdon's wedding to *that woman's* daughter. He would always think of Amelia as that. The irony of it all. She was now mistress of Kooraki, wife to the man in control of the Langdon fortunes. Amelia—who had looked at him with blazing contempt.

Bitch!

Karen hated her too. There were five messages from her in his in-box. Only *one* was he interested in. He opened that message first, read the contents—his wife was having a great time, was she?—then opened the attachment, wondering what it would contain.

What he saw made him sit down joltingly hard at his desk. How dared she? *How dared she?* A peculiar fury was racing through him. He had always had the upper hand with Ava, physically and psychologically. She had never rebelled, never protested—except at anything a bit adventurous he had wanted in the bedroom. Such a prude!

Her first and only deliberate act of rebellion had been in defying that tyrannical old bastard of a grandfather to marry *him*. Her second major rebellion had been in leaving him. Her betrayal would have left him desolated—only he knew he could force her back, and when he did he'd make her pay. No one was going to ditch him. Not even the heiress Ava Langdon-Selwyn. Her shocking lack of allegiance would cost her. He couldn't wait.

He clenched his fists in his lap, biting down involuntarily on his tongue. He tasted blood in his mouth. The attachment showed three shots of his wife dancing with some South American gigolo. As flamboyantly handsome as any matinee idol and a polo-player of all things. He couldn't believe their body language. *His* Ava! She looked like a member of some professional dance troupe, strutting her stuff. The final shot had him swearing aloud. The dance was a tango. Anyone would know that. And there was his precious frigid Ava, holding a pose that should never be. This was his *wife*, dammit! The fact that Ava could act in this abandoned way made him dizzy with rage. She wasn't going to be allowed to make a fool of him. No way!

The insufferably arrogant Langdon was away on his honeymoon with his equally arrogant wife. He hoped they had a miserable time of it. Terrible weather. Food poisoning. Lost luggage. Anything to spoil their dream time. He hated his brother-in-law with a passion. Now he hated his own wife. But he still wanted her. Oh, yes, he wanted her. He enjoyed their life together. He enjoyed controlling her. Only she had hurt him. So it was only fitting he would hurt her. The gigolo wouldn't present a problem, even if he did manage to stay on a while after Ava's parents returned home. He could easily find out when the Langdons were back in town. Arranging a charter flight to Kooraki would be easy enough.

Perhaps he ought to adopt the grieving-husband role? Enlist the gigolo's sympathies if he were still there? He was the husband, after all. It might not be far off but the application for divorce had not been filed. There was time for reconciliation. Ava knew her duty. Her duty was to him. The gigolo would see that. It wasn't as though he was after commitment. His life was in Argentina. Ava would never go there. The very thought of being away from her family would alarm her. A real cream puff was Ava.

Nevertheless, the shock of what he had seen had him still sitting in his chair a good twenty minutes later, staring all the while at a silver-framed photograph of his beautiful wife. It had pride of place on his desk. He still had her photograph on his desk at the office too. He knew Ava so well he took cold comfort in the fact she was extremely cautious by nature. No way would she have sex with a stranger. God, no! Ava had dozens of ardent admirers, who would give anything to spend a stolen hour with her. But Ava had never been unfaithful, was totally loyal. He trusted her completely. He'd had other women, of course. But that was different. Men were different. Men had different needs.

Her parents stayed on for a few days, at peace with one another and clearly enjoying themselves. They had taken a great liking to Varo, drawing closer to him every day. Clearly he was an exceptional young man who loved his family, his extended family, his country.

"Varo has a wonderful blend of sense and sensibility," Elizabeth remarked to her daughter. "It has such power to attract."

Elizabeth and Erik had derived great enjoyment from Varo's sense of humour, and his fascinating tales of Argentina and his family life there. He had invited them to stay at Estancia de Villaflores whenever they visited South America, which he hoped would be soon. The invitation had been issued with such genuine warmth both felt they might indeed take him up on it. Varo had assured them most charmingly that the *estancia* had as many guest rooms as Kooraki. His parents loved entertaining.

On the morning Ava's parents were to return home, Elizabeth sought a few private words with her daughter.

"You're in love with him, aren't you?" Elizabeth asked calmly and without preamble. She was half reclining on the chaise in Ava's bedroom, looking across at her daughter, who was sitting very quietly on the carved chest at the end of her bed.

Ava took a deep breath. She'd known this was coming. Her eyes met those of her mother. "I thought I was being *friendly*," she said, with a wry smile.

Elizabeth couldn't help laughing. "My darling, I'm a woman. I'm your mother. I understand perfectly why you're in love with him. What woman wouldn't be? He has *everything*." Elizabeth made an expansive little gesture. "He's everything Luke isn't."

Ava looked out at the gently swaying palms. "Of course he is. Do you think he loves me?"

Elizabeth smiled. "I may not have personally experienced the legendary *coup de foudre*, but I would say you two have. Your father agrees. He's very happy about it. The more the two of you attempt to play down your feelings, the more intense they appear. Have you slept with him?"

Ava felt her hot blush. *"Mum!"*

"Sorry, darling," Elizabeth apologised. "Only, you have

the radiance of a woman who is not only in love but is loved. What is Varo saying about the future?" she questioned with a slight frown. "He has deep ties to his family. He loves his own country."

Ava sighed. "I know that, Mum. All he says is, 'We wait a while.'"

"Implying?"

"I don't ask." Ava's shrug was a shade helpless. "I can't believe what is happening to me, Mum. I need a little time for the miracle to sink in. I never thought I could ever feel like this. I even thought I had a cool heart, if not cold. No, don't scoff. Luke was forever driving that point home. Maybe I can't believe it could ever work out for Varo and me. I can't even believe the divorce will proceed without incident. Luke is storing up trouble. He's like that. He'll throw anything he can in the way of holding up proceedings."

"So who's to talk?" Elizabeth asked derisively. "We're a thousand miles from anywhere. Luke knows nothing. Although I realise that dreadful girl Karen has always been his informant. Are you sure she's not keen on him herself?"

Ava shook her head. "Luke doesn't find Karen attractive. In fact he's said many an unkind thing about her. Her figure, in particular. How thin she is. He uses her, that's all."

"She could tell him about your famous dance..." Elizabeth said reflectively.

"Heard about it, did you?" Ava asked. Her parents had gone to bed before then.

"Certainly did." Elizabeth laughed. "You've always been a lovely dancer, but from all accounts you excelled yourself."

Ava's eyes were glitter-bright. "You know perfectly well how a wonderful partner can raise your performance. The tango is in Varo's blood."

"I bet!" Elizabeth laughed again. "The two of you must promise a repeat performance some time." Reluctantly she rose. "The wedding was simply marvellous. And it was lovely to hear from Dev and Amelia and know they're so blissfully happy." And now it seemed to Elizabeth her beloved daughter might have found the man of her dreams. "When is Varo going home?" she asked as they walked to the door. "He's come a long way. He will want to see lots more. The Red Centre was mentioned. Uluru and Kata Tjuta. He's so enjoying himself."

"I'm not pressing him for an answer," Ava said. "Rather the reverse."

She didn't say such thoughts and accompanying fears were never far from her mind. What would Varo's inevitable return to Argentina do to their relationship, for one? That was the burning question. She had to accept conflicts would arise. Could she give up her homeland for Varo? Could she leave the people she loved? She couldn't see that far into the future. Really, it all came down to Varo. If Varo loved her, all would be well.

Elizabeth put her arm around her daughter, hugging her close. "I want you to be happy, Ava. I pray for you to be happy. You're a lovely woman—inside and out. A wonderful loving daughter. Don't let Luke Selwyn intimidate you. I know it was the case in the past, his manipulation, though you never said anything. Dev and Amelia will be back home by the separation date—the year and the day. You have me and your father. We will be with you. Staying with a loveless marriage would be like being in a prison. The divorce *will* go through, my darling. You've a top lawyer. You're going to come out of this."

"One day, Mum," Ava said, her lovely smile a touch on the melancholy side.

* * *

She had to go in search of Varo. They had seen her parents off, and had a leisurely lunch over which they'd discussed where they would go on the station that afternoon.

It was a strange time for Ava, a euphoric time. She had the feeling the whole universe had changed. Simultaneously she wouldn't be shocked if it reverted to what it had been. Love affairs always started out with high hopes. She had even had hopes for herself and Luke, but never euphoria. Euphoria was like riding an ocean wave.

She thought she might take Varo out to see Malyah Man. The extraordinary rock formation was semi-sacred to the aboriginals on the station. It was a truly amazing spectacle, some eight feet tall, and resembled an aboriginal head atop a fiery limestone column rather like a Henry Moore sculpture or the Easter Island figures. Malyah Man stood alone in the remoteness, quite a distance beyond where they had so far gone.

She had been in awe of the rock all her life. There was something daunting about it, but it was certainly a sight worth seeing. Like all the rock formations on the station it changed colour from dawn to dusk. At midday it was a furnace-red that quickly lost intensity and became a reddish brown. By the end of the day it glowed a deep purple. She had seen Malyah Man in all his colours. What he was doing out there on his own in the wilderness no one knew.

She finally found Varo in a storeroom, crouching before a cupboard.

"Come on in." He made a wide sweep of his hand.

He looked wonderful to her eyes. Blazingly alive, exuding energy. What would she do if he disappeared out of her life? The pain would be excruciating.

Everything in life has its price.

She understood that. There might be a crushing price for her behaviour, although she and Varo had not slept together as her mother might have supposed. In any case, they had both become very aware of the proximity of her parents. It was agonising not to be together, but what option did they have? The high emotion of the wedding day had taken them by storm, sweeping aside their defences. Neither had set out with the intention of deliberately seducing the other. Fate had to take responsibility for that.

And here they were again.

Quite, quite *alone*.

She moved into the well stocked room, wondering what he was doing. "Can I help?"

"I'm after a powerful torch," he explained, turning his dark head to her. "The most powerful you've got."

"They're in the drawer over there." She pointed to the opposite wall of cabinets. "There are any number of powerful torches in use around the house. We have had floods and loss of power situations. The station store supplies the workforce."

"Presente!" Varo gave a cry of satisfaction, withdrawing a handheld torch. Ava could see the flashlight comprised an LED, not an incandescent bulb. This was the most powerful version of torch they had, with a solid waterproof assembly.

It suddenly struck her what he wanted the torch for. "You want to explore the hidden cave?" Her voice rose in sharp alarm.

"Ava, Ava… I will be very careful, you understand?" He put the torch down and came to her, taking her face between his hands.

"But it could be dangerous, Varo," she protested. "Dev hasn't gone all that far."

"Well, I intend to go a little further," he said, bending his head to kiss her not once but several times—tantalising little kisses promising much more. "It's in the nature of things, *mi querida*."

"Well, please leave *me* out!" Ava wrapped her arms tightly around him, revelling in his wonderful physicality. "As I told you, I'm more than a bit claustrophobic."

"But you *must* come with me," Varo insisted. "My concern for you will control my actions. I've done risky things. I've taken chances. I am a man, after all, and I will tell you I am considered a fine mountaineer. In my university days I led a team up one of the unexplored peaks of the Andes near the Chilean border. It was an unbelievable experience. I have made the ascent of active volcano Volcán Villarrica several times over the years. Thrilling, and not what *you* would consider safe. Climbers have fallen into lava pools and crevasses."

"Ugh!" Ava shuddered. "All in a day's climb?"

"Australia is different. You do not have our Andes, which as you know connect with the mighty Rocky Mountains."

"No, but we do have our Great Dividing Range," she reminded him with a smile. "I think it's the third longest in the world. I know it bears no comparison with the mighty Andes or the Rockies, but I still say exploring our cave system might be a tad dangerous even for you."

He traced the shallow dent in her chin with his fingertip. "I swear to you, Ava, I won't do anything foolish. Why would I? I will have you waiting for me."

The critical voice inside her started up again. *It could be dangerous.*

The problem was Juan-Varo de Montalvo wasn't your everyday man. A man of action, it would be nigh on impossible to stop him.

As a safety measure they had packed hard hats. Outside the cave the sun was at its zenith, blindingly hot and bright. Inside the cave the temperature had chilled. Varo donned his hard hat, shining the powerful torch around the cave. The great crocodile seemed to be slithering across the roof. The stick figures had picked up their dance.

It was quite spooky, Ava thought, shining her own torch. God knew how many tonnes of rock were over their heads. She couldn't help thinking of Joan Lindsay's famous story, *Picnic at Hanging Rock*. The hill country was ancient, its peaks eroded over millions of years. The thought of losing Varo, the man she knew she loved and her guest, sent waves of terror through her. Her heart was even bumping against her cotton shirt.

Varo looked down at her with brilliant eyes. "Give me your blessing."

She opened her mouth to say something, but no sound came out.

"Do not worry. I'll be fine. One kiss before I begin."

"You're crazy," she whispered.

"About you."

They kissed open-mouthed. His tongue traced the lovely shape of her lips. He stroked her cheek reassuringly and then moved away to the neck of the tunnel, bending low to make his entrance. She already knew there was a long narrow passageway, leading to a chamber where a tall man could stand up with his head clearing the roof by about a foot. Dev had told her that. She also knew cave systems could go on for miles. And that highly experienced cave explorers could and did get lost. But this was a man used to high adventure. Clearly their cave system intrigued him.

She sat down on the sand, her back against a smooth un-painted section of the wall. It took her several moments to realise she was holding her breath. Around her was absolute silence. She couldn't hear Varo at all. Knowing so much about the aboriginal people and their legends, their sacred places and their taboo places, she began to wonder if the all-powerful spirits thought of them as trespassers. She knew if the cave turned pitch-black she would scream her head off. Maybe she and Varo would never leave here, like the party of schoolgirls who had simply vanished from the face of the earth.

Get a grip, Ava, said the voice in her head. *Too much imagination.* No harm had come to Dev, although he'd admitted he hadn't been too keen on exploring all that far. For one thing their grandfather would have been furious if he'd ever found out Dev had made the attempt. Quite simply, Dev had been the most important person in the world to their grandfather. Even then the planned heir, over their father.

Varo wasn't feeling Ava's apprehension. Body and mind were set on establishing what lay ahead. He had spent a great deal of time exploring rocky caves and slopes. Here it didn't seem especially dangerous, although the air smelled strange—as though it had been trapped in the cave system for millions of years. And the entry tunnel was easily negotiated, even if it seemed to go on too long. He realised he was on a descending slope, going deeper into the bedrock. Twelve minutes by his watch and he was able to clamber out into a large cave, with tumbled boulders like devil's marbles acting as giant stepping stones to the cave floor. This was Dev's cave.

He trained his powerful torch on the roof of the cavern. No rock paintings here. The roof looked quite smooth, as did the walls. The action of water over the millennium? Who knew? There had been an inland sea at the centre of this great continent in prehistoric times. Surely proof was in that rock drawing of the great crocodile, the fish and the sea creatures? He was a bit disappointed, however. He wanted excitement, achievement.

The atmosphere had turned several degrees colder. He pointed the torch downwards. The sand beneath his feet appeared speckled with gold.

"Fantastico!" he breathed aloud. He knew Dev had felt he had to call a halt on his exploration at this point. *He* intended to go further, but without putting himself at risk. He was acutely mindful of Ava's anxieties. This entire area that the family called the Hill Country—the aboriginals would have another name for it, like all indigenous people—he knew to be honeycombed with caves.

He trained his torch on the next narrow opening. It would be a tight squeeze for a man his size…

Ava thought of going in after him then rejected the idea. She hated confined spaces. She didn't even like travelling in an elevator on her own. Even the best had problems. She had to trust Varo's judgement just as she had trusted Dev's.

But it was close on forty minutes now. How long should she wait? She wondered how much trusting she could fit inside her chest. Men and their adventuring, always tilting at death. Women spent more time considering the dangers and the consequences. Women were much more careful. Women wouldn't start wars.

She completely ignored the fact that she had given the tough game of polo a go. Her grandfather had protested on the grounds that it was not a fitting game for a female. Not because she might injure her precious limbs. Oh, no! She hadn't complied. She'd been rather good at polo, although naturally down some levels from the top notch. She loved horses and they loved her. She didn't think there was a horse she couldn't ride.

A bird—a hawk—swooped, and then flew into the neck

of the cave. She let out a strangled screech that matched the predatory bird's, but in the next moment it had flown out again. She jumped to her feet because she was so agitated.

Sounds came first. Then the beam of the powerful flashlight.

Thank God! Varo was coming back. Her emotions were bobbing up and down like a cork in a vat.

He all but swam out of the cave. Clear of the tunnel wall, his arms shot out sideways, as if he were taking wing.

"Varo!" Her cry was both relieved and anxious.

He was swiftly on his feet. He didn't even stop to catch breath. If a man's face could be called radiant, then it was his. "You have to come back with me," he said, yanking off his hard hat and thrusting a hand through his tousled jet-black waves. "It's *fantastico!*" He caught at her hand, the skin of his face as cold as if he'd been out in a snowstorm. "I've never seen anything like it before."

"Like what?" Despite herself she felt caught up in his excitement.

"I won't tell you. You must see. I should tell you first there's a narrow passageway that turned out to be a bit of a squeeze for me, but you'll slide through it."

"Am I free to refuse?" she asked, with humour and a trace of real fear.

"Of course. But there's no danger. I don't know about further into the cave system. There could be real danger there. One would need the proper equipment. But so far so good, as they say." He reached down to pick up her hard hat. "Here—put it on. You will be safe with me, my love. Bring your torch. You can't say no, Ava. You will be missing something."

He sounded and looked as exhilarated as she imagined Howard Carter might have looked and sounded when he opened up Tutankhamen's tomb ninety years before.

Ava took the hard hat from him, settling it on her head. With Varo beside her she could conquer her fears one by one.

"Lead the way," she invited.

In the "squeeze" passageway she felt a split second of overwhelming claustrophobia. She wanted to scream, but she didn't have enough air in her labouring lungs. What did the air smell of anyway? Bizarrely, she thought of shingle at low tide. Salt, sand, a whiff of fish and sea creatures. How crazy was that?

Just as she was about to fall flat on her stomach and stay there a minute or two, the passageway opened up.

Varo was through, reaching back for her. He pulled her out with as little effort as he might expend on a child. They were standing on a huge slab of limestone roughly ten feet square—one of many flat slabs descending to the cavern floor. To Ava's astonished eyes the huge area looked like a theatre, held up by fabulous twisting pillars The sight was so fantastic, so surreal, it almost hurt her to look. Yet she felt quite secure.

She pushed her shoulders back. Her breathing eased. Varo's strong arm was locked around her. She felt there was no space between them. She had fallen so madly in love the other versions of herself had faded into the past. This was the start of a whole new Ava.

"*Vaya!* Well?" He unfastened his headgear, then hers, dropping the hard hats on the huge slab.

His vitality was like an electric field. It sent charges sizzling through her. "Oh, my God!" she murmured, her awe mixed with reverence. "This is utterly fantasmagorical—if there is such a word."

Stalagmites, stalactites—she wasn't sure which was which—marvellous curtain-like draperies, giant toadstools apparently formed from ochre mud, others the shape of the water-lily pads that grew in such profusion over Kooraki's billabongs and lagoons, all filled the grand space. In one area there was an organ like structure she thought might thunder if it was ever played.

The smell of the sea inside the cavern was even stronger, yet there wasn't a visible drop of water about them. No shallow pools. Certainly no underground river. They were, however, over the Great Artesian Basin. The cave was as dry as ancient bones.

"These are natural heritage objects, are they not?" Varo asked, turning his lustrous eyes on her.

She nodded in wonderment. She was finding it hard to process all she was seeing. They were holding two powerful torches, but the brightness inside the chamber was hard to explain. She looked up. The sun might have been shining through a hole in the roof of the cavern, except of course it wasn't.

"Protected by law," she confirmed. "One can't break even the tiniest piece off. Which are the stalagmites? I should know."

"The ones growing vertically from the cavern floor," he replied. "The stalactites are the curtains. See how they touch each other, forming the draperies? This wonderful scene was formed by dripping or flowing water perhaps a million years ago. Your famed inland sea?" he suggested.

"It could well be," Ava said. Her whole being was aglow. "To think it has all been here for probably thousands of years. I should think the early aboriginal tribes would have known about these caves. And the rock paintings."

"The ones that did know would have died out."

"But they always passed on their legends. And what about all the sparkles on the floor of Dev's cave?"

A smile swept his dynamic face. "Fool's gold?"

She lifted her face to the mighty organ, with shifting prisms of light bouncing off its cylindrical pipes. "Do you think we should be here?" she asked softly. "This could be a sacred site for all I know."

"Frightened, are you?" There was a pronounced tease in his voice.

"Not with you. We're together." She had never said such a thing before. Never felt like this before. "Have you ever heard the legend of Lasseter's Reef, Varo?" she asked, prompted by the mystery glitter. Opal matrix had been found on the station. But no gold-bearing quartz veins. *As yet!*

His face relaxed into his devastatingly attractive smile. "I am sorry, but no," he said gently. He was gaining enormous pleasure from her reactions, and the fact she had conquered her claustrophobia. That was brave.

"Then I'll tell you the greatest mystery of our gold fields."

"I'm listening, but let's go down." He kept an arm around her, guiding her as they descended the staircase of toppled slabs. Memory was stirring. Something he had read somewhere, some time. That riveting word *treasure*!

"Debate continues to this day." Ava was staring around her in a wondering way. What would Dev and Amelia make of this? She couldn't wait to tell them. "Gold was the backbone of the nation then. There were huge gold strikes all over."

"I've heard."

"Prospectors came from all over the world." She crouched over the extraordinary "lily pads", awestruck. They might have been cast in stone over a living plant. "Harold Lasseter was a young prospector who became hopelessly lost when he was prospecting for rubies in the MacDonnell Ranges."

"That's the Red Centre?" Varo asked. He was looking

forward to seeing the great desert monuments. Ava *had* to be with him.

Ava nodded. "It was long ago—around the late 1890s. My family, the Langdons and the Devereauxes, were here, pioneering the cattle industry. Anyway, Lasseter claimed when he was found, starving and dying of thirst, he had stumbled across a fabulous reef of gold and taken samples. An Afghan camel driver actually saved his life. Three years later, restored to health, he went back with a surveyor. They claimed to have re-found the reef, taking bearings with their watches."

"Only to find when they got back to civilisation their watches were incorrect?" Varo guessed.

"You've heard this story," she said wryly.

Varo only shrugged.

"Other expeditions followed, but it was all too dangerous. Forbidding territory, and the tribes were well equipped to defend their land. Spearing of the invading white man was common, which meant the Government of the day wasn't keen on sending expeditions into the desert to be killed or die of starvation and thirst."

"Okay—you tell me this so we can go and find it?" he asked, amused.

"Many people believe the reef is out there." She was speaking now in a hushed whisper.

They began to pick their way with the utmost care across the floor of the cavern, avoiding all the extraordinary formations. The bone-dry sand crunched beneath their feet.

"This is out of this world!" Ava exclaimed, enraptured by such a spectacle.

"The best news is we are quite alone," Varo said "*Finally.* I do like your parents. I enjoyed their company. But I longed for us to be together." He put out a hand, bringing her to her feet. He tugged gently on the silk scarf that tied back her hair, releasing it in a flood of gold.

"You want to make love?" she asked, on a long, voluptuous sigh.

"Need you ask?"

The expression of tenderness in his eyes almost brought her to tears. "This could be a sacred place, Varo."

"What we feel is sacred, is it not?" he asked, very gravely. "You fall in love with me. I with you."

She expected her inner voice to step in. Only it didn't. There was nothing to explain this. Nothing to gainsay it either.

All was quiet. The fantastic formations might have been ancient statues, quietly watching on. This was a dream, not a nightmare.

"Come here to me."

Varo took her torch from her, set it down beside his so the combined lights spread their illumination all through the cavern. There were no dark shadows, only wondrous natural sculptures. Could any woman resist an invitation like this?

Ava buried her face against his chest. "You *made* me love you."

"Is that the start of a song?" he mocked gently.

She lifted her head, her heart in her eyes. "Neither of us planned this, Varo. I wasn't ready for it. It's all happened so very, very quickly."

"Can one call *destino* a bad thing?" His deep dark voice crooned gently against the shell of her ear.

"Destiny?" That was the way she saw it. "I'm in love with you, Varo," she admitted freely. "I'm in love with a man from another land."

Emotion made his voice rough. "I will never leave you, *mi querida*. You will never leave me."

"How can that be—?" She started to speak, but his mouth covered hers so passionately her heart contracted. She was consumed.

"You understand it will take a little time?" Slowly, almost dazedly, he lifted his head.

"I *will* be a divorced woman, Varo." She felt compelled to point that out. "Your parents, your sisters, your family might not approve of a divorced woman in your life."

"My family will have their say of course," he admitted without hesitation. "All families do—especially one as close as mine. But *I* make the decisions. Besides, you are an angel."

"No, I'm not!" Her jewel-like eyes blazed. She didn't want Varo to put her on a pedestal.

"Not you're not!" he agreed gently in his throat. "You're a woman. All woman. *My* woman."

His dark, dark gaze was ardent, diamond-bright. In one smooth motion he had her blue and white striped cotton shirt free of her jeans, easing it off her shoulders.

Was it her over-active imagination or was the cavern lit in a golden glow?

"You're feverish!" His mouth was gliding all over her satin smooth exposed skin. Shirt and flimsy stretch lace bra had since fallen to the sand.

"On fire," she whispered back.

Very tenderly he lowered her to the sand. It didn't feel crunchy at all. It felt more like a velvet quilt. He couldn't leave her after this. He *couldn't*. This was not only a ravishing physical experience. It was spiritual.

Varo bent his head to kiss the tears away from her eyes. "We pick our path, my beautiful Ava. Nothing feels wrong to you, does it?" he asked with marked tenderness.

"How could anything be wrong when we are together."

Ava knew now she would put up the fight of her life to hold on to her love.

Varo.

She had been too malleable too much of the time. Too afraid to reach out. She wasn't there yet. But she would be. That was her vow.

CHAPTER EIGHT

HE HAD little difficulty chartering a flight to Kooraki Station from the domestic terminal at Longreach. It cost him, but Luke had never felt so determined on something in his entire life. He wanted Ava back. He was going to get her back. And, by God, he would make her suffer when he did. Not physically—never physically. He was after all a gentleman. But he had special psychological powers over his wife.

She had as good as accepted she hadn't been a good wife to him. In his world, the *real* world, the *man* reigned. He had quickly learned how to control Ava's spirit. She was too gentle by far, too tender, too sensitive. She had always been frightened of conflict. That old bastard Gregory Langdon with his Midas touch must be answering for a lot, he thought with intense satisfaction. Ava had been terrified of her grandfather. And she hadn't been the only one. Most people had. Except for Amelia's beautiful conniving mother, who had been left a considerable fortune by her long-time lover. Great to know she was an outcast now, shunned by all.

There was no one about when he landed. He waited on the tarmac until the pilot turned the nose of the Cessna about. Then until he was taxiing down the runway to take off. He hated flying in light aircraft. As far as he was concerned light aircraft had a bad reputation.

Two sulphur-yellow helicopters were grounded to the right of the giant silver hangar emblazoned on its roof with the station's name. He strolled over to a station Jeep, saw with relief the keys were in the ignition. Why not? Who was there to steal the vehicle? The Langdons ruled this Outback kingdom. James Devereaux Langdon, his revered brother-in-law, wore authority like a cloak. Quickly he pitched his suitcase in the back, then climbed into the driver's seat. No way was he going to walk up to the homestead. It was a hell of a distance, and he had always hated the dry inland heat. The Jeep was a gift.

He had a plan in place. The Argentine was still there— a favoured guest. Elizabeth and Erik Langdon were back in Sydney. Karen always had kept him well informed. Pity she wasn't more attractive. Well, she *was* in her way, and extremely smart, but her fine-boned featured face was a bit too much on the hard side. Actually, Karen Devereaux was a genuine bitch. No friend to Ava, but she had come in handy over the years when he needed information.

His idea was not to confront his wife in anger. Dear me, no! He had to get this de Montalvo guy on his side. Perhaps Ava hadn't done anything wrong. Perhaps the Argentine hadn't done anything wrong either. To split them, thus bringing any budding relationship to a halt, he intended pouring his husbandly woes into Montalvo's ear. By and large *he* was the innocent party. He, the long-suffering husband. Ava had led him an excruciating emotional dance. Ha-ha—not the tango. He had accepted all the punishment she had meted out. The thing was he loved her. He adored her. He saw no life, no future without her.

He had few peers when it came to winning people around. He was, he knew, an unsung genius. He had a top job. No one was about to steal his wife away from him. Certainly not a South American gigolo.

The housekeeper was at the front door to greet him. No, *greet* wasn't the right word, he quickly saw. From the expression on her dark-skinned face she was tossing up whether to slam the door on him or reluctantly admit him. She ought to be dismissed.

Her liquid black eyes bored into his. "Ms Ava is not at home," she announced, clearly challenging him to dispute it.

For a moment he felt like giving her a good shove out of his way. Rude bitch! He had encountered her before. "That's all right," he returned very mildly, as though he had plenty of time. "Where is she? It's Mrs...isn't it?" He couldn't for the life of him think of her name.

She didn't supply it. For God's sake, didn't she know how a housekeeper was supposed to behave?

"I'm hoping to stay for a few days," he said, preparing to sweep past this formidable woman. "My wife and I need to talk. Perhaps you could show me my room? When are you expecting my wife back?" he asked, playing up the *wife* for all he was worth. They had been estranged for more than nine months now and time was running out. This surprise visit was very serious.

The woman gave a twirl of her hand. "I have no idea. Miss Ava is not on Kooraki at this time. She is showing a guest around Alice Springs and our most famous desert monuments."

He forced an untroubled smile. "That's nice. The Langdons are extremely hospitable people. I'm in no hurry. I have a week off to expedite a couple of outstanding matters. I'd like to see my room now, if it's no trouble? It was a long trip getting here. Lunch would be nice—in, say, an hour?"

With hidden amusement he watched the housekeeper inhale hard through her wide nostrils. But what could she do? Throw him out? He *was* Ava's husband, after all. He was being perfectly respectful. He had deliberately used the word *expedite*. To all intents and purposes he was here to agree to a divorce, throwing no objections into the pot. It was all politics. He spent much of his time pretending this and that.

Ava and Varo flew back into Kooraki late afternoon the following day. Nula Morris hadn't wasted a moment leaving a message for Ava at the hotel where they'd been staying—in separate rooms—so they were prepared for a confrontation of some sort. Luke Selwyn would never have dared to set foot on the station with the Master of Kooraki at home, but Dev and Amelia were currently in Rome.

To Varo it was quite simple. He was here to keep Ava from all harm. He wasn't concerned about Ava's husband. From what he had gleaned from Dev and Amelia, and around the station, Luke Selwyn was held in poor regard. He had been judged by one and all as an unsuitable husband for Ava. They had all known Ava had been desperate to escape an unhappy home life. But her hopes of happiness had sadly unravelled along the way.

Nevertheless Varo had not been prepared to meet such an outwardly pleasant and good-looking man. He resembled an English actor whose name eluded him—the one with the floppy fair hair and earnest blue eyes. It was obvious Luke Selwyn was still deeply emotionally involved with his beautiful wife. Indeed, when he had come downstairs to greet them his blue eyes had momentarily shone with tears. He appeared to be taking Ava's wish for a divorce with stoicism, and a considerable degree of pain that he sought to hide—or was going all out to create that impression. There was no sign whatsoever of fuming jealousy, hostility, let alone paranoid rage. Not that Ava had spoken out against her husband. He thought Ava was prepared to shoulder her own share of blame.

Only it couldn't be easy to throw one's husband aside, jettison a marriage. Selwyn would have to be some sort of ogre figure. He certainly didn't present himself as one. And he had risked coming out here, where he clearly wasn't wanted. But then things happened in a marriage. For better or worse.

Ava flatly refused to sit down opposite her husband for dinner. "We're finished, Luke," she told him firmly. "Why are you here?" She raised her elegant brows. She knew Luke was well into role-playing and she disapproved strongly.

"I hope it's not an inconvenience for me to come here, Ava. I wanted to say—I just wanted to clear up a few points."

He thought he looked the very picture of embarrassment to the Argentine standing at Ava's shoulder. De Montalvo was very tall and devilishly handsome, but not in any matinee idol way. He looked damned formidable. He had been hoping for a bit of a playboy. No such luck! The man had real charisma. And obviously, going on everything about him—his manner, his speech, his air of confident authority—he came from a privileged background. That was the big surprise.

Karen had spoken about de Montalvo as though his main attraction was phenomenal sex appeal. Indeed, she thought de Montalvo so sexy she could hardly contain herself. He could see the sex appeal, all right. But *daunting* was a better word. De Montalvo was no one's fool either. It would be an enormous coup to turn this man off Ava. But it was *possible*. Anyway, wouldn't a guy like that, who had it all, have a girlfriend back home? Hell, a string of girlfriends. He *was* a hot-blooded Latin, after all.

In the end Ava relented. He had been counting on that.

They were all adults, civilised people, weren't they? Dinner actually went smoothly, considering just the three of them sat down and there were so many subterranean currents. Nula was an excellent cook. He had to give her that. He was very particular about his food. And drink, of course. Kooraki maintained an excellent cellar.

For starters they were served quietly and unobtrusively with crab and mango salad and wafer-thin fresh coconut slices, followed by duck breast on a bed of hot steaming wild rice. An exquisite *millefeuille* with passionfruit curd was wheeled in for dessert. No complaints there.

Ava could put a decent meal together at a pinch, but she wasn't in the same class as her mother. But she was *so* beautiful, with her tender, angelic face. He felt like reaching out and slapping it. Not able to do that—he could just imagine how de Montalvo would react—he continued drawing the Argentine out about life in his own country as though he were really interested. They had already discussed Uluru and the Olgas, for God's sake. Been there, done that.

Of course the two of them had slept together. There was no doubt whatsoever in his mind. Ava had an astonishing *glow* about her. A luminescence that lit up her blonde beauty. Unfaithful bitch! How he didn't leap to his feet and savage them both with furious accusations he didn't know. Or perhaps he did. The upshot might have been de Montalvo knocking him flat. Instinct told him the Argentine would be quite the wrong man to cross. And he looked so damned athletic—physically superior at every level.

But did he want Ava? That was the burning question. Or did he have an affair in every part of the world he wandered into? It was hard to gauge the Argentine's thoughts. The coal-black eyes were brilliant but quite unfathomable. Surely it couldn't be an act, de Montalvo's displaying interest in what he had to say? Then again, he had been told

more than once he was an excellent conversationalist. De
Montalvo had even asked him if he had ever played polo.
He had answered regretfully that he had never had the time.
What he'd actually meant was, had he ever considered play-
ing the game of polo he would have needed his head read.
Life and limb were much too precious.

Now all he had to do was keep his cool, act brain-dead
in relation to their trip together and his wife's scandalous
behaviour, and get de Montalvo alone. He wasn't sure if he
should play his trump card. It was a horrendous lie, and it
could prove dangerous, but he suspected he might have to
use it. He had to change the Argentine's opinion of Ava,
who was still *his* wife. That called for drastic measures.

All's fair in love and war, old son!

Fortune smiled on him. He had to control a mad desire to
fall to his knees and give thanks. By an incredible stroke of
luck one of the Langdon circle—a near neighbour Siobhan
O'Hare, the one who had lusted after Langdon but lost out
to Amelia—took a trip over to Kooraki to visit. No doubt
to find out if the honeymooners were surviving the honeymoon, he thought waspishly. Obviously hope sprang eternal.
If ever the marriage broke down, the ever-faithful Siobhan
would be waiting in the wings. God knew how she thought
she could ever replace the glorious, voluptuous Amelia. But
most women had inferior reasoning powers.

Juan-Varo de Montalvo, *hidalgo* that he was, was on
hand to say hello to Ava's visitor—who, let's face it, looked
at de Montalvo with a suspicion she couldn't hide in her
eyes. Why was the glamorous Argentine still on Kooraki?
Shouldn't he have already gone on his way?

He knew exactly the thoughts that were ticking over in
little Siobhan's head. Ava was still married. To *him*. Luke
Selwyn. Blue-chip lawyer. What was *he* doing on Kooraki,

for that matter? Initially she had looked as though she had stumbled into a war zone, but with his natural charm of manner he had made it clear there was no animosity between him and Ava. She was permitted the sneaking feeling he was secretly devastated, but hiding it like a man.

To celebrate this wonderfully timely intervention he suggested to the Argentine they take a run around the station in the Jeep that was parked out at the front.

"Might be my last time here," he said, with a pained air of regret. "Ava said at dinner she intended taking you out to see Malyah Man?" He had found the weird sandstone monument bloody terrifying, but he had to get de Montalvo somewhere out there, where they wouldn't be interrupted. Malyah Man was ready to hand. "I could show you," he said, giving the other man a friendly smile.

Varo stared down at Selwyn, wondering what was going on beneath the convivial exterior. The man could be a sociopath for all he knew. He knew a sociopath's destructive qualities were not easily recognised. They could be charming when required. He had heard Ava's husband was a very self-centred man. Whatever Selwyn was, he knew he could handle him.

"You have a camera?" Luke asked, rubbing his chin.

"Sure."

"You might like to take photos," he suggested. "It's an incredible structure—rather like those Easter Island statues. The girls can enjoy morning tea and a chat without us around. We'll be back in little over an hour. It really is an exceptional sight."

When de Montalvo went off in search of Ava he stood in the Great Hall, rocking in his boots. He had gained valuable time with his wife's lover. He had to make the most of it. He would really like old Malyah Man to topple and fall in a great crush on the Argentine. He wouldn't mind that at all. But he knew it wasn't going to happen.

Ava wasn't at all happy Varo had agreed to go for a trip around the station with Luke. But what could she do? If she said she didn't want him to go with Luke, it might appear to him as if she had something to hide. Her way to prevent Luke from giving his side of the story.

She hesitated, her mind racing. Luke was up to no good. She knew him too well. He would be out to squeeze the last little drop of sympathy he could out of Varo. That was the role he had chosen to play. The wronged husband. Helpless to keep a wife who no longer wanted him or needed him. She came from a rich family, but now she had no sense of dependency on anyone—much less her husband. Her grandfather, thinking she would never be able to stand on her own two feet, had made her totally independent for life.

Ava's nerves were jangling. She couldn't help feeling a creeping apprehension. If Luke couldn't have her, Luke would be out to destroy her. Or her one big chance at happiness.

"Well?" Varo questioned humorously, as she hesitated.

"I had intended showing you Malyah Man myself." She tried not to show any trace of her inner agitation.

Varo shrugged. "Then Selwyn and I will go some place else. There—that's decided."

Siobhan's clear voice piped up from the seating area behind them. She could feel Ava's tension. And why wouldn't she be tense? It was obvious to her there was something between Ava and the dashing Argentine. Luke Selwyn must be feeling it too—not that she had ever liked him. But one *could* feel pity. "Oh, Malyah Man is marvellous, Varo. You must see it before you go home," she enthused.

Ava took a breath. "Well, I suppose if Luke wants to show you, then go by all means."

"Not if you're upset about it?" Varo took no heed of the overly curious neighbour. It was all he could do not to draw Ava into his arms, hold her tight against his chest.

Ava raised a smile. The last thing she should appear was anxious. Or, even worse, *guilty.* "Of course not. Don't be long."

"Just over an hour, Selwyn said."

"Lunch at one," she reminded him, turning to her uninvited guest, whose ears and eyes were agog. "You're staying, of course, Siobhan?"

Siobhan pinkened up. "Love to," she gushed. She couldn't wait to tell her mother all about this. The Argentine was so sexy she felt a throb in her own blood.

Poor old Luke!

Blazing sunlight flooded the plains. On the far side of them the jagged outline of the ancient Hill Country stood fierily against a cobalt sky. Never until the day he died would Varo forget the sublime experiences he and Ava had shared.

He had seen many extraordinary and extreme sights so far in his life, taken many adventurous journeys. He and two friends had once loaded their backpacks and climbed to the top of a spurting volcano, where they'd had to don masks and protective gear. With the same companions he had gone extreme white-water rafting in turbulent waters. He had visited Antarctica—amazing beyond belief—and the Galapagos Islands with their wonderful evolutionary marvel the giant Galapagos Turtle and magnificent marine iguanas—the only sea-going lizards in the world.

He had followed the Argentine revolutionary Che Guevara's journey on his own motorcycle, half believing in the Curse of Che. It was well documented that the Bolivian politicians and generals who had shared responsibility for his death had later met with violent accidental deaths themselves. He had visited all the wonders North and South America could offer. He had seen the great awe-inspiring desert monuments of Central Australia.

But he had never before made passionate love to a woman while lying on the velvety sand of an ancient cavern with fantastic pre-historic formations gazing down at them. It was an experience that had great meaning for him, because he knew the passion he felt for Ava was true.

Luke Selwyn's voice jolted him out of his lingering euphoria. "Almost there," he announced, with a sidelong grin. "He looks a cantankerous old bugger, Malyah Man. I know Ava was always frightened of him. But then Ava has phobias." He paused for a moment, gnawing his lip. "I love her, you know."

"Love her or want to hold on to her?" Varo asked bluntly, glancing across at Ava's husband.

"Of course I want to hold on to her," Luke freely admitted, almost banging his fist on the wheel. "What man wouldn't? She's so beautiful."

"She is. But she has many other qualities to be greatly admired," Varo clipped off.

"Of course, of course," Luke agreed at once. "She's the loveliest person in many ways. But it broke my heart that she didn't want children. I know what was at the bottom of it, of course," he said with deep regret. "For all the fact she was a Langdon, she had a miserable childhood. She was terrified of her grandfather. He was an immensely powerful, tyrannical man."

Varo felt his heart flip over in his chest. Ava didn't want children? Could Selwyn, who appeared genuinely brokenhearted, possibly lie about something like that?

He suddenly remembered how his eldest sister, Sophia,

had sworn she would never go through the experience of childbirth again after Alvaro, his nephew, had been born after a prolonged and difficult labour. Sophia, however, had changed her mind. She had brought adorable little Isabella into the world, with none of the trauma associated with Alvaro's birth. Maybe his beautiful Ava felt threatened by the pain of childbirth? Men couldn't totally understand. He had friends who had been overwhelmed by their wives' first pregnancy. Over-protective, over-anxious—living the pregnancy. He felt he might be like that too. One's wife would be the most important woman in the world.

"Are you okay?" Luke was asking with concern. "You've gone quiet on me."

"Have I? I was thinking about my sister, actually," he said, choosing his words. "You were telling me Ava doesn't want children?"

Luke took a deep breath before continuing—a man trying to calm himself. "I was. It blew me away. There was never a hint of it before we were married. I naturally assumed Ava would want children as much as I do. My parents were longing for a grandchild. But Ava's attitude firmed with every passing day. I wanted her to have counselling about it, but she flatly refused. Please don't think I didn't try to calm her, Varo. I believe she really fears childbirth. Some women do. It got to the point where I was getting a bit paranoid myself. And then we discovered she *was* pregnant. My God!" he said quietly. "I was the *enemy* from that moment. Something must have gone wrong with her contraception method. It happens. I have to confess when she told me I couldn't help but be *thrilled*. The longed-for child! I promised Ava I would do anything—everything—to support her, that we would get her safely through pregnancy together—" He broke off, overcome by emotion.

The towering figure of Malyah Man loomed ahead, but

Varo was seeing it through a blinding haze. He had to grit his teeth. Even his breathing was constricted. Out of the clear blue he was abruptly unsure of anything. He might just as well have stepped off a cliff. Ava was in his bloodstream. He had come to think of her as part of his destiny. But what did he *really* know of her? Indeed, what did she know of *him*? The two of them had been swept away by the force of their feelings. It was a classic case of the heart ruling the head, the fatal *coup de foudre*. Still, a big part of him was highly suspicious of Selwyn, the self-styled wronged husband.

"Let's park the Jeep first," Selwyn suggested, like a man trying to buy time. "I can't go on for the moment. I get too damned upset. Ava was the centre of my world. A child would have made us complete. I was *absolutely* certain Ava would come around. I really felt that her peculiar fears would pass. A kind of phobia, I suppose. Not all women long to have a child. Many elect to go childless these days. Some don't even want a man as soon as they become financially independent. Sorry if I'm drawing you into this, Varo," he said, with an apologetic half-smile. "But it's good to be able to talk to someone. You know—like strangers on a train. I can't talk to my parents. I wouldn't dream of talking to our friends—"

"But surely you have Karen Devereaux's ear?" Varo broke in, feeling the heat of anger but fighting it down. He wanted to grab hold of Sewlyn, drag him out of the vehicle, beat the truth out of him. Yet his question was asked suavely, with a touch of sarcasm.

Selwyn responded at once, as though anxious to clear that point up. "As though I'd talk to Karen about Ava!" he exclaimed, lifting one hand off the wheel and throwing it up for emphasis. "Poor old Karen has been competing with my wife all her life. She is horrendously jealous of Ava. She has every reason to be. No, I couldn't confide in Karen," he said ruefully, shaking his head, "although she likes to keep in touch. She rings me from time to time. Karen doesn't trust many people, but she trusts me."

Varo kept silent. His nerves were drawing tighter every second. He could see Selwyn wanted to tell him more. He wasn't at all sure how he would react. He would never have thought for a moment Ava might not want children. He had assumed she was a woman who loved children as he did. Now he was no longer sure of anything. He would bide his time, hear Selwyn out.

Like the vast desert monuments Uluru and Kata Tjuta, rising as they did out of the featureless plains, so too did Malyah Man. The striking sandstone pillar was set in the middle of nowhere, surrounded by grassy flats that were thickly sewn with some pink flowering succulent he later learned was *parakeelya*—an aboriginal word. The stock liked to feed on it.

"Fantastic, isn't it?" Selwyn commented, as they stepped out of the Jeep. "Ava never would come here alone."

"So you said." Varo walked to the foot of the ancient formation—probably the only remaining relic of some pre-historic plateau. He tried to keep his mind focused on the natural formation. It reminded him strongly of tribal sculpture. African or Toltec-Mayan. There was a great dignity to the extraordinary "human" head. Certainly it wasn't a welcoming figure. It was a *guardian* figure. He was sure of it.

Selwyn was somewhere behind him, obviously keeping his distance.

Varo turned around. "It seems you suffer your own apprehension?" he said with a vague taunt.

"Well, he *is* a scary-looking guy." Selwyn tried a laugh that didn't quite come off. But to prove himself he moved over to where Varo was standing. "I hope I haven't upset you?" he asked, studying the Argentine's handsome profile. It was set in stern lines.

"In what way?" Varo glanced sideways, stared the other man down.

"A man would have to be blind not to notice you're attracted to my wife," Luke offered, holding up his hands in peace.

"I would think any man that laid eyes on her would be attracted," Varo returned. He rested a reverent hand against the sandstone folds of Malyah Man's "cloak".

Luke sighed. "I just wanted you to get things right," he said. "There's so much I could tell you."

"Go right ahead," Varo invited, covering the deep stabs of anger.

Luke lowered his voice, as though talking to himself. "I have to get this off my chest, Varo. It's been killing me. You have no idea how lost and wretched I feel. I'm a man who believes in marriage. I believed in *my* marriage. I love Ava with everything I am. Body, heart and soul."

"Apparently you weren't able to convey your deep feelings to her?" Varo said, shooting his companion a derisive look.

"You don't understand." Luke rubbed fiercely at the nape of his neck. Something had stung him, dammit! "The pregnancy ended in catastrophe." His voice dropped to a hoarse whisper. "Ava—my beautiful Ava, who looks like an angel—aborted our child."

This time Varo couldn't control himself. He lashed out on instinct, grabbing hold of Selwyn by his smarting neck. "You're lying," he rasped.

He looked so daunting Luke Selwyn moaned aloud. "Please…" Luke struggled to get free, but the Argentine held him fast. He was inches taller, fitter, stronger, and his black eyes were glittering with rage. "You don't *want* to believe it. I understand. I *have* to tell you. I refused to believe it too. Only it's too true. Ava aborted our child. She confided in Karen. At least Karen was always there for her. Her family don't know. I *know* it sounds appalling. It *is* appalling. I realise now I shouldn't have told you. This is something I should have kept to myself. Forgive me, but I thought you deserved to know. I'm sorry."

Varo didn't loosen his grip. On the contrary, he strengthened it, knowing he was spinning out of control. Selwyn was lying. It couldn't possibly be true. Ava had aborted a child? Unthinkable. He *loved* her. He knew now he had never fallen in love before. How could he not be shaken to his very core?

"Varo?" Luke Selwyn's voice quaked. He had taken a risk and now it looked as if his desperate ploy had backfired. His heart started to thump. He had never felt so exposed. For all he knew the Argentine was going to kill him.

Out of nowhere a hot, gusting wind suddenly blew up. It was so fierce Luke felt a kind of desperation to find shelter. Not so the Argentine, who seemed to be part of it all. Was a desert storm about to roll over them? The Outback was such a dangerous, unpredictable place.

Even as he wondered, de Montalvo thrust him away as if he was beneath contempt.

How dared he?

Luke fell heavily, wondering if something terribly untoward was on its way. His wife's lover, of all people, intended to beat the living daylights out of him. And in the middle of a dust storm. They might have been in the Sahara. He could taste red dust in his mouth, clogging it, preventing speech. He looked up, as if impelled. It was a mistake. At that precise moment a fist-sized rock broke away from the towering sandstone formation, sending him into a cowering position. The rock appeared to hang for a split second

in mid-air, before it fell with a clunk on his head—although
he was covering it, and his ears.

Hell and damnation!

He felt the throb. There was probably a horrible amount
of blood.

For a second even Varo was transfixed. The wind that had
gusted up so violently in the next minute had fallen away.
It was a perfectly clear day. Not a cloud in the densely blue
sky. He looked to Selwyn, huddled on the ground. "Are
you okay?" He wasn't going to offer comfort, but he had to
check on the man.

"I'm not right at all!" Selwyn yelled, spluttering and mut-
tering invectives. "The blasted rock hit me." He staggered
to his feet, holding a hand to the side of his head.

"I assure you, *I* didn't throw it," Varo said, turning to
stare up at the regal desert monument. "Maybe Malyah Man
didn't like what you were saying?" he said, with a hard, cutting laugh.

"Don't be ridiculous!" Luke examined his right hand. It
was streaked with blood. He would have thought the blood
would be more copious…

"Better get it cleaned up," Varo suggested with no trace
of sympathy. "I'll drive."

"It's *hurting*, I tell you." Selwyn was now holding his
head with two hands. He kept moaning, a continuing stream
of colourful expletives flowing from his lips.

"Could have been worse," said Varo, giving Malyah Man
a parting salute. He had seen many strange things at different times, but nothing the likes of that.

Selwyn was already sprinting away to the Jeep, obviously fearing a barrage of rocks.

I can't—won't—believe what he has told me.

Yet how could he ask her? If it were the truth she would
be mortally wounded, exposed. A lie and she would be furi-

ous with him for even giving it a moment's credence. Either
way, he was compelled to find out.

But what if it is true? It will change everything.

He couldn't begin to go there. There were life-changing
moments along the way.

Selwyn was still moaning as they made their way into
Kooraki's homestead. Ava, on trigger alert pretty well the
whole time they had been away, was on hand to meet them
in the Great Hall.

She wore a smile that faded the moment they entered
the front door. "What on earth has happened?" She looked
from Varo to her husband. She hardly recognised him. Luke
stared back glassy eyed, his fair hair standing up in tufts,
streaks of red dust all over his face.

"I'll tell you what happened." He drew a harsh, rasping
breath. "Montalvo here seems to find it a joke. A big rock
fell off that pillar. Size of a meteor, it was. It hit me on the
side of the head. It could have *killed* me." Real tears glinted
in his eyes.

Varo didn't mean to, but he laughed. "Actually, I really
and truly believe it was Malyah Man who pitched it at you,"
he said, with no trace of humour. Indeed his temper was
rising.

"You're saying a piece of sandstone fell off the monument? Is that it?" Ava asked, feeling sorry for the usually
impeccable Luke. He looked such a mess he might have
gone through a turbulent experience.

"Not *fell* off," Luke gritted. "The bastard aimed it right at
me," he said, setting about putting his hair to rights. "Don't
look so surprised, darling. You were always frightened of
the thing."

"In *awe* of, Luke," Ava corrected, seeing Varo visibly
tauten at the "darling". "I didn't think Malyah Man was *threat-*

ening. Well, not to me. But I wouldn't have offended him for the world." Ava's eyes met Varo's. "You okay?" she asked.

Something more had happened out there. She could tell. There was something *different* about Varo. She couldn't place it. But it was in the quality of his brilliant black gaze. It was as if he was looking at her with fresh eyes. Luke would do anything to sully her good name. The possibility he had attempted to do so was real. She didn't have an inkling what he might have said.

"I keep on the right side of the Ancients too," Varo said.

Ava was having trouble even thinking about Luke and his cracked head. Up until the time they had left, Luke had been playing the good guy. That alone made her stomach contract with nerves. Luke simply *wasn't* a good guy. He was a man who liked to get square. A man who would always seek revenge for the slightest hurt or word out of place. What had he said to Varo that made him look at her differently? What was there *to* say, for God's sake? She had always been gentle, respectful, restrained. She had never looked sideways at another man, even when she'd known plenty of men looked at her.

Finally she threw out an impatient hand. "Let's get you cleaned up, Luke, shall we? Is it painful?" God knew, Luke was no super-hero. He had always made a terrible patient, even with a head cold. "Do you think it might need a few stitches?"

"Of course it doesn't," Varo broke in, sounding incredulous. "It was more in the nature of a shot across the bows. Let's hope it worked."

Ava's eyes swept Varo. She dearly wanted to know exactly what Varo had meant by that, but she couldn't ask him there and then. It would have to wait for later. Or maybe she would never find out?

Luke was complaining wanly that he needed "peace and quiet". He could have his peace and quiet. He could stay the night, but she had organised the first leg of his trip back to Sydney for the following day. Station supplies were being flown in mid-morning. Luke could fly out with the freight plane. He could take care of himself after that. She still didn't know why he had come. They had discussed nothing. No doubt he was biding his time.

Luke was. He moved off in the direction of the first-aid room, comforted by the fact his ploy was actually working. He'd got the bandwagon rolling. All he had to do was sit back and watch proceedings. Innocent or guilty, it was a well-documented fact mud stuck. He could see how upset the Argentine was, even if he was doing a great job of keeping his feelings under wraps. Particular lies had a huge advantage. How could Ava ever prove her innocence? She could protest, sure. But would de Montalvo believe her? Would *anyone* believe her? He knew he had Karen on side. Karen would back him. Uphold his lie. You had to understand Karen's powerful jealousy of her cousin. *He* did. It had worked for him in the past. Lies could and did ruin affairs of the heart.

Luke felt no pang of guilt. Ava was his wife. She would take her punishment and then they could get on with life. The Argentine was a man who would want children. Probably a dozen or more. De Montalvo's perceptions of his angelic Ava had already shifted. He had almost heard the crash as Ava had fallen off her pedestal.

Serve her right!

He also blamed her for that whack on the head. People liked to pretend there were no such things as spirits and guardian figures. They should visit the Outback. He would swear he'd heard old Malyah Man make a deep throaty sound like *yahggh* as the rock began to fall. Weren't the old Kadaitcha Men supposed to have hissed that over their dying victims?

* * *

There was no opportunity for Ava to speak to Varo. Lunch was served, and Luke had recovered sufficiently to leave his sickbed. She could see he wasn't altogether happy with salad Niçoise and seared Tasmanian salmon escalopes. No starters. There was, however, a lemon tart to save the day.

Siobhan gave him lots of sympathy, thinking someone had to. The Argentine had a hard impatience etched on his stunning face. Ava was trying to hide some upset. "It's a wonder you weren't concussed," she said in a show of solidarity. Her tone was sugary at times, even cloying.

Luke frowned. "Perhaps I *am*." His injury was still hurting. He would need another couple of painkillers. He had to ready himself for a little talk with his wife. In his head he was tweaking it. All a man had to do was stick to his guns.

"One never knows," Siobhan pondered, looking towards her silent hostess. "When I was little I toppled head-first off a trampoline. Everyone thought I was fine but I had a concussion."

Luke didn't respond. He was always bored with problems outside his own.

Ava had to stop herself from sighing aloud. Siobhan was overdoing the sympathy. Was it deliberate? She could see Varo stir restlessly. The sooner Siobhan was on her way the better. She had flown over in her father's helicopter. Siobhan was Outback born and bred. A woman of the land. She would make a grazier cattleman an excellent wife. Of course she had been in love with Dev for years. Still was. Ava had been reminded of that constantly, with Siobhan's questions about the honeymooners. Ava hoped Siobhan would get over Dev soon. There had only ever been one woman for Dev. That woman was his wife.

CHAPTER NINE

VARO offered to drive Siobhan to Kooraki's airstrip, which seemed to cheer her immensely. She blushed.

Ava, however, spoilt the twosome by saying she would come too. After Siobhan had flown off home she would suggest to Varo they go for a drive. Maybe back to Malyah Man, as he appeared to be active. She was desperate to know what the barely perceptible change in his manner was all about. But it was there. The familiar easy charm hadn't been as much in evidence over lunch, although he had responded to all of Siobhan's thirty or so questions. One might have thought Varo came from an unknown part of the planet about which Siobhan knew nothing...

"All right, then. Goodbye." Siobhan smiled up into Varo's handsome face. "I expect you will be going home soon, Varo?"

"No, no—not *soon*," he responded, drawing out the *soon*, knowing Siobhan was storing up all she had seen and heard for relaying her family.

His response cut the goodbyes short.

Siobhan climbed into her Bell helicopter and in no time at all ascended into the wild blue yonder.

Ava looked at Varo, asking rather hesitantly, "Would you like to go for a drive?"

"As you wish," he answered smoothly.

It wasn't the answer she wanted. "Is something wrong?"

"Why would you think that?" he parried.

She gave a short laugh. "I've seen you in different moods, Varo. Sometimes I allow myself to believe I know what you're thinking."

"So what am I thinking now?"

A sudden uncharacteristic anger took hold of her. Her eyes flashed like jewels. "It's Luke, isn't it? What did he say to you?"

"What could he say?" Varo shrugged, not knowing which way to go with this. He would be so glad to be rid of Selwyn. He was even glad Siobhan O'Hare had flown off home.

"He sees you as a rival," Ava said hotly. They were, she realised with a shock, on the verge of their first argument. "Please don't answer my questions with a question, Varo. He said something to upset you. That seems clear to me. He may not have exhibited that side of him, but Luke is an extremely possessive man." Even the words in her mouth tasted bitter. "You didn't get into a fight, did you?"

Varo's voice was amused and disgusted. "Believe me, Malyah Man struck your husband the blow. I didn't have to do a thing."

"So you're not going to tell me?" Ava said. Her whole body felt as if it was going into a dejected slump.

He couldn't help touching her cheek. Her skin was as soft as a flower petal. He could smell the scent of her skin. Wound up as he was, he still wanted to take her in his arms, hold her body in an arc of intense pleasure tautly against him. Instead he said, "Let me get you out of the sun. We can't afford to bake your beautiful skin."

Ava didn't say anything until they were almost at the Jeep. "I don't want to go back to the house, Varo," she said in a strained voice. "Not with Luke there." This time her voice registered her disdain.

"So we go for a drive." Varo held the passenger door, waiting for her to get in before he closed it.

He took his time walking around to the driver's side. Luke Selwyn's disclosures had shocked him to the core. He couldn't deny that. At the same time he couldn't accept them either. His beautiful Ava not wanting children. Let alone cruelly terminating a pregnancy. He couldn't imagine the overriding guilt a woman might feel. But the Ava he knew seemed utterly guilt-free. One part of him wanted to tell Ava what Selwyn had said; the other part urged him to remain silent. Selwyn could be an utter scoundrel, a pathological liar. His reasoning would be if *he* couldn't have Ava no one else would. He couldn't bear to see Ava upset, the lovely colour gone from her face. But he actually feared he would do more harm than good confiding in her.

"So, where to?" he asked, putting the vehicle into gear.

She touched her slender fingers to her forehead. "Blue Lagoon," she said jaggedly. "We can sit on the bank beneath the trees. I know you're finding it hard to talk to me, Varo. And I know there's a reason. Luke told you something about me that has you terribly disappointed in me. In all fairness, don't you think you should tell me so I can defend myself?" she appealed to him.

Varo turned a grave face to her. She had a point. "I could be doing entirely the wrong thing, Ava," he said after a moment's consideration, "but I need to ask you. Have you ever been pregnant?"

Ava felt her heart jump in her breast. There was a long and awful ringing silence. Luke had told Varo she had fallen pregnant at some time? She literally couldn't speak she was trying so hard to control her outrage. "Excuse me—would I have kept that from you?" she demanded, fully communicating her anger.

"I don't really know, Ava," he answered quietly. And he

didn't. He wasn't by nature a judgemental man. And this was the woman he loved. "It is, after all, your business. I can understand if you had a miscarriage you might not like to talk about it. The memory could be too painful."

Ava was torn between bursting into tears and ordering him to stop the vehicle so she could jump out. "You hit Luke, didn't you?" she accused him. "Not that Luke wouldn't have had it coming."

"Would a jaguar swat a fly?" Varo returned bluntly. "I certainly wanted to—but, no, the rock fell away from the sandstone pillar. I watched it. For a split second it was stationary in mid-air, and then it dropped with a satisfactory crunch on your husband's head."

"My husband?" That hurt. Ava stared straight head. "He's *my husband* now?"

"He *is* your husband," Varo pointed out quietly.

"And you're my lover?" she asked with surprising fierceness. The writing was already on the wall. She was going to lose Varo. One way or another Luke had seen to that.

"I'm very seriously involved, Ava. We both know that." He turned off the main track, driving too fast towards the chain of lagoons. But what was in their way? These were the vast empty plains. Varo sensed she wanted to get out of the Jeep. He was finding it desperately confining himself.

"Involved? Is that the precise word?" Ava was losing the battle to keep her voice steady. "Not in love with? No? You prefer *involved*?"

"You haven't answered my question." The expression on Varo's striking face was unreadable. "I can understand if you kept it from me. You weren't sure how I would deal with it. How I would react."

"How you would react?" Ava exclaimed, her lovely face suddenly flushed with blood. She closed her eyes tight, shaking her head from side to side.

Varo believes Luke, that miserable, beastly liar. Don't men always stick together?

Luke was out to harm her in the most horrible way. He *knew* she had fallen in love with Varo. How could she hide it? Even she knew there was a special glow about her. Now she had to suffer for her perceived betrayal. She could picture the two of them talking out in the desert. Luke playing the tortured husband to the hilt. Varo feeling horrified and let down because she had kept such an event from him. She could see the residual anger still in Varo's brilliant eyes. If he hadn't actually made a physical attack on Luke he had erupted, not far off it.

"Stop the Jeep, Varo," she said furiously, and then made a huge attempt to lower her voice. "I want to get out. It seems you don't know me at all."

Varo ignored the order. He threw out a strong restraining arm across her breasts. "Sit still," he said tautly. "We're almost there."

Even the birds seemed to be singing melancholy songs. Ava stalked away from Varo down to the water's edge. This beautiful lagoon had always calmed her. Here she and Varo had sunk beneath its glittering emerald surface to steal heavenly kisses out of sight. She looked for a long time at the glorious flotilla of water lilies that steeped the lagoon in so much beauty. Nut grass and little wildflowers of flashing colours wove a sweet-scented tapestry, cloaking one area of the pale ochre sands. She had always thought this particular lagoon cast a primeval spell, but today it couldn't calm the tumult of her mind.

What else did Luke say while he was at it? She had been unfaithful? Not once but several times? Of course he had forgiven her. He could even have gone the whole hog and suggested he might not have been the father of the child? The child that never was.

She wouldn't put anything past Luke.

"Ava!" Varo called to her.

She turned back to where he was standing, in the shade of a line of feathery acacias. Such a wonderfully charismatic man. She loved him with all her heart. It was a hot, sultry, breezeless day. Shade would be welcome. Earlier in the day she had heard a series of muted thunderclaps that just as suddenly stopped. It was possible they would have a short, sharp afternoon shower. It might even be accompanied by a burst of hail. There were a few big, tumbled clouds appearing on the horizon in a peacock-blue sky.

"Let's sit down," Varo said, not knowing how to proceed exactly if Ava wouldn't confide in him. "I'm sorry if I've upset you."

Ava sighed deeply, thinking the wonderful harmony that had existed between them was as good as wrecked. She gave a raised right hand gesture, almost signifying defeat, and then sank onto the warm dry sand, drawing her legs up and clasping her arms around her jeans-clad knees.

Varo put out his hand, turning her head to him. His long fingers had a life of their own. They caressed the satin smoothness of her cheek and jawline. "Talk to me," he urged quietly.

Ava jerked her head away more forcefully that she'd intended. Her long blonde hair broke out of its clasp, spilling down her back and over one shoulder. "About what?" she asked bleakly.

"The truth. That's all I ask," he replied gravely.

Her eyes were gleaming with unshed tears. Luke had pushed all her buttons. He knew how she would react. Wind her up and let her go. "Which implies you believe I haven't been entirely honest with you?" she countered angrily. "For that matter, have *you* been entirely honest with *me*, Varo?" She was going out on the attack she was so overwrought. "Have I learned *everything* I need to know about you? You're nearly thirty years of age. You're not only a striking-looking man—a man who would compel the eyes of women—you're a man of strong passions, sexual vigour, high intellect. It's inconceivable you haven't had many affairs these past years, which you naturally don't want to expose. It's even possible you could have fathered a child and not known anything about it. It has happened countless times before today."

Varo too felt anger spurt into his veins. Anger Luke Selwyn's disclosures had caused to erupt. Now this! "Don't insult my good name, Ava," he said curtly. "I won't allow it—even from you. If a young woman had fallen pregnant to me she would have known to come to me. I would never desert such a woman, the mother of my child. However, no such woman exists. I've had my affairs. Of course I have. But I had come to believe I had never truly been in love."

"Past tense?" she said bitterly.

"It's not *me* I wish to talk about, Ava," he said, trapping her hand and holding it fast. "I have been entirely honest with you. I am, I hope, a man of honour. I was brought up to be. You are changing the subject."

"The subject being that I was pregnant to Luke?" she said hotly. "I lost my baby and I neglected to tell you about it? What is it you want me to say?"

"I've told you. I only want the truth."

"And you get to ask the questions?" The bitter note rang in her voice. She loved him so much and he didn't trust her.

"When did this happen?" he asked, feeling her anguish, desperate to understand.

At that point Ava totally lost it. She raged out of control. Her right hand—the hand nearest him—came up with the full intention of slapping his dark, handsome and arrogant face. Only he caught her wrist, bringing her arm down to her side.

"Let go of me." She couldn't endure his touching her. She began to struggle wildly, only he continued to hold her captive.

"Do not be frightened. I would never hurt you." Still, there was a little flame in his lustrous eyes. "I should never have asked you this."

"No, you *shouldn't*!" She managed to get in a sharp little punch to his chest.

The thought of losing him filled her with dread. But it was inevitable, wasn't it? She was doomed to losing the only man she could ever love. She didn't know what was happening to her because all of a sudden she was fighting him, her face flushed, her movements frantic. Anger and hopeless desire were mixed up inside her. Her every movement held an erotic charge. Not only to her. But to him. Their desire for each other was like a powerful drug that raced unchecked through the bloodstream.

Of course with his man's strength he triumphed. She was soon lying flat on her back, her body pinned to the sand. It felt much coarser than the velvety sand of the cave. Varo loomed over her, holding her down as easily as if she were a child.

He was breathing heavily, biding his time until the wild tumult of passion that was inside him miraculously cooled. This was Ava, and he was treating her with hard male dominance. The tiny top button of her pink cotton shirt had come undone. As she struggled so did the next. Now her lacy bra was exposed, and the shadowed cleft between her white breasts. His head was swimming. Her body was exquisite. He needed it so badly he almost felt like pleading for it.

"Are you going to let me up?" Her clear voice challenged him. This was a new side of Ava.

"The moment your anger passes," he announced very tensely. "A woman has never attempted to slap my face before."

"Even when you badly needed it?"

A violent hunger was washing through her. She wanted him to take her. Drive into her. Leave his brand. No way could she deny it. She was simply playing sex games. Desire was never far from them—even now, when there was so unexpectedly furious anger. The fury was actually inciting them. And it wouldn't go away. It was pumping strongly through both of them. She thought she couldn't stand it, but her body's response was just the opposite.

Still holding her arms, Varo sought her beautifully shaped sensuous mouth. He kissed her deeply, passionately, until she stopped struggling and was quiet while his hands moved over her. She should have been shamed by her surrender. Instead her senses were so exquisitely sharpened she abandoned herself to this feverish sexual onslaught. He was immensely desirable to her. Her arms came around him. Locked.

I'll never let you go.

The reasoning part of Varo was stunned by his intense hold on her delicate woman's body. Only she was egging him on, glorying in his tight embrace, even if they both remained grimly silent. There were no tender words of love. Tenderness had no place here. The hunger was boundless; the opportunity to make the other suffer as they suffered…

They were naked, their limbs tangled, bodies forming, re-forming, responding to their own rhythms that nevertheless matched perfectly. Her long blonde hair was wildly mussed. Together they were caught in a tempestuous love dance with a total lack of inhibition, willing slaves to the senses. But what kept Ava from screaming out how much she loved him? What kept Varo from responding with great ardour how much he loved her? Both were stubbornly holding on to the raw hurt and confusion Luke Selwyn had sparked.

They were one body. He brushed hard against the swollen bud of her clitoris, augmenting the pleasure. Then he was buried so deep inside her she gave an involuntary cry that swiftly softened into satiated little gasps. At such a crucial point, when nothing else existed outside of the pounding waves of pleasure and excitement, she could do nothing other than cry out his name.

Varo was unable to control his own massive response, his thrusting deep, his possession of this woman total. He felt as if his whole being was going out of him into her.

Above their heads the sun filtered down through the trees. And still neither of them spoke.

When Ava was finally able to get to her feet she had to lean against him for support. "At least I know you want me," she said, her voice low-pitched and trembling with emotion.

She was astounded at the wild abandon with which she had responded to Varo's lovemaking. It couldn't have been wrong because it had felt so right.

"As you want me," he rejoined. "Forgive me if I was a little too rough."

She gave him a soft look. "I was as caught up as you, Varo. Just give me a minute and we'll go. I have the feeling we could get a heavy shower of rain. Maybe even hail."

"Let's hope so," he said tautly. He kept one arm around her waist, absorbing her body heat. "I for one need cooling down."

We were so happy!

Ava drew back her hair, fastening it once more with the gold clasp. Finally she looked up, regarded him with the glitter of tears in her eyes. "It's all so sad."

The greatest part of him wanted to tell her he loved her,

adored her. She was his woman. He would never let her go. His fears were too dominant at that moment. Difficult to accept Ava might fear having children. But that could be handled with lots of tender loving care and support. And the rest? He couldn't bring himself to reveal anything more Selwyn had said. In fact he believed in his heart it was a lie.

"You ought to talk to me, Ava," he said, pinning her sparkling gaze. "Not now. But later." Varo was striving for a detached calmness he did not feel. His desire for her would never abate. Nevertheless he said, "Both of us need a little time to cool down and reflect."

Ava turned away sharply. Her body was still throbbing. Her nipples, her breasts, her sex. She would simmer for hours. It was a new Ava Varo had set loose. A new woman he had called forth. She had lost too much time dissociating herself from her painful past. Her defeats were many. Her triumphs were to come. Nothing was going to stop her having it out with Luke. She would even holler at him if she had to. She—ever so peaceful, confrontation-hating Ava. She felt shame for how biddable she had been. A great deal of it had to do with her childhood. She was a woman now.

They both got splashed with rain and light hail as they ran from the Jeep to the short flight of front steps. Ava paused, shaking the quickly melting hail from her hair. The strong smell of ozone was in the air. Both of them had remained quiet on the journey back from the lagoon. Both knew much had to be said.

Luke watched them return. He stood at the French doors of his guestroom—not as large or as handsomely furnished at the spacious room he and Ava had always occupied, he thought with fierce resentment. He would get square. He would go back and have more of a rest before he showered,

dressed and went down to dinner. He was actually looking forward to it. Knowing Ava as he did, she would have
reacted to any accusations de Montalvo might have made
with her usual pained silence. Ava was all politeness. She
couldn't assert herself for love or money.

He didn't have to do a damned thing. All he had to do
was bide his time. The Argentine wouldn't waste a moment
getting himself organised to leave Kooraki and the beautiful Ava behind. Before the separation time was up he was
convinced he would have his wife back. With more revenge
to come. Ava had let him down very badly. How could she
avoid punishment? Subtle, of course. He had learned exactly
how to manipulate her. Not that he hadn't had *his* affairs,
but there was no question his wife could have one and get
away with it. Punishment had to fit the crime.

Some time later, when Ava burst in on him, he looked
up with genuine astonishment. "You could knock," he said,
displaying his annoyance.

At the sight of him lounging on the bed Ava's fury increased. "You were *not* invited to this house, Luke," she
said. "You are *not* a guest. We are separated. I am filing
for a divorce. All this is known to you, yet you came here.
Now I know why. To cause me as much pain as you possibly could."

"Don't imagine you don't deserve it," he said in his cold-
est voice, rising slowly from the bed. He would never forgive her for what she had done, but he now felt a driving
sexual hunger. Ava had never really given herself to him.
He knew that. He knew he had never truly aroused her.
Something inexplicable to him. He had no such trouble with
other women. She looked fantastically beautiful, as though
she had suddenly stepped down from her white marble pedestal to become *woman*.

"I never deserved *you*," she said, her remarkable eyes

flashing. "I've arranged for you to fly out with the freight plane tomorrow, Luke, so you might as well do your packing tonight. The plane arrives at midday. It doesn't take long for the station supplies to be unloaded. Be ready."

Her fierce ultimatum only served to increase his rage. "You're not serious, are you, my darling?" he asked with a disbelieving sneer. "You're my wife, Ava, and don't you forget it."

"Don't dare to threaten me," Ava warned, keeping her sparkling gaze on him. "I want you *out*. If you don't choose to go quietly, I assure you I'll have you thrown out."

"By your lover?" He moved threateningly towards her.

"There will be no need to involve Varo," she said with disgust, not falling back a step as he'd expected, but holding her ground. "Any man on the station would be happy to do it. No one has any time for you, Luke. They never did. I blinded myself to your faults. You kept your true form well hidden until after the wedding ceremony. I've paid for my mistake."

"No, you haven't!" he exploded, feeling a rush of hate and hunger. "You seem to forget I could easily raise objections to your filing for divorce. Why, the separation time isn't even up and you're having it off with another man. Shame on you, Ava."

She laughed at the hypocrisy of it. "The shame is all yours, Luke. You told Varo I had a pregnancy that ended in miscarriage. That was a lie."

He came to a halt, like a statue. "And how exactly are you going to prove that?" he asked, wondering what had possessed her all of a sudden. The change in her seemed profound.

"I would think a medical check-up might do it," she retorted. "I have *never* been pregnant, Luke. I didn't want a child with you."

"But, my darling wife, you confided in Karen," he pointed out, his voice dripping acid. "Don't you remember? Karen surely will. She was as shocked as I was. Angelic old you! You have well and truly blotted your copybook. Karen knows the story."

Ava visibly paled. So he had drawn her cousin into his web. "Even Karen would stop short of telling such a lie for you," she said hardily, praying it would be true.

"Only it *is* no lie." Selwyn kept his eyes on her. "Karen suspected. You simply confirmed it. I was *thrilled* you were carrying our baby. But you aborted it, didn't you?"

Ava was seized by a pain so bad it was agony. "You told Varo I *aborted* my baby?" she cried, blazing with anger. "I don't believe it."

"Didn't he mention it?" Luke asked silkily, shaking his fair floppy head. "I suppose not. I think he was much too shocked to bring up that sad fact. He'd be Catholic, wouldn't he? Practising, no doubt—and his entire family, with their Spanish background. But you did it, didn't you? At some time we all have to take responsibility for our actions, Ava."

"Who would do this kind of thing?" Ava implored. "You disgust me, Luke. You're a truly bad man." Her voice fell away to a whisper.

Heartened, he went to her, grasped her strongly by the shoulders.

She broke away, stepping back sharply. "Keep your hands off me," she warned, very deliberately.

This was too much to tolerate. His meek, vulnerable Ava, blazing like a firebrand. "Ava, I love you," he said, injecting high emotion into his tone. "I understand your shame, your sense of guilt. You did a terrible thing. And the worst part is there was no great pressure on you, Ava—no extenuating circumstances. You weren't single, on your own with little or no money, no support. You had me and my family.

You had a choice and you chose very badly. You *know* you should be punished. What goes around comes around. You need de Montalvo to believe you. Swallow your story. But he won't. He's no fool. Okay, you let him seduce you. You've had your little bit of illicit excitement. Frankly, I didn't think you had it in you. You're such a frigid little thing."

"Not with Varo," she pointed out with pride. "And it hasn't been a case of illicit excitement, Luke. I'm deeply in love with him."

"Rubbish!" Luke exploded, seeing a red mist before his eyes. "Mark my words, you pathetic creature, de Montalvo will very soon be on his way. You're damaged goods, as the saying goes."

Ava was silent a moment longer. "Men *have* caused damage in my life," she admitted in a low voice. "My grandfather…even my father separating from the mother I loved. We weren't able to go to her. Grandfather stopped that. And *you* have done me damage, Luke. You have very dark places in you. You're a narcissist. *Your* needs are the most important thing in the world to you. You don't love me. You don't know anything about love. I entered into a precipitate marriage against all good advice. You enjoyed controlling me. You enjoyed marrying a Langdon—such cachet!"

Ava stepped forward, adrenaline coursing through her. Without another moment of hesitation she hit her husband spontaneously across the mouth. She had known in her bones Luke would provoke her into some sort of action.

Luke was genuinely shocked. He had not been expecting any such action from her. Their life together had been free of physical confrontation. He had played the psychological game. The cat and the mouse. Only the mouse had at long last found its roar.

The blow wasn't heavy, but the antique ring Ava frequently wore had managed to split his lip. He reared back from her, as astonished as if she had morphed into a virago. "Are you *mad*?" he exploded, unable to believe meek and mild Ava had done this.

"Far from it. I've never had this sense of power. It's great. You tried so hard to rob me of all confidence, Luke. That's the ugly side of you." She picked up a handtowel he had left on the bed and threw it at him. "Don't bleed on the carpet. And don't attempt to come down to dinner. I'll have a tray sent up. I mean what I say, Luke. I want you off Kooraki midday tomorrow. I never want to lay eyes on you again."

She went to sweep past him—only in a burst of over-whelming rage he grabbed her.

"I'm the only man you've got," he gritted, close to screaming. There was a wild look in his eyes. "I'm your *husband*—get it?"

That wild look should have made her very nervous in-deed, but it didn't. "Let me go," she said, ice-cold.

Luke's good-looking face went white with fury. He shook her hard, much the stronger of the two. "Do you really think I'm going to let you make a fool of me?" he shouted. Then an odd smile spread over his face. "I'm a lot more danger-ous than you think, my darling." He began to rock Ava in his arms. "No way can you leave me, Ava. Till death do us part, remember?" One of his hands closed painfully over her breast. "I won't be going tomorrow. But the Argentine will. You must take your punishment. Then we can get on with life."

Varo had had no intention of allowing Ava to confront her husband with no back-up from him. She had been adamant about his not accompanying her, which was fair enough, and he had made it appear he acquiesced when his true in-tention was to hold himself in readiness some place nearby. He knew the layout of the house well by now. He would take the rear staircase to the gallery. He knew which room Selwyn was in.

Selwyn had deliberately tried to sabotage the relationship between Ava and himself. He had divulged Ava's secret, determining the relationship would quickly burn out. Selwyn wanted his wife back. No one could blame a man for that. But Selwyn wasn't a man. No one who had come close to him would think that. Malyah Man had meted out what could be taken as a genuine warning. Selwyn was *trouble*.

He'd given Ava a good five minutes to mount the main staircase and walk the short distance to Selwyn's guest-room, which was at the far end of the west wing, then made his move. His whole being had felt electric with tension. Even his scalp had prickled. He'd had only one purpose. That was to keep Ava from danger.

At the top of the staircase he'd heard voices. He had seen with gratitude that the door of Selwyn's room was very slightly ajar. Ava had evidently thought it wiser to leave it that way. In his mind he had Selwyn ripping into Ava with his accusations.

Silently he'd moved the short distance to stand just to the side of the heavy mahogany door with its ornate brass knob. Selwyn had been speaking. He'd heard him very clearly.

"Karen suspected. You simply confirmed it," he was saying. "I was *thrilled* you were carrying our baby. But you aborted it, didn't you?"

Selwyn had laughed suddenly with what Varo thought was venom and violence.

My God, was it true then? Was he about to learn the stark facts?

Ava hadn't responded. Perhaps overcome by her feelings, the trauma she had suffered. Then all of a sudden she had exploded. "You told Varo I *aborted* my baby?"

There had been rage in it, but to his ears it had sounded like righteous rage. She'd been utterly incredulous. Was this the most terrible revelation of her whole life brought out into the open, or was it Selwyn's monstrous lie?

Ava had gone on the attack. The attack of the innocent, not the guilty. He had wanted to cry out in triumph. He'd wanted to applaud. An enormous burden had been lifted from his shoulders. Instead he'd stood there, awaiting the right moment when he would thump on the door, then enter without permission.

Selwyn's accusations had continued to stream out. Ava had called him "a bad man". Her voice had been barely audible but the tones were heartfelt. In the next breath she'd switched to a shout.

"Keep your hands off me."

Time to move in on them, Varo had thought grimly. Selwyn was in full flow. He'd called Ava—beautiful, passionate Ava—*frigid*. Anger had welled up in him until he'd heard Ava's impassioned statement like a momentous declaration.

"I'm deeply in love with him."

In love with me! That's brilliant!

Selwyn had put up his worst, and Ava had had her chance to respond. Varo had found himself hanging on her every word. She'd sounded strong, independent. He had felt the fierce pleasure of pride in her. That was what Selwyn would hate—a strong, independent woman. He wanted a woman to control. Ava had broken free of her chains.

Perhaps he should not intervene, but walk quietly away. She was handling the situation on her own.

He was almost at the top of the staircase when he'd heard Selwyn roar, "Are you mad?"

It was followed by Ava's ice-cold retort, "Let me go!"

In a flash he turned back, understanding Ava was in

need of him. He threw open the door so violently it crashed against the wall, rattling a valuable *famille noir* Chinese porcelain vase that miraculously didn't fall over and break. Only who would have cared? Ava was grappling with the brute of a man she had married for all the wrong reasons. He had his hands clamped around her white neck. God, was he trying to *strangle* her?

Varo swooped, his black eyes glittering, his power-ful shoulders hunched forward like a heavyweight boxer waiting his moment to unleash his strength. Selwyn was howling now, knowing he was trapped—moreover by a man who looked as if he was about to kill him.

"She had it coming!" he panted. "Everything I told you is the truth."

He got no further. A heavy fist slammed into his ribs, knocking the breath out of him and slamming him back against the French doors.

"Get up." De Montalvo's voice was deadly quiet.

Blood was oozing from Selwyn's lip after Ava's unprec-edented attack. Now he faced possible cracked ribs. He threw up his hands as if in defeat.

Concern over what might happen lent Ava strength. She clamped her two hands around Varo's hard-muscled arm. "Leave him, Varo. Please do what I say. He's not worth it. He'll be out of here by tomorrow. I'll lock him in."

She meant it. She wasn't going to have Luke free to wan-der the house. He wouldn't get out through this door. He wouldn't dream of trying to scale the front façade. He was no mountaineer.

A hard edge was in Varo's voice. "Why don't you let me teach him a lesson?" he rasped.

"I'll have you up on an assault charge," Luke the lawyer suddenly yelled, his expression ugly.

A voice at the back of his mind was telling him Ava

would always come to his rescue. Though no woman would ever measure up to him. Few men either.

"Don't make me laugh!" Varo bit off. "What do you suppose the law would make of a man who attempted to strangle his wife? Can you see the red marks on Ava's neck, you brute? I am witness. I will call the staff to testify. You don't deserve Ava. You never did. Haven't you learned that by now?" He took several steps closer to Luke, who recoiled.

"Don't come any nearer."

"Varo, we don't want more trouble. Leave him." Ava felt her anxiety growing. She knew in her bones she couldn't find a way to Varo. He was tremendously upset.

"This poor excuse for a man doesn't deserve pity," he said with utter scorn. "What if I hadn't been there, outside the door? It doesn't take long for a man to strangle a woman. Particularly a mad man." The tension in his body was like a tightly coiled steel spring. "Get up, you gutless worm."

Luke Selwyn didn't do guts. He remained where he was, holding a hand to his ribs and making weird whimpering sounds.

Varo apparently couldn't care less. He stepped forward and gave Luke a clip across the head. "Count yourself lucky!" he exclaimed. "I believe Ava is the one who should press charges. It would and should end your career."

Luke looked past the menacing Argentine to Ava. "You wouldn't do that?" he asked, like a man amazed. "I'm your husband. I wouldn't have hurt you. I was only trying to shake sense into you."

To his horror, he received another clip over the head. "Strangle, you mean. You're on your knees, so apologise to Ava," Varo told him harshly.

Apologise? Never!

"Can't hear you," Varo said.

"Oh, God, leave him. It's not worth it." Ava's low, mellow voice had turned hoarse. She touched an involuntary hand to her bruised neck.

At that telling hoarseness Varo's strong hand came out, ready to clip Selwyn again.

"Varo, *please*. Leave him for my sake."

Varo gave her a brilliant sideways look. "I will and I am," Varo insisted. "But first the apology. Go ahead, Selwyn. While you're at it, admit your lies. You do realise you're in a very bad position indeed?"

Selwyn was silent.

Varo turned to Ava. "Looks like he's not going to do it. Ah, well!" Contempt was in his face as he stared down at the other man.

Selwyn didn't do bravery either. He broke into a choked apology without actually admitting he had lied. "I only did it because I love you, Ava. I hope you realise that?"

"Thank you, Luke," Ava said. "Tons of self-pity, no genuine remorse. The sad thing is you believe you're a good person when you're a man who knows nothing about love or even empathy. You have no capacity for it. You'll find painkillers in the bathroom cabinet. Take a good long bath. I want you off Kooraki. The chapter in life we shared is *over*."

They were almost at the door when Luke, now up and swaying on his feet, made a final attempt to inflict more wounds and more doubt. "Ask Karen if you want to know the truth," he said, addressing Varo directly. There was a gleam of triumph in his eyes. "Women—even angel-faced women like Ava—are seldom what you think they are. What I told you should be enough to stop you from making a terrible mistake. Heed my warning. Take the path I suggest and see where it leads." He flashed Varo a smile that had nothing to do with friendship or warmth.

Varo didn't smile back. "It's important you stop now, Selwyn," he warned, looking very tense. "It's possible you may have a cracked rib or two. What about a broken nose?"

Luke's moment of feeling back in control crumbled. He had no reply to that. Ribs were one thing. A broken nose would seriously affect his good-looks. He was a man women noticed.

Luke, the king of lies, Ava thought bleakly. *Luke, the rotten liar.* He had taken lying to new heights. The truly depressing thing was that liars had a long history of being believed.

A familiar sick feeling grew in her stomach. Varo *wanted* to believe Luke was a pathological liar, but had all his suspicion fallen away? Luke had had a lifetime of practising lying. Practice had made him very convincing. She fancied she saw an element of doubt in Varo's dark eyes. If he made the decision to speak to Karen she knew she would never recover. Karen was no benevolent soul. Karen harboured the demon jealousy. She had always been Luke's ally in the past. Even so Ava thought her cousin, connected to her by blood, would not go so far as to condone such an enormous sick lie.

Right now all that mattered to her was that Varo believed in her innocence. Where would they be without trust? Trust between two people who loved each other was crucial.

Luke was locked up for the night. A generous tray had been sent up, so there was no danger of his dying of starvation. Another tray was delivered at breakfast.

When Luke's eyes locked with those of the formidable housekeeper, who clearly hated him, he began to wonder if she might have put something in his food. The orange juice tasted a bit funny. He left it aside.

He was burning up inside with fury. As soon as he got

back to Sydney he would arrange to meet Karen; probably he'd take her to dinner if he was fit enough. Put a spin on what had happened. He fully expected Karen to lie for him. He had always had a way with women. Even the strongest of them were weak. Even now he couldn't believe Ava, his wife, no longer loved him.

Give her time, said the voice in his head.

He could almost tell the future in his guts. The Argentine would go away. fade right out of the picture. His accusations would stick. He just *knew* he would have the last word.

Right or wrong, good or bad, Ava's mind was resolved on a single purpose. She had to ask Varo what he intended to do. She wanted a straight answer. If he intended to consult Karen—and even without telling her Karen would soon let her know—she could rule out her heart's desire. Varo would go. And he would go fast. Varo wouldn't be the first man to be blinded by lies. Up until now their hearts had been ruling their heads. Luke's poisonous intervention had changed all that. Luke had brought them to the *big* question.

Did Varo trust her or not?

Varo escorted Luke to the airstrip. He fully intended shoving Selwyn on the freight plane, standing by to make sure he didn't attempt to get off. From the moment they'd get inside the Jeep Selwyn had started up again.

"Beautiful women have a great deal of power. Remember that. They attract sympathy even when they don't deserve it. Men are always the losers. They lose their wives. They lose their kids."

Varo had turned to glance at him. "You never give up, do you?"

"Of course I don't. And you seem to forget I am a practising lawyer. A very good one."

"And you came close to being a criminal. You'd better remember that. You may have missed the bruises on Ava's neck, but no one else did. They will all come forward to speak out against you. I can understand in a fashion why you tried so hard to convince me of your lies, but I assure you I have no need to check out your story with Ava's cousin. I was standing outside your door earlier than you think. It wasn't difficult to believe Ava might have suffered a miscarriage and didn't want to speak about it. Impossible to believe she had her pregnancy terminated."

"Listen—"

"Be quiet now," Varo warned, his mouth twisted with distaste. "In a very short space of time Ava will apply to the court for a divorce. The separation time is almost up. You will offer no resistance. You may harbour a sick desire to hurt her, but you never will. Ava has a powerful brother. And she has *me*."

An hour passed. It was evident Varo had driven off somewhere to think. Ava walked through to the kitchen to have a word with Nula, who was waiting to prepare a late lunch. "I have to go for a walk, Nula," she said.

The housekeeper looked at Ava with concern. Ava was very pale and the marks around her lovely white neck stood out in the first flush of bruising. "A walk where?"

"Oh, just around the garden," Ava said vaguely. "Don't worry about lunch. Varo seems to have gone for a drive. We can have a sandwich and a cup of coffee later."

Ava tried for a smile. Then she walked away.

What had delayed Varo was his offering assistance to the two station hands who had been allotted the job of off-loading the station supplies. At first they seemed a bit embarrassed, he supposed because he was a guest, but he took no notice. Three pairs of hands were better than two. Besides, he liked to talk to them about what they did on the station.

When he returned to the house, Nula told him before he even had time to ask that Miss Ava had gone for a walk in the garden. It wasn't any city man's idea of a garden. It was bigger, in fact, than the gardens of Villaflores, which were extensive. No matter—he would find her. He would find her wherever she was. At the ends of the earth. He had come to this extraordinary country for the wedding of a friend. He had found a woman who had caught instantly at his heart and at his imagination. He had found his future wife.

Ava heard a man's footsteps crunching on the gravelled path. Instinctively she opened her mouth to call, "I'm here, Varo. On the stone bridge." This was it. Decision time.

Varo lost no time changing direction. He had come to know the Full Moon Bridge well. It spanned a man-made pond where the great buds of white lotus flowers slowly opened, their giant leaves almost reaching the base of the semi-circular bridge. The sun blazed out of an Outback sky of intense sapphire, lending emerald-green waters a blazing patina of gold.

Ava was standing in the middle of the bridge, gazing down at the glittering water adorned with the great gorgeous blooms. He went to call out an apology because he was a bit late for lunch, only she turned to him as he approached— such a sad, serious expression on her face.

"Ava, what is it?" His heart rocked.

"I thought you might have gone off to think," she said, lifting her remarkable blue-green eyes to him.

"Think about what?" He snaked an arm around her back, letting it fall to her narrow waist.

Slowly he led her off the bridge to one of the small

summerhouse structures in the garden, where it was a great pleasure to sit down in the shade, surrounded by wonderful scents and a wilderness of blossom. The birds and the butterflies loved this place. It was no wonder the Langdons took such pride in the magnificent gardens they had achieved over generations in the wild, he thought. He had already quizzed Ava about many of the native plants, thinking they could do very well in the gardens of Villaflores.

"Well?" He gave her a soft, tender look, fighting down his inner rage at the damage Selwyn had done.

Ava bit her lip. "I don't really know where to begin."

"'Begin at the beginning and go on till you come to the end: then stop,'" he said humorously, quoting Lewis Carroll.

She had to smile. "You're always surprising me, Varo."

"I've got another one of Carroll's," he said, much more seriously. "'I can't go back to yesterday, because I was a different person then.'"

Tears came to her eyes as though they were saying goodbye. "That's true, isn't it?" she said. "But no matter what you do—what you decide to do—no matter where you go, I will never forget you, Varo."

He frowned, then said, "So what is this? You're telling me to go?" She had that look about her. She was so pale. Was she about to break his heart?

"No, no," Ava cried out in a kind of agony. "I thought you would *want* to go. I thought you might have some lingering doubts. Luke is such an accomplished liar. He's made lying an art form."

"You think I doubt you?" Varo asked in amazement. "I may have briefly considered you had a miscarriage and couldn't bear to talk about it. I would understand that. But the rest—never! You are my dearest, most beloved Ava. I trust you with my life. I trust you with my heart. Here—I give it to you." He cupped his elegant hands, held them out to her. His accent was becoming more and more pronounced as his feelings grew. "You *cannot* turn me away. I won't allow it." There was real worry on his stunning face.

"Let you go? You're crazy!" Ava exclaimed, letting her head fall against his shoulder. "I love you, Varo. You are the most wonderful thing that has happened to me in all my life. I would never have experienced *love*—true, undying love—if I hadn't met you. You *can't* go away." She gripped him around the waist, tried to shake him. "I won't let you. The first pregnancy I will ever have—the first baby I will ever hold—will be part of *you*. *Our* child. I should tell you I want at least four children. Two boys, Two girls. I think that should do it."

Varo stared into her lovely face, his expression deeply serious. He chose that very moment to slip out of her arms, only to drop onto one knee before her. "Some of us are greatly blessed in life," he said with emotion, because he was not a man who was afraid of emotion. "We find our soul mate. You are mine, Ava. I beg you to do me the honour of becoming my wife. Moreover, I insist on it. We will be married wherever you like. If you can't leave your homeland, I will—"

Ava leaned forward and sealed her mouth to his. It was a deep kiss, with an intensity of which there was no doubt. After a while she lifted her shining blonde head, her whole being aglow. "'For whither thou goest, I will go; and where thou lodgest, I will lodge: thy people shall be my people, and thy God, my God,'" she quoted. "I certainly believe in Him. He brought me *you*."

She held out her hands in a gesture of raising Varo to his feet. Then she too stood, to go into his waiting arms. They closed strongly, protectively, adoringly around her.

The moving finger had written. Time now for it to move on.

This was their destiny. They were ready to accept it and all life's challenges head-on. The power of love was awesome. It would overcome all else.

EPILOGUE

WHEN Karen Devereaux was asked by Luke Selwyn to back his shocking claim she refused point-blank, livid with outrage. None of it could be proved. She just *knew* Luke Selwyn had made it all up. Ava had never breathed a word to her about any pregnancy because she had never fallen pregnant to Luke. Karen was furious, deeply resenting the fact Luke was trying to use her. It would be much better if she broke off their so-called friendship.

Word was Ava and Varo were having two wedding ceremonies: one at Kooraki, the other at the Estancia de Villaflores in Argentina. She dearly wanted to go to both. There was even a chance Ava might ask her to be one of the bridesmaids. She had seen a great deal of Europe, the United States and Canada, but she had never been to South America. This was a wonderful opportunity to go.

Dev and Amelia were back from their honeymoon. There was bound to be a *huge* engagement party. She and Ava had always been close. Now she would make it her business to draw closer to Amelia, the mistress of Kooraki. Hadn't they always been a trio? Really good friends? She had always loved and cared for her cousin Ava. Or so she told herself. Luke Selwyn was someone from the past…

* * * * *

CATTLE RANCHER, SECRET SON
Margaret Way

PROLOGUE

FATE, DESTINY, CHANCE: call it what you will, it has a hand in everything.

Gina Romano, a young woman of twenty-four, whose classical bone structure, golden skin, lustrous dark eyes and hair richly proclaimed her Italian heritage, was walking to her friend Tanya's front gate. It had been a lovely relaxing afternoon with Tanya and her beautiful new baby, Lily-Anne.

Tanya, cradling tiny Lily-Anne, naturally the most beautiful baby in the world, was standing at the front door, waving Gina off: Gina's hand was on the wrought-iron gate making sure it was closed securely after her, when she felt a tingle like an icy finger on her nape. It alerted her, bringing on a familiar feeling of alarm. Every time she felt that icy finger, and she had felt it many times in her life, she took it as a signal *something* was about to happen.

She pulled away from the gate, moving swiftly out onto the pavement, hands shaking, legs shaking, head humming as if it were filled with high tension wires. She was no clairvoyant but she had come to accept she had an extra sense most people either didn't have or didn't get to develop. It was a gift, simultaneously a curse; an inheritance handed down through the maternal line of her family as other families claimed the second sight.

The *noise* came first. One minute the leafy suburban street was drowsing under a turquoise sky, the next, a range of things happened. An early model car with its engine roaring and trailing grey-black clouds of exhaust fumes turned into the street without slowing at the corner. Gina watched the driver correct the skid, only to gun the engine even though the left front wheel was wobbling. Gina estimated he was doing a good fifteen to twenty kilometres over the fifty kilometre speed limit.

From the property directly opposite, the real estate agent overseeing the forthcoming auction, camera in hand, strode out onto the pavement on the way to his car. He stopped, took in the situation and cried out. Simultaneously a flame-haired cherub called Cameron from the house next door to Tanya's came bounding down his unfenced driveway and ran pell-mell onto the street without so much as a glance in either direction. He was totally oblivious to danger, his mind was set solely on retrieving his blue beach ball, which was fast bouncing away from him into the opposite gutter.

The estate agent, a man of sixty, to his everlasting horror was assailed by such a terrible feeling of helplessness he simply *froze,* but Gina, who didn't even hear Tanya yelling frantically so focused was she on the child, reacted like an Olympic sprinter coming off the blocks. Adrenaline poured into her body, causing a surge of power. She *flew* after the little boy, at one point her long legs fully extended front and back as she rose in an extravagant leap. Or so it appeared to the neighbours alerted by Tanya's screaming and the awful din set up by the smoking bomb. As one of them later confided to the television reporter, "It was the coolest thing I've ever seen. The young lady was moving so *impossibly* fast she was all but airborne. Ought to make the headlines!"

So this then was much more than a simple good deed. It was seen to be on the heroic scale. But Gina herself felt no sense of valour. She did what she thought anyone would have done in the circumstances. A child's life was on the line. What option did she have but to attempt to save it? Her very humanity demanded she act and act *fast*.

Heart almost bursting through her rib cage, she scooped up the child in the bare nick of time, her body sparkly all over as though wired, and then flew on to the safety of the grassy verge thinking there was no way she could avoid taking an awful fall or being pulverized by Tanya's formidable brick-and-wrought-iron fence. She had a vision of herself lying on the grass, moaning because of broken bones, maybe even covered in blood. But for now, her main thought was how to cushion the child whose vulnerable little head was buried against her breast.

Please, God...please, God! Every atom in her body braced in case He didn't hear her.

She needn't have worried. It had been decided all would be well. What could so easily have been a tragedy— glittering metal pulverising two tender bodies—turned into a feel-good human-interest story. A workman built like a double-door refrigerator but as light on his feet as a ballet dancer in his prime appeared out of nowhere to gather Gina and child in like it was a set piece of choreography. Little Cameron, now the drama was over, broke into frightened howls of *"Mum-eee! Mum-eee! Mum-eee!"* the *ees* mounting ever higher.

A distraught young woman, with orange locks that refused to lie down, was running to him, calling repeatedly, "My darling, my darling, my baby!" Gina, her own body trembling in aftershock handed Cameron over to his mother to an outpouring of thanks. Cameron, for some reason common to children, stopped his heart-wrenching wailing and began to laugh merrily. He reached into the pocket of his little blue shorts to hand Gina a couple of jelly beans he hadn't touched, presumably as a reward.

Incredibly it was all over in a matter of seconds, only now there was a small crowd surrounding them who burst into spontaneous applause as though they had witnessed a great piece of stunt work. The battered car, scruffy young man at the wheel, didn't stop or even slow though he did flash a nonchalant hand out of the open window, obviously taking the philosophical view "all's well that ends well."

Angry fists were raised in his direction, cries of condemnation. A silver-haired old lady added a few words one would have thought she wouldn't even know, much less use, but he accelerated away, apparently with a clear conscience, mobile now glued to his ear. He would later be picked up by the police who were delighted to have his licence number handed to them on a plate. There was also the matter of a stack of parking fines he had completely ignored.

Praise shifted to the real estate agent. Belatedly, he had done something right. Momentarily transfixed by horror he might have been, but he had immediately swung into action on witnessing Gina's spectacular transformation into "Wonder Woman you'd have to call her! Used to love that show!" He was ready for a laugh now. Hadn't he snapped out of his sick panic to get "the whole blessed thing" on film?

Thus it was, Gina Romano found herself an unwilling heroine and would remain so for some time. Cameron's immensely grateful parents later went on television to say they would never forget what Ms Romano had done. In fact, viewers got the decided impression Gina was now part of the family. Tanya took the welcome opportunity to show off her beautiful baby to the larger world, added her own little bit. "Gina's so brave! Why, only a few months back she saved Cameron from a big black dog."

"Let's hope there won't be a *third* time for wee Cameron!" the woman reporter joshed, smiling brilliantly into the camera.

Gina, the heroine of all this, prayed inwardly: *Don't let anyone recognise me.*

But recognised she was. By her colleagues and friends, just about everyone who knew her at her local shopping centre, the inhabitants of the small North Queensland sugar town a thousand miles away where she had been born and raised, and most crucially by the last person on earth she wanted to see her captured image: the man she had fallen hopelessly, madly, irrevocably in love with four years before. The man Fate had denied her. The man she had so carefully hidden herself away from. Not even her closest friends even suspected she knew him. Or *had* known him.

Intimately.

Gina never discussed her former life, her secrets and her haunted past. She had a good life now for which she was very grateful. It had all the trappings of normality. She had an attractive apartment in a safe area with importantly a lovely little park nearby with a kiddies' play area. She had a well-paid job with a stockbroking firm who valued her services. She had men friends who admired and desired her. At least two of them definitely had marriage on their minds, if mentioning it meant anything. Men, generally speaking, had to be helped along in these matters.

She couldn't commit. And she knew why. Hardly a day went by that she didn't think of the man who had taken her: body, mind and soul. Trying to forget him hadn't just been one long struggle: it was a battle she had come to accept she was doomed to lose.

CHAPTER ONE

Coronation Hill Station
The Northern Territory

FROM the crest of Crown Ridge, tumbled with smooth, near-perfectly round boulders like a giant's marbles, Cal sat his magnificent silver-grey stallion, watching a section of the lowing herd being driven towards the holding yards at Yering Springs. From this incomparable vantage point on top of the ancient sandstone escarpment, the whole of Jabiru Valley was revealed to him. Silver billabongs lined by willowy melaleucas and groves of pandanus wound away to the left and right, the sun flashing off surfaces as smooth as glass. He could see the flocks of magpie geese and whistling ducks congregated around the banks and exploding from the reed beds. Wildlife was abundant in the Valley: native mammals, reptiles, trillions of insects and above all, the *birds*. The gloriously coloured parrots, the cockatoos, galahs, rosellas and lorikeets, countless other species, the beautiful water birds and, at the top of the chain, the reigning jabiru. It was the great numbers of jabirus, the country's only stork, fishing the billabongs and lagoons that had given the Valley its name.

The Territory was still a wild paradise with a mystical feel about it that he firmly believed derived from the aboriginal culture. The *Dreaming*. The spirit ancestors had fashioned this ancient land, creating everything in it. Where he now sat on his horse had provided natural art galleries in its numerous caves and rock shelters. Many of the walls were covered in ancient rock paintings, art treasures fiercely protected by the indigenous people and generations of McKendricks who had taken over the land.

In whatever direction he looked, the landscape was potent with beauty. He supposed he would have made a good pagan with his nature worship. Certainly he was very much in touch with the natural world. He even knew, like the aboriginals on the station, the places where great *energy* resided, certain sandstone monuments, special caves, rock pools and particular trees. The lily-covered lagoons on Coronation Hill were filled with magnificent waterlilies of many colours: pink, red, white, yellow, cream. His favourite was the sacred Blue Lotus. Underneath those gorgeous carpets it had to be mentioned, glided the odd man-eating croc or two. They had learned to take crocs in their stride. Crocodiles were a fact of life in the Territory. Don't bother them. They won't bother you.

God, it was hot! He could feel trickles of sweat run down his nape and onto his back. He lifted a hand to angle his wide-brimmed Akubra lower on his head, thinking his hair was getting much too long. It was curling up at the back like a girl's. He would have to get it cut when he found time. The mob had been on the move since the relative cool of dawn but now the heat was intense. The world of sky above him was stunningly clear of clouds, an infinity of burning blue. He loved his home with a passion. He loved the colours of the land. They weren't the furnace-reds of the Centre's deserts but cool blues and silvers, the deeper cobalts and amethysts. Instead of the rolling red sand dunes of the central part of the Territory, in the tropical north, the entire landscape was covered in every conceivable shade of lustrous green.

And flowers! Extraordinary flowers abounded in the Valley. The grevilleas, the banksias, the hakeas, the native hibiscus and the gardenias everyone knew, but there were countless other species unique to the far-away regions that had never been named. No one had ever had the time to get around to it. Australia was a dry, dry continent but oddly produced the most marvellous wildflowers that were becoming world renowned. Everywhere he looked exquisite flowers unfurled themselves on trees and shrubs, others rode the waving tops of the savannah grasses that could grow after the Wet a good four feet over his head, and he was six feet two.

It was here in the mid-1860s that his ancestor, the Scot, Alexander Campbell-McKendrick, swore an oath to found his own dynasty in the savage wilderness of the Australian Outback. It was quite an ambition and a far, far cry from his own ancestral home in the Borders region of Scotland. But as it stood, a second son, denied inheritance of the family estates by the existence of an elder brother, Alexander McKendrick, an adventurer and a visionary at heart, found an excellent option in travelling halfway across the world to seek his own fortune in the Great South Land, where handsome, well-educated young Scotsmen from distinguished families were thin on the ground. McKendrick had been very favourably received, immediately gaining the patronage of the governor of the then self-governing colony of New South Wales.

The great quest had begun.

It had started in the colony of New South Wales, but was to finish far away in the Northern Territory, the wildest of wild frontiers, where a man could preside over a cattle run bigger than many a European country. This was the mysterious Top End of the great continent, deeply hostile country, peopled with a nation collectively called the *Kakadu*.

McKendrick had been undaunted. It was from this very escarpment he had named on the spot Crown Ridge because of its curious resemblance to an ancient crown. He had looked out over a limitless lushly grassed valley and he had recorded as "knowing in his heart" this was the place where the Australian dynasty of the Campbell-McKendrick family would put down roots. Land was the meaning of life. The land endured when mighty monuments and buildings collapsed and dissolved into dust.

So that was my great-great-great-great-grandfather, Cal thought with the familiar thrill of pride. *Some guy! And there is* my *inheritance spread out before me.* The McKendricks—they had abandoned their double barrel name by the turn of the twentieth century—were among the great pioneers of the Interior.

By late afternoon he was back at the homestead, dog-tired, bones aching after a long, hard day in the saddle. It was truly amazing the amount of punishment a young man's body could take. His father, Ewan, so recently a dynamo, had slowed down considerably this past year. Ewan McKendrick was a legendary cattleman like the McKendricks before him. There had only been one black sheep in the family, the third heir, Duncan, the supposed *quiet* one, whose exploits when he came to power got him killed by an unerring aboriginal spear, the terrible consequence of ill-treating the black people on the station. It was a crime no McKendrick had committed before him and none ever did again.

Cal found his mother and father and his widower uncle Edward, his father's brother, in the library enjoying a gin and tonic and talking horses, a never-ending topic of conversation in the family. Their faces lit up at his arrival as if he had just returned from an arduous trek to the South Pole.

"Ah, there you are, darling," cried his mother, Jocelyn, extending an arm.

He went to her and put his hands lightly on her thin shoulders. A beautiful woman was his mother. She had made a great wife to his father, a fine mistress of Coronation Hill but she had never been a particularly good mother. For one thing she was absurdly wrapped up in him when, sadly, she had spent little time or attention on her daughter, his younger sister, Meredith.

"Settle this for me, will you, son?" His father immediately drew him into an argument he and Ed were having about blood lines. The McKendricks had a passion for horses. Coronation Hill, named at the time of settlement in honour of the British queen Victoria, was very serious about its breeding and training programme, not just for their own prized stockhorses, horses capable of dominating not only rodeos, gymkhanas and cross country events, but the racehorses on the bush circuit. Bush race meets were enormously popular, drawing people from all over the far-flung Outback.

Ewan clapped gleefully as Cal confirmed what he had been maintaining was correct. "Sorry, Uncle Ed." Cal slanted his gentle uncle a smile. "You were probably thinking of 'Highlander.' *He* was a son of 'Charlie's Pride.'"

"Of course." Edward nodded his head several times. Edward had never been known to best his elder brother. Though the family resemblance between the brothers was strong, Edward had always been outshone by Ewan in all departments, except, Cal thought, in sensitivity and the wonderful ability to communicate with children and people far less fortunate than the grand McKendricks.

"Thanks for arriving just in time," his father crowed,

giving his loud hearty laugh and stabbing a triumphant finger at his brother. "Fancy a cold beer, son? I know G&T's aren't your tipple."

"I'll go and get cleaned up first, Dad," Cal replied, quietly dismayed at how much pleasure his father took in putting his brother down.

"Did you sack young Fletcher?" Ewan grunted, shooting his son a startling, blue glance.

Cal shook his head, not prepared to alter his decision. "I've decided to give him another chance. He's young. He's learning. He takes the pain."

"Very well" was all his father said with a rough shake of his handsome head, when once he would have barked, "You're not running Coronation yet, son."

Except these days he was, or close enough. It was, after all, his heritage. Irresistibly, Cal's gaze went to the series of tall arched stained-glass windows that dominated the library. The sinking sun was starting to stream through the glass, turning the interior of the huge room into a dazzling kaleidoscope of colour: ruby, emerald, sapphire, gold. Ceiling-high mahogany bookcases in colonnaded bays were built into the walls on three sides of the library housing a very valuable collection of books of all kinds: literature, world history, ancient and modern, mythology, science, valuable early maps, family documents, colonial history. It was a splendid collection that desperately needed cataloguing and maybe even re-housing. When his time came he would make it his business to hire someone well qualified to carry out this long-needed important work. Sadly neither his grandparents nor his father and mother had felt impelled to have the arduous task begun. Uncle Edward knew better than to interfere. Since he had tragically lost his wife to breast cancer ten years before, Ed had lived with the family.

Cal had no family of his own yet. No woman to share his life, ease the burden. Kym Harrison was the girl he was supposed to have married. He had been briefly engaged to her a couple of years back. He was still marvelling at how he had allowed it to happen. Of course, his mother had never let up on him to "tie the knot." But it hadn't been right for him, and Kym deserved better. Six months the engagement had lasted. Six months of fighting something too powerful to be overcome. Passion for another woman. One who had betrayed him. Every loving word that had fallen from her beautiful mouth had been a *lie*.

How could he have been so blindly mistaken? Even at near twenty-five he'd been no naive young fool. He was supposed to be, then as now, one of the most eligible bachelors in the country. He had to know it. The women's magazines kept him constantly in their lists. But there had been no serious attachment since. Just a few pain-free encounters, pain-free exits. Not that there was any such thing as safe sex. Someone always got hurt. It wasn't just a question of taking his time, either, of being *sure*. It was more a battle to exorcise those memories so vivid, they denied him the power to move on with his life. Yet he had tried.

He had known Kym since they were children. They connected on many levels. But compatibility, similar backgrounds, close family ties, weren't enough. Not for him anyway. Their relationship lacked what he had learned, to his cost, truly existed. *Passion*. Wild and ravishing; emotion that took you to the Heavens then when it was ruthlessly withdrawn dropped you into your own pit in Hell.

Hadn't he wanted her from the very first minute? The memory surfaced.

"Good morning, sir. Another glorious day!"

No shy dip of the head, but a calm, smiling, near-regal greeting, as if she were a princess in disguise. A princess, moreover, of uncommon beauty, even if she did happen to be folding towels.

He had stood there transfixed, desire pouring into him like burning lava. And it wasn't desire alone. He honestly felt he had no other choice but to fall madly in love with her. It was his fate. He hadn't been looking for any holiday fling; certainly not with a member of the island staff. Yet he had wanted this woman to have and to hold. *His woman.* God, in his secret heart she still remained *his woman.* What an agony love was! It forced itself on you, never to let go.

Gina!

How could he remain faithful if only in mind to a woman who had utterly deceived him? Kym had been his parents' choice almost from the cradle. Kym was the daughter of his mother's best friend, Beth Harrison. The Harrisons were their nearest neighbours on Lakefield. A marriage between them was a fantasy both mothers had harboured. His mother who had told him all his life she adored him—his mother was the classic type who doted upon the son—was still trying to come to terms with the split up. He had spent most of his childhood fighting off his mother's possessiveness, so it had been almost a relief to go away to boarding school even if it meant leaving his beloved Coronation Hill. How differently his mother had treated Meredith! Not unkindly, heavens no, she loved Meredith in her way, but rather as though daughters didn't matter all that much in the scheme of things. His mother's special love had been directed to *him.*

No little girl child should have to suffer that, he thought. When he married and children came along he would make sure any daughter of his would be treasured. Kym, an only child, enjoyed full parental love. It had been lavished on her. No son had come along in the Harrison family so Kym would inherit Lakefield. "You couldn't find a better match, my darling," his mother always told him. "No other woman could love you more than Kym does. Outside me, of course." This with a bright laugh. "Kym is perfect for you."

His mother didn't know about Gina unless his aunt Lorinda had told her. Lorinda had sworn she wouldn't. Lorinda, his mother's only sibling, had helped him in a remarkable way back then. He was very grateful to her for her kindness and empathy. She always had been enormously supportive. It had to be true about Kym's really caring for him. They were still friends, despite everything. Or maybe Kym was just hanging in there until such time he realised she really was his best choice. Maybe compatibility could be made to work. Obsession, after all, was a disaster. He gave a small shake of his head, warding his visions off. How could a man keep a woman's image burning bright when it was all of four years since her desertion? He had taken Gina's betrayal not just hard. It had near crushed the life out of him when up to then he had shown no fear of anything.

He had hated her at first. He had thought hate was a way out. But hate hadn't worked. Having loved her, he found it was less corrosive to hate himself. That's when he had allowed himself to become engaged to Kym, convincing himself Kym was the path to healing. That hadn't worked, either. It was just as impossible to remove Gina from his bloodstream as live without a heart.

He was passing his father's study when Meredith called to him, "Got a minute, Cal?"

"Sure." He walked into the room, his eyes ranging over her face. Usually his sister had a welcoming smile for him, but this afternoon she looked serious, even sad.

"Hey, there, what's up?" His voice echoed his concern. Meredith was three years his junior. They were the best of friends. In fact, he would have to think really hard to remember a cross word between them. Their isolated upbringing had forged strong personal loyalties between them. He had always looked out for his little sister, though, like all the McKendricks, Meredith had grown tall with the slim, lithe build of the athlete she was.

She was a marvellous horsewoman. She had won many cups and ribbons over the years, nearly as many as he had but no one had thought to display them as they did his. Once when they were kids, he had pinned her ribbons and rosettes all over her and taken pictures of her, both on and off her horse. He had hung on to those early photographs, too. The best one he'd had enlarged and framed. It sat on the desk in his bedroom along with a few other family portraits of them both. Great shots all of them.

He had to admit all his family were exceptionally good-looking. Genes were responsible for that. Meredith was beautiful but she made no effort to play up her looks. Rather she seemed to work at playing them down. She wore no make-up, just sunscreen and a touch of lipstick, jeans, neat little cotton shirts, her rich brown hair bleached gold at the temples by the sun, pulled back into a section of thick plait that ended in a loose ponytail. Even without her making the slightest effort, men turned to look at her.

There were lots of things he wished for his sister—a fuller, more rewarding life, a man she could love and who loved her, marriage, children, but none of this was happening. For *either* of them. His father had frightened most of Meredith's serious suitors off. Their dad could be a very intimidating man. Although, it wasn't as if Meredith was the apple of his eye as anyone might expect with an only daughter. Meredith came well down the line when she should have been right up there. But that's the way it was. Nothing he nor Meredith could do about it. He was eternally grateful she had never blamed him. There had been no sibling rivalry, no wrenching jealousy. It had been bred into Meredith that sons, not daughters, were the ones who counted. As for suit-ors, most guys knew not to apply unless they could come up to scratch, and McKendricks' scratch was a very hard call.

"Take a look at this," Meredith was saying, breaking into his reverie. She laid a sheet of newspaper flat on the mas-sive partner's desk, smoothing the crumpled surface. Such graceful hands, he thought, but regretfully getting knocked about with hard work. His sister did a lot more than pull her weight. She handled most things so quietly and effortlessly her capabilities tended to be overlooked or at the very least taken for granted. Meredith was not only beautiful but she had brains to spare. She would make some lucky guy a bril-liant partner.

"What is it?" He rounded the desk, to stand beside her, topping her easily. "Oh, my God!" He felt the ground open up beneath his feet....

Watching him keenly, Meredith's face filled with anxi-ety. "Look, I'm sorry if I've done the wrong thing, Cal. But something inside told me you'd want to see this."

Physically and mentally reeling, he still managed to put a reassuring hand on her arm. "That's okay, I do."

"I thought so," Meredith breathed more easily. "You really loved her, didn't you?" She glanced at her brother's strong profile, registering his shock, and the way the muscles had bunched along his strong jawline.

"It's been a job trying to hate her," he answered, trying to control the grating harshness of his tone. He stared down at the beautiful unsmiling face of the girl in the newspaper photograph. "I always knew this day would come."

"I think I did, too," Meredith murmured quietly.

"How did you get a hold of it?" He glanced at the top of the page, seeing it was a Queensland newspaper. The State of Queensland adjoined the Northern Territory. They didn't take this newspaper.

"It came wrapped around some supplies Dad ordered," she said. "I almost screwed it up and threw it away. Something stopped me." Meredith paused, involuntary tears welling into her deep blue eyes. "She's still as beautiful as ever. More so now she's a woman. The first time I saw her back on the island I thought she looked like a very young Roman goddess. Full of grace, but there she was beavering away as a domestic. She had such a *look* about her."

"Enough to stop your breath." His mouth had turned so dry it was difficult to speak.

"I so liked her," Meredith lamented, even now wondering how she could have been so mistaken in Gina. "She seemed as beautiful inside as out."

"Error of judgement," he said with a humourless laugh. "I just couldn't believe it when Lorinda told me Gina had gone." Cal made a big effort to shove the old agony away. "She didn't even bother to give notice. She just took off."

Meredith recalled it well, her own shock and dismay, as Cal continued speaking. "The odd thing was Management didn't seem perturbed about it, when anyone would have thought they would be angry at the way she'd left them in the lurch. I could never figure it out."

"Aunt Lorinda would have had a private word with them," Meredith said quietly, "or her pal did. Ian Haig owned the island. Still does. Obviously to avoid further upsetting you, they dropped it."

"I guess so," Cal said, nodding. How did one learn to shut down on images that persisted? In his mind's eye, he saw Gina lying back on the white sand, the sea breeze all around them, him bending over her, ready to claim that lovely, moulded mouth. "We've been there, Mere." He sighed. "No one is going to take the ground from under my feet again.

No point in going over it. Whatever the full story, Lorinda tried to help in any way she could."

"Not much use, was she?"

Cal's mahogany head, sun-streaked like his sister's, jerked towards her in surprise. "What is that supposed to mean?"

"Well, she could have persuaded Gina to at least attempt to explain herself to you," Meredith said. "I would have, but Gina didn't confide in me. As for Aunt Lorinda, I haven't exactly forgiven her for interfering in my pitiful fling with Jake Ellory."

Cal grunted, "Ellory wasn't half good enough for you, Mere." He lay a sympathetic hand on her shoulder.

"Okay." She had to acknowledge that. "Point is I was able to see that for myself. I know Aunt Lorinda means well. She dotes on you, always has. She's very nice to me, too, but she's a master manipulator just like Mum. They're as thick as thieves. The facts were she was all in favour of Kym. Kym was the blue-eyed girl. Gina was the seductress. I guess we're never going to know exactly what happened. I could have sworn Gina was as madly in love with you as you were with her. The *feeling* that was generated between you two turned the air electric!"

"That wasn't electricity, my dear, that was hot air," Cal said flatly, his handsome features grown taut. "Gina didn't have the guts to tell me what she told Lorinda. What she had going was a great holiday fling. The reality was, she already had her serious boyfriend back home. Italian descent just like her. Marrying him was obviously very important in her family."

Meredith could accept that as true. Italian and Greek communities were very close. "Well, it was a sad, sad business. That's all I can say. But how does someone who readily puts her life on the line for a child act in a spineless manner? It doesn't make sense. Look at her face. It's not just a beautiful face, it's a *brave* face. I'm not surprised she did something like this. I can see her doing it, can't you? Why then didn't she try to explain herself? Why did she allow herself to get in so deep in the first place, given she was virtually promised to someone else? Perhaps she was frightened of her dad? I got the impression from something she let drop, he was super strict. I know all about strict dads."

Cal, re-reading the article, turned his remarkable gaze back on her.

A McKendrick in every other respect, the height, the splendid physique, the handsomely chiselled features, Cal had inherited his emerald-green eyes from their mother. Devil-green, one of Meredith's girlfriends called them, always trying to capture Cal's attention with her bold, sexy glances.

"I'm going after her," he announced.

"You are?" Somehow that didn't shock her. She even wondered if she hadn't deliberately set it up. She could have thrown away the article. Instead she had kept it for him. Was it possible this time he and Gina could make it work? Gina's wedding plans with her Italian boyfriend hadn't come off, it seemed.

"You bet!" Cal rasped, radiating determination. "How come she didn't marry that guy? It says here, Gina Romano." He stabbed the paper with a tanned forefinger. "That's her maiden name, not Gina Falconi, or Marente or whatever. Another guy she left with a broken heart. She's still unmarried. I want to know *why*." Cal threw up his head, unable to control the thoughts of revenge.

Meredith made no attempt to dissuade him. Cal had the bit between his teeth. When Cal decided to do something, it was done and pretty damned quick. She knew Gina had broken his heart. She knew he had been trying to forget her ever since. He deserved the chance to find out once and for all if Gina Romano simply wasn't worth all his pain. Cal was approaching thirty. He had to move on. Their parents were desperate for him to get married. They needed Cal to produce an heir, give them their first grandchild. Needless to say they would be hoping for a boy.

"What are you going to tell Mum and Dad?" she asked. "You run the station. You can't just vanish."

"I'm going to tell 'em I'm in need of a short break," he answered tersely. "Steve can hold the fort while I'm gone. He's well capable of it. He carries his old man's genes, even if Lancaster won't acknowledge him." Everyone in the Outback knew Gavin Lancaster, Channel Country cattle baron, was Steve Lockhart's biological father. Steve might as well have had *Lancaster* stamped on his forehead. "Even Dad concedes Steve has turned out just fine when initially he was against taking him on. Didn't want to get on the wrong side of Lancaster I suppose. Lancaster's one mean man."

Meredith's expression was wry. "They call Dad a son of a bitch behind his back," she reminded him.

"Maybe. But he's not *mean*. Mostly he's generous. Steve is shaping up to be the best overseer we've ever had. Had he been granted a bit of Lancaster money he could have bought a property of his own and worked it up."

"Well, that's not going to happen," Meredith spoke briskly, hoping the heat she felt in her veins didn't show in her cheeks. "Gavin Lancaster will go to his grave refusing to acknowledge Steve. One wonders why. His wife is dead. His other son doesn't measure up from all accounts. One can only feel sorry for him. Ah, well!" Meredith threw the issue off with a shrug. Usually she kept her thoughts about Steve Lockhart under wraps. She had learned the hard way to feign indifference to any man who attracted her, a man, moreover, who was a McKendrick employee and Gavin Lancaster's illegitimate son to boot. As far as her parents were concerned there was a *huge* gulf between family and staff. She found life easier if she kept up a pretence. No one was to know what went on inside her.

"I'll take this," Cal was saying, folding the sheet of newspaper so it fitted into the back pocket of his jeans.

"Be my guest. I suppose this just *could* be a mistake, Cal," she offered gently, feeling a sudden obligation to warn this brother she so loved and respected.

"That's just a chance I'm going to have to take." Cal started to move off, his stride swift and purposeful. At the door he turned to give her his heart-stopping smile. It was a smile Meredith shared, though she wasn't fully aware of it.

"It's been four years?"

"It only seems like yesterday."

Meredith blinked rapidly at the expression in his eyes. She knew the struggle he was having trying to keep his passionate emotions in check. The newspaper clipping had come as a revelation. "What are you going to do when you find her?" She realised she actually *wanted* Gina Romano back in their lives. Her memories of Gina were of a beautiful young woman strong but gentle with a great sense of humour and highly intelligent. The sort of young woman she would have treasured as a friend. She knew she couldn't speak for her mother and father. She had the sinking feeling they would be strongly against someone like Gina. Gina wasn't a PLU. It was the snob thing, PLU meaning People Like Us.

Cal took a moment to reply. "I'm going to demand she tell me to my face why she *lied*."

The words were delivered with chilling force.

CHAPTER TWO

GINA parked outside "Aunt" Rosa's modest bungalow made beautiful by the garden Rosa lavished such love and attention on. Taking the myriad scents of the garden deep into her lungs, Gina walked slowly up the stone-paved path to the front porch decorated with flower-filled hanging baskets. When Rosa had bought the bungalow three years back, Gina had helped greatly with the clean-up operation, cajoling a few of her sturdy male friends to join in, especially when it came to hauling in the rocks Rosa had used as natural features. In those days there was *no* garden, a few straggly plants, but Rosa had turned the allotment into a private garden paradise. The stone paths led through a wealth of flowering shrubs, camellias, azaleas, peonies, hydrangeas, through cascading archways of roses, all strongly fragrant, the floribunda wisteria, "Alba," and groves of lush ferns. There was always something happening in Rosa's garden, something to lift the heart.

Rosa was her godmother, her mother's bridesmaid at her first disastrous marriage which had produced Sandro and her. The great tragedy of her life was the disappearance of Sandro, her brother. Two years her senior, he had run off at the age of sixteen after a violent argument with their father, the most difficult and demanding of men. Sandro had not only run off, he had vanished from the face of the earth.

How did one do that? Gina had asked herself that question countless times. How did one lose one's identity? How did one go about obtaining a driving licence? What about credit cards, a Medicare card? Could Sandro be dead? Something inside her told her no, though he had never contacted her or their mother to tell her he was safe, not a single phone call or a postcard. His disappearance had almost killed their mother and caused her, his loving sister, deep grief that continued right up to the present day.

Rosa knew all about her family's deeply troubled past. Rosa had been there. *"One day, cara, Sandro will return to us. You'll see. It was just that he could no longer live with your father."* What Rosa felt Gina's father to be was always delivered in impassioned Italian. Rosa was a woman of volatile temperament.

Yet their father had worshipped her, his daughter. She could do no wrong. She was his shining star. She might have been marked down for future canonisation. *"My beautiful Gianina!"* Until the night she confessed she was pregnant. Then her virgin image had been well and truly shattered.

Rosa had always kept in touch with her. Indeed, Rosa had offered to take her in, after her father had literally thrown her, the fallen idol, out. It had truly been the never-darken-my-door-again situation she had hitherto thought only existed in novels. But the last thing she had wanted was to bring down trouble on Rosa's head even though her godmother had sworn she could handle the likes of Ugo Romano.

"He's a great big bully, you know!"

When Primo, Rosa's husband, died at the early age of fifty-four Rosa sold the old sugar farm and travelled to Brisbane to be near her goddaughter. Rosa, a warm, generous woman had not been blessed with children, a great sorrow to her. *"Poor Primo, he couldn't manage it."* Otherwise

Primo had been a good, good man. Everyone in the community had agreed on that.

"Someone has to look after you!" Rosa announced when she arrived on Gina's doorstep, followed by a torrent of curses aimed at Gina's father. At least one of them must have worked because Gina's father barely eighteen months later had bounced off a country road, the old farm utility turning over a few times before landing in a ditch killing him in the process.

"God has spoken," Rosa, never short of an explanation, pronounced at the funeral. *"Now everyone is safe. My poor Lucia, maybe, might find herself another husband. One to cherish her. I see Vince Gambaro over there."*

Gina's mother, Lucia, was pardoned by both her daughter and Rosa. Though desperately unhappy in her arranged marriage, she had been too cowed by her husband to leave him though the friends who cared for her had begged her to do so.

"Sometimes poison isn't all that bad!" muttered Rosa, with black humour.

Before Gina was even at the door, painted cobalt-blue and flanked by matching glazed pots bearing a wealth of pink camellias, Rosa, unconventionally, but eye-catchingly dressed in her own creations, was out on the porch, smiling a welcome.

"He just loves this cartoon," she said. "Lots of giggles, clapping, singing, dancing, peals of laughter. Such a beautiful sound, a child's laughter! I think the video is nearly through."

"Has he been a good boy?" Gina bent to kiss her godmother's satin-smooth cheek. Rosa was a striking-looking woman with a passionate, lived-in kind of face. She was also very queenly in a gypsy fashion. And she had admirers. Rosa had always had admirers, though she had never once succumbed to temptation in all the years of her marriage. One admirer was very much in the picture, a well-to-do widower, a retired bank manager. Gina had met him on several occasions, thinking him a nice man but lacking Rosa's broad cultural interests.

"Always a good boy! Impossible not to love him." Rosa was stroking Gina's arm, showing the depth of her affection. Her goddaughter had filled a vacuum in Rosa's life, but nothing could erase the sorrow of not having children and grandchildren of her own. Gina and Roberto came somewhere in between.

"Mummy!" Now Robbie was at the door, holding up his arms.

Gina picked him up and hugged him to her while he covered her cheeks in kisses. "Hello, my darling," she said, her heart melting with love. "So what happened at preschool today?"

"I learnt lots of things," he told her proudly, then frowned. "I think I've forgotten now."

"No matter. It will all come back."

"Are you coming in?" Rosa asked, standing back from the door.

"For ten minutes," Gina smiled. "I've got something for you."

"For me, too?" Robbie asked hopefully.

"Something for you *both*," Gina said, setting her son down. Goodness, he was getting heavy and he was tall for his age.

"I hope mine comes in a bottle." Rosa flashed another dark-eyed grin. Rosa was a wonderful cook and something of a wine expert, partial to a really good red, preferably a Shiraz.

"It got highly rated," Gina told her.

"Bellisimo!" Rosa cried, throwing up her arms and going into a spirited little dance that made the gold hoops in her ears sway and Robbie laugh. Rosa was far more of a grand-mother to Robbie than ever his real grandmother was, now living far away on a New Guinea coffee plantation.

They walked through to the kitchen, Robbie running ahead. Modest from the outside, inside the bungalow was a reflection of Rosa's exuberant, artistic nature. The walls of the house were covered in her paintings. The warmly welcoming yellow-and-white kitchen was dominated by a large painting of a wicker basket filled to overflowing with yellow lemons and their lustrous leaves, the leaves spilling onto a white tablecloth. Gina loved it. Rosa had given her several of her paintings to decorate the apartment.

They were home in less than ten minutes. She settled Robbie in front of the television in the living room so he could watch the end of the video while she went through to her bedroom to change out of her smart business clothes. Inside the walk-in wardrobe she reached for a comfortable caftan that was still rather glamorous, fuchsia silk with a gold trim. She'd been out to a business lunch, which she thought should carry her through dinnertime. Maybe a light salad? Robbie wanted his all-time favourite which she allowed him once a week—sausages and mash. She always bought the best quality pork sausages, wrapped them in bacon, which he liked, and let him have tomato sauce, which surprise, sur-prise, had turned out to be one of the dwindling number of things good for everyone. Once a very fussy eater, Robbie now enjoyed his food, eating the healthiest food for most of the time. The great news was she now had him eating banana porridge before he went off to school. He refused point-blank to eat cereal or eggs. *Yuck!*

She was passing through the hallway when a knock on

the apartment door startled her. Visitors had to buzz through to her video-intercom and identify themselves before being allowed through the security door. It had to be Dee from the Body Corporate Management. If parcels arrived and couldn't be delivered because she was at work, Dee usually took care of them. Dee was a good sort, ever helpful, kind and gentle with Robbie. And why not? Her beautiful little son was a gorgeous child with the sunniest of natures. Everyone loved him.

She didn't open the door immediately. She checked through the peephole but could only see someone holding up a large bouquet of yellow roses. They looked like her favourite, Pal Joey. Nat Goldman, a very nice guy she worked with, had taken to sending her roses, but they were usually red. Shaking back the long tumble of her hair, she threw back the door, a smile on her face.

And there was Calvin McKendrick; the power elite!

There had been no icy tingle this time to warn her. Her powers had deserted her. Or his powers were stronger. The blood roared in her ears and she wrapped her arms tightly around herself as if the action could prevent her from falling. No trace of her smile remained.

Four years were as *nothing*. His presence was as vividly familiar to her as if their separation had only been fleeting moments. Yet she stood rooted to the spot, unable to move, unable to speak, struck dumb with wonderment. Then very gradually her entire body began to react. She felt an unbearable urge to throw herself into his arms, feel them close powerfully around her. She wanted to inhale his marvellous male scent. She wanted to kiss his beautiful mouth. She wanted to *taste* him. Hadn't she suffered grievously these past years? Instead she took a long, deep breath, widening her eyes in surprise.

"Cal!"

"Ah, you've remembered!" he said suavely. "Do please go on." There was a dangerous edge to the civility of his tone. It matched the glitter in his remarkable eyes, as green as emeralds, and as cold.

"Go on?" She groped for the door behind her so she could close it. He couldn't be allowed to see Robbie. She had to keep him from it. She was too frighteningly vulnerable, now as then. He could take her beloved son off her, or curtail her time with him. That prospect she couldn't bear. The McKendricks were powerful people with an army of lawyers at their disposal and limitless funds. That alone inspired fear.

"Well, surely you're going to add you're surprised to see me?" The voice she had so loved, was filled with mockery.

"I am, *very!*" Even to her own ears her voice sounded strangled. She was trembling all over, her heart kicking against her ribs. "How did you find me?"

He tut-tutted. "And you, the heroine?"

Of course. The newspaper story that had even made it onto the television. People still pointed at her in the street. Some even came up to her, congratulating her on her bravery.

What can I do? She couldn't get her head around the dilemma that now faced her. It was imperative she pull herself together.

"Have you someone with you?" he asked, seeing the agitation that was written all over her. His eyes went beyond her to the entrance hall; a small console, a striking oil painting above it, two Victorian lustres, emerald-green glass, decorated with tiny white flowers and gold leaves; all very pretty.

Gina scrambled to nod her head, though she felt dazzled and dazed.

"Are you asking me to come back another time?" Perversely he found his eyes consuming her. She was a wonder-ful-looking woman; more beautiful than ever, if that were possible. Her classical features were more clearly defined, her eyes deep, dark bottomless pools. Her masses of hair, neither straight nor curly, fell in thick sinuous coils half-way down her back. Desire over which he had no control streamed through his blood, like a river in full spate. He was a greater fool than even he had thought.

"Please don't come back, Cal," Gina begged, spinning very quickly as she heard Robbie, his programme over, moving to join her. "There's absolutely nothing we could have to say to one another after all this time." Galvanised, she tried to shut the door but Cal deliberately blocked her efforts with one foot against it.

No, Robbie! the voice inside her shrieked.

But Robbie came on, dead-set on finding out who his mother was talking to. Robbie had great social skills. He loved visitors. Just as she feared, he rounded the partition that divided the entrance hall from the living area, running to Gina and grasping her around the hips. "Hello!" he said brightly, addressing Cal. "Are you a friend of Mummy's?" He gave an engaging little chuckle, looking at Cal with the greatest interest.

But Cal for once in his life was literally struck dumb. He stood pulverized by shock. Whatever scenarios he had considered on his long trip here, it was never this! He found himself rocking back on his heels as the truth came roaring for him like an express train.

God! There was nothing irreverent about his silent oath. Recognition shot simultaneously to his heart and his brain. This was his child. This was his son! There could be no mistake. The child resembled him too closely.

He dragged his eyes away from the beautiful little boy, to pin Gina's treacherous, dark gaze. She looked frightened, utterly wretched, as well she might! "I'd like to come in, if I may." He fought to keep the tight rein on his voice, for the child's sake. "It seems, Gina, we have things to discuss." He put out his hand to his son: dark copper curls like petals, framing an angelic little face. In adolescence those dark copper curls would turn a rich mahogany like his. He had the McKendrick features, but even more tellingly the black-lashed eyes so brilliant a green, they were often described as emerald. There was the McKendrick cleft in his chin, not deep like his father's, more shallow like his. Uncle Ed had a cleft chin. Meredith had a distinctive dimple.

"Hello, there, Robbie." Cal showed the child all the gentleness and warmth he denied the mother. "I'm Cal. Calvin McKendrick. I am an old friend of your mother's. I'm so very pleased to meet you at long last, though I think I would have known you anywhere." Anywhere on this earth, he thought, trying to come to grips with Gina's treachery.

"And I'm pleased to meet *you*," Robbie responded, sweetly, unlocking his grasp on his mother and extended his hand as he'd been taught.

Cal thrust the beautiful yellow roses into Gina's rigid arms before taking the child's hand. "So, Robert?"

"*Robbie.* I've been watching my favourite cartoon."

"Really?" Cal spoke normally, though naked shock was showing in his eyes.

"You can see my video if you like," Robbie offered graciously.

"That's very nice of you, Robbie," Cal said.

"Have you got time now?" the little boy asked hopefully, obviously having taken an immediate liking to Cal.

"Darling," Gina interrupted, "Cal only called in for a minute." She drew Robbie back against her, giving Cal a pleading look.

It had no effect on Cal whatsoever. "No, that's okay!" He shrugged a rangy shoulder. "I wasn't going anywhere special. Do you mind, Robbie, if I come in?" Cal gave his son an utterly winning smile.

"Oh, *please*, Mummy, can he?" Robbie stared up into his mother's face, a highly intelligent child, trying to puzzle out the atmosphere. "I haven't had my tea yet," he told Cal. "It's bangers and mash. Would you like some?"

"If there's any to spare." Cal twisted Gina a hard, challenging smile. He was absolutely certain he wouldn't be able to eat anything, but he definitely wasn't going away.

"Oh, goody!" Robbie put out his hand to take Cal's. "Oh, your hands are rough inside!" he burst out in surprise, as baby-soft three-year-old fingers met up with hard calluses.

"That's because I'm a cattleman," Cal explained.

"What's that, a cattleman?" Robbie asked with great interest, beginning to pull Cal through the door. "Do you own cattle, cows and things?"

Cal nodded. "One day I'll show you."

"Promise?" Robbie's big beautiful eyes lit up.

"Let's shake on it."

"You're a very nice man," Robbie pronounced, taking the handshake as a promise.

"Thank you," Cal replied. "It must be getting along to your bedtime soon?" he asked, desperate to have it out with this woman who had so betrayed him.

"Seven o'clock." Robbie lifted his head to scan the face of this tall man he seemed to know somehow, but couldn't understand why. "That's when I go to preschool. I can stay up a little later at the week-end. Will you be here when I go to sleep?"

"Bound to be," Cal said.

Somehow they kept up a reasonable pretence until Robbie went to bed. His mother kissed him as she always did when she tucked him in. "Good night, my darling."

"'Night, Mummy."

"Sleep tight."

"Don't let the bed bugs bite." Robbie giggled as he finished off the nightly ritual, then he put out a hand to Cal.

"You're going to come back and see us, aren't you, Cal?" he asked hopefully.

"Count on it."

Gina watched Cal lean down and touch her little boy's cheek with the most exquisite tenderness.

"That's good. I really like you," Robbie said, the glow from the bedside lamp turning his eyes to jewels.

"As it happens I really like you." Cal smiled, watching his son sigh contentedly, then close his eyes, dark lashes heavy on apricot cheeks.

They returned in a fraught silence to the living room. Gina was amazed tears weren't streaming down her cheeks. She had never seen Robbie respond to anyone like he had to Cal.

Blood will out!

Carefully, she shut the door that led down the corridor to the bedrooms, grateful Robbie slept very soundly, especially when he was overexcited as he was tonight.

"You hate me," Gina said. His face was a taut mask.

"Who in hell would blame me?" Cal replied in a tone so contemptuous it cut deep. "Why did you do it?" He went to her and seized her arms with controlled fury. "So you ran back to your boyfriend! Why didn't you make a fool of him like you made a fool of me? When you realised it was my child you were carrying, why didn't you try to pass it off as his? Didn't think you'd be able to pull if off, eh? Worried he might kill you when he eventually found out? Where did the green eyes come from, the copper curls? Robert is the image of me when I was his age. I have stacks of photographs to prove it, as though we *need* proof." He released her so abruptly, Gina stumbled and had to clutch at the back of an armchair to stay upright.

"I'm sorry if you feel hurt, Cal," she said, tonelessly. "At least it proves you're human."

"Human? What the hell are you talking about? And you're *sorry*? God!" He began to pace the carpet like a caged tiger. "Is that all you can say, sorry? I had a right to *know*. Robert is three years old. Just think what I've missed! Or haven't you any heart at all? For three years I've had a son I didn't even know existed. I wasn't there when he was born, when he took his first steps, when he started to say his first words. I've missed his birthdays. I've missed loving him. I've missed the joy of having him love me. What's wrong with you? How could you do that to me?" He fell down on the sofa, throwing back his head and covering his eyes with his hands. "What the hell were you thinking about? Dear God, Gina, are you devoid of all conscience?"

She stared back at him, trying hard not to burst into tears. "Don't, please *don't*! I had to cope any way I could."

He flung up his handsome head, tension making his features more hawklike than ever. "And that meant absenting me from your life?" He stared about him at the large room, decorated with style and care, the furnishings, the art works, the fresh flowers. "You live here?"

"Of course I live here." She thrust the heavy fall of her hair over her shoulder.

"Alone with Robert?" He shot her a challenging glace.

"Yes." She dared not add, "As if it's any of your business." He was furious, shocked, a pallor beneath his dark tan. She was frightened of him; of what he might do. She just knew something was going to come of that newspaper article.

"You work?" The question was terse. "Sit down, why don't you?"

Demolished she took a seat opposite him. Her heart was beating so fast she thought she might be sick. Low voiced, she named her firm of stockbrokers.

"It must be a darn good job!" He let his eyes move insolently around the attractively furnished room.

"It is," she answered shortly, regaining her breath. "All you see here is mine."

"Bravo!" he crowed.

"What do you want, Cal?" She cut across him, the room thick with tension.

"Who looks after Robert until you get home?" His eyes lanced.

She hated this interrogation, even as she knew she had to endure it. "My godmother, Rosa. She's a wonderful woman. Roberto loves her."

"What's the wonderful Rosa doing down here in Brisbane, or is *everything* you told me a pack of lies?"

"No!" she protested, shaking her head. "When Rosa's husband died she sold the farm to be near me. She takes her responsibilities as godmother very seriously."

"Her prayers couldn't prevent you becoming an inveterate liar," he countered bitterly.

"I never lied to you."

He laughed harshly. "God, you're lying *now.* You were the one who told me you loved me. You told me you never dreamed there could be such happiness. You told me you wanted to be with me always. If they weren't lies, may I ask what in hell *were* they?"

Fearful only a moment before, Gina's magnificent dark eyes flashed. "Why weren't *you* truthful with me?" she demanded, the pain of the past as raw as yesterday. "You had a girl back home you were expected to marry. I even know her name, Kym Harrison. Don't look so shocked. Men are notoriously unfaithful. I saw a photograph of you together in a magazine. You were at the Melbourne Cup. Calvin McKendrick and his lovely fiancée, Kym Harrison. I still have the clipping somewhere to remind me of your treachery. Why didn't you tell me about your Kym?"

He couldn't answer for a minute so taken aback was he by her use of the word *treachery.* "Why are you drawing Kym into this?" he retaliated, heavily frowning. "As soon as I met you there *was* no other woman. No Kym. You were everything I wanted. *My* woman. Getting engaged to Kym came after. It shames me to say it, it certainly wasn't my finest moment, but I became engaged to Kym to forget *you*!"

She stared at him, this man who had haunted her, the father of her child. "It didn't work?" Her tone was deeply hostile. She was out to wound as he was wounding her.

"No more than your relationship with your Italian boyfriend," he countered, sending her a glittering glance that would have crushed her, only she was too startled by his mention of a boyfriend.

"I beg your pardon?" she said, disdainfully, lifting her chin.

He laughed at the hauteur. "Oh, come off it! How easily you assume the regal demeanour. Sure there's not a Contessa or two in the background?"

"I wish!" There was a curl of her moulded lips. Those lips he had kissed so often. "I had *no* Italian boyfriend if that's your idea of an excuse. My father frowned on boyfriends. I was a virgin when I met you. You *know* that."

Colour mounted to his prominent cheekbones. "Yes," he admitted, "but we did use protection."

"One time we didn't."

He buried his head in his hands. "Then my responsibility was far greater than yours. You were just a girl. I was mad about you. Absolutely crazy with love and longing. The last thing I wanted to do was hurt you."

"Am I supposed to believe that?" Her tongue lashed him. "You *did* hurt me. More than you will ever know. I've suffered, but I have my beautiful Roberto."

"And Robert is a McKendrick family name. I recall telling you that."

"Maybe you did—" she shrugged "—but I named him after my brother, Alessandro. Roberto is his middle name." She didn't tell him both factors had influenced her.

Cal studied her with a frown, suddenly remembering how she had told him an older brother had defected from home. "You're talking about the Sandro who went missing when he was sixteen?"

"Aah! You actually remember something!" Her voice throbbed with scorn.

"I remember *everything*!" he corrected her harshly. "He's never contacted you?"

She shook her head, sadness replacing the scorn. There was a long, long list of Missing Persons. "He could be dead for all we know."

Even through his shock and anger, her obvious sorrow reached him.

Gina swallowed on a dry throat. Before her she saw a man who had matured a good deal since she had last seen him. He looked every inch a man of power and authority. The sweetness, however, that had been so much part of his expression had disappeared.

The fear returned. "Please, Cal. Can you reassure me you wouldn't be so cruel as to try to take Robbie from me? I adore him. He's my son."

"He's *my* son, too, Gina," he said curtly, rising to his feet and looming over her. "Tonight I claim him. Fortune has at long last decided to turn my way. I have every intention of taking him back to Coronation Hill. He's a McKendrick. Coronation is his home. It's his heritage. He's my heir."

Anger and fear boiled together in her great dark eyes. "He's my heir, too, I remind you! Romano blood runs in my son's veins. Just when do you think you could take him? Go on, tell me that. And what about me? Do you really think I'm going to stand back and let you take Roberto from me? You'd have to kill me first."

His expression, unlike hers, was astoundingly cool. He took hold of her wrist, letting her feel just a touch of his vastly superior strength. "No need to kill you, Gina," he drawled. "*Marrying* you suits me better."

For a moment she thought she would faint. "Because I have your child?" she cried passionately. "I wasn't good enough for you before." She pulled away violently, rubbing her wrist. "Marriage between us would never work."

He went down on his haunches before her. "Listen and listen carefully." He spoke softly but his demeanour conveyed forceful determination. "I want my son to have a proper upbringing. No broken home. I want him to have a mother and father. That's the two of us. Are you going to tell me there's someone else on the horizon? Someone prepared to take on another man's child? Not that he would have to. I'm intent on getting custody of Robert. I don't think the court would look too *favourably* on you and your deceit. Your brother, Sandro, isn't the only one in your family who likes to disappear. Tell me this? How can a woman who put her own life on the line to save a child, lack the guts to come forward? To stand up and be counted. Or were you overcome with guilt?"

She kept her head lowered, not daring to look into his mesmeric eyes. She was overwhelmingly conscious their faces were mere inches away. "Even when you were making love to me, making our baby, you were lying," she said wretchedly.

He made a sound of the greatest impatience. He caught

her chin sharply, holding a hard thumb to it to keep it up. "You could get any acting job. You're great!" he scoffed. "It's the Italian thing. You know how to exploit emotion. I told you I loved you. I never meant anything more in my life. That part of it is over. I can never trust you again. These past four years I've learned to *hate*!"

"And I have hated, as well. A nice basis for a marriage!" Gina looked him right in the eye, her tone inflammatory. Damn him, damn him! Being so close to him was tearing her in all directions. "And what about your so lofty family?" she demanded. "They wouldn't have accepted me then, why now? Although I don't include your sister, Meredith, in this!"

He stood up, rigid with disgust. "Lord, what a fake you are, Gina. Don't try to drag my family into this. Why don't you just admit it? I was your last big fling before you settled down and became a good little Italian wife. You were going home to marry your boyfriend, the one *Papa and Mamma* had picked out for you." Unforgivably he parodied an Italian accent.

"You were the one going home to marry your Kym." Her great eyes flashed. "So you see, liars on both sides." Suddenly she saw clearly her version of events would clash with his own. She had had her knowledge from his aunt, but at this point she didn't want to draw his aunt into the whole tragic mess because it would only serve to further anger and alienate him.

"Well, we got our just reward," he said with deep irony. "My engagement didn't work. Your marriage prospects were doomed to failure. It's the old story, isn't it? Damaged goods. Hate that expression myself. I have to say motherhood has done wonders for you." He made it sound like she'd once been an ugly duckling. "The dewy girl has turned into a woman. You didn't answer me about your current love life? Not that it matters a damn whatever you're going to say."

She stared across at him, feeling a tightness in her chest. She had loved him as much as she was capable of loving anyone outside her son. *Their son.* "You're serious, then? You're going to force a marriage on me?"

"You bet!"

The hard light in his eyes swallowed all her breath.

"I seem to recall your telling me your parents' marriage was arranged?"

"And it was desperately unhappy as any marriage between us would be." Remembrance of her unhappy family life shadowed her face.

"You omitted to tell me that. I suppose another lie?"

"So, I'm an accomplished actress and an inveterate liar?" She gave him a scathing glance.

"Maybe the two sometimes go together! And how are the Romanos?" He used his suavest tone.

She was racked by a little convulsive shiver. "My father is dead. My mother has remarried. She and her husband live in New Guinea now. I rarely see her."

He lifted supercilious black brows. "She didn't waste much time?"

"She's trying to make up for the lost years," Gina said crisply. "My father had a very difficult temperament."

"I'm sorry to hear it. I suppose that's why Sandro took off?"

"My father was very hard on him. Not at all kind."

"Yet you gave me the strong impression he adored you?"

Adored her? When she exactly matched his vision of her. She sometimes thought her father couldn't have coped with a pregnant daughter, in or out of wedlock.

"What, no answer?" He stared across at her, so wanting to pull her into his arms he had to grip the sides of his chair.

"I'm not going to allow you to question me further," she said angrily. "You McKendricks are cruel people."

That stung him. "Don't you think you should wait to meet them before you decide that?"

"I've met *you*." Her great dark eyes dominated her face. "Let me say again. A marriage between us couldn't work."

He steepled his lean hands, as though considering. "Given you're the mother of my son," he said finally, "I suggest you try to make it work. Or sit it out."

"Sit it out?" she gasped. "I would never, never choose to sit my life out. I want what every woman wants—a man to love her, children, a happy home. We have nothing in common."

"Apart from our son. Never forget that. And unless I'm very much mistaken we're still physically attracted to one another. We could still have the sex. That might keep us pinned together. The sex hasn't gone away, has it?"

She could never deny it. But she *did*. "Oh, stop that!" she said sharply. "Sex is out of the question."

"But I've never forgotten it. You were terrific, Gina. I wanted you to the point of madness. Pathetic how you made me feel! You made me so weak with longing I couldn't see straight. I used to go around all the time my body aching with pain and desire. I was *nuts* about you." He could barely contain his hostility.

"But that was it, wasn't it?" she retorted. "You just loved having sex with me."

"Why not? Sex with you was Heaven. And so disastrous!"

"Some relationship!" she muttered bitterly. "Well, I paid for it."

"Not just *you*!" His expression hardened into granite. "If

you can spare a thought for me, who was never told he was a father. How long will it take you to get yourself organised?" he asked crisply. "I assume you'll have to give notice to your firm. You'd better make it as short as you can. There'll be no difficulty taking Robert out of play school or whatever it is."

She put a hand to her pounding temples. "I can't do this," she near wailed. "You're quite mad."

"My dear Gina, I've never been saner." He leaned back in the armchair, the picture of nonchalance. "If you fight me I promise you, you'll lose. Your best course—indeed, your only course—is to try to make a go of this. *I'm* prepared to."

His arrogance made her livid. "*You're* prepared to!" She totally forgot herself and shouted.

"Keep it down," he warned, turning his head towards the bedroom area.

"Don't tell me what I should do in my own home," she hissed, saturated in hot feeling. "I can see you've grown ruthless."

"If I have it's because of you," he retorted on the instant. "If it makes you more comfortable I give you my solemn promise I won't touch you until you're ready."

"And what makes you think I'll *ever* be ready?" She stared at him coldly.

"Let's have a little test run, shall we?"

He confounded her by rising from his chair.

An unbelievable thrill shot through her. "No test runs!"

He hauled her to her feet, holding her so she had no chance of getting away. "Not so easy to run now, is it, *Gianina*?"

Passion came boiling to the surface. Will subservient to the flesh. Past merged into present. "Don't accuse me of running one more time," she gritted. She hadn't run. She'd been persuaded it was the only thing she could do. The honourable thing.

"Or you'll do what?" His eyes rested compulsively on her full mouth. "Don't try playing the innocent victim with me, Gina. It won't wash. You're a born seductress. You don't have to do anything but look at a man. *Kiss* me."

"Too many kisses," she said, yet her whole being was thrown into a sensual upheaval. No one touched her like he did. She tried to call on her pride and her sense of self-esteem. It would have been easier to call up thunder and lightning. "Damn you to hell!" she cried weakly as his grip tightened.

"I've been there." He spoke with great bitterness, sweeping her fully into his arms. There he held her as though that was where she belonged and nowhere else. She wondered how, after so much pain, her body could respond so brilliantly to his touch; but shamefully it did. It was no mock-up test kiss. It was incredibly turbulent, profoundly vengeful. Deeply suppressed emotions erupted as if at the touch of a detonator.

When they finally broke apart, both were breathing heavily. Cal waited only a speechless moment before he pulled her against him again. "So it's not all over then?" His emerald eyes glittered as though he had won an important battle.

How could she find the words to deny it anyway? He had ruined her utterly for other men. "You said it yourself. All we've got is sex."

"And it's *good*," he ground out harshly, before covering her mouth again.

Hungrily his hand sought her breast, shaped it, his fingers taking hold of the erect nipple, tightening *exquisitely.* She couldn't help her quick gasps that he muffled with his lips. There was a hot gush of feelings inside of her as powerful chemicals were released into her bloodstream.

Surely it was a type of cruelty this power he had over her? she thought fiercely. Would she never be safe from him, safe from herself?

It wasn't just Cal's strong arms that were holding her hostage.

Gina could deny it all she liked, but it was her own heart.

Hours after he had gone back to his hotel, Gina lay in bed sobbing as she hadn't sobbed for years. All the suffering came back to haunt her. Her parents' unhappy marriage; her mother's inability to stand up for herself or for her children, in particular Sandro; her father's periodic rages and she the only one they were rarely directed at; Sandro's disappearance after that last dreadful fight. Later the miracle of the island that had touched her with such radiance, then left her an outcast. The terrifying discovery she was pregnant; her own banishment from the family home, the all pervading sense of loss. Just seeing Cal again brought it all rushing back like the incoming tide to the shore.

She could never have survived on her own without the small stash of money her mother had secreted from her father and stuffed inside a pocket of her suitcase, all the while crying broken-heartedly, without the courage to intervene. More financial help had come from Rosa and Primo; and all through, Rosa's tremendous support. Gina had known the background of her baby son's father, scion of a rich and powerful family, but she had never considered contacting him. She didn't need to be paid off. She had her pride to sustain her. The love she had felt for Cal McKendrick, the ruling passion that had altered the course of her life, was soured by betrayal.

In the last couple of years she had found her feet, but the memory of him had shadowed her life, making it near impossible for her to embark on another relationship. Now he had marched right back into her life, filled with a violent outrage she had kept the existence of his son from him. She tried to block out the harshness and devastation that had been in his voice. Did she really deserve such condemnation? Perhaps she did. She understood his pain even as she feared his power and influence. The time had come for him to assert his rights; to claim his son and as a consequence his son's mother.

"This time you're not getting away, Gina. You're going to do exactly what I tell you."

She rose from the bed to change her tear-drenched pillows, turning her head to look at her bedside clock. 2:10 a.m. She reminded herself she had to get up early in the morning. She had to shower and dress, wake Robbie, get his breakfast, then ready him for preschool, drop him off, then continue on into work where she had to do what he had instructed her to do. Hand in her notice.

CHAPTER THREE

YARDING up had gone on all day. Steve was closing the gates on the portable steel yard when she rode up on him. He knew even before he turned his head it was Meredith. That's how sensitised he was to her presence. She had helped out all day on a tough job. Too tough for a woman, he thought, but there was no dissuading her. She was a McKendrick. Most of the young guys on the station were in love with her. Fat lot of good it would do them, the only daughter of the "Duke and Duchess" Ewan and Jocelyn McKendrick.

"I think I can say it's been quite a day!" She sighed lustily from behind him.

"You did more than your fair share," he said as he turned, using a matter-of-fact voice. It was the usual way they talked to one another. Keep it businesslike. "Any news of Cal?"

She dismounted, and he took the reins from her, knotting them around a rung of the fence. "Plenty." She was dressed like he was, in jeans and a cotton shirt. He had a bold red bandana around his throat. Hers was blue to match her shirt, but the colour paled into insignificance against the sapphire of her eyes. Both of them wore cream felt Akubras low over their eyes. Even the late-afternoon sun had a real bite to it.

"Big secret, is it?"

She didn't smile and she had the most beautiful smile in the world. Lovely white teeth, finely cut mouth. An aristocrat yet with no vanity or ostentation. "I guess you're going to know about it soon enough," she said, "but I'd like you to keep it to yourself."

"Sure."

She nodded, knowing he was as close lipped as she was and very loyal. "Let's walk down to the creek, shall we?"

He dared not speak. What could he say? I'd walk to the ends of the earth with you? He'd been on Coronation Hill the best part of two years with hardly a day when she hadn't been stuck in his head. Truth be known he was well and truly smitten with Ms Meredith McKendrick. Enormous effrontery but he'd learned from early childhood how to cover up his feelings. The men, never slow to catch on, hadn't a clue, though Tom, the retiring overseer, had muttered to him just before he left: "Reckon you could handle McKendrick, son. Why don't you have a go?"

He would, too, only he had precious little to offer a woman like Meredith McKendrick. He couldn't even offer her a clean name. All because of Lancaster! It had been tough growing up, as he had, in a family with various shades of blond hair when his was as black as a crow's wing. His eyes, instead of being the Lockharts' azure-blue, were more gold than brown. Eyes were a dead give-away. They showed one's ancestry. Meredith, for instance, had the McKendrick eyes. They were so blue in some lights they looked purple. Cal had his mother's eyes—dark green with a jewel-like quality. Steve was barely ten when he discovered his "foreign" colouring didn't come from his mother's side of the family as she had always claimed. His colouring came directly from Gavin Lancaster.

He remembered hiding out on the verandah, listening to his mother crying in the bedroom until her tears must have blinded her. He remembered Jim Lockhart berating her, full of an impotent rage now the secret was out. No one could touch Gavin Lancaster. He was too powerful. But Gavin Lancaster could make life very hard for a stockman like Jim Lockhart and his family. He had two half brothers and a half sister. All of them, including his mother, had long since packed up and moved to New Zealand, putting the Tasman between them. The Outback was Lancaster's territory. A man needed to be frightened of Gavin Lancaster and his vengeance.

All except him. He sure as hell wasn't frightened. He had remained. No one was going to separate him from the land he loved. Certainly not the man who had sired him.

He followed Meredith's lead down to the bubbling stream, a small tributary of a much larger billabong, their boots bruising hundreds of tiny wildflowers he thought were native violets.

"Let's sit here," she said, sinking wearily onto the pale golden sand and throwing off her wide-brimmed hat. She had beautiful hair…long and thick and gleaming, burnished at the temples with streaks the colour of champagne. He would love to see it out, streaming over her shoulders. A dream?

Slowly, he lowered his long length beside her—he was six-three—relishing the moment but keeping a respectful distance. "Problems?" he asked, slanting her a glance. No one would have known he was suffocating inside, just to be near her. The two of them alone together. It rarely happened. He calmed himself, feeling the slick of sweat on his brow.

Meredith stared across the creek that could swell to a river in the Wet. The late-afternoon sun was flooding the area with light, throwing rose-gold bands across the rippling surface of the water. "I'm telling you this, Steven, because I trust you. Cal does, too."

She was the only one to ever call him Steven. He loved

his own name on her lips. "You know anything you tell me remains private."

She nodded. "It will all come out eventually."

"It can't be that bad if it has to do with Cal?"

"I'm hoping with all my heart it will be good," she burst out emotionally. "This all has to do with a woman."

"Most things do." He sounded solemn.

"The only woman for Cal," Meredith said. "It started four years ago. Some of the family took a long holiday on a Barrier Reef island, a small privately run luxury resort. A friend of my aunt's owns it. Our group, extended family and friends took over the island. It only caters to around thirty. On the island was a very beautiful young woman called Gina. She was working in the university vacation as a domestic, waitress, whatever was required. Cal fell madly in love with her and I could have sworn she fell madly in love with him. It was really something to see them together."

"Sounds like it ended badly?" he said, feeling truly sorry. How could anything end badly with a guy like Cal McKendrick who had everything?

"Very badly," Meredith said. "Gina left the island without saying a word to Cal. He was devastated. She didn't say anything to me, either, though we quickly got to be friends. She did, however, speak to my aunt."

Aah, Steve thought, gazing off to the opposite bank where graceful sprays of crimson flowers were blossoming amid the trees. The uppity Aunt Lorinda. A fearful snob like the rest of them except Cal and Meredith who were totally devoid of that defect.

"Gina told my aunt it was just a mad fling," Meredith said quietly. "It didn't look like it at the time. Anyway, Cal has never forgiven or forgotten her."

"Yet he got himself engaged to Kym Harrison?"

Meredith ran a finger down her flushed cheek. "I know.

But it was a big mistake. There's always been a lot of pressure on Cal."

"His shoulders are plenty wide enough," Steve said admiringly.

She turned her face to him, surreptitiously studying his profile. Steven Lockhart was a great-looking guy, the golden eyes, the inky-black hair, the strong, regular features. He had an inherent authority to him. The Lancaster Legacy, though he'd bust anyone in the nose for saying it. "Cal thinks a lot of you, too."

"That's good," he reacted with dry amusement. "I always get the impression your dad would like to see me move on."

What could she say? I don't know why my father is as he is? Maybe her father had intercepted one of her stray looks in their overseer's direction. "That won't happen while Cal's around," she assured him. "Cal is running the station, as you know. Dad has more or less semiretired. Cal's very happy with you. Didn't he leave you in charge?"

He turned his sleek black head to look smilingly into her eyes. "I thought *you* were?"

"Me?" She gave a bittersweet little laugh that nevertheless was music to his ears. "I'm not in charge of anything. No, that isn't true. I run the office. I do lots of things."

"Too smoothly," Steve said, unconsciously echoing Cal. "You make the job look too easy. People take the super-efficient for granted. Anyway, go on. I want to hear this story. I've sensed, underneath, Cal is far from happy on the personal front."

"Who is?" she asked, suddenly serious. "Are *you* happy, Steven?"

I've been happier than I've ever been in my life since I met you.

He couldn't tell her that, instead he managed casually,

"I'm happy sitting here with you. Or aren't I supposed to say that?"

She caught the metallic glint. "You've got a big chip on your shoulder, Steven Lockhart."

"I've got a big chip on *both* shoulders," he commented. "That's why I'm so well balanced. So this trip of Cal's is connected to Gina?"

"It's all about Gina. He's dead-set on bringing her home."

"What, here to Coronation?" That stopped him in his tracks.

"This *is* his home."

"So they've reconciled after all this time?" he asked more quietly.

"There's more."

"Of course there's more." He picked up a pebble and sent it skittering across the ruffled surface of the water. "There's *always* more."

Meredith could still feel the shock of her brother's revelation. "Gina had a child, a little boy," she said simply. "His name is Robert, Robbie."

"And the child is Cal's," Steve finished for her.

Meredith released a pent-up breath. "Apparently he's the image of Cal at the same age, even to the green eyes. He's convinced Gina they should get married."

Steve gave a little grunt. "So marriage it will be, knowing Cal. What do your parents think?" He knew perfectly well the McKendricks still had their hopes set on Kym Harrison, who was a nice enough down-to-earth person, but no match for Cal.

"They don't know anything about it as yet," Meredith told him, her tone tinged with worry. "It's going to come as an enormous shock and they don't like shocks. Cal rang me to tell me the news. Cal and I are very close."

"I know that." He picked up another pebble. He had to

do something with his hands. "How do you feel about it? I mean, you have a nephew you didn't know about."

With a sigh she fell back against the sand, looking up at the luminous sky that was filling with birds homing into their nests. "And I can't wait to meet him. It will be wonderful to have a little nephew to love. I want to love Gina, too. I know Cal has never stopped loving her. Cal feels very deeply. I could tell he was shocked out of his mind to find he had a son but I could hear the joy, as well. This is what he truly wants."

Steve put a hand to his head, painfully aware of the length of her slender body beside his; the swell of her breasts, the curve of her hips, her lithe thighs and long legs. He got a tight rein on his feelings. *Man, don't let go or you'll go straight to Hell!* But didn't she realise the way she was lying back like that presented a danger? He felt he was teetering on the brink. Relaxed around women, he was like a cat on a hot tin roof with Meredith. To counteract it he said almost sternly, "Why didn't she tell him? I can't see Cal turning his back on her, or his child!" The likes of Lancaster certainly, but not Cal McKendrick. "I don't think I could forgive a woman for doing that to me. Just think what he's missed out on. The boy must be…three?"

"They'll have to work it out, Steven," she said, and her voice wobbled a little. "Gina is from a migrant family. Italian. They had a sugar farm in North Queensland. Her heritage shows. She's very beautiful."

"More beautiful than you?" Now, why the hell had he said that? He never got too personal. It was taboo.

"Most certainly," she said, flashes of excitement heating her body. She was deeply attracted to Steven Lockhart. She'd known that for a long time. Just as she knew his prime concern had to be survival. At twenty-eight he'd made overseer on one of the nation's premier beef-producing stations, which was no mean feat. He was well paid, lots of perks. He had a future, providing he didn't get on the wrong side of her father. An adverse word from Ewan McKendrick could harm him in the industry. There was *no* future as Gavin Lancaster's illegitimate son. Lancaster refused to acknowledge him.

She shut her eyes, so now Steve was free to look down at her beautiful face. She had lovely clear skin, with a healthy gloss to it. He loved the soft dimple in her chin. He loved her finely cut mouth. He wanted to kiss it. *So badly.* He wanted to pull her long thick hair out of its plait. He wanted to arrange it the way he had often imagined himself arranging it around her face. "Don't you want to hear you're beautiful?" he asked, unable to keep some of the spiralling sensuality out of his voice.

Meredith's dark blue eyes flew open. The very air was trembling.

"Not from *you*, Steven," she said, swift and low.

He pulled back. Looked away. "Right! I get it. I'm out of line." Some part of him wanted to teach her a lesson. One she wouldn't forget. He wanted to reach for her and haul her into his arms. He could feel the dark force in him, the driving male need. Managed to get it under control, but hell, did it have some power!

"I'm not sure you *do* get it," she said, swinging up into a sitting position. "I didn't mean to offend you, Steven. I know that came out badly. I'm sorry. We're rarely alone together. I'm nervous. What I was trying to say is, *we* can't go anywhere."

His golden eyes had sparkles of light in them. "I didn't think we could, actually," he returned, his tone as cutting as a blade.

She put out a shaking, conciliatory hand; let it hover. She was frightened to touch him. She was frightened what touching him might do to her. She could see the lick of sweat on his darkly tanned skin. She wanted to put her tongue to it. "I've hurt you."

"*Never*, I hope." He flashed her an upbraiding look. "Relax, Meredith. I've put the man back in the box. I'm the dumb employee again So when are they arriving?" Crisply, he changed the subject.

The snap in his voice stung. "Cal is coming home Saturday. Gina and Robbie will follow at a later date."

And the Duke and Duchess didn't know? Only Cal McKendrick could pull that off.

"Well, I hope with all my heart it comes off." And he meant it. Cal McKendrick was not only his boss but a good friend, a supporter.

"That's very nice of you, Steven," she said softly, feeling, inexplicably, about to cry. And she *never* cried. She had learned early not to.

"I'm a sweet guy," he said with an ironic twist to his truly sexy mouth.

"No, you're not." A little laugh escaped her. "You're a good person but that's not the same thing. You're a very complex man. You're carrying a lot of baggage."

"And you're not?" His black brows shot up in challenge. "Now, aren't I being outspoken today?" Extreme sarcasm charged his expression.

She stared back at him, wanting for a long time to know all about his life, aware of his deep reserve. "It must have been tough for you growing up?" she asked gently. "When did you find out about Lancaster?" The question should come as no surprise. Everyone knew the story.

He was silent for so long she didn't think he was going to answer. "I'm sorry if I'm intruding on a private grief. You don't want to talk about it?"

"I'm surprised you want to hear," he said, his mind spin-

ning, as all of a sudden picturing himself having a child
with her.

"No, you're not!" She surprised him by saying. "You
know I want to hear. I like you, Steven."

"How very gracious of you, Ms McKendrick." He didn't
hold the sarcasm back.

"Does it help to mock me?" she asked, turning her eyes
on him.

"It does actually." He shrugged. "The difficulties of our
situation and so forth. To answer your question I found out
that Lancaster had fathered me when I was around ten. The
man I thought was my father, Jim Lockhart, had always
been a bit uncertain of me. My mother explained away my
colouring as being on her side of the family. She was a
honey-blond. I was the black crow among all the white-
feathered cockatoos. Lancaster, strangely no great womaniser, took a fancy to my mother—she was, probably still is,
a very pretty woman. She said he raped her." He laughed
harshly. "You can bet your life it was a lie. That was just
a story to serve up to poor old Jim. Even he wasn't fooled.
Lancaster didn't have to rape any woman. He could have
any woman he wanted. Mum loved Jim, the father of three
of her children. But sleeping with Lancaster was like sleeping with a god. A wicked one at that. She wasn't supposed
to get pregnant."

"But it happened."

"It must have. *I'm* here. I'm so much like him we don't
need any DNA. They took off for New Zealand where
Lockhart had family. I hear from them from time to time.
Jim could never take to me, especially after, but he did his
best."

"So when was this? When were you on your own?"
Sadness jolted her heart.

"Fourteen. I couldn't go with them, too difficult for Jim,

my mother explained, too destructive to the marriage. I was sent to boarding school for the next three years. They must have had to dig deep. It was a top school. My friends came from Outback properties all over Queensland. That's how I finished up as a station hand."

"Who very quickly rose to the top," she reminded him. "Have you ever spoken a word to Lancaster?"

"I couldn't trust myself to speak to him," Steve said, tasting violent anger at the back of his throat. "I despise the man. He's supposed to be Gavin Lancaster, the big man, the cattle baron! He's a spineless, gutless, wimp. One day we're going to come face-to-face. One day—"

He broke off, his expression so dark, Meredith caught a glimpse of his inner demons. "You don't need him, Steven. You're going to make your mark on your own."

"I intend to," he said. Somehow he knew he was capable of extraordinary things. "You know, I've got half brothers everywhere. A Lancaster, two Lockharts. A half sister— she was a sweet little thing—yet I feel connected to no one. Cal comes the closest."

Meredith's tender heart smote her. She saw in her mind's eye a vision of the fourteen-year-old left all alone while his family started a fresh life in another country. "Give me your hand," she said very gently, reaching out to him.

His tall, powerful body went taut. "I don't think that's a good idea," he warned, knuckles clenched white, obviously agitated when he was usually so in command.

"I want you to think of me as your friend." It seemed very important to her he did. "*Please*, Steven. I told you. I like you. I…"

She never got to finish that hopelessly inadequate sentence. With an explosive oath, he lifted her forcibly, effortlessly into his arms, so she was lying across his chest, staring up into a face brilliant with a passion he couldn't control.

"You can't try the teasing, Meredith. Not with me, you can't!"

Teasing? She had no thought of teasing in her head. "But, Steven, it's not like that!" She was so agitated she had difficulty speaking.

"Then you should be more careful," he rasped, lowering his head with such a look of hunger it overwhelmed her. Heartbeats shook her body. She was aware of an acute sense of trepidation. She had imagined something like this happening, though she had held it a secret deep within her. What if the reality fell far short of those imaginings? What if…

He kissed her until she was swooning in his arms, the excitement breathtaking. His beard was slightly rough against her soft skin, grazing it, yet it was so wonderful! He was cradling her, covering her face and neck with kisses, as if only she could make his hunger and pain go away. His hands closed around her face as he kept returning to her yielding mouth, over and over, his tongue slipping around the moist interior, exploring it and the shape of her teeth.

It was astonishing as though it were all happening in the most voluptuous slow motion. Meredith didn't see how it could go on without their shedding their clothes, rolling naked on the sand. Her shirt was already off one shoulder. She was crushed against him, the pressure of her breasts against the hard wall of his chest, going along with this tumultuous tide, with not a thought in her head of fighting it. She could smell him, the wonderful male scent of him, something *warm* and intoxicating like the smell of fine leather and warm spices.

"Do you know how beautiful you are?" he muttered. "No, stay there." He had unloosened her thick plait; now her hair was swirling all around them releasing the herbal scents of her shampoo. He took a handful of it, kissed a lock, then her cheek, inhaling her skin. She'd been working all day yet she was so fresh. Always was.

Meredith had never felt so weak in her life. Her body had turned boneless. She didn't think she could possibly stand up or find her balance if she did. She was making no attempt to block his moving hands. She didn't want to. It was all too thrilling. Now his hand was reaching into the neck of her shirt, moving down to her breast; long strong fingers reaching further down, seeking the nipple, already erect.

How could she stand it? She was unravelling like a bolt of silk. She had to do something. God, what? This was *ecstasy.* She'd had little of that. She wasn't a virgin—a few, mostly pleasant experiences—but she'd never known anything like this or felt so remotely close to someone. And they were only kissing. *Only!* His fingers had reached her nipple, stimulating it further, setting her off wildly. Sensation was spreading down to her groin. She had to squeeze her legs together, when she wanted to throw them wide apart. Her heart was pumping madly She didn't know it but her nails were sinking into his back. Stars exploded behind her tightly shut eyelids, a kaleidoscope of colours.

Easier to put out a fire before it reaches a conflagration.

The warning voice in her head tried to call a stop, but she was too caught up in sensation. Calling a halt was so totally against her desire.

Meredith, you're losing yourself. Stop now. The voice came again. This time it had the power of a scream! She could so easily fall pregnant. It was a long time since she had taken the Pill.

Somehow she stayed his hand, though the effort nearly

split her open. "*Please*, Steven." Her voice was no more than a ragged sob.

For a moment, an eternity, she thought he couldn't or wouldn't heed her plea. She was unsurprised. She should never have let him go so far. But, oh, it was ravishing, electric! And she had learned a few things about herself she had never known. She was electric only for *him*.

Steve's anguished groan came from way down deep in his throat. How was he supposed to let go of her after that? Didn't women understand a man couldn't just shut down at the flick of a switch? He didn't know how to protect himself from the pain. He buried his face in her sweetly scented neck, his hands breaking off caressing her. He could have howled aloud. "I don't know what to say," he muttered, as much to himself as her.

"You don't have to say anything," she tried to comfort him, feeling as if they were sealed off from the rest of the world.

"I frightened you for a moment, didn't I?" He threw his head back to stare into her eyes, his own glowing.

"Maybe," she whispered, not hiding from the truth. "I frightened myself, too."

He gave a strange laugh. "See what happens when you ask to hold my hand?"

"It's been coming a long time. But you know what they say? Forewarned, is forearmed." She tried to joke, when she had never felt so emotional, allowing her forehead to rest against his. "I care about you, Steven. I don't simply like you. I really care."

He accepted that now. All that wild passion wasn't only on his side. The tremors that shook her had been real. For long moments there he had thought she would let him do anything he liked with her. Let him peel off her clothes, run his tongue over every inch of her satiny body, find every little secret crevice. "If someone saw us and reported to your dad I'd be out of here this same afternoon," he said wryly, thinking it would have been well worth it. "Even Cal couldn't save me."

She felt bolder, stronger, than she had ever felt in her life. "*I'd* save you," she said, planting a kiss near the corner of his eye. "My father has played the heavy in too many of my relationships. God knows why. It's a puzzle. Cal is the one my parents love and adore. Not me."

"They must be mad," he muttered thickly and with disgust. "A wonderful daughter like you to fill their lives?"

She gave him another sweet kiss, this time on the cheek. "I must get up. Go home, Steven." Life went on. Reality replaced rapture. She had to make a big decision. She had to decide what she really wanted out of life. She had to decide if the emotion that had ripped through her like a hurricane could move on from a powerful sexual attraction to something deeper, stronger, more permanent. She realised she expected it with a man like Steven Lockhart. There were deep waters beneath that calm, controlled exterior, deep surging passions.

A kiss can be life changing. Strange but true.

With her hair undone it was blowing this way and that in the late-afternoon breeze. "You've wrecked my hair," she said, smiling down at him, the warm flush in her cheeks highlighting the burning blue of her eyes.

"You wouldn't say that if you could see yourself. A woman's hair truly is her crowning glory." He sat looking at her, his heart ravished, as she rebuttoned her shirt, then set about replaiting the gleaming masses. "How is it going to be from now on, Meredith?" he asked, his tone very serious. "I couldn't have made it more obvious how I feel about you. Now everything has changed. How do we handle that?"

She flicked her thick plait over her shoulder, making the decision to speak the truth. "I want…I want *you*, Steven."

He nodded as though she had revealed something very important. Then, "Talk around the station is, your parents want you to marry that McDermott guy. Are you going to do it?"

She began to brush sand off her clothes. "Nope."

"He's got a lot to offer," he persisted. The McDermotts were a wealthy pastoral family and McDermott was a likeable guy, a great polo player.

"I suppose. Everything but love." She didn't tell him Shane McDermott had already proposed to her. Twice.

"So where are you leading me, Heaven, or Hell?" He stood up; looming over her, a superbly fit young man, his golden-brown eyes searching her face.

"What about the stars?" she suggested softly, wishing the two of them could stay like this for ever.

"I'd snatch them down for you if I could." He pulled her tight…tighter.

"I'll remember that." She leaned back against his arm.

They stayed like that for long moments staring into one another's eyes, then he released her. She turned away to pick up her hat, settling it jauntily on her head. It was very difficult trying to return to normal again. Steven was right. Every second of their explosive lovemaking had brought them closer and closer together. Everything had, indeed, changed. Her desires, her longings, her hopes had been dredged up from some deep quarry inside her. She had to start thinking about wanting *more* instead of settling into a pattern of accepting *less*.

"Let's move slowly," she said, blue eyes going back to him, seeking his understanding. "One day at a time." She knew opposition from her parents would be fierce if she came out with her feelings for Steven Lockhart. "Okay?"

She sought some gesture of agreement. "I don't care if we're seen together often. I'm past pretence." She waited nervously for his answer, frightened he might move back from the brink, seeing himself as a man with a lot to lose and probably nothing to win.

He inclined his raven head. "Whatever you say." How he wished he had more to offer her. Right *now*. He knew he could get it, but it would take time. "I guess your family will have enough on its hands welcoming Gina and their little grandson."

She sighed in agreement. "You'll be hearing about it." She held his gaze, wanting to make sure he understood the opened lines of communication between them really mattered. Changes came through making decisions and carrying them through. If she wanted Steven Lockhart—and she realised she did—she knew she would have to give up her ingrained reticence and *reach* for him. He had suffered too much rejection and he was a man of pride.

To her relief he gave her a little salute. "At the end of the day, this is going to affect us all."

It was only after she rode away that the voice in his head began. It whispered words of caution that dropped, heavy as a pile of stones.

Remember who she is, Steve.

Yet she had come willingly and without resistance into his arms. She was as powerfully attracted to him as he was to her. That much he knew. Or had they both simply surrendered to an overwhelming temptation? And what about the McKendrick rules? Cal had broken them. Even for him it hadn't been simple. How much more difficult for Meredith?

When Meredith went downstairs some fifteen minutes before dinner—which was always at 7:00 p.m. on the dot, dress please, no jeans, slacking not accepted—her mother called to her the moment she saw her.

"There you are, dear," Jocelyn spoke brightly. "Join me for a moment, would you?" She beckoned Meredith to follow her down to the library, leaving behind her a light trail of her very expensive signature perfume.

"Anything wrong, Mum?" Meredith asked when they were inside the room. It was huge, but wonderfully atmospheric and welcoming despite the size. She loved books. Couldn't live without them. For years she had wanted to make a start on cataloguing the library—Uncle Ed had been keen to join her—but they both realised they were going to be refused the project.

Don't bother me now, Meredith. When I decide the time's right I'll call in a professional. Someone who knows what he's about.

He. That was her father, the quintessential chauvinist.

The ambience of the library settled her slightly when, truth be known, she was a bundle of nerves what with Cal's affairs and hers. Cal couldn't come home soon enough so far as his sister was concerned.

Jocelyn turned about, delicate brows raised like wings. "Why should anything be wrong, dear? No, no, I was planning on asking Kym to stay for the week-end." She settled herself gracefully into a deep comfortable chair, upholstered in a rich paisley, indicating to Meredith to take the one opposite. "I thought you might like to ask Shane. Make up a foursome." She gave her daughter an encouraging smile. "You're getting on, my dear. Time to settle down. One should have one's children young. Your father and I did."

"I'm not twenty-six yet, Mum," Meredith said, thinking subtlety often eluded her mother.

"Twenty-six is getting on," Jocelyn said, her voice firm.

"Not what anyone else would call over the hill," Meredith

murmured dryly. "And aren't you forgetting something, Mum?"

"Remind me." She put a hand to her triple string of large, lustrous pearls. She was rarely seen without them even if they were half hidden by collars or under sweaters and the like. They were a wedding present from her husband and very valuable.

"Dad has made an art form of scaring off my admirers," Meredith pointed out. As if her mother didn't know! And often condoned.

"Don't be ridiculous!" Jocelyn now studied her slim ankles. She had kept her tiny waist and youthful figure and was very proud of it. "Only the fortune hunters, dear. Shane isn't one of those."

"No, indeed, he's *one of us*," Meredith lightly mocked, thinking in some respects her mother was a throwback to far less egalitarian times. "Shane and I aren't going anywhere, Mum. Sorry to disappoint you. I like him. I value him as a friend, but I'm not and never will be in love with him."

Jocelyn's equable temper suddenly flared, putting diamond chips into her glass-green eyes. Jocelyn thoroughly disliked having her plans thwarted. "Who said anything about love?" she demanded to know. "There are far more important things than love in a marriage, my girl. Love can fly out the window as fast as it flew in. You have to consider more lasting qualities. Similar backgrounds, shared interests, liking and respect. Friendship is very important. Friendship between the families, as well. I'd like you to know—"

"Did you love Dad when you married him?" Meredith interrupted the flow, wondering if her authoritarian father had ever been a lovable person.

Jocelyn did effrontery exceedingly well. "Of course I loved your father. How could you ask? We are *still* in love."

Meredith supposed they were in their own way.

"And we're excellent friends. Your father and I see eye to eye. We've been greatly blessed. We have our wonderful son. A better son no parent could ask for. And we have you. You're a beautiful young woman, Meredith. Or you could be if you ever decided to do something about yourself. You could take a leaf out of Kym's book there. She's always marvellously turned out. All I ever see you in is jeans with your hair scraped back. It's scraped back even now."

Meredith put a hand to the loose curls that lay along her cheeks. "And here I was thinking I had prettied it up. Could the fact I do a lot of work around the station, as well as in the office, have anything to do with the way I dress, do you suppose? It might come as a surprise to you, but Kym has often told me she'd give anything to look as good as I do in jeans."

Jocelyn lifted a porcelain ornament—eighteenth-century Meissen—off the small circular table beside her, then put it down again gently. "Well, she is a bit pear shaped," she conceded with a smile. "So what about it? We ask them both, Kym and Shane. Give the poor boy a chance, dear. You won't have any trouble with your father. I've already spoken to him. We like Shane."

Meredith clasped her hands together. Looking down at them she was sure she should be taking more care of them. Especially now when she had never felt more a woman. Bring on the hand cream! "Be that as it may, Mum, you're wasting your time. I don't think this week-end is a good time to invite anyone. Cal won't want to come home to find Kym here. Do you never stop hoping?" Meredith looked at her mother with pitying eyes. Jocelyn had gone through life getting what she wanted. Maybe that was why she couldn't seem to give up on Kym. After all, she and Beth Harrison had dreamed of a marriage, uniting the two families and eventually uniting the two stations.

"Never!" Jocelyn gave a shake of her beautifully groomed head, dark hair swept back off a high brow. "Kym suits Cal perfectly."

"Kym suits *you* perfectly, Mum," Meredith corrected. "There's a big difference. The engagement didn't work. It's never going to work. Please don't ask Kym over. It won't be any nice surprise for Cal, believe me. He may have a few surprises of his own."

Jocelyn, who had settled back, sat up straight, her unlined forehead suddenly furrowed. "Meaning what? Are you trying to tell me something, Meredith? If you are, I'd advise you to be out with it. You surely can't be inferring Cal has someone hidden away?" She looked aghast at the very idea.

"Why don't you wait until he comes home," Meredith advised, and went to stand hesitantly by her mother.

"What is it, Meredith?" Jocelyn looked up to meet her daughter's gaze directly. "You know I hate surprises. I like to know *exactly* what's going on."

Meredith let her hand rest on her mother's shoulder. "Cal does have some news, Mum, but it's not my news to tell. He'll be home on Saturday. You'll have to be patient until then."

CHAPTER FOUR

THEY were all gathered around the long mahogany table in the formal dining room listening to Cal deliver his momentous news. It was an elaborate setting, Meredith thought. The table, for instance, had always reminded her of the deck of an aircraft carrier. Around it were ranged Georgian chairs, tied with elaborate silk tassels, convex gilded mirrors on the walls, a magnificent Dutch still life over the sideboard—fruit, vegetables, game birds. Only one of the great chandeliers was on. Even then the light was dazzling. The room was only used for gala occasions—but it seemed as good a place as any for her brother to tell his extraordinary story.

Cal told it simply, but movingly. He had to convey to them how powerfully Gina Romano had affected him from the very first moment he saw her. He had wanted no other woman. No way could he tell them in bringing Gina here he was bending her to his will. He had to stick to the charade. He must have been convincing, because Meredith's expression was soft and tender. She looked thrilled.

And thrilled Meredith was. If Steven could feel the same way about her as Cal did about his Gina, what a priceless gift that would be! The rest of the family greeted Cal's news with a ringing silence.

This was never meant to happen!

Meredith's eyes flew to her brother's, renewing her support. Still, the family continued to sit there as if they'd been turned to stone; or Cal had spoken in an unfamiliar tongue and they were struggling to decipher it. Meredith gritted her teeth, her throat aching with tension.

Their father, for once, was plainly at a loss. Nothing in response. He started to speak, then stopped. Their mother held her fingers to her temples as though she had suddenly developed an appalling headache, which, indeed, she had. Uncle Ed continued to stare down at the gleaming surface of the table as though amazed at the shine.

"I don't believe this," Jocelyn finally burst out, in evident anger and confusion. It tore at her, making her blind to anyone else's feelings but her own. "This is the most appalling news. This Gina doesn't sound the sort of girl you would bring home. Let alone *marry*."

Meredith winced, hardly daring to look at her brother to gauge his reaction. "Mum, *please*!" she begged, excruciatingly embarrassed by her mother's outburst.

Jocelyn ignored her, beginning to cry, but Cal's handsome features showed no softening. They hardened to granite. He thrust back his chair and then stood up, addressing his mother. "How did you get to be such an appalling snob, Mother?" he asked, his voice tight. "I'm sure the Queen of England wouldn't carry on like you. You've gone on with your PLU nonsense ever since I can remember. There has to be an end to it."

He sounded so disgusted that Jocelyn, who was used to the greatest respect from her son, started to pull herself together. "Lorinda did warn me," she said, in that moment of stress letting the cat out of the bag. "She was most concerned."

Cal's heart tightened up like a fist. "When was this?"

Jocelyn didn't answer. Instead she made a small agitated flourish with her hand.

"Are you saying you knew back then?" Suddenly Cal had to confront the fact Lorinda, the aunt he had always trusted, had deceived him.

"Of course we knew, son." Ewan McKendrick reached out to take his wife's shaking hand. "And she had your child?" The question ended upwards in a kind of wonderment.

"Your grandson, Dad," Cal told him, strong emotions etched on his face. "It's just as I told you. I never knew."

"I'm certain you didn't," Ewan responded on the instant. "You're a man of honour."

"Honour short of *marriage*, you mean, Dad?" Cal asked bitterly. "Provide for her and the boy. Sweep it under the carpet. Get on with life. I'm afraid that's not on. I'm going to marry Gina. I'm going to bring her and my son home."

Jocelyn blew her nose exceedingly hard when she was always so dainty about such things. "But how can you love her after all she's done to you?" she cried. "She's a heartless woman. Not worth knowing. You probably wouldn't look at her now," she added, though it didn't make a lot of sense.

Meredith rushed to support her brother. "Gina is a beautiful person, Mum. Anyone would be proud to welcome her into the family."

Jocelyn burst into fresh tears. She had no desire whatever to meet this Gina person. But Gina's son? That was a matter of great concern to her. The boy was Cal's heir.

"Let me repeat, I'm going to bring Gina and our son home." Cal didn't know it but he looked colder and harder than his father ever had.

"And is he going to be page boy at the wedding?" Jocelyn stopped her tears, to enquire with great sarcasm. "Where is this wedding going to be held, may I ask? Not here. I won't be humiliated in front of the world. I couldn't bear it." She followed up that announcement with an exaggerated shudder.

"Steady on, Jocelyn." Ewan held up a warning hand. He knew his son if Jocelyn didn't. No way could he allow his son to take leave of the family. Ewan knew Cal would, if pushed.

"What do you think, Uncle Ed?" Cal looked across the table at his uncle who had remained silent throughout as though being seen was one thing, heard another. Not that anyone could get a word in with Jocelyn.

Ed spread his hands. His sister-in-law was behaving in a disastrous fashion but he was living in the family home. Hell, he had a right to it, come to that! "Anything that makes you happy, makes me happy, Cal," he said with obvious sincerity. "I'm sure your Gina is as beautiful as Merri says. I can see you're stunned, but your mother and Lorinda have always been as thick as thieves."

Jocelyn gasped. "Shame, shame, shame, Ed McKendrick. Lorinda is a loyal sister and she *adores* Cal," she rebuked him. "Lorinda acted on the highest motivation, love and concern. It was your Gina who ran off, Cal, back to her own world. Is that how to love someone, deceiving them then running away? Utterly spineless I say."

Cal strove to keep the fury and confusion he was feeling out of his voice. "I think the less you say, the better, Mum. This is a fait accompli. I've found the mother of my son. I'm finally going to bring them home. Her and Robert."

Jocelyn's green eyes gushed afresh. "Damn it, damn it, damn it!" she cried, her whole body trembling under the force of her shock and anger. "No wonder you didn't want Kym over, Meredith." She turned on her daughter as though she were greatly to blame. "Kym will be devastated when she hears about this."

"For God's sake, my dear, you're flogging a dead horse," Ewan McKendrick groaned, raising a hand to stay his wife. "I have told you."

Jocelyn stared back at her husband, feeling greatly undermined. "The point is *you* wanted Kym, too, Ewan. She was *our* choice. Not some young woman who won't belong. Had Cal and Kym married, in time Lakefield would have been added to the McKendrick chain. It was all so suitable."

"Business is business and PLU is PLU, eh, Mum?" Meredith couldn't resist the dig.

Her father turned cold blue eyes on her. "Please don't speak to your mother like that, Meredith."

"I'm only stating an evident truth, Dad. Why don't you stop treating me like a child?"

Jocelyn broke in irritably. "I don't think I'll ever forgive you for not warning me, Meredith. I've suffered a betrayal. I'm terribly, terribly wounded."

"Then I'm sorry, Mum. But as I pointed out at the time, it was Cal's story to tell."

"Exactly! I told Meredith to leave it to me," Cal confirmed in a clipped voice.

"What, keep the truth from me, Calvin?" Jocelyn asked piteously.

Ewan wasn't attending to anything being said. "I haven't met my grandson and he's three years of age," he murmured, very poignantly for him. "Who does he look like?" He turned beseeching eyes on his son.

Cal sat down again, sighing heavily. "Like you, Dad, like me. He's a McKendrick, but he has Mum's green eyes."

"My green eyes!" Jocelyn spluttered, as though only one other person in the world was entitled to them. "You're the one with my green eyes, Calvin. It's impossible, I tell you. She can't come here." Jocelyn's small face started to crease up again. "I won't be grooming a total stranger, to take over from me. Not that she could," she added scathingly. She stared back at her son. No adoration there, only anger and condemnation.

"If Gina isn't welcome here, *I* don't stay." Cal laid down the ultimatum, looking grimly resolute.

There was no question in at least three people's minds he meant it. "I can wait it out until it's my time to inherit. You don't own Coronation Hill, Dad. You're the custodian. Just as I will be for *my* son, my son Robert."

But Ewan McKendrick was way ahead of them all. "As though I would ask you to go," he cried, exhibiting great dismay, and not looking at his wife. "When is it you want to bring Gina and the boy home?"

Oh, thank God, thank God! Meredith gave silent praises. When the chips were down, their father always chose the smartest course.

Cal shot a wry glance at his sister, reading her mind. "By the end of this month. This house is big enough to swallow up the lot of us. We wouldn't have to see one another if we didn't want to," he added satirically, though it was perfectly true.

"Good God, son, we don't want you to go into hiding!" Ewan exclaimed. "Dear me, no. What's happened, has happened. Now we must move forward. The sooner the better."

"Thanks for that, Dad," Cal said, the severe tension in him easing fractionally. "In view of what I've just heard I need to have a talk with Aunt Lorinda." Anger and disillusionment flinted from his brilliant eyes.

"Well, you'll just have to wait now, won't you!" Jocelyn cried in a kind of triumph. "She's in Europe."

"She'll be back," Cal answered shortly. It was important

he get to the bottom of the matter. Gina hadn't said anything that implicated Lorinda in her decision to flee the island, but the fact his aunt and his mother had discussed their blossoming romance had suddenly opened up a Pandora's Box.

"So when do you plan to take your marriage vows?" Ewan was asking, busy looking at the situation from all its angles in his head. Wouldn't even make a nine day wonder he shouldn't be surprised. Times had changed dramatically, if only Jocelyn could see it!

"I'm not entirely sure." Cal glanced across at his sister. What better sister could a man have? Yet he couldn't tell her Gina wasn't exactly ecstatic about marrying him. He was forcing her into it. He wasn't happy about that, but he was determined on his course. Robert was a McKendrick. His place was on Coronation Hill. Robert needed his parents together, not apart, two people to love and raise him. He couldn't risk Gina marrying someone else, providing an alternative father to *his* son.

"If you're going to go ahead with this it will be better if you marry her at some register office. Brisbane, Sydney, Adelaide, whatever," Jocelyn said bitterly. "I'm sure your sister will be delighted to act as a witness."

"Absolutely! I'd be honoured," Meredith said. "I think it's a miracle Cal and Gina have come together again."

"With *your* help!" Jocelyn bitterly accused her daughter, so often the scapegoat.

"No register office," Ewan broke in, his stern glance silencing his daughter who was about to respond to her mother. "The wedding will be here on Coronation."

Jocelyn looked at her husband with betrayal in her reddened eyes. "You can't mean it, Ewan."

"All the McKendricks have been married from here," he answered, with blunt force. "Including you, Ed. We've all had huge weddings, great celebrations. We're going to do things right."

"And if I refuse to be here?" Jocelyn threw down the challenge.

Ewan reached out to pat her shoulder. "But you won't refuse, will you, my dear? You've always been an excellent wife." He turned his arrogant, handsome head towards his son. "Would you like that, Cal?"

"That's what I want, Dad," Cal said. "But nothing big."

"Frankly I don't see how we can avoid it." For the first time Ewan smiled. "You've been through a tough time."

"*Gina* has been through a tough time," Cal said, mustering up his most caring tone.

"That's absurd." His mother might have seen through him she gave such a scoffing laugh.

"She must be a strong person," Ewan cut in, frowning on his wife. Ewan McKendrick was every inch the diplomat whenever an occasion demanding diplomacy arose. "Bring Gina home, son. We'll make her welcome." He ignored his wife's bitter exclamation, but turned on her a rare, cold eye. "I can't wait to meet my grandson. Especially if he looks like me."

Would a little granddaughter have fared so well, I wonder? Meredith thought, then immediately chided herself for being so mean.

"Thank God that's over," she said an hour later, after she and Cal made their escape to the garden. "It was a bit of a surprise learning Aunt Lorinda was busy informing Mum of everything that went on at the island. Do you suppose she had anything to do with Gina's abrupt departure? Now that I think about it, I wouldn't put it past her, though she was always sweet to Gina."

"Yes, she was." Cal was forced to admit it, but inside he

was hurting badly. He had blamed Gina for years, when it now seemed he didn't know the full story.

"Gina didn't explain why she left?" Meredith read his mind.

"She certainly didn't say Lorinda made any decision for her."

"So what was Gina's decision based on?" Meredith frowned. "Wouldn't she say?"

Cal stared up at the brilliant clusters of stars. "Merri, Gina made it quite plain she wants to shut the door on the past. She refused to get into any discussion, but I gathered she thought at the time she wasn't good enough for me. Pretty damned silly, I know. But I suppose looking at it from her side she was made aware there was plenty of money being splashed around. She came from an ordinary family with I imagine little money to spare on luxury holidays. Perhaps she felt overwhelmed. People do. You know that."

"But Gina gave no sign of it," Meredith said. "Her manner couldn't have been more natural. Gina could take her place anywhere."

"She was so *young*," Cal said. "Maybe that accounts for it. She got frightened off."

"Did you ever mention Kym to her?" Meredith persisted. "The fact Mum and Dad cherished hopes the two of you would marry?"

"God, no!" Cal protested violently. "I never gave Kym a thought. There was only Gina. But she found out later about Kym. She saw a photo of us in some magazine. Kym and I were engaged at the time."

"Oh!" Meredith gave a little anguished moan. "Do you suppose Aunt Lorinda might have told her about Kym? She saw a grand love affair unfolding right under her nose. Time to put a stop to it. We now know she contacted Mum."

"I'll get to the bottom of it, don't you worry," Cal said with quiet menace. "Gina had her opportunity to denounce Lorinda. If there was anything to denounce. She didn't."

Meredith pondered it all in silence. "So what happened to Gina's boyfriend? I imagine the marriage was well and truly off when Gina discovered she was pregnant?"

"Now *that's* the strange thing. Gina claims there was no boyfriend," Cal answered. "She must have gone into denial. I'm fairly sure she was frightened of her father. He's dead, by the way." He held back a curling palm frond from his sister's face. "Did you get around to telling Steve any of this?"

She nodded, grateful for the cloak of darkness. "You said I could. He was very sympathetic. Steve's on your side. He's had a hard life. He understands a great deal."

"You like him, don't you?" Cal spoke directly.

She felt the heat rush into her skin. "I do." Meredith was beyond pretence. She had to get a life. "He's quite a guy. But can you imagine if *I'd* told Mum and Dad tonight I was pregnant and Steve was the father, what their reaction would have been? Krakatoa! Do you really think Dad would have jumped in to say we must be married on Coronation? The crazy ironies of life, brother. We live by a different set of rules."

"They're not *my* rules, Merri," Cal said, with the greatest regret, knowing her assertion to be true. "Dad and Mum—especially Mum—have to lighten up." He broke off to stare down at her. "Say, you're not telling me in a roundabout way you *are* pregnant?"

"What would be your reaction?" she asked, confident she knew what it would be.

They kept walking. "If he loved you and you loved him I could only be happy for you, Merri. Love is all that matters."

"Tell that to Mum," Meredith replied. "No, I'm not pregnant, though Mum has recently told me I'm leaving it almost too late to have kids. She wanted to invite Shane over this week-end. Shane *and* Kym."

"Struth!" Cal exclaimed wryly. "I just hope Mum hasn't been giving Kym false encouragement. That would be too cruel."

"I don't think Kym needed anyone's encouragement," Meredith said. "I think she has just been waiting for you to come to your senses, as it were."

"Some people are just one-track. I'm sorry if Mum's going to take it out on you, Merri. It's too bad the way she does that."

"It does tend to fray the nerves," Meredith admitted, "but I'm here for you, brother." She tucked her arm through his, as though anchoring him to the moment.

"And I'm here for you, Merri. Never forget that."

Gina didn't put her apartment on the market. There was no way she could tell if a marriage between herself and Cal would work out. But what real alternative did she have but to try? There was no way she could risk not having her beloved Robbie with her all the time. A custody battle would be costly, time-consuming and in the end she would be the loser, forced into, at best, sharing custody with Robbie's father and his family, all locked away in their private stronghold. No wonder she had simply folded like a pack of cards.

She didn't dare look deep inside her heart. Except sometimes at night.

You're still in love with him. You are and always will be.

Always the inner voice to never let her escape.

Cal McKendrick was and remained her incurable addiction. Maybe they would have a chance if he were an ordinary man, a colleague like Nat Goldman. She had met

Nat's family. They would have been delighted if the friendship between her and Nat had become more serious. She remembered Cal's beautiful sister, Meredith, on the island. Meredith had always been so friendly yet she had the sense there was a considerable gulf between them. Such wealth as the McKendrick family had, was quite outside her experience. She had never witnessed anything like it. She hadn't started the affair with Cal. An affair had never occurred to her. She had been too much aware of her position on the island to offer any male guest the slightest encouragement, let alone *him*. She had been hired as a domestic/waitress, whatever was needed. She certainly needed the money to help her through her final semester. She was the first in her family ever to attend university. That in itself had been a great source of pride to her father. She had scored the highest rating. At university she had once been voted the girl with the three *B*'s. Brilliance. Beauty. Brains. Just a fun thing. No one had mentioned anything about Luck.

Her family had had little money to spare, however hard her father had toiled. Theirs had been a small sugar farm, not a plantation. There was no way she would have embarked on what in the end turned out to be the most momentous, the most unforgettable, the most painful course of her life.

Cal McKendrick had been her lost love.

Until now.

When she told Rosa about Cal's re-entry into her life, Rosa had barely been able to contain herself.

"What's he want this time?" she asked, her voice, as always, fiercely protective.

Even Rosa had been silenced when Gina told her what Cal McKendrick wanted was marriage.

"You still love him?"

"I can't help it." No point in covering up from Rosa. Rosa would see through it.

"Gran Dio!" In response, Rosa balled up a rock melon and pitched it through the open kitchen window into the backyard where it narrowly missed a visiting cat who took off shrieking for safer territory. "Tell him I come with you for a week or so, perhaps a month. We face this family together. You and Roberto are *my* family. I am Aunt Rosa. You cannot do without my support."

When Cal phoned, Gina passed on Rosa's message, which was more or less an ultimatum. If she had expected some kind of sarcastic comment, even downright opposition, he had only laughed. "That's nice!" Cal phoned often. Probably checking on her whereabouts, if he didn't already have someone on the job. She had even started to check if there were any strange cars parked for any length of time in front of her apartment block. No way was she going to be allowed to abscond with his son.

Then there was Robbie. She had spent a good deal of time pondering what she would tell him, but if she had agonised over what to say—that the man Robbie had met only a short while ago, the man he had taken such a liking to, was in reality, his father—Robbie wonder of wonders took it near effortlessly on board.

"He's my daddy?" he asked, his eyes full of amazement and a dawning delight. "Where is he right now?"

"Are you listening to me, Robbie? Cal's your *father.*" She hadn't expected it to be this easy. She was worried he didn't fully understand. Bright as he was he was still very young.

"Yes, Mummy," Robbie replied blithely, "but where *is* he?"

She had swallowed the hard knot in her throat. "He's back home, Robbie. His family is what is known as cattle barons. That means they own vast properties in the Outback they call *stations*."

"Like train stations?" Robbie nodded knowledgeably.

"No, darling. A train station is a stopping place where passengers get on and off," she explained. Robbie had never been, in fact, on a train. He had always travelled by car. "In Australia we call really huge farms with lots and lots of land, *stations*. There are cattle stations and sheep stations and sometimes sheep and cattle together. The McKendrick holdings—they have a number of what they call *outstations*—are cattle stations. You must have heard cowboys in the videos you watch call them *ranches*. That's the American word. We say stations."

"Wow! So Cal's a cowboy?" Robbie asked in such delight his greatest ambition might have been to be one.

"Well, a cattleman like he said."

"That's *wild*!" Robbie breathed. "Cal said he was going to show me some time." So at the tender age of three, Robbie was taking in his stride what might have shocked an older child or cast him into a state of panic.

"The time's almost here, Robbie," Gina said. "Your father is coming for us at the end of the month. Not long to go now. We have to leave Queensland and live in the Northern Territory. I'll show you on the map where it is. It borders Queensland, but it's a long, long way from here."

"How do we get there…by train? Gosh, I hope so." The excitement showed. "The great big long one on the TV. The Ghan, they call it. It travels through all that red desert with no one in it."

Gina shook her head. "I'm sure we'll travel on the Ghan one day but your father will be picking us up in the family plane."

Robbie's eyes went as round as saucers. "My daddy flies a plane?" Seated on a chair facing his mother he suddenly dropped to his knees, staring up at her and squeezing her hands.

"It's not a great big plane like you've seen at the airport," Gina hastened to tell him. "It's much smaller."

Robbie dramatically collapsed on the carpet. "He must be very rich!"

"Sort of." Gina didn't want to stress that side of it. "Your father and I are going to get married. How do you feel about that, my darling boy?" She gazed down earnestly into his beautiful little face.

Now all of a sudden Robbie looked deeply flustered. "I don't know. Do you *have* to?"

She couldn't begin to imagine what she would do if he suddenly burst into tears. "Your father wants us to be a family, Robbie," she explained very gently. "I will become Mrs McKendrick. You will become Robert McKendrick. We take your father's name."

Robbie rolled onto his stomach. "It sounds very nice," he said after a few seconds of consideration. "He likes to call me Robert, doesn't he?"

"Yes, he does, like I often call you Roberto. I don't want you to forget your Italian heritage. That's why Rosa and I speak Italian to you, as well as English."

Robbie gave a perky little nod. "My friend Connie speaks Italian just like me. Jonathon speaks Greek and Rani speaks Vietnamese. We think it's fun being able to speak another language."

"And so it is. So the answer's yes, Robbie?" she asked. "Your father and I will be getting married."

Robbie jumped to his feet, and then threw himself into his mother's arms. "I guess it's all right. But what is going to happen to Aunt Rosa?"

Gina silently applauded her son's caring nature. "Rosa is going to come with us." Her arms closed around her precious son, while a tear slid down her cheek. "At least for a little while to help us settle in."

"Goody, hurray!" Robbie lifted his head from her shoulder to give her a beatific smile. "I'd hate to leave Aunt Rosa behind."

"We'll never lose Aunt Rosa," Gina said.

It was a solemn promise.

CHAPTER FIVE

TEN minutes before the plane was due in, many of Coronation's considerable complement of staff began to assemble. They lined the airstrip in front of the giant hangar. This was a day of celebration. Cal was bringing his family home, the young woman soon to be his wife and their three-year-old son. Everyone had been told an aunt of Cal's fiancée was to accompany them. Whatever the lovers' star-crossed past, everything was set to be put right. A big barbecue had been planned for the staff starting around seven. The latest addition to the McKendrick clan would probably be tucked up in bed fast asleep, but the family was expected to look in on proceedings at some part of the evening.

Whatever Gina had expected, it wasn't a welcoming party. As they came in to land she could see all the people assembled on the ground. Even Rosa who had determined on being unimpressed, rolled her eyes and gestured with her hands. "Like something out of a movie!"

It was true. The aerial view of the great station complex was fantastic. It looked like an isolated settlement set down in the middle of a vast empty landscape that stretched away in every direction as far as the eye could see. Gina remembered reading somewhere the Northern Territory had less than one percent of the population of Texas in the U.S.A.

although it was twice the size. So there was a long way to go in the Territory's development. It was still frontier country and perhaps because of it wildly exciting.

She couldn't begin to count the number of buildings. The homestead had to be the building that stood apart from the rest, set within an oasis of green. It appeared to be enormous if the roof was any indication. The airstrip was at a fair distance from the homestead. It was easy to pick out from the huge hangar that had a logo painted on the silver glinting roof. It appeared to be a stylised crown. Beside the hangar stood a tall mast with the Australian flag flying from it. Farther away she could see holding yards jam-packed with cattle, three circular dams, probably bores. Beyond the complex lay the vast wilderness.

Some areas of it resembled jungle, other areas were almost parkland. Dotted all over the landscape were winding streams and smaller tributaries she supposed were the billabongs. They were quite distinct in character from the huge lagoons mostly circular and oval, where palms and pandanus grew in profusion. She could see a huge mob of horses running down there. Wild horses by the look of them, the Outback's famous brumbies.

Robbie, who had been alight with excitement at his very first plane trip, had actually slept for most of the flight. Now he was wide-awake and raring to go.

They were dropping altitude, coming in to land. Her stomach muscles clenched in anticipation, though it had been a remarkably smooth flight with Cal, a seasoned pilot, at the controls. He gave every appearance of a man who thoroughly enjoyed flying. With great distances to be covered, she began to appreciate how private aircraft in the Outback would seem more a necessity than a luxury, although she knew this particular plane cost a good deal more than one million dollars.

"Steady on, matey!" Robbie cried out in gleeful excitement, clapping his hands together. This was the adventure of a lifetime.

"Sit still now, little darling." Gina placed a calming hand on him.

"Who are all those people down there?" he asked in wonderment.

"Station staff," Gina whispered back.

That thrilled Robbie and made him laugh. More people appeared as if they had been hiding in the hangar.

"Big, *big*!" Rosa exclaimed, gesticulating with evident awe.

It was big all right!

The tyres gave a couple of gentle thumps on the tarmac, the brakes screeched, then Cal cut back to idle as they taxied towards the hangar. There he cut the engines, making his afterchecks. A few minutes later they were walking down the steps into the brilliant Territory sunlight.

"These are *our* people, Robbie," Cal explained, swooping his son high in his arms.

"Why? Are you a prince or something, Daddy?" Robbie asked, touching his father's face and staring into his eyes as though Cal was the font of all wisdom and authority. Robbie had learned all about the Queen and the royal family at nursery school. There was a picture of the Queen in a beautiful yellow dress in his old classroom. The teacher had told them a famous Australian artist called Sir William Dargie had painted it.

"A prince? No way!" Cal laughed. "I'm just an ordinary person."

That had to be the understatement of the year, Gina thought, trying to calm her own jittering nerves. Robbie had taken to calling Cal "Daddy" in the blink of an eye. No working up to it. It was as though her little son had longed to use the word. Both of them, man and boy, appeared to be going on instinct. Cal and his son had reached a place from the outset where the relationship was set. She was proud of the fact Robbie had found enormous security with her, his mother, but there was no denying the very special role of a father. It was as Cal had said. Robbie needed *both* his parents. Their son was revelling in the family wholeness.

"Other kids have a mummy and daddy. Now so do I!"

That observation had been delivered with tremendous satisfaction. Why had she ever thought him too small to notice her single-parent status?

With Rosa standing excitedly at her shoulder, Gina watched as a tall, very slender young woman—it had to be Meredith—broke ranks and rushed towards them.

"Welcome, welcome," Meredith was crying happily.

Gina was enveloped in a hug. "I've thought of you so often, Gina," Meredith said. "It's wonderful you're here."

"It's wonderful you're here to meet me." Gina was unable to prevent the emotional tears from springing to her eyes. "Meredith, I'd like you to meet my aunt Rosa. She has always been a great support to me."

"Lovely to meet you, Rosa." Meredith smiled warmly, both women taking to each other on sight. Meredith had been expecting a "motherly type" figure but Aunt Rosa was a striking, very sexy-looking woman with remarkably good skin.

"Lovely to meet *you*, my dear." Rosa, well satisfied with what she saw, put her arms around Meredith and hugged her back.

Meredith turned excitedly to her brother and the little boy in his arms. "Well, I recognise *you*, young man," she said, laying a gentle, faintly trembling hand on Robbie's flushed cheek. "You're the image of your daddy." Her brilliant eyes went to her brother's. "This is truly marvellous, Cal."

His triumphant smile flashed back at her. "Isn't it just? This is your aunty Meredith, Robbie." He introduced them with pride. "I told you all about her, remember? Meredith is my sister."

"Merri," Robbie said. "You called her Merri, like Merry Christmas."

"Merri it is," Meredith said, shaking the little hand Robbie gave her. "Do you want to come and meet the rest of the welcoming party?" she asked. "They're longing to meet you."

"Oh, yes, please," Robbie said, wriggling to get down.

"We're right behind you." Cal set his son down, watching him catch hold of Meredith's hand with the utmost trust and confidence. He was an amazingly friendly little fellow, remarkably self-possessed for his age. It was easy to see from his general behaviour and his advanced social skills Gina had raised him with a tender, loving hand. He also spoke very well and gave every appearance of being highly intelligent. He was a little son to be proud of.

A group of children had materialised—they had been kept in the shade of the hangar—making Robbie even more excited. They were the children of Coronation's staff, educated until the age of the ten at the small one-teacher schoolhouse on the station. All in all, it took some twenty emotion-packed minutes before the welcoming party broke up with another round of cheers led by the station's overseer, a very dashing young man called Steve Lockhart, before Cal was able to drive them to the homestead.

"That was the greatest thing ever!" Robbie exclaimed with satisfaction. "Everybody likes me."

"And why wouldn't they?" Meredith laughed, looking over Robbie's glossy head into his mother's eyes. "You're a great little boy!"

Time enough to see if Cal's parents like me, was Gina's

thought. It didn't strike her as odd that Cal's parents hadn't come down to the airstrip to greet them. She supposed they might be people like the aunt Lorinda she well remembered. Cal had carried off the introductions with marvellous aplomb. No one looking at them both would have suspected things weren't as they seemed. As they had walked down the receiving line he had kept an arm lightly at her back, an expression of pride in her etched on his dynamic face. Steve Lockhart, she recalled, had been observing them closely behind the charming welcoming smile. There was some strong connection between Meredith and Steve. She felt it keenly. But she also felt as far as the senior McKendricks were concerned staff would be expected to keep their distance. How then would that affect any friendship between Meredith and the station's impressive overseer? Gina recognised the quality in him.

They were received in the library. *Good heavens, what a room!* Gina thought. She could have fitted her entire apartment into the huge space. And *received* was the only way to put it. Cal's mother, a beautiful, well-preserved woman, dressed as though she were going to an important luncheon minus her hat and bag—glorious pearls—was seated in a wing chair. Cal's father, a very handsome man with piercing blue eyes was standing behind her. Another man, also standing, a few feet away, and bearing a close resemblance to Cal's father, had to be Uncle Edward. Uncle Edward for a mercy looked kind and approachable. He was smiling, a lovely warm smile. Gina returned it with gratitude. This was certainly one good-looking family! But that was okay! The Romanos hadn't been behind the door when good looks were handed out. Rosa, too, was immensely attractive. Uncle Edward certainly appeared to think so going on his expression as his eyes came to rest on her.

Rosa, for her part, wasn't worried about the McKendricks. She could take them in her stride. What she was worried about, was how they would respond to her goddaughter. Looking after Gina was the reason Rosa was here.

Cal took the direct approach, making introductions. His mother remained seated. They were all obliged to go to her. Gina could feel the little waves of resistance that emanated from the seated figure though Jocelyn spoke the right words as though she had learned them from a script. *Obviously she believes I've brought disruption and disgrace to the family*, Gina thought, shaking Jocelyn's unenthusiastic hand. There was no question of a hug much less a kiss. The handshake was as much as Gina could expect to get.

Cal's father, Ewan, after an initial moment of what appeared to be shock was quite genial by comparison. Gina caught him giving his wife a sharp, rebuking glance. She must have got the message because the charged atmosphere lightened somewhat. Friendly and outgoing as Robbie was, he had been half hiding behind his mother. Now Cal picked him up in his arms.

"This is your grandmother and grandfather, Robert. And that gentleman over there is my uncle Ed, your great-uncle. Say hello."

"Hello, everybody," Robbie piped up sweetly, looking around them all. Even at three he could recognise family going on appearance alone.

There were two spots of colour high up on Jocelyn's cheeks. Her green eyes that had appeared unfocused suddenly rested with great clarity on the little boy. "What a beautiful child you are!" she now exclaimed. "Come give Grandma a kiss." She held out her hand.

"Why, he's the living image of you, Cal!" Ewan McKendrick burst out in triumph, his eyes settling with approval on the beautiful, self-composed young woman his son had brought home with him. This Gina, who he and Jocelyn had worried had no background at all, looked magnificent! He was quite taken aback. But what a blessing! "I want you to know, Gina, you're most welcome to the family. Most welcome."

Gina made no answer, but graciously inclined her head, unaware how very regal it appeared.

"And how good of you to accompany her, *signora*." Ewan's blue glance swept on to Gina's decidedly attractive companion. She was a damned sexy-looking woman. "May I call you Rosa?"

"But of course!" Rosa replied graciously.

"What, not going to shake hands with your grandfather, young man?" Ewan asked the little boy jovially, absolutely thrilled the boy was so clearly a McKendrick. What a plus!

Robbie went to him immediately. "I'm happy to meet you, Granddad."

Jocelyn chose that precise moment to burst into tears motivating Ed to jump into the void. "You must all want to rest after such a long flight?" he suggested, his eyes alighting more or less compulsively now on Rosa. She positively radiated life and vitality! Things couldn't get any better.

"Long but very smooth," Rosa assured him, meeting his gaze straight-on. There was a natural voluptuousness running like a ribbon through the accent Rosa had never lost. Now she took to studying with equal interest this tall, gentlemanly man with the blue, blue eyes and chivalrous expression. A widower, she had been told. There was a strong attraction already between them. Could there be a little love for her around the corner? It was astonishing when and where love turned up.

Meredith, who had been busy watching proceedings, spoke up. "One of the men will have taken your luggage to your rooms. I'll come up with you…help you settle in." It would give her mother time to compose herself, she thought.

"That will be lovely." Gina bestowed on her a grateful smile.

"You're coming, too, Daddy?" Robbie asked, looking back to his father with a melting smile.

"You bet I am," Cal assured him, though he remained where he was, a bracing hand on his mother's shoulder. "I'll be with you in a minute."

"Didn't you promise me you were going to teach me to ride a horse?" Robbie asked as though they might start the lessons now.

"A *pony*, Robert. I'll get one in especially for you."

"Oh, bravo!" Ewan McKendrick cried heartily. "It's only natural you have the love of horses in your blood, Robbie." My word, this was turning out well, Ewan thought. Jocelyn would just have to pull herself into line.

"Make this work, Mum," Cal bent to murmur in his mother's ear.

"Who said I haven't?" she replied haughtily, when the party were out of earshot. "At least she's beautiful." Even as she acknowledged the fact, Jocelyn felt a fierce stab of jealousy. She had always been Number One in her son's life. She had expected to remain Number One even if he had married the amenable Kym. This Gina was something else again. It wasn't easy to be supplanted. "As for the other one!" She threw up her hands.

Now it was Ed's turn to stun them. "Spellbinding, wasn't she? I just might ask her to marry me."

His handsome face wore a wide grin.

"You're joking of course!" Jocelyn looked at her brother-in-law with extreme disfavour.

Wasn't he?

* * *

Jocelyn, who had hardly eaten anything at dinner, said good-night early and withdrew. Ewan, who couldn't completely disguise his anger with his wife, made his departure some time after.

Count on it. There would be words upstairs, Cal thought, angry and disappointed with his mother. He had never seen her so stiff and ungracious, even if he recognised her nose was out of joint. Both Gina and Rosa had that ineffable thing—glamour.

"You can stand in for me, Cal, at the party," Ewan said over his shoulder. "All they want is to see more of *you*, and Gina, not me!"

An overtired, overexcited Robbie had long since been tucked up in bed.

Rosa and Ed, who had hit it off extremely well over dinner, the attraction continuing apace, had talked art among other things, Ed all the while staring at her in admiration. Now they expressed the desire to go along with the young ones to join the barbecue, which was in full swing judging by the sound of country-and-western music filling the air. Rosa who had wisely taken a short nap to look her best, showed no sign whatever of fatigue. Meredith, looking really beautiful, was also eager to join the party.

Cal detained Gina as the others moved off, chatting happily like old friends. "Let's go out on the terrace," he suggested. He needed privacy as two members of staff continued to hover in the dining room, checking that everything would be left just so.

"As you wish." Gina let him take her arm, unable to control her body's response to his touch. It made her feel extraordinarily vulnerable.

"Well, we lived through that," he offered dryly when they were out in the gardenia-scented night air. Inwardly, he was wondering if his father was going to throttle his mother.

"Your father is trying," Gina answered. "And Meredith and your uncle Ed are so kind, but it's just as I expected. Your mother doesn't, and never will, like me."

My mother is jealous, Cal thought but couldn't bring himself to say it. "My mother is used to being in total control of the situation," he said by way of explanation. "This time she isn't. Don't let her bother you too much, Gina. She'll come around."

"If only for Robbie's sake." Gina took a calming breath. Inside love and hate were battling for her soul. "It's as well he looks like you. He'd have had no chance had he looked like me."

Cal glanced down at her, trying unsuccessfully to numb his own strong feelings. He had been watching her all night. She wore her hair the way he liked it. Loose, centre parted, flowing over her shoulders. Her dress was short and lacy, gold in colour. The low neckline showed her beautiful bosom to advantage, the skirt-length revealed her long sexy legs. "It so happens I'm praying for a daughter who looks just like you."

"You may have a long wait," she said coolly.

"Then I'll just have to seduce you all over again. That's what you think I did, isn't it? Seduce you? Because, you know, I thought the attraction was mutual?"

"I don't remember." She turned her face away.

"Liar." He led her down the short flight of stone steps. "Ed seems to have taken quite a shine to Rosa?" There was amusement and surprise in his voice.

"Sometimes you just never know what people are capable of," Gina said. "Your uncle has been alone a long time?"

"Ten years. His wife, Aunt Jenny, was a lovely person. I remember Meredith crying her heart out at the funeral. I wanted to, but couldn't. Men don't cry and all that. I had to bite my lip until I drew blood."

"So you do have a heart after all?"

It wasn't a tease. She sounded serious. "Oh, well, while we're at it, where have you stowed yours?"

She tossed back a long sable lock. "I have Robbie. My son is everything in life to me. That's the only way you got me here, Cal. You gave me no option but—"

"To stage a battle you'd very likely lose," he finished for her. "Now, what about if we call a truce while we're on show. Remember, we're supposed to be lovers, cruelly separated for so long now to be gloriously reunited in marriage."

She laughed though her heart was beating like a drum. "Don't think I'm taking off on any honeymoon," she warned. "And don't think we're going to finish up in the same bed."

"*Gianina, mia*, it's not as though I've actually asked you to have sex," he mocked. "But never fear. I will get around to it." His voice grew more serious. "I thought we might defer the honeymoon until Robert is more used to the family. Or we could take him with us?"

She stopped moving, visibly agitated. "Where on earth are you thinking?"

"Need you ask, the island?" Now, what was the matter with him, baiting her like that, because she reacted like that was the cruellest thing he could have said.

"You must be mad."

He shrugged. "That's the sad thing. You *made* me mad. Good and mad. Tell me what happened on the island, Gina. You can make it brief if it pains you to speak."

She glanced up at the twinkling fairy lights strung through the trees. Their glow swept the grass and illuminated the garden beds that were filled with rich tropical flowers, the fragrance intoxicating in the warm air. "What are you trying to trap me into saying? I told you I don't want to discuss the past. Suffice to say I fell in love unwisely but too well."

"You jumped right in."

"So did you."

"I shared your reckless streak," he freely admitted. "You were my Juliet. The girl I thought I could die for."

"No tragedy, a farce."

"We have Robert, don't we?" he said in a low voice.

"Yes," she answered quietly.

"I should tell you I intend to have a long talk with my aunt when she gets back home. I have an idea she had more to do with events than I'd realised."

"The past is ancient history. I'm determined to move forwards. So where is your aunt? Does she take off on her broom stick now and again?"

It was said with such scorn, he stopped in his tracks. "Where did that come from all of a sudden?"

Immediately she made a rueful face. "That was a slip. I withdraw it." She had to close a door on the past now that this new door had opened. His aunt would always remain family. She would always be around. "I would never go back to the island," she said, changing the subject. "It was another time."

"I wouldn't go back, either," he said crisply.

"You were just being cruel then?"

"I feel cruel towards you once in a while."

She felt her heart contract. "Small wonder I'm scared of you."

"I should think you would be," he replied, glancing down at her.

They walked on through the tropical night, the path over-shadowed by magnificent broad-domed shade trees. "I don't want any big wedding, Cal," she said nervously.

"So why don't you make a list of a few close friends?" he

suggested in a suave tone. "I don't want any big wedding, either."

"I have no intention of dressing like a bride, either."

"What?" He brought them to a halt. "When you'll make a *glorious* bride?"

She bit her lip, her body aching at his closeness, her mind bent on running away. "I'm the mother of a three-year-old boy."

"High time you got married then," he commented. "I have to insist you dress the part. I'm not going to be denied my trophy wife. That's part of the deal."

They moved on. "Would you like me to ask your Kym to be a bridesmaid?" she asked silkily.

"You'd have to be really crazy to do that."

"Stranger things have happened. I know someone who invited all his old girlfriends to his wedding."

"You were one of them?"

"Never! I'm a one-man woman at heart." Damn, why had she said that?

"I'll disregard that. The only man you'll ever be allowed to get romantic over is *me*."

"That's not going to be a lot of fun."

"Why are you working so hard to hate me?"

She gave a brittle laugh. "That's a lot of question, Cal. Loving you turned out to be very, very painful."

"Surely you made me pay keeping Robert from me." His hurt, his sorrow, his impotent rage burst through his lips.

Gina reacted fiercely. So fiercely Cal was forced to pull her to him, silencing any tempestuous outburst of hers by covering her mouth with his own. "People can see us," he muttered, against her gritted teeth.

How very stupid of her! An anguished moan escaped her throat. People, of course. She had to keep her wits about her, yet every time she was alone with him she thought them sealed off from the rest of the world. Ever so slowly she managed to pull herself together. Even that wildly discordant kiss had made her knees buckle.

"You shouldn't say things like that to me," she censured him, shaking back the silky hair that was spilling around her hot face.

"I'll let you go when you say sorry."

She could hear the taunt in his voice. "You'll let me go *now*. I'm just mad enough to scream. Besides, I can't run away."

"That's right," he agreed. "You can't. You look beautiful. Did I tell you? I love that dress."

"I thought you might like it," she said, tartly.

"Oh, I do. It shows off your beautiful figure. Your mouth tastes of peaches and champagne."

"I've had both," she pointed out. "Shall we walk on?"

"Why not?" he agreed suavely. "Arm in arm like a happily married couple."

"And just how long do you think this marriage will last?"

"Well, let's see now. It's the start of the twenty-first century," he said musingly. "Hopefully we'll have a good fifty years, probably more. The thing is, when you said yes to marrying me, Gina, in my book that means *for ever*."

The expression on his handsome face looked a lot more like ruthless than loving.

Steven had reached the stage where he thought she wasn't going to make an appearance that night. The evening was a great success. No effort had been spared to ensure Coronation's staff would find it memorable. The food was great—as always—Coronation's premier beef, numerous side dishes, hot and cold, salads galore. Icy-cold beer was on tap to stimulate the appetite, soft drinks and fruit juices for the children—they were still running around—wine for the ladies. The dessert table—a mecca for anyone with a sweet tooth—was a long trestle covered with a white linen cloth. It was laden with dishes that looked like they had been prepared by a master chef dedicated to that sort of thing. He circulated constantly—it was part of his job— still, she didn't come.

Then he saw her.

His mood lifted to the skies. She was walking with Gina's aunt Rosa and Edward McKendrick. He really liked Ed, who was vastly more approachable than his elder brother. Gina's aunt, he realised, was an unconventional dresser but he thought she looked great in her vividly coloured outfit. It was sort of gypsy-ish, embroidered with something glinting. From the body language Ed seemed to think she looked fantastic. *Good for you, Ed,* Steven thought. It was a tragedy what had happened to Ed's wife—a lovely woman from all accounts—but eventually one had to get on with life.

Meredith stopped his breath. She wore a dress, a beautiful deep blue dress. He had seldom seen her in a dress, not even at the polo matches or informal functions Coronation hosted from time to time. She mostly wore jeans or tailored pants. Why not? Hers was the ideal figure to show them off. But tonight she wore something filmy and to him desperately romantic. Romance his soul craved. Did women realise men were every bit as romantic as they were? The fabric of her floaty skirt wrapped itself around her lithe body as she moved. Her wonderful hair was loose, falling in a shiny waterfall down her back.

Ed came towards him, extending his hand. "Everything going well, Steve?"

"Everyone's having a great time, Mr McKendrick." Steve returned the smile and the handshake, shifting his gaze to Meredith and Aunt Rosa. "Good evening, ladies. May I say how beautiful you both look?"

"Certainly you may!" Rosa nodded her dark head, her thick hair short and expertly cut. "I think there is something a little bit dangerous about you, Steven." She waved a finger.

"No worries." Steve smiled back at her. "It's just that I like women. Are Cal and Gina coming?" He glanced towards the main path.

"Right behind us," Meredith said, surprising herself greatly by going to him and taking his arm. Never once had she done that. "I think I'd like a cold drink. What about you?" Her gaze moved from Rosa to her uncle, who overnight looked ten years younger with a renewed zest for life.

"You two go on ahead," Ed answered in a relaxed voice, "Rosa and I will stroll for a bit."

Rosa took Ed's arm companionably. "You must tell me everything I need to know about your magnificent gardens, Edward." Her intriguing accent made not two but three sensuous syllables of *Ed-ah-ward*. "I'm longing to explore them by daylight."

"And I'd be delighted to show you," Ed responded gallantly. "That wonderfully exotic fragrance on the air is from the many, many beds of yellow-throated Asian lilies, the pinks, the whites and the creams."

"Why, yes, I can see them glowing in the dark," Rosa said. "I would love to paint them."

"Then you must have your chance."

"Why is it I think Ed has taken a great liking to Gina's aunt Rosa?" Steve asked as Ed and Rosa moved away across the grass.

"She's an extremely attractive woman and a woman of culture." Meredith smiled. "She and Ed got into a discussion on art at the dinner table. Both of them are well informed, but I could see Dad was rather bored. He and Ed look very much alike but their personalities are completely different."

"How did the little dinner party go?" Steve asked. "Are your parents going to make an appearance tonight?"

Meredith shook her head, mightily relieved. "Mum retired early. Dad followed. I expect they might have a few words when they're alone. Mum scarcely pretended a veneer of charm over dinner."

"That's awful." Steve winced. "I would have thought your parents would be delighted to have such a beautiful woman for a daughter-in-law. And Robbie is a great little kid, full of life and so well spoken for his age. Mother and son made a really good impression with the staff. So did Rosa. Everyone on the station is full of praise for them and delight for Cal. That's why the evening is going so wonderfully well. Everyone's happy."

"Are *you* happy, Steven?" She stared up at him, the bronze of his skin in striking contrast to the snowy white shirt he wore with his tight fitting jeans. For herself, she was glowing inside, certain now she was in love.

"I am now you're here," he said softly, gazing down at her. "I was beginning to get worried you mightn't make an appearance."

"Nothing would have kept me away." She gripped his arm tighter, a gesture Steve found utterly enchanting. It was all he could do not to turn her into his arms. Alas, there were too many people around. "I meant it when I said you look beautiful. You dazzle me. You're a *dream* in a dress, especially one that floats all around you."

"Why, thank you, Steven." She smiled, stars in her eyes.

He bent his head to her urgently. "I want to kiss you."

"I want to kiss you back."

Only voices intervened. *"Hi, Steve! Good evening, Ms McKendrick!"*

"Hello, there!" Meredith responded brightly, lifting her hand to return the greetings.

"Can't we go somewhere *quiet*?" Even as he said it Steve couldn't help laughing. They would have to get right out of the home compound to find silence. Someone had turned the music up louder. Someone else toned it down a little. People were dancing.

"Not tonight I'm afraid." She sighed with deep regret. "Cal and Gina will be along soon. Why don't we join in the dancing?"

"Do you think that's wise?"

"It's too late to talk about being wise now, Steven," she said, yearning to be in his arms.

Steven came back to himself for a minute. "I don't want to put you into any stressful situation. Your happiness is very important to me, Meredith."

"So you're *not* going to dance with me?" She tilted her head to one side.

"Are you asking me if I'm game?" he responded to the challenge.

"Something like that, Steven Lockhart."

His smile faltered slightly. "But I'm not a Lockhart, am I? I'm not a Lancaster, either. What *am* I to you, Meredith?"

She reached up to gently touch his mouth, tracing the outline of his lower lip, beautifully cut and undeniably sensual. "You're too touchy."

"I want to touch *you*," he said, his voice mesmerizing. "I want to very gently unwrap you from your beautiful clothes. You can't be wearing a bra, not in that dress?" His golden-brown eyes moved over the tiny bodice with its thin straps, cut to reveal her décolletage.

"There's one built into the dress," she explained, aware her voice shook. It felt like he was stroking her. Featherlike strokes that ranged over her throat and down to the upward curves of her breasts.

The music had changed to a ballad.

He took her into his arms. Wasn't this what he had been longing for all night?

Other couples were dancing beneath the trees, some were twirling down the paths. Some were just having fun. Others were intent on each other.

He was a beautiful mover. She knew that from the way he walked.

They were perfectly quiet. There was no need for words. The intense communication came from the sizzling proximity of their bodies. She was falling fathoms deep into a bottomless lagoon of sexual hunger. It surpassed anything she had felt before. She had to go further, much further than kisses. She let him steer her this way and that, her heart beating madly. If only they didn't have to stop. She wasn't even sure she *could* stop.

"Meredith!" Somewhere a little distance off, amid the babble of laughter and music, her father's voice cracked out.

"God, it's your dad," Steve muttered, "and he's heading this way."

He didn't release her, however. He made no move to. "I thought he was supposed to have retired for the night?" he asked, the merest thread of humour in a dead calm voice.

"I thought he had."

Still, he held her.

"Good evening, Mr McKendrick," Steve greeted his boss smoothly. "We weren't certain if we were going to have the pleasure of your company this evening."

Ewan McKendrick stopped right in front of them. "So you took advantage of the situation by thinking you could dance with my daughter?" he retorted in an insufferably arrogant tone.

Steve kept a tight rein on his temper and his tone low. People were starting to look their way, aware things weren't quite right. "Excuse me, sir, is there a law against that?"

There was no trace of insolence in his voice, just a simple question requiring a simple answer.

Meredith's nerves were fluttering badly. "Please, Dad! You're drawing attention to us."

Her father ignored her. Fresh from a humdinger of an argument with his wife, he was ready for blood. "Would you mind letting my daughter go?" he said thickly, reaching out to shove Steve away, but Steve, a good thirty years younger and superbly fit, didn't budge. He did, however, drop his hands, not wanting to further inflame an already inflammable situation.

Some distance away Gina felt that warning finger on her nape. She began to walk faster.

"It's good you're so eager to join the party." Cal laughed, stepping it out with her.

"Something is wrong up ahead," she told him, sounding serious. "I feel you should be there."

Cal didn't ask her what she meant. He had seen in Gina a lot of things beyond her physical beauty.

It was as she said. Cal saw with dismay his father give Steve Lockhart a hard shove in the shoulder. It had no effect so far as he could see on Steve, but it told him all he needed to know. A head-to-head confrontation was already in place. Meredith's body language spoke of embarrassment and anguish. Poor Merri! She looked so beautiful tonight. She didn't have to take this sort of thing. Their father was as dictatorial a man as he had ever met, whereas Steve had earned his trust and deserved respect.

"Your parents would do well to step into the twenty-first century," Gina murmured, shaking her head. It was inevitable she would be on Steve's side.

"I can't help but agree," Cal gritted, increasing his pace. "They run Coronation Hill like their own kingdom." It wasn't something he was proud of. He glanced down at Gina, not wanting to draw her into it. "You might like to stay here."

She shook her head. "I'll come with you."

"It might get sticky."

"I have no doubt you can handle it."

They closed in on the trio fast. "Hey, everything okay here?" he called, the heavy tension in the atmosphere coming at them in a wave.

Ewan McKendrick rounded on his son. "You *can't* be talking to *me*!"

"Actually, yes, Dad," Cal said, coolly quiet.

Out of the corner of her eye Gina saw people moving quickly away from what looked like shaping up to be a war zone. Most of the staff would have taken note of the fact their very popular overseer was dancing with the boss's daughter. Not only that, but *how* they were dancing. Hadn't she divined an involvement between Meredith and Steve Lockhart, within the first few minutes?

"You're upset, Dad," Cal spoke to his father soothingly, knowing words had most likely passed between his parents. "Why don't I accompany you back to the house?"

"What am I supposed to make of this?" Ewan demanded of his son. "I come out for a breath of air and to make an appearance and what should I be confronted by but my daughter snuggling up to this fella here." He stabbed a condemnatory finger in Steve's direction. "Didn't you see what was going on?"

"Dancing, Dad. All quite respectable," Cal answered reasonably. "You've overreacted. Merri can dance with whomever she pleases."

"Not while she's under *my* roof," Ewan returned furiously.

"Your roof, certainly," Cal agreed. "My roof, Mum's roof, Merri's roof, Ed's roof."

"No need whatever to include me!" Gina broke in ironically, vividly reminded of how her own father had tyrannized her male friends.

"Gina, darling," Cal stressed, "you and Robbie go with *me*." He returned his attention to his father. "Let's go, Dad. Don't spoil what has been a pleasant evening. I think you owe Steve an apology. He's done no wrong."

Ewan's handsome face reddened. "He hasn't, eh? I gave you more credit, Calvin. Lockhart here has a larger purpose than being our overseer. Mark my words. He has designs on my daughter, *your* sister, I might remind you."

"You're absolutely right, sir," Steve broke in, "I do think the world of Meredith."

"Indeed!" Ewan thundered, now totally enraged. "You just keep away from her, fella. I have in mind someone from a fine family for my only daughter. Not a no-one like you!"

They were all startled by his tone, swept with vehemence.

"That's it, Dad!" Cal got a firm grip on his father before Steve lost it. He was about to, judging from his expression. "It would help a lot if you come away."

Ewan McKendrick shook his head several times as if to clear it. "The fella's a bastard!" he ground out heavily. "No way could you ever be good enough for my daughter. You're fired, Lockhart. Don't try to go against me, Cal. I'm still in charge of Coronation and don't you forget it."

"I'm not forgetting it, Dad," Cal said very quietly, yet his voice carried an effortless authority. "But I'm relying on you to regain your common sense. Steve is very good at what he does. You can't expect me to carry the burden without him. Come along now. Your blood pressure was up the last time the doctor took a look at you."

"Why wouldn't it be up in this family?" Ewan McKendrick glowered, but he allowed himself to be led away.

Gina reacted first. She reached out a hand to the distressed Meredith, who clasped it tightly. "My father used to interfere in all my friendships, Meredith," she lamented. "I was never allowed to bring a boy home. Only girlfriends were allowed. As I got older no one was good enough for me. I was my father's 'shining star.' He always called me that. When I fell pregnant he literally threw me out."

Meredith and Steve were so shocked by that admission they momentarily forgot their own outraged feelings. "Gina, how dreadful!" Meredith was aghast. "I never thought—"

"I've never spoken about it," Gina said. "My mother gave me whatever money she had spirited away. Somehow I was able to finish my degree. I didn't show until the seventh month, which helped a lot. I didn't tell anyone. Only Rosa knew. I couldn't have done without Rosa. She's been an enormous support to me and wonderful to Robbie. You can't allow your father to run your life, Meredith. Please don't think *I* am now interfering in your personal affairs. I do so out of my own experience and concern for you."

"I know that, Gina." Meredith shook her head, utterly dismayed. "Does Cal know this?"

Gina smiled sadly. "One day I'll tell him."

"You should tell him now."

Gina shook her head. "There are still a few issues we have to work through. I'll know the time."

"Of course you will." Meredith backed off. "How mortifying this all is. What must you think of us?"

Gina spoke directly. "Your mother doesn't like me, Meredith. I doubt she ever will. Your father will try. But I'm not sure I can live under the same roof as a mother-in-law who so clearly doesn't approve of me."

"What are you saying, Gina?" Meredith's voice rose in alarm.

"I'm saying if I'm not happy here I mightn't be able to stay." Gina's beautiful face took on an adamant cast. Gina had had more than her share of dysfunctional families.

"You've told Cal how you feel?" Steve asked. He was still fuming inside, having come very close to punching McKendrick in the nose. Cal had known it. That was why he had spirited his father away.

"No, but I will if it becomes necessary," Gina said, with a note of resolve in her voice. She knew, if Meredith and Steve didn't, Cal wasn't about to let her leave. For *any* reason. By the same token she knew he wasn't going to allow his mother to continue on her present course. She looked back into two distressed faces, as much for her as themselves, she realised with gratitude. "I was surprised and very touched by my welcoming party when we arrived," she told them. "I'd like you to know that. I suppose it's normal enough for your mother, Meredith, to have difficulties accepting me. I'm not the daughter-in-law she wanted. Kym, wasn't it? Your aunt, Lorinda, told me all about her." In the stress of the moment that withheld piece of information spilled out.

"So it had to be when we were on the island?" Meredith's face darkened with a frown.

Immediately Gina made a little dismissive gesture with her hands. "Sorry. I've said too much already. Cal doesn't know. I'd prefer the past to stay in the past, Meredith. It will do no good to rake it all up. Now, if you'll excuse me, I'll carry out Cal's wishes and mingle with the staff for a while. I expect he'll be back soon."

Meredith looked at Steven in sharp dismay. She could see he shared her feelings. "Please remember Cal needs you desperately, Gina."

Gina didn't answer but turned away with an enigmatic little smile.

Cal needs his *son* desperately, Gina amended in her own mind.

Left alone, Meredith put a conciliatory hand on Steve's arm.

"Careful," he warned, his lean body taut.

"Please don't be like that, Steven," she begged. "I am so sorry, but it's not my fault."

Or maybe it *is*, she thought wretchedly. She should have protected Steven. That meant leaving him well alone.

"It would have given me a great deal of pleasure to have punched your father in the nose," he said tightly.

"I think we all knew that, Steven. My father can be unbelievably arrogant. In some ways my parents don't know a lot about *real* life."

"They're too protected by their wealth," Steve diagnosed accurately. "But I suppose it's not all that surprising. Isn't God a McKendrick?"

His tone cut. "He *can't* fire you."

"He *can* fire me," Steve corrected, his attractive voice oddly harsh.

"Cal will speak to him. He'll listen."

"You think so?" Steve threw up his hands. "I think it more likely you'll disappear overseas. Join your gadfly aunt who appears to have done some mischief whether Gina wants to keep her out of it or not. As for you, you'll come home and marry your father's nominee. None of your family will accept me, Meredith, outside of Cal and Gina. And that would only make it hard for them both."

Anger came, swift and unexpected. "Shouldn't you be worrying more about whether *I'll* accept you?" she cried.

That settled it for Steve. "I'll be out of here by midday tomorrow, okay?" he said curtly. "Maybe sooner. It's been great knowing you, Meredith. Tell Gina if she wants a normal life then she sure picked the wrong family."

She ran after him, mortified. "Steven, please don't go." She made an effort to catch his shirt, and almost lost her footing on the exposed root of a tree.

He didn't notice and kept going, taking swift, powerful strides away from her.

Meredith gave up. Her father had made sure of it calling Steven a bastard. How dare he?

See what you've gone and done? the voice in her head taunted. *You should have left him alone. You knew what was going to happen. You fool you! Getting to think things might be different. Nothing will ever change around here. Not until it's Cal's turn to reign.*

Steven, she knew, had been sitting pretty as Coronation's overseer, a position of trust and responsibility. He had security and earned good money. It would be highly unlikely he could find a comparable position in the near future. She wasn't even sure if Cal could persuade her father to relent even if Steven agreed to stay. And that didn't look like it was happening. Not from the way he had stormed off.

Meredith returned to the house feeling sick to her soul.

CHAPTER SIX

READY for bed, Gina looked in on Robbie, whose bedroom was just across the hallway from hers. She opened the door very quietly, widening the opening so a golden ray of light fell across his face. She had left a small night-light burning in any case. It was possible he could awake some time during the night and feel disorientated in a strange house. She didn't really expect him to. It was Robbie's practice to fall asleep as soon as his head hit the pillow, sleeping right through until she woke him by pulling the lobe of his ear very gently in the morning. It was a trick that always worked.

Just as she thought, he was fast asleep, clutching his favourite teddy bear. Her face softened into an expression of the utmost maternal tenderness. Robbie wouldn't go anywhere without that bear. His father had promised him the room would be redecorated in any way he liked. Maybe a few lighter touches here and there, but it was a beautiful big airy room with French doors leading out onto a broad verandah. It was a full moon outside; the big copper moon of the tropics. She had to say it affected her.

She wanted Cal. She wanted him to come to her. She wanted to hear his voice.

How could you love a man so passionately when he had broken your heart?

Gently, she closed Robbie's door. His room had a different view from hers, overlooking the extensive gardens that led to the large stables complex at the rear of the house. Coronation Hill's homestead was very impressive, she thought. A huge substantial house, it had evolved, so Cal had told her, from the original single-storey stone colonial cottage. One would never have known it. Today it was a lofty two-storey structure with the central section linking two long wings. Obviously the generations of McKendricks had spared no expense developing a homestead that befitted their station.

She returned to her own room, feeling bruised, emotionally and spiritually. How could this possibly work out? Even Meredith's developing relationship with the extremely attractive Steven Lockhart seemed heading for a shipwreck.

"Damn!" she said out loud, giving one of the pillows several good thumps.

"Bad as that, is it?"

She looked up to see Cal standing in the open doorway. His handsome face wore a brooding expression. It was obvious he, too, was deeply disturbed.

"Need you ask?" Another minute and she would have shut her door. Would he have knocked?

He sighed in a way that told her the events of the evening had well and truly taken their toll. "May I come in?"

She shrugged. "Shut the door after you. Robbie's asleep. So tell me what's happening about Steve? Did you manage to persuade your father to change his mind about sacking him?"

"I can handle my father," said Cal, thrusting a hand through his thick mahogany hair. "It's Steve I'm worried about. Meredith has come back to the house in a hell of a state. Sometimes I think there's not a guy in the world who would pass first base with Dad."

"Meredith can't live her whole life being dictated to."

Cal shrugged. "Of course she can't. But I don't think there's been anyone who really mattered to her up to this date. No one to really push for. Steve would seem to be different. She said he told her he was leaving in the morning."

"Oh, no!" Gina looked back at him in dismay. "Have you spoken to him?"

"I'm giving him some space. Hoping he'll cool off. He can't get anywhere until the freight plane gets in around noon."

"And Meredith?"

"What about her?" His jewel-like eyes moved over her, studying her hungrily. The muscles of his thighs tensed as his body stirred. No make-up, long hair tied back at the nape, a shell-pink satin robe sashed tightly at the waist, slippers on her feet. She still looked glorious, he thought with a hot burn of desire that was exposed in his eyes.

"Is she going to give in without a fight?" Gina's breathing started to come rather fast. Labour as she might, she still couldn't keep her physical yearning for him under control. Just to look at him triggered a response.

"*We* did, didn't we?" He suddenly flung himself down on the end of her huge four-poster bed, falling backwards with a groan.

Ohhh! Gina didn't feel she was any way near strong enough for such temptations. "Why was your father so horrible to Steve?" Autocrat or not Ewan McKendrick's reaction had seemed excessive.

"Because Dad can be bloody horrible sometimes." Cal addressed the ornately plastered ceiling. "For a man like my father, a family liaison with a staff member is *verboten.*"

Gina moved well away from the bed. Hadn't her liaison with him been forbidden? "*Mein Gott,* German!" she said with a flash of sarcasm. "And the *bastard* bit? That was appalling. I was shocked."

Cal remained lying where he was, as though it would cost him too much of a physical effort to get up. "Steve is the natural son of one of our biggest beef producers," he explained. "A man called Gavin Lancaster. Lancaster took a fancy to Steve's mother many long years ago and Steve is the result. He's so much a Lancaster everyone in the Outback knows."

"And Lancaster knows, presumably?"

"Of course."

"But he chooses not to recognise his own son?" There was a throb of outrage in her voice.

"I'm very sorry to say the answer's yes."

Gina felt a great rush of pity for Steve Lockhart. "This Lancaster can't be a man of character and heart. That's terrible, Cal. And Steve's mother?"

"She was married at the time. Somehow managed to patch the marriage up. The family—he has two half brothers and a half sister—moved to New Zealand when Steve was fourteen. He's been on his own since. Surprisingly, however, they did put him in a very good boarding school before they left."

"Oh, that was nice of them!" Gina scoffed.

"Wasn't it? He was with other boys from landed families. That's how he remained on the land. Love for the land is something that runs deep in the blood. Steve has it."

"Poor Steve!" Gina looked towards the moonlit verandah and beyond that the night under stars. "The barbecue must have folded. The music has stopped."

"I think Dad's performance put paid to the evening," Cal groaned. "But they got a good few hours in."

"Steve's in love with Meredith," Gina said, a poignant expression on her beautiful face.

"He may well be but he's a proud man. Come here a moment." He raised his dark head slightly off the bed.

"You can't stay." She didn't move.

"Shall I get out now?" he asked, and gave a low laugh.

"No, you don't have to go *right* now."

"Many thanks, *principessa*!" he mocked. "Bear with me for a little while. That's all I ask."

All? She was near mad for him to touch her. Their sexual attraction was so strong she did right to fear it. Excitement was growing at a great pace inside her. She tried, but failed to keep it down. He knew exactly how to press her every last button. To move nearer the bed, would be akin to going in at the deep end.

When she was little more than a tentative foot away, he suddenly made a grab for her. "Gotcha!" He pulled her to him with a fierceness that still held an element of cherishing.

They were both on the bed in one swift motion, he half on top of her, running his hand down her shoulder to her waist to the top of her long slender leg, stopping while he looked deep into her eyes.

"I finally get you home and it's all bad news. Well, not entirely. Robbie has the magic key to everyone's heart. I'm sorry for the way my mother behaved at dinner. I apologise for her. I get mad just thinking about it, but it wasn't the time to bring on a big family argument. That might have to wait, but you can bet your life she got an earful from Dad."

Gina felt like she was about to cry but decided she could not. He lowered his face into her neck, his mouth moving against her skin. "Oh, you smell *wonderful*! Like a million wildflowers!"

She could feel the weight of his head on her shoulder. He had his eyes closed, just lying there breathing her in. "Things have got to change, Gina," he muttered against her skin. "Just hang in there. I'm going to make them change. I know how." *I can't lose her,* Cal thought. *Not all over again.*

The ache of tears was in Gina's throat. She couldn't help herself. She placed her palm very tenderly against his cheek. When she surrendered, she surrendered. It was part of her nature. What was the point of all this alternating between love and hate? They were tied to one another, weren't they? They shared their son.

"Gina?" He opened his eyes to stare at her. She had never seen eyes like his before she had met him. That amazing jewel-like green. Now she had a child with those same eyes.

Cal lifted his torso supporting his body with his strong arms. "Would you let me love you?"

Heat grew to flame. She knew he would be true to his word, giving her the opportunity to say yes, or decline his advances. If she said no would she always look back at this moment and regret it? Or should she open herself up to him? She had kept maintaining the past was best forgotten. She even acted on it, in not implicating his aunt in her banishment from the island. Shouldn't she look to the future? Shouldn't she take the first step?

As if to goad her the voice inside her head said: *Because you want it...want it...want it!* Sexual needs had their own sovereignty. Her need for him was urgent.

Cal saw the change come over her. He saw the powerful feelings that drove her. Feelings that left little place for pride or any other consideration. Nothing could stand up against the raw passion they had for each other.

Gina's hand came up compulsively and found the buttons of his shirt. She slid them free from their buttonholes. She could smell the special male fragrance of his skin, as intoxicating to her as her fragrance was to him. She could feel his warmth, the texture of the whorls of dark hair on his chest, spearing through it with her fingers while his whole body tensed. She must have been taking too long because abruptly he helped her, stripping his shirt roughly from him and flinging it away.

His shadow fell over her. He held her hands away as he bent to kiss her open mouth, pouring such passion into and over her she was drenched. Then he was removing her clothes, folding his face into them, and when she was naked his hands began to move over her, commanding her body to obey. It was a primitive kind of mastery; dominant male over female; but it was made all the more fantastic because it seemed to Gina to be overlaid with a ravishing tenderness. He wasn't so much intent on his own pleasure. He was intent on *hers*.

"Tell me you can find it within yourself to love me?" His hands enclosed the golden globes of her breasts, the darkening rose-coloured nipples swollen and erect.

"I *did* love you." Her eyes were closed to him, as though open they would reveal too much of herself to him.

"Or so you said." His hand began to trace a line from her navel down to the quivering apex of her body with its delicate cleft. He dipped his head and kissed her there.

Sensations shot through her as keen as a blade.

She shuddered, her voice barely audible. "I believed all *you* said to me then." Her back began to arch and flex. The impact of his mouth on her sex was enormous.

"But you can't believe me now?" He took his time over his ministrations, all the while watching her face, a clear barometer for the raging emotions he was arousing in her.

"All I want is for our son…to…be happy." She could only gasp out the words, her body was in such a throbbing state of arousal.

"*I* don't matter?" Now his fingers found their way inside her.

"Of course you matter," she gasped, her back arching off

the bed as he explored deeper. "I can't talk. I can't *talk*." Sensation was eclipsing everything else, requiring her most intense concentration.

"You're going to marry me."

His voice sounded deep in her ear.

"Yes!" she moaned hoarsely.

He levered himself over her, a lean powerful man yet she couldn't seem to feel his weight. She *adored* his body on top of hers. Worshipped it. Now her own hand began to move, certain of what he wanted. She heard with a certain triumph, the harsh catch of his breath.

"Gina!" He groaned as if he were in the most exquisitely excruciating pain.

"I'm here!" She carried on tormenting him, until he could scarcely bear it. Then in a galvanic surge he reversed their positions. She was on top of him, her legs locked around him, muscles taut, her long hair tumbling forwards as she bent to kiss his marvellous mouth.

"Will this pass for love?" she softly taunted, armed with the knowledge in her lovemaking he found her faultless.

His voice was a near-satiated growl in his throat. "If it isn't, don't let it ever end."

From long habit Cal awoke in the predawn. The sky outside was a luminous pearl-grey, the horizon shot through with filmy layers of pink, gold and mauve. They were lying spooned together, front to back, her beautiful body curved into his, his arm lying over the top of her, the tips of his fingers resting on her breast. He felt his body instantly react, but first he just wanted to look at her sleeping face, to savour the miracle of her presence beside him. He no longer had just memories to live with. He had the woman. Whatever the difficulties of the past, the difficulties that lay ahead, this part of their relationship was perfect. He couldn't imagine lovemaking more ravishing. He swore he could hear the beat of her heart. Surely it matched his own?

She sighed deeply and began to turn, eyelids flickering, a frown shadowing her face, her lips murmuring, *"No!"*

His hand tightened over the satin slope of her shoulder. "Gina, you're dreaming." He shook her. "Gina?" There was real anguish in that moan.

A handful of seconds later and she opened her eyes, huge and velvety dark. "Cal!" She looked as if she were still lost in a wilderness of emotions.

"Are you okay? You were having a bad dream."

She shivered though the room was pleasantly warm. "I was back on the island."

"So why did it make you want to cry?"

She stared up into his eyes. "What *did* you really feel for me then, Cal, *what*? Please tell me."

He pushed her back gently into the pillows. He couldn't bear to tarnish the memory of what they had.

She closed her eyes against that telling expression on his face. "I'm sorry."

"You should be sorry." He bent and kissed her. A kiss that seemed to go on and on for ever. "I'm crazy about you," he muttered as he withdrew his mouth from hers. *"Crazed."*

This time when they made love it couldn't have been more different from the night before. This time their coming together was more a clash. It was almost as though each was still out for revenge. Unresolved revenge for four long years of pain and grief. Were they damned by all their complex issues? A man could be crazy about a woman without wanting it, without even loving her. Gina had believed herself abandoned at the most crucial turning point in her life. She had had to bring a child into the world without the love and support of its father; Cal felt himself betrayed by the girl, who in the shortest space of time, barely six weeks, had become everything in the world to him. The girl who had the power to destroy his ordered life. The girl who had denied him all knowledge of his son. There were, without question, powerful issues yet to be worked through.

But physically, they thrashed in the bed together, in an orgy of desire, playing out their past torments while their demons were let loose. Cal thrust into her powerfully, one hand behind her high arching back, her hoarse little cries serving only to drive him on.

When it was over they lay back utterly shaken by the primitive forces that had taken them over.

"Did I hurt you?" God, had he intended to, even for a moment? he castigated himself.

"No, though I seem to have left my mark on you." She could see her nail marks on his shoulders and on the small of his hard muscled back. "Let's take a shower," she suggested, aware her voice sounded as fragile as she felt. "That's when I can get my breath back."

"Here, let me help you." He rose from his side of the bed and came round to her, the splendid male, lifting her naked body high in his arms.

Under the warm silver stream of water, she let him cover her with a soft lather of sandalwood-scented soap: over her face, the long stem of her throat, down over her breasts, the smoothness of her stomach, between her legs, right down to her toes. She had thought herself satiated, yet she was trembling all over again, her stomach sucked in. She realised she couldn't get enough of him. Quite simply he filled her with passion in every pore of her skin. He was holding her strongly beneath the arms as the torrent of water washed over them; virtually holding her up. Her back was pressed up against the cold, slick tiles. He was moving into her body, moving rhythmically, driving slow and deep until he found her very core. The expression on his downbent dark face glistening with water was heart-poundingly rapt.

Gina had the strangest sensation they were becoming one person. Then all thought was lost in a rush of violent desire.

Cal had been sitting outside the overseer's bungalow for maybe ten minutes before Steve drove up. He got out of the station ute, mopping the sweat from his face with the red bandana he had worn around his neck. He walked up the couple of steps with no sign of surprise.

"I've sent Mike and a couple of the boys to bring in the cleanskins at the ravine."

"Good." Cal nodded. "Have you decided what you're going to do?"

"I reckon your dad decided that," Steve said. "Look, would you like a cup of coffee?"

"I won't say no." Cal stood up, both men going inside the comfortable bungalow furnished in a simple palette of white with a turquoise-blue feature wall in the living area to offset the polished timber floor, the big Thai coffee table and the brown leather sofa and matching armchairs. The station had provided all the furnishings. Steve had added a few pleasing touches.

"Take a seat. This won't take a minute." Steve walked into the small kitchen and set to making the coffee with excellent freshly ground arabica coffee beans brought in from New Guinea.

While the coffee was perking he rejoined Cal, taking a seat opposite him in one of the armchairs.

"I don't want you to go, Steve," Cal said. "You do a great job. I rely on you and I trust you."

"I appreciate that, Cal. I really do but I can't have one of the McKendricks for me and one bitterly against."

"What about Meredith?"

Steve fought to speak calmly. "What have I got to offer her, Cal? A woman like that."

"Okay, so we can fix things," Cal said. "Do you love her?"

Steve lowered his head. No response.

"Steve?"

When Steve looked up there was misery in his golden eyes. "I was in love with her from the word *go*. Nothing has happened between us, Cal. Just a few kisses."

"One kiss can change a man's life, Steve."

"Tell me about it. It's not as if I've even got a name to offer her. My own mother and Lancaster did that to me."

"That's quite an indictment," Cal said.

"You don't know what it's like, Cal. I know you feel for me but you can't really put yourself in my shoes. You're a McKendrick. That's a proud, pioneering name. You know who you are."

"And you know who *you* are," Cal responded. "You're a top man. Every last person on the station likes and respects you."

"You're leaving out the most important people. Your parents."

"It's quite possible to love one's parents or some member of the family, for that matter, without liking them. I know my father and mother have a certain view of themselves that doesn't jell with the times. Right from the early days Coronation Hill was run more or less on feudal lines. Even Dad's extraordinary attitude to Merri's suitors, and she's had quite a few very serious about her, is feudal. It's the sheer size of the place and the isolation."

"Plus the money, the power and the influence," Steve added harshly. "I really should have taken my mother's maiden name instead of staying with Lockhart. But I guess it's too late to change now."

"Meredith will be tremendously upset if you go."

"I'll think of something," Steve said, his mind jam-packed with mostly crazy ideas. How did a working man win an heiress? A working man with pride?

"I've thought of something," Cal said. "Want to hear it?"

"Just let me get the coffee," Steve said, rising and moving back to the kitchen.

"Thanks," Cal said when Steve returned with a tray wafting a rich aroma. "What do you think about this? What if I send you to Jingoll?" Jingoll was a McKendrick outstation close in to the McDonnell Ranges in the Territory's Red Centre. "And bring Cash Hammond back here. He's a good bloke. He's not you, but he does the job."

The constriction around Steve's heart eased up slightly. "But wouldn't your father object to that, too, Cal?"

Cal looked untroubled. "Dad's the king of the castle in name only these days, Steve. You know that. *I* run the chain. If I say I'm sending you to Jingoll, Dad will accept it."

"And I never get to see Meredith?" Steve drank his coffee too hot.

"That's up to the two of you, Steve. Merri has a sizeable trust fund."

"God, Cal!" Steve set his mug down so hard it might have been a hammer on an anvil.

"Hear me out," Cal said, holding up a hand. "I'm well aware of your scruples, Steve. All I'm saying is Meredith has the freedom to do what she likes."

"But if she came to me then your parents would give up on her?" Steve met Cal's eyes directly.

"It all translates into choices, Steve. We all have to make our own choices in life."

* * *

When Cal returned to the homestead an hour later he went in search of his sister. He needed to tell her what had transpired between him and Steve. Steve moving away from Coronation Hill was an undoubted loss for the station, but a plus for Jingoll. He didn't know what Meredith would think of it, however. Jingoll was around eight hundred miles away, the distance between Darwin in the Top End and Alice Springs in the Red Centre being close to a thousand miles. He entered through one of the rear doors of the house, hearing voices coming from down the hallway. As he drew nearer to his father's study he recognised the voices. His mother and Gina were having a discussion. Ordinarily he would have let the sound of his boots announce his arrival, but this time for some reason he trod very quietly along the thick Persian runner, hesitating a few feet from the open doorway.

"So that's how it was done?" Gina was saying, her voice resonating with what Cal thought was quiet resignation.

"Something had to be done," his mother snapped back. "My son was to marry his childhood sweetheart. They were as good as engaged even before that unfortunate holiday."

"So that was the plan," Gina continued as though she was scarcely listening to his mother. "Your sister—a most convincing, beautiful society lady—told me Cal was to marry the girl the entire family loved. It had been known for ages. Sadly for me, I was little more than a bachelor's last fling before Cal tied the knot. A few months on he would be settling down to a splendid marriage—one made in Heaven."

"And so it was!" Jocelyn responded, her tone showing not a skerrick of remorse.

Again Gina didn't sound as if she were listening. It seemed more like she was simply speaking her thoughts aloud. "So you and your sister came up with a plan. She told Cal—who trusted her implicitly—and why not? I saw how sweet and loving she was with him—that I had gone to her, begging her to have me spirited off the island. She was a powerful lady. I was in awe of her. I was so young, the product of an ordinary working-class family. I thought your family lived on a scale I couldn't even imagine. The owner of the island was your sister's good friend. She could do anything. So the two of you concocted the story that I had confessed to her I had given my promise to marry *my* childhood sweetheart. My *fictional* childhood sweetheart. My father was a control freak, Mrs McKendrick. Something like you. I had no boyfriend. Then your sister told Cal I'd become panicked by the situation I found myself in. I had got myself in so deep I wanted only to run away. I was already promised to a young man my father approved of. I remember the exact words she used to me. She seemed so kind, so wise and mature, trying to prevent me from making a fool of myself, but she was playing me for the naive girl I was. *'My dear child, you do realise my nephew is very far above you?'"*

"True, too true!" Jocelyn answered so strongly. Cal winced. "Only by then it was too late. You were already pregnant."

"How could I possibly regret it?" Gina said. "Nothing was easy. My father was so devastated by my fall from grace, he banished me from our home. But I had Cal's son, my beloved Robbie. It may not be what you want, Mrs McKendrick, but Cal and I will be married very soon. Our son is the most important person in the world to us. If you wish to hold on to your son's love it might be in *your* best interest to turn over a new leaf."

There was a shocked silence, then his mother's well-bred voice rising in outrage. "You're advising me, are you?"

Cal judged it high time to make his appearance. He stood framed in the open doorway of the study, trying to keep calm if only on the surface. His mother was wearing her famous pearls. She was seated behind the huge partner's desk that was singularly free of paper work. Meredith, the unsung heroine, took care of all that with her usual quiet efficiency. Gina was standing in front of the desk, with her back to him.

His mother saw him first, her skin draining of all colour. "Cal, how long have you been there?" she quavered.

Gina spun around. Her face, too, betrayed shock. "Cal, we never heard you."

He closed the distance between them, folding an arm around her. "For once I was eavesdropping. I should do it more often, especially with so many dishonest people about."

Gina's sigh was ragged. "We didn't mean for you to hear anything." She had been trying to effect a private understanding with her future mother-in-law, not drag Cal into it.

"I did tell you to shut the door," Jocelyn snapped, some colour returning to her face. As ever she was determined on braving it out.

"I'm sorry. I should have, but you rather upset me..."

Jocelyn sucked in a breath. "And I'm *not* upset?"

"If you are you deserve to be, Mother," Cal told her bluntly. "You and dear Aunt Lorinda. Just goes to show what a fool I was back then. I *trusted* her. She was family. She'd never shown me anything but love. She's a wonderful actress, too. I was sucked in good and proper."

"Exactly what she wanted," Gina said bleakly. "I believed her, too."

"Let's be very clear here," Jocelyn interrupted, a frown between her eyes. "Lorinda's only motivation was love and concern. She didn't want you, Cal, to make a terrible mistake."

"The terrible mistake was getting engaged to poor Kym. The fact is the two of you conspired to ruin my relationship with Gina," Cal said with a hard condemnatory note Jocelyn had never heard in his voice before. "I won't forget!"

"But, Calvin, we did what we thought best." Jocelyn threw up her hands. "You were set to marry Kym. She was just right for you. I was very grateful to Lorinda for letting me know what was happening on that island. It might be hard to believe now, Gina, but Lorinda quite liked you. She thought you very beautiful and clever, but unfortunately not one of us. She was seriously worried that you may have got hurt."

Gina gave a brittle laugh. "I did get seriously hurt, Mrs McKendrick."

"Please don't let's overlook the damage done to me," Cal broke in, his expression severe. "I'm only just getting to know my son. Robbie is only just getting to know his father. Or did the three of you think it was all *women's* business?" He turned his head to stare Gina down.

Gina didn't answer. Jocelyn sat stricken under her son's weight of judgement.

"What, no replies?" Cal asked, curtly. "No sorrow, no remorse?"

Jocelyn delicately licked her chiselled lips. They were bone-dry. "Robert is a splendid little fellow," she offered like it was some sort of olive branch. "A true McKendrick. I'm sure the two of us will become great friends. Your father is already very proud of him, Cal. Robert is a beautiful child."

"You would never have laid eyes on him, only Merri happened to see that article about Gina in a paper," Cal pointed out coldly. "It was Merri who drew my attention to it. We have her to thank for bringing Robert into our lives."

"Fate sometimes takes steps to put things right," Gina murmured, lifting her drooping head.

"So where does that leave us?" Jocelyn asked.

Cal clipped off his answer. "It leaves us with the hope *you'll* take a good long look at yourself, Mum. You cross Gina, you cross me. Gina is to be my wife. She's the mother of my son. I love you—you know that—but I won't tolerate your trying to destroy the life the two of us want for our son. You messed up once. You're not allowed to do it again."

Cal turned about and stalked from the room, leaving the two women staring at one another. It would have been an exaggeration to say they were suddenly allies but they both felt the weight of his deep abiding anger.

Robbie, running around the ground floor, in an ecstasy of exploration, found Jocelyn some time later in the big room with all the plants. It was a dazzling world for a small boy used only to the confines of a two-bedroom apartment. In the room where his grandmother was, there were *trees* that nearly reached the ceiling. There were lovely big fat pots taller than he was, like the pots full of golden canes Aunt Rosa had in her garden. Huge hanging baskets were suspended from the ceiling, tumbling masses of beautiful ferns and flowers. He had never seen so many flowers in his life.

Mummy always had flowers in the apartment. He and Aunt Rosa used to go out into the garden late afternoon and pick some for her before she came home. Mummy liked lilies. There were beds and beds of lilies out in the garden, which seemed to him more like the Botanical Gardens Mummy used to take him to. He had never seen anything in his short life like this place called Coronation Hill. Not just the great big castle, but all the little houses and long dormitories for the stockmen grouped around it. There were no streets or streetlights, no highways, on Coronation; no tall buildings, no buses or trains, nor lots of cars whizzing up and down. There were no coffee shops and restaurants, none of the shops where Mummy normally went to buy things. Instead there were planes and a helicopter, lots of heavy machinery, thousands and thousands of really marvellous-looking cattle, emus, kangaroos—he'd heard *crocodiles*—zillions of birds and best of all *horses*. He couldn't wait until the special pony his daddy had ordered for him would arrive. But above all there was this enormous, empty land! It spread out to the horizons and they had it all to themselves! That was amazing! Coronation Hill was an enchanted kingdom. And it was his home.

"Hello, Nanna!" he carolled, delighted to see her. His grandmother was sitting quietly with her back to him so he ran around the front of her, stopping short in dismay. "Oh, Nanna, you're *crying*!"

Jocelyn tried very hard to stem the flow. She had been sitting there coming to terms with what was going on in her life. It seemed to her she had never been so alone, darn near ostracised. Of course she was to blame. Her attitude was so negative. Even she could see that. Ewan was very upset with her. Their argument the night before had badly affected her. Cal, her beloved son, was starting to think badly of her. Of course she was jealous. *Go on, admit it!* She had been the Number One woman in her son's life. She wasn't any more. That was hard to take, especially for a possessive woman like her. A winner all her life it seemed to her all of a sudden she could finish up a big loser if she persisted with the hard line she had taken. Maybe there was something dreadfully wrong with her? The only answer was to express an abject apology directly to Gina, her soon-to-be daughter-in-law, and suggest they start again.

"Nanna?" Robbie asked uncertainly, worried his grandmother might be sick or something.

Jocelyn came out of her unhappy reverie. "Just a few little tears, darling boy. Nothing for you to worry about. I'm fine now. What have you been up to?" she asked, trying to speak brightly.

Robbie moved close to her, putting his elbows in her lap and staring into her face. "Why are you so sad?"

Jocelyn gave a funny little groan. "How can I be sad with you around?" She gave him a lovely trembling smile.

Robbie leaned upwards and kissed her on the cheek. "It's so wonderful here, Nanna. I *love* it. It's my home now, isn't it?"

"It certainly is," Jocelyn responded, the icebergs that had all but held her heart fast, starting to melt away. "Coronation Hill is where you belong."

"And Mummy?" Robbie asked earnestly, taking her hand. "Don't you think she's beautiful?"

Jocelyn saw a far-reaching question in her grandson's highly intelligent eyes. *Her* eyes, wasn't that remarkable?

"Yes, darling, I do," she said, allowing herself to be drawn to her feet. "Mummy is very beautiful and she's raised you beautifully. She should be very proud. We're going to have the greatest time ever on the wedding day. I expect you want to be page boy?"

"Page boy, what's that?" Robbie looked up at her a shade anxiously.

"Come along with me and I'll show you," Jocelyn said. "I can show you photographs of your daddy when he was page boy at several big society weddings. That was when he was around four or five. He said he was too old thereafter and refused. Aunty Merri was flower girl at lots of weddings. It's all in the albums."

"Please show me," Robbie said with the greatest interest. "Are there photos of you, Nanna? Mummy said you would have been a fairy-tale bride?"

Jocelyn's gratified smile flashed out. She bent and kissed the top of her grandson's glossy head. "Oh, I was, my darling," she said. "I can show you. I used to have hair like your mummy's. It flowed all the way down my back."

"Like Rapunzel?" Robbie giggled.

"Rapunzel didn't stand a chance!" Jocelyn joyfully squeezed his hand.

CHAPTER SEVEN

MEREDITH rode until she and the gelding were close to exhaustion. It was the gelding's condition far more than her own that had her reining in at the creek, a place that she loved, all the more so now, because it was the place she and Steven had first acknowledged what they could mean to each other. The lead up had been slow—the going was tough—but finally when left alone together caution had given way to feelings of the heart. She just knew in her bones Steven wouldn't stay after the harshness of the way her father had spoken to him. He had insulted Steven in the worst possible way. It was so cruel, so unfair. Steven was the victim of the illicit affair between Gavin Lancaster and his mother. Steven was blameless. Yet he had been saddled with a burden almost too heavy to carry for most of his life.

Meredith sat down on the bank beneath the willowy melaleucas, with hundreds of little wildflowers, purple with yellow, black-spotted throats, growing all around the base of the sweet sapped trees. Above her, she could see chinks of the smouldering blue sky. There could be a late tropical thunderstorm though a cooling breeze had sprung up. It was moving its fingers through her hair and quelling the heat in her skin. A pair of brolgas were standing on their long legs amid the reeds at the water's edge. Brolgas mated for life.

These days humans weren't taking sacred vows all that seriously. When she married she wanted it to be for ever.

She thought about the way Steven had kissed her; the way he held her; the depth of feeling he had transmitted to her through his mouth and his hands. Yet she had been much more certain yesterday that he loved her than she was today. At least *in love* with her. That very first kiss had been, to her, the start of something big. She asked herself if it had really been that way for him.

A flight of pygmy-geese with their glossy green upper parts and breast bands had arrived, hovering above the mirror-clear surface of the water as though admiring their reflections. On the opposite bank brilliantly coloured parrots were alighting in the trees with wonderful flashes of emerald, deepest sapphire, scarlet, yellow, orange. Australia was famous for the numbers and varieties of its parrots. Almost certainly they had originated on the ancient southern continent of Gondwana. For once the sight of them didn't give her the usual pleasure. At that moment she felt as though all pleasure had been drained out of her.

She *had* to speak to Steven.

Back home at the stables, she turned the gelding over to one of the stable hands to take care of, and then she cut through the home grounds, narrowly dodging her uncle and Rosa who appeared to crave one another's company. She made for the staff quarters beyond the home compound, encountering no one along the way. She prayed Steven would be at the bungalow even if he were packing to leave. It amazed her now, the amount of interference in her affairs she had tolerated from her father. She had to stop living that kind of life. But it also struck her Steven was the first man she was fully prepared to fight for. She had taken a long time to truly fall in love. Maybe that was it.

She was running up the short flight of timber steps when Steven faced her at the door.

"Hi!" he said, his strong face impassive.

"May I come in?" She felt incredibly nervous.

"Sure." He stood away from the door. "You look tired." There were shadows beneath her beautiful, intensely blue eyes.

"I couldn't sleep. How could I what with everything that's going on."

"Would you like some coffee?" he asked. "Cal was here. I made him some, but I'm ready to make fresh."

She shook her head. "No, don't bother unless you want some. I haven't seen Cal. I've been for a ride because I was in the mood for a darn good gallop. Trying to clear my head. So what did you and Cal decide?"

"Sit down, please." It struck him she looked more fragile than he had ever seen her.

Meredith sank into an armchair, looking around her. The bungalow was comfortably and attractively furnished. Steven had kept it immaculately. No one could describe him as a careless man. "Two years later and this is the first time I've ever been inside your bungalow." She gave a brittle laugh. "Doesn't that say something?"

"It says you're Ms McKendrick and I'm the overseer," he clipped off.

She swallowed on her dry throat. "May I have a cold drink if you've got it?" she asked.

"Mineral water?" He glanced back at her, wanting desperately to take her into his arms. Determined not to.

"That'll be fine." She clasped her hands together. "Well, how did you end up?" she asked when he returned. "I must know."

"How did we end up?" He put the frosted glass into her hand, his shapely mouth compressed.

"Steven, please answer me," she begged. "You know how much I care about you."

"Enough to take off with me today?" He stood staring down at her, his expression taut and challenging.

Her heart jumped. "What, on the freight plane?" *Could she, would she? What could she throw in a bag? Where would they go? Their flight from Coronation would be the talk of the Outback.*

"Yes," Steve said. "You look mighty nervous."

"But it's a stunning suggestion, isn't it, Steven?" Her sapphire eyes pleaded with him to understand.

"You'd come if you loved me."

She thought, *Is that right? Is that what I should be prepared to do?* "I don't know, Steven." She shook her head from side to side. "I just don't know." She needed a little time.

"It's okay," he replied, as if he never for a moment expected her to say yes. "I'll put you out of your misery. Cal has made the decision for me. I'm to go to Jingoll and Cash Hammond is to come here."

"What?" For a moment she thought she would burst into tears. But shouldn't she be used to hiding her feelings by now? "Jingoll is outside Alice Springs."

"So?" His heart rose a little at her evident distress.

"How do I get to see you?" she demanded emotionally. "I wanted to learn to fly the plane but Dad wouldn't hear of it. Even Cal couldn't shift him. What am I supposed to do, drive all darned day and all darned night?"

"You've got money." He shrugged, pretending indifference to her plight. "You could call up a plane just like that! Fix it with Jim Pitman today. He could fly you down to me. Stay a week or two." *To hell with it! Make it easy for her to make the break.*

"Do you love me, Steven?" she asked with her heart in

her eyes. "Or are you just a little bit *in* love with me? We don't entirely know one another."

"No, we don't," he replied soberly. He could see the way things were shaping up. Put to the test she was getting cold feet. And why not? He had no reputation to protect. *She* was Meredith McKendrick. "I should be finishing off packing," he said, just short of dismissively.

A tight hand closed over Meredith's heart. "Maybe we can meet again in a little while?" She stood up, trying unsuccessfully to pin his eyes.

"Why not? There are always rodeos, bush races, and what not."

Her head dropped. "I'm sorry, Steven. So sorry for everything." She went to move past him to the door, fighting down a storm of tears, only he suddenly caught her to him, golden eyes glittering. He forced her head back into the crook of his arm, his mouth coming down on hers. Passionate. Heated. Punishing.

When he released her she put a hand to her breast. Her heart was hammering unnaturally.

"Just something to remember me by," Steven offered tonelessly.

Steve headed almost directly south to the McKendrick holding that was situated close to the fantastically coloured McDonnell Ranges of the Red Centre. Here the landscape was as different from the tropical north as it could be. The Red Centre seemed as old as time itself, the mystique of the place amazing. Jingoll ran Brahmins, beautiful cattle crossed with the best Queensland Brahmins and, going further back, fine American Brahmin stock. Jingoll's Brahmins were well-known in the industry.

The change-over went remarkably smoothly. Steve assuming the top job of manager caused no problems what-

ever with the staff. Everyone knew he had been the overseer at the McKendrick flagship, Coronation Hill, but the
rumour was, as Cal McKendrick's man, he had been sent
to make Jingoll an even bigger outfit than it was. That was
okay by all. Steve Lockhart might be young but if he'd been
overseer on Coronation, he really knew what he was about.

Steve set about proving it from day one. The best way he
could cope was to bury himself in hard work. Work shifted
the burden of his wretchedness a little. But he thought about
her every minute of the day. Then again he had to admit
Jingoll gave him a breathing space, while he tried to think
how best to go about the difficult task of wooing an heiress which was far more a hindrance than a help. During
his first few weeks he made several trips to Alice Springs
or "The Alice" as everyone called it. The Alice almost in
the dead centre of the continent was a big supply depot for
the outlying cattle stations, mines, and aboriginal settle-
ments. In addition to being an important commercial centre
it was also an enormously popular tourist spot for visitors
from around Australia and overseas. The Alice was the
jumping-off point for the Red Centre's great monuments
and beauty spots: Uluru, Kata Tjuta, Mount Connor, the
Devil's Marbles, Rainbow Valley, King's Canyon and the
extraordinary Palm Valley, a sight Steve found staggering,
blooming as it did in all its tropical splendour in the middle
of the red desert.

On that particular day Steve having completed station
business allowed himself a couple of cold beers and a big
wedge of Mediterranean sandwich, a freshly baked round
loaf stuffed with half a dozen delicious ingredients, before
he made the long drive back to the outstation. He was sitting
at the bar counter alongside a chatty local called Pete, when
an old fellow with the long grey hair of an ancient prophet
and a matching grey beard burst through the pub doors jab-

bering something with his mouth wide-open. Despite that, his voice was so agitated, so high and reedy, most of those in the pub couldn't make out what he was carrying on about.

"What did he say?" Steve asked, not really interested. Pete was polishing off his own sandwich with gusto. It was seriously good.

"Hang on!" Pete swung around in his chair. "That's old Barney. Should be Balmy. He's a terminal alcoholic. Has been for the last forty years." Barney was still into his high decibel hollering but it took a moment for everyone to work out what he was on about. By the time everyone did, the humming bar inhabited by tourists, locals, and stockmen having a day off in town, shut down to a stunned silence.

"Struth!" said Pete as though someone important had just died without warning. As, indeed, they had.

The pub owner, ponderously moving his huge frame and smoothing back his remaining strands of sandy hair, came from behind the bar. "News is just in, folks," he announced. "No need to mind Barney though he got it right for once. I have to tell you Gavin Lancaster, his son, the station overseer and another passenger, not yet identified, have been killed in transit to Darwin. Their Cessna with Lancaster at the controls went down some thirty kilometres north-east of the ranges. Apparently there was no emergency call, nothing. The wreckage was spotted by the Flying Doctor on a routine flight. So there it is! Lancaster is dead, when most of us thought he'd live to be a hundred."

Pete immediately swung to face Steven, studying him with unblinking light blue eyes almost too big for their sockets. "God, mate, that's your dad, isn't it?" he burst out. "Isn't Lancaster your dad? Hell, you're the living spit of him. I spotted it right away. I tell yah, mate, I'm shocked. *Shocked!*"

Steve didn't say anything. He couldn't trust himself to

open his mouth even if he could find his voice. Instead he had the urge to bolt. As always he had been aware of the curious stares coming his way ever since he had entered the pub. It happened all the time. What could he possibly tell this guy, Pete, he didn't already know?

"Do you think there are things like justice in this world, mate?" Pete put the question to him in a philosophical kind of way.

"What's your point?" Finally Steve managed to find his tongue, though even to him it sounded like a croak.

"My point, Stevo, is this!" said Pete. "And remember you got it from me. They've always said Lancaster was scared of nobody—but maybe he was a little bit scared of the Almighty? I know I am. It could well be Lancaster decided to do the right thing at long last and put you in his will."

Steve wrenched up a sad, bitter laugh. "He didn't know me." He stood up wanting to get out of the pub as fast as possible. For one thing everyone was now staring his way. That's what happened when you had the Lancaster brand on your forehead.

"I dunno, mate," Pete said, shaking his head, "my feeling is you're being a bit hard on yourself. I recognised you right off. Didn't say nuthin' then, o'course. Didn't want a punch in the nose. Only jokin', mate. You look a real good guy. Different from old Lancaster, God rest his soul," he added piously. "My bet is, you might be hearin' from his lawyers yet."

"*You've* got a better chance of hearing from them, Pete," Steve said, and moved off.

When he got back to Jingoll homestead, several voice messages were waiting for him. All of them related to the crash of the Lancasters' plane. The news had circulated through

the Outback with the speed of a high-priority cyclone. One
message was from Cal saying he was sorry so many lives
had been lost. No more. The family would be attending the
Lancaster funerals as a matter of course. These Outback
courtesies and marks of respect were understood.

*Well, the high and mighty McKendricks might be there,
but I sure as hell won't,* Steve thought, though the news had
powerfully upset him. Lost lives he supposed. Light aircraft coming down in the Outback was a fact of life. One of
the dead was his biological father, another his half brother
Brad. Even so he wouldn't be attending any funeral. The
family had never had any use for him. He had no use for
them, either.

But there he was wrong.

Once again Fate had made the decision to step in.

The day of the funerals was one of scorching heat with
banks of grape-coloured clouds shot through with streaks
of living green piled up on the horizon. No one took much
notice. Outback skies could turn on truly ominous displays
without one drop of rain falling. The heat and the threatening sky didn't prevent mourners from all over the country making their pilgrimage to the Channel Country in the
extreme South West pocket of the State of Queensland. This
was the stronghold of the cattle kings. The select band of
families and pastoral companies ran the nation's greatest
concentration of beef cattle in their unique, riverine desert. The Lancaster fortress, *Euroka*, an aboriginal word
for *blazing sun*, was the flagship, but the Lancaster chain
like the McKendrick empire spread its life lines through
adjoining States.

Gavin Lancaster's two daughters, Catherine and Sarah,
both in their early forties, tall, elegant women, stood tear-
less, but their faces spoke of controlled grief. Standing with

them at the graveside was their half brother, Steven. It was Catherine, the elder sister, who had persuaded Steven to attend. She had been adamant he should finally take his rightful place by their side. It was something Steve found enormously touching and, yes, *healing*. The family resemblance between all three siblings was so strong it made it much easier for them to identify with one another. The husbands were unable to attend so Steven stood in for them both. One was a brilliant economist at present a speaker at an overseas conference; the other a cardiologist with a very tight schedule.

Much had happened in the week since the fatal plane crash. The man who appeared to have ignored Steve's existence for all of his life had left him by virtue of his elder half brother's death a sixty percent controlling interest in Lancaster Holdings. It had been a shock on a monumental scale. Steve had gone on to learn from the family's high-powered lawyer, who strangely enough had looked and acted more like a kindly parish priest, that Gavin Lancaster had secretly supported him for most of his life. Lancaster had made it possible for him to attend his prestigious school. Lancaster, too, working behind the scenes, had been instrumental in those early days, when Steve was fresh out of school, in getting him placed on a top station.

There were more shocks in store. Steve learned Lancaster had kept copies of his school reports and his sporting achievements along with a whole batch of photographs. Steve in his wildest imaginings had never conceived of such a thing. Looking through the photographs, he'd had to swallow many times on the hard lump in his throat. So the man Steve had spent most of his life despising had looked out for him all along, though Gavin Lancaster had chosen to live his life without his *other* son.

Perhaps his wife wouldn't have tolerated me beneath their roof, Steve thought. Who would know?

Steve could hear the Lancaster lawyer's voice in his head. *"I never truly understood why your father did what he did, Steven. You're obviously a fine young man, but he tried to make up for it in the end. You won't have any problem whatever with the daughters. They're women of depth and character. Both married now to outstanding men with no connection to the industry. Their interests lie elsewhere, so you'll have a free hand to run Euroka. Cal McKendrick speaks very highly of you, so you're up to it. Needless to say my firm is ready to support you in any way we can."* He had smiled encouragingly as he took off his glasses. *"Let me be the first to offer my congratulations. It's your father's wish that you be known from henceforth as Steven Lancaster. And perfectly right it is, too!"*

Rags to riches! Steve thought. But riches couldn't be measured against the lifelong abandonment of a father. So far as he was concerned they could take it all away in exchange for the chance of having belonged.

Afterwards at the reception at Euroka homestead, Steven found he couldn't have been treated better. Amazing what being handed a grand inheritance could do, he thought cynically. Some of the mourners even greeted him with a touch of reverence. Overnight a lot of power had been put into his hands. He and his half sisters made their way around the two large reception rooms briefly greeting people with a few words and a handshake. It might have been kind of crazy, but Steve felt he was supporting Cate and Sarah, far more than they were supporting him. But then it was obvious they had loved their father no matter what his faults and they had certainly loved their brother who, they had told

Steve, had been overwhelmed by the thought of his future responsibilities.

"You see, Brad wasn't a cattleman," Cate had told him with tears in her eyes. *"The thought of stepping into Dad's shoes used to terrify him. Brad really wanted a quiet life. Now he's got it. None quieter than the grave."*

Steve turned to find himself face-to-face with the McKendricks. To anyone watching—and a great many were—it would have appeared the Lancaster heir was being comforted and consoled by close family friends.

Ewan McKendrick even got a little carried away with his words of reconciliation, Jocelyn McKendrick offered Steve her sincere condolences when she really meant congratulations. "I'm sure Catherine and Sarah are going to depend on you a lot!" She gave him a little encouraging pat on the arm.

Now I'm *one of them*! Steve thought, just so tired of all the hypocrisy.

Cal and Gina came to him, saying exactly the kind of thing he wanted to hear. When they moved off he was left alone with Meredith.

"Isn't life amazing?" He spoke with great irony.

"Maybe that's why it's so interesting?" she said, staring up at him, soaking him in. From somewhere he had found a beautifully tailored black suit, pristine white business shirt, obligatory black tie. Probably one of his half sisters had organised it, getting it in from the city. It fitted perfectly. He looked extraordinarily handsome and strangely daunting. Almost another person. "How are you *really*?" she asked, striving not to feel rebuffed.

"Well, most importantly I'm *rich*. Even your mother and father are prepared to accept me. Let bygones be bygones and all the rest." He glanced over her head to where Cal and

Gina were standing at the centre of a small group. "Cal and his Gina make a beautiful couple. Where's young Robbie?"

"He's at home with Rosa and Uncle Ed. After ten years on his own, Uncle Ed looks set to remarry. Rosa has reminded him of all the lovely things he had forgotten."

"Good. I like your uncle Ed. He deserves to rediscover some happiness. Cal and Gina working things out?" Gina, as if sensing she was being spoken about, suddenly turned to give them a little smile and a wave.

Meredith waved back. "They *appear* to be, yet I feel both of them are struggling with a lot of hurt. We've since found out there was a conspiracy going on to keep them apart. My mother and my aunt Lorinda, I'm sorry to say."

"Why doesn't that surprise me?"

His tone stung.

"You'll be getting your invitation to the wedding," Meredith continued, very uncomfortable beneath his searing gaze.

"I expect I will. *Now.*"

"I know how you must feel." It was a great strain being with him in this mood.

"You don't know how I feel, Meredith." The sight of her was playing havoc with his nerves. He wanted to haul her into his arms and scream at her, as well. "How could you? You look lovely, by the way. Black suits you." With her long arched neck and her hair pulled back into some sort of roll she was as graceful as a swan.

Meredith stared over to where her brother and Gina were standing. "Cal wants to take us home, Steven," she said, aware of the flight plans. "I made a mistake coming here. The family is represented. I'm sorry."

"You *didn't* make a mistake, Meredith," he said crisply, his manner changing. "We have to talk."

She looked up at him, startled. "About what? You're in a strange mood."

"Why wouldn't I be? I've had so many shocks this past week I scarcely know how to handle myself."

"You look perfectly in command to me. Your half sisters genuinely care about you. I've spoken to both of them."

"They're lovely women." His expression momentarily softened. "I'll never forget it was they who approached me. Far too much of my life has been wasted."

"You can change all that, Steven," she said gently.

"Sure!" His tone was falsely expansive. "I have the solution to all my problems. I have money, position, the running of one of the country's legendary cattle stations. I can even get the girl I want. I can't buy her, of course. She's got money of her own. But I'm pretty sure if I talk to her dad, he'll give me the green light."

Her hands were trembling. "Do you think that's all you need, my father's approval?" She threw up her gently determined chin.

"Meredith, did you think I was talking about *you*?" he asked suavely. "Wait and see if I don't make the most eligible list like Cal. There won't even be a scandal. The media will turn it all into a biblical tale. Prodigal son comes home. All anyone cares about is *money* and who's got it!"

She pressed her palms together to steady her hands. "On the contrary, *I* don't care about money, Steven. I don't think I even care about you any more. You're eaten up with bitterness."

He shook his head at her, a demonic sparkle in his golden eyes. "While *you're* a rich young woman who hasn't yet learned to stand on her own two feet."

Sparks rose into the air around them. "I'm surprised you saw anything in me in the first place," she said. "I'll say goodbye, Steven. I hope you have a good life. I mean that."

"How sweet!" He surprised her by catching her wrist, locking his fingers about it. "You leave now and you'll never see me again." He bent to her, speaking very quietly.

The strangeness of his manner was undermining her. "Surely you can't be asking me to stay?"

"I'm *telling* you to stay." Now his voice was full of authority. "Did you really think you could get away from me as easily as that?" He drew her so close to his side, its significance couldn't be lost on the room.

"You're mad!" There was no way she could break away without causing a scene.

"That's too ridiculous. I'm nothing of the kind. Pop along now and tell the family you're going to stay over. Tell them I have lots to tell you. Tell them your new life begins *now*."

It was inevitable at some point Cal and Gina would encounter Kym. Sad occasion or not Cal could see the simmering jealousy just below the surface of Kym's murmured greetings, so civil and proper. Cal knew she took not the slightest pleasure in meeting Gina, but she was doing a fairly good job of hiding it. Though not from Gina, he fancied. Gina was extraordinarily intuitive. Kym was busy assessing her from head to toe, working very hard to find a flaw.

You won't find one, Cal thought, wishing all the hurt would seep out of him, believing it would take time. His big question was, why when Gina had found herself pregnant, did she not try to contact him? Even had he been engaged to Kym—never mind that hadn't happened—but even *if*— he would have broken his engagement and married her. He had put the question to her heavy heartedly and she had recoiled.

"My worst fear was you would take my baby from me."

"How could you possibly have thought such a thing?"

"Because I was scared. Scared of you. Scared of your family. Why are you trying to blame me?"

The sad truth was, he *did*.

As for Kym, desperately unhappy after the break-up of her engagement to Cal, she now found herself desperately unhappy once more. It showed in her paleness which she hoped would be interpreted as sadness. She had truly believed—with Jocelyn's encouragement—she only had to bide her time and Cal would come to his senses, accepting she was the best possible choice for him. Now he had presented them all with the object of his mad passion from years back. Not only that, a ready-made heir, who according to a besotted Jocelyn was "the image of Cal." In one fell swoop Cal McKendrick, the man Kym had fixated on for so many good years of her life, was lost to her. She had ceased to exist for him. She could see it in his eyes as they rested on her, the outsider.

Even as she entertained such thoughts, Kym was murmuring to this woman who had stolen her heart's desire from her. "I do hope we're going to be friends, Gina. May I wish you both much joy." It was a lovely little speech and it tripped sweetly off her tongue. She would *hate* it to be barred from Coronation Hill. Hate it still more not to retain Cal as her friend.

"So that was your ex-fiancée?" Gina remarked quietly as Kym drifted away. "She still loves you." Her voice softened with pity. Gina knew all too well the pain of loss.

Cal couldn't be drawn. He had caught sight of some people he wanted Gina to meet. "Kym will find the right guy to make her happy," he said. "I certainly hope so. She's wasted years of her life on me." He began to steer Gina across the crowded room.

First, Kym has to forget you, Gina thought. She doubted she and Kym would ever become friends. Thank God for Meredith! It made Gina happy to know she had Meredith supporting her. Their friendship had progressed rapidly. Meredith was a lovely person. She deserved happiness, a full life. Gina had the presentiment all roads led to Steven Lockhart, or Steven Lancaster as he was now known. She'd had to bite down hard on her lip when Cal's parents had offered Steven their condolences. The acquisition of land and a proud pioneering name really did make extraordinary things happen, she thought.

CHAPTER EIGHT

By MIDAFTERNOON the last of the mourners had left the station in their private planes, charter planes, helicopters, trucks, one bus and all manner of four-wheel drives. Catherine and Sarah were among them. The sisters had spent a few hours of the afternoon discussing Lancaster family matters with Steven, grief-stricken about the deaths of their father and brother, but enormously relieved, even jubilant at the back of their minds a Lancaster would take over the running of Euroka and its several outstations.

"Lord knows what would have happened had Fate not brought you into the family frame, Steven," Catherine said.

Both women were anxious to return to their children; each had two girls, not present at the funerals, because the sisters hadn't deemed it advisable to uproot them from school, and if the truth be known, their father and brother had shown little interest in any of them. Both sisters put that down to the fact they were all girls. It was a sad fact of life—one that Meredith could attest to—some fathers had little use for their girl children.

"Fortunately *our* girls' fathers adore them," Cate assured them.

Steve's response was immediate and sincere. "Well, I want to meet them at the earliest opportunity."

"Oh, they'll love you!" Sarah had turned to him, blinking tears out of her golden-brown eyes.

Another prophecy that turned out perfectly true.

Meredith and Steve returned to the empty homestead in a near silence. Both of them had been treading around one another almost on tiptoe. It was amazing how greatly humans tortured themselves, suffering in silence, often unnecessarily, devising strategies for containing emotions, strangely frightened to reveal what was really in their hearts lest they be met by rejection. Love was such a terrible ache.

Meredith went to stand at the balustrade staring out at the horizon. The sky was piling higher, ever higher incandescent storm clouds, great plumes of purple, indigo, black, slivers of silver. Their depths shot through with the crimson rays of the sinking sun. It was a fantastic sight against the burning red of the pyramids of sand that lay to the north and the south-west of the station. The mirage was abroad, busy playing its usual tricks. Silhouettes of tall, slender trees stood out amid the wavy silver lines. Little stick people ran about in the somnolent heat and in the roughest driest areas blue lagoons glittered like polished mirrors, overshadowed by thickets of palms. These were the phantom pools and water holes the explorers of old had been tricked into trekking towards with no hope of ever reaching their destination. If only they had met up with some aboriginal tribe, Meredith thought. Aboriginals knew the exact location of wells and springs in the most forbidding country. She knew of many pioneer lives that had been saved by the kindness of the tribal people, including her own family.

The heat had increased not diminished with the closing hours of the day. It was difficult to believe such an extraordinary celestial display might not amount to a powerful electrical storm. *At least it might clear the air,* she thought.

Doug Winstone, the station overseer, was making his way towards the homestead. He had a curious rolling gait, the result of a serious injury some years back when an enraged bull had gored his leg.

"I'll go and have a few words with him," Steven called.

"Righto, and please tell him to thank Julie once again." Meredith lifted a hand to Doug who doffed his dusty hat.

"Will do."

It was Doug's wife, Julie, who had cooked and cleaned for the homestead over a number of years, but she and Doug had never been asked to take up residence in any part of a very large house. Instead, Julie had gone back and forth from the overseer's bungalow. It was she and the other station wives who had served at the funeral reception, although Cate had ordered in the mountain of sandwiches, biscuits and small cakes that had disappeared beneath the mourners' famished onslaught.

She watched the two men talking earnestly, no doubt discussing job priorities. She, herself, had been greeted most respectfully as if everyone on the station expected that she and Steven would make a match of it after an appropriate period of mourning. They looked an odd couple, Steven and Doug. Steven so tall and young man lean, Doug short of stature, top heavy, with a bull neck, powerful shoulders and a barrel chest. He and Steven had reached an understanding right away. It showed in the body language. These were two men who already trusted each other.

She moved back from the balustrade that badly needed re-painting. The verandah wrapped the lower floor but not the top floor. She thought that a shame but it could easily be added on. The homestead was a mix of Regency and Victorian architecture. It had symmetry about it, but it was definitely not a welcoming place. All houses had an aura and this house badly needed its aura changing. It was an

unremarkable building compared to Coronation's homestead, but she was certain it could be turned into something
far more impressive. The size was there. The interior rooms
were all large, with high ceilings, and well proportioned.
A lot of charm could be added to the exterior simply with
adding some decorative details; certainly a repainting of
the shutters on the large sash windows and all the timber-
work, columns, balustrading, fretwork, etc. The broad,
canopied verandah was very attractive, but the timber columns needed to be wreathed in flowering vines, maybe a
beautiful violet-blue to go with the shutters that could be
painted darkest green. She knew *exactly* what had to be
done, even if she could see it would be a big ongoing job.

They had seen Cate and Sarah off at the airstrip. Neither
sister had appeared the least bit surprised she should stay
back with Steven. There was only one possible reason for
that, Meredith thought. They believed what Doug and Julie
Winstone believed; she and Steven were lovers. Her breath
came sharp and jagged at the very thought. She felt herself
on the very brink of a major turning point in her life, even
if it looked as though the two of them were in retreat. It was
a travesty of her true feelings.

The two men concluded their conversation. Doug tipped
his hat to her once again. She responded with another wave,
while Steven strode back to her. How she admired the wide
line of his shoulders, the narrow waist, the lean hips.

"What exactly am I doing here?" she asked him as they
moved into the unattractive entrance hall when such an
area should always be inviting. It was long and fairly narrow with a timber staircase that led to the upper floor set
just outside the drawing room. Something else that needed
relocating.

"I would have thought that was obvious." Steven spoke
with a false nonchalance, thinking all this past week he had

been moving in a dream. He, who had always been on the outside, was in overnight. "You're keeping me company. Otherwise you would have gone home with your family."

"I suppose!" She answered coolly enough, when she was all but delirious with anticipation. She was, after all, quite, quite alone with him and she had taken steps to ensure she was safe.

"So this is Euroka homestead," Steve muttered, as they moved into the drawing room. "It's rather a scary old place, isn't it?" He lifted his handsome dark head, staring about him. "That was my dominant impression. It could even be haunted."

Meredith couldn't control a shiver. "It does seem to have a coldness at its heart." She too began to look around her, making changes inside her head. It wouldn't be all that hard to make the room look more natural and inviting simply by pulling down the heavy velvet curtains. Velvet in the Outback! She would introduce cool colours for a start. Maybe citron and white? The drawing room was furnished with a number of fine antique pieces—indeed, to Meredith's eye it looked like a drawing room of the Victorian period—but the spacious room had an air of neglect about it. It even looked dusty though there wasn't a speck of actual dust in sight. Julie Winstone and her helpers had made sure of that. But a home was not complete without the woman at its heart.

Steven's voice broke into her reverie. "No woman!" he said, echoing her own thoughts. "No woman's touch! How long ago was it the girls' mother died? They didn't say and I didn't like to ask."

"Quite early I think. Cate and Sarah are in their early forties. I think their mother died when they were still in their twenties." Meredith fingered the heavy velvet curtains, wanting to give them a good yank. They were stiff with age. "I know both of them married young."

"Probably broke their necks to leave home," Steve observed dryly. "Hell, this is a terrible place. It looks like it's been caught in a time warp."

"It's *your* place now," Meredith reminded him. "Men left alone generally let things slide. The house is shabby, but that can be easily fixed."

"It's not only shabby. It's unnaturally quiet."

Indeed, the only sound was the soft fall of their footsteps on the massive Persian rug. That at least was splendid, all jewelled medallions and floral arabesques. "It knows one era has ended and another has begun," Meredith hazarded, into the deathly quiet.

"Maybe the house doesn't approve of me." Steven had caught sight of his reflection in a tall gilt-framed mirror. It seemed to him he had changed. Maybe it was the sombre funeral clothes Cate had flown in for him. He had never owned such clothes in his life. "Have I changed or is it just me?" He turned to Meredith, a strikingly handsome young man who now had a chance at achieving some measure of greatness.

She didn't have to consider. "Yes, you have."

"In what way?" He didn't know if he liked the sound of that.

"You're a cattle baron now and you're behaving accordingly. Or to put it another way you've been given the opportunity to be your own man."

The corners of his mouth compressed. "It might come as a shock to you, Ms McKendrick, but I thought I *was*."

"Oh, please, I didn't mean to offend you." Meredith gave a little grimace. "You know what I mean. Money gives one confidence if nothing else."

"It hasn't given confidence to *you*."

"You want to hurt me back?" Her intensely blue eyes met his.

"I suppose I do." He shrugged, slanting her a half smile. "A little anyway. This place is unnerving me. How am I going to make a home here?"

"You will." Meredith continued to gaze around her. She might have been an interior designer he had called in with all the answers at her fingertips. "Some pieces should be kept, others put into storage. You need new custom-made sofas, new curtains, a cool colour scheme. Maybe the sash windows knocked out and replaced with French doors. One or two Asian pieces wouldn't go astray and an important painting. I like the mix of different styles, don't you? This is just one of those awful days."

"Isn't it just!" He sighed deeply. "I've buried a father and a half brother I never knew. Wouldn't you have thought my half brother at least would have tried to meet me?"

Something in the way he said it brought her perilously close to tears. "You've heard enough about Gavin Lancaster to know he was a strange, hard man, Steven. I'm certain he had great power over his family. He probably ordered them not to make contact. Your existence was no secret, but he had decided to shut you out." Meredith half turned away, quite upset over it.

"At least I now know Cate and Sarah had wanted to meet me." Steven spoke in a gentler voice. "I'm most grateful for that. But things could have been so different. No use talking about that now, of course."

"Fate has stepped in," Meredith said. "You were always meant to come home."

His expression was disbelieving. "You're not saying Euroka is home?" That idea struck him as downright peculiar.

Meredith nodded. "You can't damn your father for everything. At the end he gave you back your heritage. Your job is to keep it safe."

Steve picked up a smallish bronze sculpture of a horse and rider, balancing it in the palm of his hand. It was a work of art. "He didn't know he was going to die. He didn't know his son and heir would die with him."

"Fate, Steven," Meredith repeated. "We have to leave it at that."

They were at the far end of the drawing room, moving into the adjoining room when Steve asked, "Are you sure there's not someone following us?" The hairs on the back of his neck were standing up.

"You've got a lot of imagination for a tough-minded man," Meredith countered briskly, when she really felt like grabbing his hand.

"And I'm not on my own. *You* can feel it, too," he accused her. He knew if he touched her he wouldn't let her go.

"I wish I couldn't," Meredith confessed. "I don't fancy sleeping on my own."

"Who said you had to?" He gave her a down-bent golden glance. He was overwhelmed by her loveliness yet he felt an immense pressure on him to behave well. He didn't lack commitment, but the last thing he wanted to do was panic her.

"*I* said. I'm here on the understanding you keep your distance." Deliberately, she walked ahead of him, in retreat again. They were in a smaller room, a sort of parlour. It was enormously gloomy even with the lights on. There were a number of portraits hung on the walls around the room and she went to study them one by one.

"Not a one of them seems happy!" Steve observed, looking over her shoulder. He had the urge to place his hands on her silk clad shoulders, to bend his mouth to her beautiful swan's neck and kiss it but he kept his hands and his mouth to himself.

"They do look a touch subdued," Meredith remarked. "You've inherited the family face."

"Meredith, I've heard that for years and years," he told her in a satirical voice.

"Well, it's a very handsome face. It could have been ugly."

"That wouldn't have worried me if I'd had a *name*."

She moved on to the portrait of a very fragile-looking lady in a white silk morning gown. "It was all very sad, Steven, but you've been acknowledged now."

"Yes, indeed!" he agreed dryly. "My new status has certainly made a huge difference to your mother and father. Let's get a glass of something."

"I wouldn't mind a glass of wine," Meredith said, all her nerves jumping. She knew she couldn't count on herself not to surrender to anything he wanted. Indeed, she felt her entire tingling body belonged to him. Wasn't that proof perfect she loved him? "I don't expect there's a wine cellar."

"This isn't Coronation Hill, Ms McKendrick," he pointed out suavely.

"There might be, you never know." She sounded hopeful. "Let's take a good look upstairs before we go in search of one. I want to take this dress off anyway. It's depressing me. Sarah left me a couple of things to tide me over until I go home *tomorrow*," she stressed. "We're pretty much of a size."

His glance swept her. It held so much heat it sizzled her to the bone. "Sarah's actually thin," he said a little worriedly. Sarah was, indeed, too thin. "But you're very slender and lithe. You stand very straight. I like that. But I know what you mean. I'll change myself, then we can hunt up some food. The piles of sandwiches didn't take long to disappear and I had nothing."

"Neither did I."

"Nevertheless funerals evidently make a lot of other people hungry."

"And thirsty," Meredith added, thinking it hadn't just been tea and coffee that had quickly been downed. Whiskey decanters had been drained.

"I don't like this staircase," Steve said, not able to prevent himself from admiring her legs. High heels on a woman were infinitely sexy.

"Neither do I," she said, not about to let him in on the idea she had for relocating the staircase. She had her reasons for keeping him guessing. In fact, she had to confess to herself she was rather enjoying it, even on such a sombre day.

"So which bedroom do you want?" Steve asked, as they moved along the wide corridor.

Meredith spoke up so casually they might have been cousins. "I'll take Cate's. It's been aired and made up. Julie has been so good. She's quietly seen to a lot of things." She walked into the large old-fashioned bedroom that looked towards the front of the house. A verandah to walk out onto would have been perfect, but that would have to wait.

What am I thinking, for goodness' sake! She was actually redecorating the house in her head.

"What about you?" she asked airily, stepping back to admire the embroidered silk coverlet on the bed.

"I think I'll just head across the hall." He turned his crow-black head in that direction.

"To Sarah's room?"

"I don't want to get *too* far away," he told her with a mocking smile. "You're not mentioning you're damned nervous, but I know you are."

"It's an unfamiliar house," she replied, defensively. "Moreover, one expects some kind of nervousness on such a day." In reality she was spooked.

He nodded, beginning to walk away. He might pretend to be at ease but all his senses were doing a slow burn. "All the signs augur for a thunderstorm during the night. If you're frightened you don't have to wait for an invitation to come over."

"Sorry, Steven," she called after him. "I come from the Territory, remember?"

He paused at the door, his face the face of the portraits downstairs. "It might shock you to learn, Ms McKendrick, the electrical storms here are even worse. Now, I'm going to change out of this undertaker gear. Knock on my door when you're ready to go in search of the wine cellar. Let's hope Julie has done us a service leaving us some food."

Left alone Meredith looked quickly at what Sarah had left her. A pretty loose dress in an ink-blue and white pattern, a sort of trapeze dress with short ruffled sleeves and a double ruffle at the hem. That would do nicely, lovely and cool. There was a pair of navy flatties a half a size too big but she was glad of them. She rarely wore high heels; a pink cotton nightdress, pintucked and embroidered with tiny grub roses, matching robe, very virginal. Both sisters were easy to like. She saw how life might have been hard for them without their mother, and knowing they had a half brother somewhere they had been forbidden to meet.

Meredith went to the solid mahogany door and closed it, without actually turning the lock. Would she forget to lock it tonight?

"I'll be damned if this isn't the best room in the house," Steven was saying, his surprised glance sweeping the large cellar with its attractive rustic ambience. The ceiling was dark beamed, the walls stone, as was the floor with a wide stone archway dividing the wine storage area with its long rows of racks from a seating, dining area if needs be. There were two big leather armchairs in front of a fireplace obviously well used—the desert could grow very cold at night— and a long refectory table with eight Jacobean-style chairs set around it. There was even a strikingly realistic rural oil painting of a herd of cattle fording a coolibah-lined creek.

"Someone spent a lot of time here," Meredith observed, hunting at the bottom of the canvas for the name of the artist.

"So what do we want?"

"White for me," Meredith said, shivering a little because the cellar was so much cooler than the house. "A sauvignon Blanc."

"A sauvignon Blanc it is." Steve picked a bottle up, passing it to her while he hunted up a Shiraz for himself. Maybe there was a steak or two in the fridge? Euroka was a cattle station after all.

No steaks, but a leg of ham, bacon, plenty of eggs, cream, milk, cheese, a basket full of bright red tomatoes, a brown paper bag full of mushrooms; and in the bread bin a loaf of sour-dough bread, obviously freshly baked.

"Looks like ham and eggs," Meredith said. "We can pretend it's breakfast."

"Ah, to think we really *will* be having breakfast together," Steve said, mockery in his expression. But the emotion was there. "Look at you, a little housewife!" Meredith had tied a clean apron around her waist to protect Cate's dress.

"Do you think you can get away with this because we're on our own?" she asked, briefly lifting her eyes to him. He was wearing a red T-shirt with his jeans and he looked extraordinarily vivid, vibrating with a physical energy that was like a force field around him. It was very impressive.

"Get away with what exactly?" he asked, though he knew precisely what she meant. He was goading her. He didn't want to, but he was.

"Your resentments are evident, Steven," she said, but went no further. The atmosphere between them was inflammatory enough.

He shrugged. "You're better off with me than at home, I'd say."

Meredith didn't acknowledge that, either. She took six large eggs out of their carton. "Shall I scramble them? There's plenty of cream."

"Are there no ends to your talents, Ms McKendrick?" He tipped out the mushrooms that needed a wipe over. "Scrambled will be fine. Why don't you have a glass of the red while you wait for your wine to chill?"

"I think I'd drink anything at the moment." She gave a faint sigh. The strain was telling on both of them. She began to break the eggs into a bowl, adding the cream.

"I'll find us some glasses. *Nice* glasses." Steve hunted through the numerous cupboards before he hit the mother lode, crystal. He filled two glasses and put one beside Meredith's hand.

"Thank you." Meredith took a good sip of the wine. It was ruby-red and very good.

A sudden gust of wind blew strongly through the back door, pungent with bush incense. Steve went to close it. "I know we'll get rain," he said. "I just know it."

Lightning was a dazzling white illumination, searing the retinas of her eyes. Meredith hid her head beside a stack of pillows. She could have pulled the curtains but she had no desire whatever to sleep in the pitch-dark. The bedroom was oddly cold. Could she risk getting up and finding a blanket? Why not? Steven wasn't going to come to her. She had to bow low before him. The truth was he hadn't forgiven her for her apparent rejection.

You'd come if you loved me.

And if you don't, I'll disappear out of your life.

That had been the implication. What had she done? She'd waffled on about meeting up again in a little while. That had been a mistake. Now, apart from ensuring she had stayed with him, he was acting as cool as you please.

"Good night, Meredith!"

"Good night, Steven." She was far from happy, but she managed to sound as cool as he.

Both of them had been hungry, leaving not a morsel on their plates. There was ice-cream to follow; she found a tin of peaches. They finished the wine and then Steven made coffee. Afterwards they talked a good deal about running a big operation, something with which Meredith was well acquainted. She made a number of suggestions that he picked up on immediately, saying they were excellent and facetiously offering her a job. They talked about what would be expected of him, who might replace him on Jingoll, anything and everything except their personal relationship and where it was going, if anywhere. It was a huge jump from desire to consummation. She realised she wasn't going to be allowed to get away with that perceived humiliation.

Surely he realised she couldn't have turned her back on everyone and eloped with him on the spot? She had obligations. It would have taken her a little time to put her affairs in order, then pack her bags if that was what he wanted; not that she didn't understand where he was coming from. Steven had lacked real commitment from childhood. His family had virtually abandoned him by the time he reached adolescence. What a blow that must have been! What a heartache for a young boy! When he had suggested she go with him to Jingoll, a *yes* answer had been crucial. In some ultrasensitive corner of his mind she had failed him, even if he could rationalise the difficulties of her position.

Then there was her parents' embarrassing back flip. Who could blame him if he was contemptuous of that? Surely he couldn't think his change of fortune had had any influence on her? All her adult life she had kept herself very much under control. She had been waiting for the right moment to make her move. She had, in fact, been working steadily towards it when Fate stepped in.

Around three in the morning the rain advanced from the north like a large army on the march. Meredith heard it coming minutes before it actually arrived. Then when it did, the storm broke with ferocity, a driving deluge that changed direction within seconds as the wind chopped this way and that. Now it was pelting through the open casement windows, whipping up the curtains that went into a wild dance.

Meredith turned on a bedside light, then sprang out of bed, but by the time she got to the windows the rain was lashing the bedroom floor. Half blinded, she managed to get one window down without much trouble, apart from being drenched—indeed, the flimsy nightgown was almost ripped from her body—but the sash on the middle window abruptly broke as she was lowering it. It came crashing down with fragments of glass flying like steel chips.

Instantly she jumped back before the chips could stab her, curling up her bare toes against the broken glass that now lay on the floor.

"Meredith?"

It was Steven banging on the door, his voice charged with anxiety.

"It's open!"

He burst into the room, shirtless, his jeans pulled on in obvious haste, zipped but not buttoned. She could see the low line of his navy hipsters. "Don't move!" he ordered, taking in the situation at a glance.

"You've got bare feet, too," she warned him, rain all over her face and in her eyes.

He yanked up a cushion and swished it a few times over an area of the wet floor. Then he pitched it into a corner. One armed he lifted her away and carried her that way, back into the centre of the room. "You're soaking wet."

"I *know*. So are you!" His black hair, his bronze skin and his upper body were glistening. Yet he felt warm, whereas she was chilled.

"Hang on, I'll get a few towels." He rushed to turn on the lights in the bathroom, but she went after him, her wet nightgown draped to her body like a second skin.

A few seconds more and she was swaddled in a large bath towel while he took a smaller one to her hair. "You'd better get out of that nightgown."

"*Excuse me*, not while you're looking!" She spoke huskily from behind the towel he was so energetically wielding.

"Then I'll turn away."

He did, throwing down the towel and turning his wide bare back.

"What are we going to do about the rain pouring in?" she asked, pulling the nightgown over her head in a kind of frenzy. Her heart was beating much too fast. She knotted the pink towel around her like a sarong, feeling incredibly nervous but her whole body aroused.

"We'll have to pray the storm passes over quickly or the wind changes. Or I can rig up something. Can I turn around now?"

"Yes." She had never been more conscious of her own skin.

"Actually I could see you in the mirror."

She found that so electrifying her whole body broke out in a fabulous flush of excitement.

"Only joking," he murmured, his fingers reaching out to tidy her tumbled hair.

"Then I'm not amused."

"Neither am I. I've never felt less like laughing in my life." His eyes dropped the length of her body, and as he did so, his handsome face picked up a sharp shadow. "Your foot is bleeding."

"Is it?" She hadn't been aware of any cut or sting.

"Let me take a look," he said with concern. "Sit on the chair."

"Aren't we're supposed to be fixing the window?" She knew where all this was going but she wasn't about to stop it even for a tornado.

"I'll fix it when the rain stops. Right now I want to take a look at your foot."

"I don't remember standing on any glass." How could she when she was concentrated on him? The bright light cast a mosaic of glittering jet on his hair, the whorls on his chest, the dark gold of his face, the skin of his shoulders, his strong arms and his sculpted torso. Who could blame her for feeling such piercing desire?

"You must have." He balanced her narrow foot in the palm of his hand. "It's not bad, just a bit of blood." He reached around for a box of tissues that were sitting on the counter. "I'll hold it until the bleeding stops." He glanced up at her, glittering sparks in his eyes. "You know, your toes are as pretty as your hands."

It might have been the most thrilling compliment she had ever received because she was instantly on fire. "Not a lot of people know that." She spoke shakily, finding the sensation of her foot resting in his hand incredibly erotic. She could even hear her heart banging furiously above the wild orchestration of the storm. It seemed to her to be passing over the roof in a dipping rush before swinging away.

He lifted her foot higher and pressed his mouth to her high instep. Then he began to lick it, curling his tongue over her soft skin down to her toes.

"Steven!" A moan came from the back of her arched throat.

"God, you're beautiful!" He said it in such a tender voice she couldn't help it. She burst into tears.

"Meredith!" His expression so frankly sensual, changed to concern. "You're all right? You're okay?"

She let her head fall forwards onto his shoulder, her breathing deepening. "I've missed you. Oh, God, how I've missed you! I want you back."

"And I want *you* back." He rose from his haunches, gathering her close up against him. "Tell me you love me. I'll never let you go otherwise."

She sank against his marvellous lean body, letting his chest hair graze her cheek. The pleasure she felt at being back in his arms was tremendous. "That's all right! I'm happy here." She gave a voluptuous sigh, pierced through with love.

"But I want to take you back to bed. *My* bed." His eyes had turned very dark with emotion. "You can't stay here anyway."

She lifted her face to him, blue eyes overbright, her hair in riotous disarray. "You're saying you want to sleep with me?"

"That's not the worst of it. I'm *going to*!" His gaze travelled down over her smooth shoulders to the cleft between her breasts barely concealed as the pink towel kept dipping lower and lower. "Surely you're overdressed in that?" he asked huskily.

Yearning poured into her. She no longer felt the need to deny or repress it. "Can I keep it on while I ask you a question?"

"Fire away." He pulled her in very tight, trapping her within his arms. "Ask me anything."

It rippled out with laughter. "What are your intentions, Steven Lancaster?"

He spoke against her lips. "Devilish!" His palms were running down over her silky shoulders, her sides, his fingers playing very gently with the folds of the towel. "Surely you already know? I want you. I'll never stop wanting you. I want to marry you."

She could see so clearly how wonderful that would be. Overcome with emotion, she dropped her head, barely able to speak.

"Look at me." He cupped her chin.

Tremors were shooting through her. She could feel the heat rising from his skin. She caught his musky male scent, the evaporated rain, saw the little pearl drops that still clung to him. She leaned forwards and tongued a few off. They tasted like some powerful aphrodisiac putting her in a fever of want.

"Would you have come to me if all this hadn't happened?" he asked. "Or would you have lost your nerve?" It was a serious question demanding a truthful answer.

Her throat was suddenly crowded with words. Then they came tumbling out as though to withhold them any longer would choke her. "Never. I'm so sorry what happened that last time, Steven. I wanted you to understand so badly. I know you felt I failed you. No, don't say anything. You *did*. But I was planning all the while. You stamped your name on me. Body and soul. I swear, I was never going to let you go." Her nerves were fluttering badly. She lifted her arms to lock them around his neck. "*Please* believe me." She was frantic he would. "Nothing and no one would have stopped—"

She got no further. The flow of words was as abruptly cut off as the drumming rain.

His mouth was over hers, covering it, his tongue opening it up fully to his exploration. He kept going and going, thoroughly aroused, kissing her, staggering her with the force of his passion. The towel fell away unheeded, falling in a soft pile at their feet. She strained against him, while he grappled with her satiny naked body, her breasts crushed against his bare chest. For a long moment he held her back from him, studying her body, his glance alone ravishing her. She rose on tiptoes. She had never thought it possible to feel like this. He lifted her as though she weighed no more than a feather pillow.

Naked he put her down on his bed, leaving his strong hands on her shoulders, revelling in her expression that was wild with longing. For *him*!

"From this day forward we're bound together," he said in triumph, desiring her so much his entire body throbbed. He wanted nothing more than to bury himself deeply within her, feeling the clutch of her around him. He wanted to merge himself with her. All his wildest dreams, his hopes, his expectations, so seemingly impossible, had come true. He had made a great discovery. Meredith was the love of his life.

Blissfully, she sank back into the pillows and shut her eyes.

When she opened them again, *her man*, her lover was bending over her, staring down at her with such a world of longing in his eyes her limbs turned liquid.

She cried out his name in an ecstasy of need. "Steven, my true love, come here to me."

He obeyed, awed by the realisation he was about to take this wonderful woman in a way he hitherto had only dreamed about.

CHAPTER NINE

LIFE was always dealing out surprises. Almost overnight Jocelyn had undergone a remarkable sea change. The histrionics disappeared. Previously unable and unwilling to conceal her dismay that things were not what she had hoped for, Jocelyn now set about making the best of things. Robbie had a lot to do with it, Gina thought. There was no doubt in anyone's mind Jocelyn really loved Robbie. He was a beautiful child, his father's son, of course, natural, easy, comforting and loving with his grandmother. That was the irony of it, Gina thought. If Cal had brought only Robbie and not her back to Coronation Hill, Jocelyn would have been over the moon. As it was, Jocelyn had discovered it wasn't pleasant being the odd man out. Ewan and Meredith had accepted her. In fact, one would have thought she was the girl Ewan had in mind for his son all along.

Even Steven Lancaster—the young man Ewan McKendrick had appeared to hate so much—was now very much in the picture. Meredith had come home from the Lancaster stronghold, so happy, so radiant, so obviously very much in love, her imminent engagement to Steven was received with exclamations of congratulations and every appearance of pleasure. Even Jocelyn knew better than to risk a sarcastic comment.

"Marvellous, isn't it?" Meredith commented later to her brother. "It seems I've done something right at long last!"

Gina found Robbie in one of his favourite places, the beautiful Garden Room Jocelyn always called the Conservatory. He was sitting at a small circular table flanked by Rosa and Uncle Ed who had taken over elements of his education. A big picture book was open in front of him, his glossy, dark head bent over it. Rosa saw Gina first.

"So where are you off to, *cara*?" Her brilliant dark eyes swept over Gina. She was in riding costume, which pretty well answered the question. It really suited her, Rosa saw with pride and pleasure. Her Gina had a beautiful body. She wasn't so sure about Jocelyn McKendrick as a teacher for her beloved godchild. But it appeared Jocelyn had been a fine rider in her day and still rode, though not as frequently. She had offered to give Gina riding lessons on the quiet. It was to be a big surprise for Cal.

"Mummy, Mummy," Robbie broke in excitedly, "Uncle Ed found a book for me all about the planets. Do you know what the word *planet* means?"

Gina went to him and kissed his warm rosy cheek. "No, my darling, I don't. Please tell me."

"It means *wanderer* because the planets wander across the sky."

"Well, that's what the ancient Greeks *thought*, Robbie," Ed told him. "In fact, the planets all circle the Sun. They move in the same direction, in much the same plane and each spins on its axis as it orbits." He demonstrated with a finger and a twirling movement of his hand. "You have a very bright boy here, Gina." Ed looked up to smile at her. "He just soaks up knowledge. It's a pleasure for Rosa and me to have anything to do with his education."

Rosa reached out and covered Ed's hand with her own.

They'll probably beat Cal and me down the aisle, Gina thought as she moved off. But they'd have to be awfully quick. The wedding invitations had been sent out. It was to be a small wedding. No more than fifty people. Neither of them wanted a big affair. Each night he came to her. Lying beside her on the bed until she finally went off to sleep, her body wanting nothing more after the tumultuous passion they aroused in each other. Their sex life was glorious. It could hardly have been bettered, but their trust in each other lagged behind. The lost years, the old grievances, the needless suffering, needed time to be erased, before each had full confidence in the other. Both of them desperately required forgiveness of themselves and one another.

They had decided for Robbie's sake they wouldn't openly share a bedroom until after the wedding. Gina couldn't wait. They had talked about a honeymoon. They didn't want to leave Robbie. The love between father and son had developed at a tremendous rate. That was Cal's big problem with her, Gina thought sadly. She had deprived him of his son for three of the most precious years of life. Cal had taken that greatly to heart. She was terrified that deprival might in time be forgiven but never forgotten. What Cal required of her from now on, was her total allegiance.

She arrived at the stables complex a minute or so late. It was set amidst beautiful trees, with a training yard, almost a small track, enclosed by a high white painted picket fence facing it. Jocelyn, looking very trim and youthful, was waiting for her in the cobbled courtyard. Their horses had been saddled up by one of the stable boys—and there appeared to be quite a number. Gina's mount was a pretty liver-chestnut mare called Arrola—which meant *beautiful* in aboriginal— with a star on its forehead and four white sox.

"Just the horse for a novice like you," Jocelyn had decided briskly.

Arrola, who really did have a lovely nature, extended its velvety muzzle to be stroked. Gina made an affectionate, low clicking sound she had learned from Jocelyn that appeared to work. That first time she had prayed she would stay on. She was still praying after half a dozen lessons, but she had settled a good deal. She had to admit Jocelyn was an excellent teacher, very patient, showing no sign of disappointment or disapproval when Gina couldn't perform as expected. Gina had come to the conclusion— and she was being very hard on herself—she wasn't a natural as all the McKendricks were and Robbie would prove to be, but she was quickly gaining an acceptable level of expertise. Jocelyn wouldn't tolerate less.

Jocelyn always chose the route they would take, always away from where the men would be working. This was to be a surprise for Cal after all. The two of them always rode alongside, Jocelyn constantly offering instruction on some aspect of posture and handling of the reins. Today was a new route along a chain of billabongs densely wooded around the banks. The onset of the monsoon season had brought in a few storms but the earth beneath them was hard, giving Gina a feeling of security and solid leverage. Her leg and thigh muscles didn't ache half as much as they used to, either.

After twenty minutes or so, Jocelyn gave the order to quicken the pace. Ahead of them the giant landscape glimmered in the heat. The fragrance of wildflowers tossed up by the storms carried on the wind. In the distance, glittering through the thick screen of trees, some of them covered with scarlet flowers, were the billabongs alive with native birds and maybe the odd crocodile.

Gina, feeling a rush of excitement, lightly kicked Arrola's

flanks. She was beginning to appreciate how enormously exhilarating a gallop could be.

Riding up from the stream, Cal heard the drumbeats of hooves before he actually sighted the riders. Then as he cleared the trees a single rider burst into view, billows of dust rising as the rider's horse galloped out of control. A second rider came hot in pursuit; an expert this time. He recognised his mother's small frame.

"God!" he shouted, scarcely able to believe his eyes. Here was a tragedy waiting to happen. Galvanised, he swung into action, squeezing his big bay gelding's sides hard, urging it up the bank, then into a gallop. It couldn't be, it shouldn't be, but it was happening. That was Gina out there and she was in terrible danger. It struck him with tremendous force the devastation he would experience if she were injured. Or worse. He could see she had lost her hat, her long hair streaming on the wind. He recognised the horse. It was the little mare, Arrola, normally such a mild animal. Now it was clearly in a mad panic, galloping wildly towards the line of trees with Gina clinging desperately to its back. Her stirrups appeared to be lost. If she got flung off—and God knows how she was staying on—she would come down in a fearful mass of broken bones. If she managed to stay on, the mare would only continue its crazed gallop on to the trees. There she would have no hope. She would plough into a tree-trunk, or be hit by a large branch, her neck broken, her limbs snapped.

His heart froze. Why had he held back on telling her how much he loved her? he flayed himself. Why had he continued to blame her for not contacting him when she found herself pregnant? He had the right to know, sure, but why had he wanted to keep punishing her? Maybe she had kept a momentous event secret from him, but she must have suffered carrying their child alone. He had wasted so much time nursing his hurts, instead of trying to let them go. Even when he found out Lorinda and his mother had plotted against them, he had still kept on blaming Gina. She should have come to him. He could have put things straight. She hadn't trusted him. The grievances had gone on and on.

Now *this*?

There suddenly existed, right out of the blue, the dreadful possibility he might never get to tell her how much he loved her. How desperately he wanted her. There had not been enough talk about matters of the heart. He had laboured to hide his very real love for her and he had to bitterly regret that. She could go to her death not knowing. That was unimaginable. No way could he let it happen.

His mother's horse, Dunbar, was a splendid animal. It never stumbled. It was eating up the ground but he realised it would never overtake the little mare. The mare must have had a considerable lead, he calculated, his heart twisting in pain at the fleeting thought his mother could have been in some way responsible. Even as the thought came into his mind, he rejected it absolutely. His mother had her faults but she would never do anything to harm anyone. Even her efforts to break up his island romance didn't come under the heading of a malicious act. She and Lorinda would have truly believed, however mistakenly, they were doing the right thing.

He rode like he had never ridden before, his face blanched with fear and a boiling dread. If there was a God in Heaven, He couldn't do this to him. To have refound the woman he loved only to lose her to a violent death? How could he survive such a tragedy without undergoing some tremendous alteration in his character?

He galloped on. A lesser horseman would never have

closed in on the runaway so fast. The gelding was won-
drously surefooted in the rough. It didn't have the speed and
power of his favourite stallion, but it was responding mag-
nificently. They were coming at the runaway from an angle,
cross country, whereas his mother was pounding straight
after them. His mother, too, was in mortal danger, but still
she kept going. She would have to get Dunbar under control soon, or she, too, ran the risk of getting pulped amid
the wilderness of trees.

A final powerful surge and he was pulling the big gelding alongside. Immediately it and the little mare began to
jostle for supremacy, the tall gelding easily winning out. On
Gina's beautiful face was exhaustion and despair. "Hang
in there, Gina!" Cal shouted, finely judging the precise
moment to lunge after her reins.

Please, God, don't fail me!

The first line of trees, brilliant with flower loomed up.

His nerve held iron-hard.

Got them!

Now it was a ferocious battle to control two horses. He
reined back hard. The gelding responded, the mare just
wanted to keep on going as if it had a death wish. Superb
horseman that he was, Cal had to fight against being pulled
from the saddle. Again he yanked back. The little mare was
still putting up a mighty fight, hell-bent on hurling herself
and her rider into the trees.

He gave her a bit of head, and then pulled back as violently as he dared without bringing them all down. "Whoa,
now, easy, easy, easy…"

With the compliance of the gelding, so responsive to his
every demand, he got the mare under some sort of control.
"Easy, girl, easy!" The mare began to centre herself.

The thicket was no more than twenty-five yards away.

* * *

Gina fell into his arms, collapsing against him, burying her face against his chest. His strong arms encircled her as though he would never let her go. All his defences, all his efforts to keep his real feelings in check were swept away.

His mother rode up, her face paper-white. "My God, Cal," she gasped, chest heaving. "Only *you* could have done it. Gina could have lost her life." She spoke with the tremendous relief of a person who had seen a horror averted.

One arm still strongly around Gina, Cal went to his mother's assistance helping her dismount. There were tears coursing down her face. "My fault, my fault," she kept saying. "I'm so sorry, son. We wanted it to be a big surprise for you."

"Whatever happened?" His mother looked too distraught to really question, but he had to know at least that. Gina was in shock. She was very pale and trembling. So far she hadn't spoken a word.

"A bloody kangaroo!" His mother who rarely swore, swore with gusto. Anything to relieve her pent-up feelings. "Gina has been doing so well I thought we could try a little gallop. All would have been well, only the 'roo just popped up in front of her, spooking that silly mare. Spooked good old Dunbar, too, for that matter. He did quite a dance. If Gina had had more experience she could have reined the mare in. Instead Arrola took off as though she was going for the post in the Melbourne Cup. I didn't know she had it in her. I'm so dreadfully, dreadfully sorry. I would never have forgiven myself if anything had happened to Gina." Jocelyn looked into her son's eyes, frightened.

"I know that, Mum," he said gently.

At his response Jocelyn rallied. "Well, we'd better get her home," she said, already swinging herself back into the saddle. "A shot of brandy should do it. Some good strong black coffee. Always helped me. I'll ride ahead. Get one of

the men to bring the Jeep. Bear up, Gina, girl," she called
down to Gina in such a bracing voice Gina might just have
been blooded. "It's a miracle you managed to stay on. I can
think of any number who would have fallen off."

Jocelyn kicked her sweating horse into a gallop, determined to outrun her lapse of judgement. The girl had guts.
Damned if she didn't!

Gina remained within the half circle of Cal's arm, drag-
ging in fortifying breaths. She was very pale but he thought
it unlikely at this stage she would go into a faint.

"This is just a suggestion," he murmured quietly. "I could
take you up before me on the gelding. You would be quite
safe and we'd meet up with the Jeep quicker. If you prefer
not to, shake your head."

His tone was so gentle and comforting Gina nodded her
head. "Okay!"

"Okay what, Gina?" His expression relaxed a little.

"I'll ride with you." She turned up a face that showed a
mixture of trepidation and bravery.

"I'll never let you come to harm," he said, making no
effort to hide his depth of feeling. "Just trust me."

"I do," she whispered. She had the sense many of the
defences he had put up against her had toppled.

"I really don't deserve it." His brief laugh was ragged.

"You saved my life. Whatever would have happened to
me if you hadn't turned up?"

"Don't even think about it." Cal shuddered.

"Death by freak accident."

"Hush!" Of course, it happened. Freak accidents weren't
uncommon in station life.

"It was all for you, the riding," Gina wanted to reassure
him. "Your mother had faith in me. I let her down."

"God, no," Cal protested violently, greatly upset even
if he appeared in control. "The best station horses can be

spooked. Horses are such nervous animals and the 'roos have a bad habit of popping up out of nowhere. You'll learn how to keep a horse under control."

"Is that why you want me to get on one again!" She gave a ghost of a laugh.

"Not today if you don't want to." His arm tightened around her. It was a relief to hear her voice strengthening and see colour coming back into her cheeks.

"Then I have to tell you the only one I'd do it for is *you*!"

Back at the homestead Gina found herself being fussed over.

"You can go off now, Cal," Jocelyn said after about an hour and several cups of tea later. "Gina will be fine now. We'll look after her, won't we, Robbie, darling?"

"We'll spoil her!" Robbie stoutly maintained.

Cal stood up, looked down at Gina, reclining on the sofa. "I'll stay if you want me to." God, he'd do *anything* she wanted.

"That's okay, I know you've got lots to do. I'm fine. Really!" In fact, she had never felt so safe and sound.

"We'll look after her, Daddy." Robbie gazed up at his father. "Won't we, Nan?" Robbie had taken to calling Jocelyn Nan of his own accord. "It bothers you, doesn't it, Daddy, Mummy got such a fright?"

Cal smiled down on his very perceptive little son. "You can say that again, pal!"

"Mummy's brave all the time," Robbie announced proudly.

At that moment, Rosa, who had been taking a leisurely drive with Edward, rushed in, closely followed up by a concerned-looking Edward, their gazes falling on Gina. "What is this I hear?" Rosa asked worriedly.

Gina thought it time to move. She swung her feet determinedly to the floor. "No fuss, Rosa, dear. I'm fine."

"You look upset?" Rosa's dark eyes flashed accusingly

around the room, focusing on Jocelyn. Her baby needed protection.

"Mummy doesn't want to talk about it, Rosa, okay?" Robbie jogged over to Rosa and took her hand in his. "She got a fright when her horse bolted, but Daddy saved her from any danger. No one is as good as my daddy. He's a marvellous rider. Now we're helping Mummy get over it. Would you and Uncle Edward like a cup of tea?"

Rosa blinked and caught her breath. "Coffee, I think, sweetheart," she said. "I must admit I panicked."

Jocelyn stood up immediately, all graciousness. "I'll go organise a pot. It won't be too long before it's ready."

For the rest of the day Gina took it quietly, but by evening she was over the worst of her shock. She was alive when she could have been a serious casualty. Or dead. Everyone appeared enormously grateful. For the first time there was genuine accord around the table, Jocelyn leaning over to touch Gina's hand several times during the meal. Even Ewan put his hand on top of Gina's and gave it a little squeeze. Gina didn't realise it but everyone thought she was standing up to a very frightening incident awfully well. Meredith, who had been staying with Steven for a couple of days working out how best to refurbish Euroka's homestead, had been startled and upset by the news when she phoned in earlier in the evening.

"It must have given you a tremendous fright, Gina," she said. "And Mum, too. When I spoke to her she was trying hard not to cry. What a miracle Cal was around to save you. You'll have to make it up to him tonight, girl!" This she proffered with a smile in her voice.

The very least I can do! Gina felt a rush of affection for her soon to be sister-in-law.

* * *

The household settled around eleven o'clock and a short time later Cal tapped on her bedroom door.

He stood looking down at her, a bottle of champagne and two flutes in hand, a white linen napkin draped over his arm. "Room service, madam."

"Please come in," she said, as though he were exactly that, but her whole body was instantly a-pulse.

"Sometimes nothing else will do but champagne," he offered smoothly.

"It certainly helps." Gina turned and saw them both reflected in the mirror of the dressing table; he with his impressive height, densely, darkly, vividly masculine; she with her flowing hair and glowing skin, dressed only in a satin robe, the quintessential image of alluring woman. As an image it appeared incredibly erotic. "Do we have something to celebrate?" Her dark eyes watched him.

"You know we have. This has been quite a day." He leaned to graze her cheek. "There *is* a God," he announced.

"Of course there is." Gina moved to take up a position on the invitingly cosy chaise longue covered in a lovely pale green silk. "I've never doubted it."

"And I never will again!" Cal said, his voice filled with real gravity. He didn't think the memory of the immense blessing they had been granted that afternoon would ever leave him. Gently, he twisted the cork from the bottle, muffling the loud *pop* with the linen napkin. "I should have brought a wine cooler," he said, partially filling one flute then the other. "You do realise the silk on the couch is the same colour as your robe?"

"That's why I'm sitting here," she said, her voice silken cool. Gracefully she accepted her flute from him, deliriously close to swooning. "Sit beside me. There's plenty of room." She patted the smooth surface.

He gave her his achingly beautiful smile. "The damn thing is almost as wide as a double bed. We might try it here one night." Emerald eyes glittered as he moved slowly towards her. "To us!" His breath ended on a faint groan. "For gut-pulverising moments this afternoon I thought I was going to lose you."

They clinked glasses, their eyes locking. "You do want me around then?"

He continued to soak her in. "How can you say that?"

She pushed back the long cuffed sleeve of her robe. "You've been very…conflicted, Cal. You can't deny it. I could tell."

He smarted inside, knowing the charge was right. "Tonight is going to be different," he promised, low voiced. "You tore the heart from me, Gina. Afterwards…" He paused, shrugged a shoulder, then settled opposite her on the chaise. "Some things you can't help."

"I know. I've gained a lot of experience these past few years. It wasn't supposed to happen like it happened," she said with profound regret. "I should have done something."

"*I* should have done something." The admission continued his liberation. "Think how different it would have been." He captured her free hand, studying her pearly fingernails, inflamed to be near her. "I should have married you four years ago. I had the wisdom to fall in love with you. I lacked the wisdom to see through Lorinda. She was enormously convincing and she was family. I believed she loved me and had my best interests at heart."

"And so she did, by her lights." Gina spoke with intensity. "That's what made the deception so easy. You trusted her because she was family. I trusted her because I truly believed I wasn't good enough for you."

His hand pulled away. "Is that what she said?" he asked sharply, his face tautened into an angry mask.

Gina glanced straight head. A fresh arrangement of exquisite tropical orchids had been placed on the nearby table. "I believed it," she repeated, thinking it wasn't a good thing to store up the mistakes of the past. Life wasn't long enough to hold on to thoughts of vengeance.

"And what do you believe now?" he demanded, swiftly draining his glass, then setting it down.

She hesitated a moment. "*You* mightn't be good enough for *me*!"

He laughed aloud, charmed and amused by the little expression of hauteur. "Drink up," he ordered. "I'm going to make love to you far into the night."

"Really?" She exhaled voluptuously, unable to hide her sensual pleasure. "That will be wonderful! But I need more from you than desire, Cal McKendrick, however ravishing."

"Desire is only part of it, *Gianina*," he assured her. Those moments of terror when he had thought she could be killed, had clearly shown him his own heart. He loved her so much he wanted to go down on his knees before her.

"Then tell me about the other part," she invited, holding her empty flute for a refill.

He stood up. "You have a mind to make me wait?" He glanced back over his shoulder, seeing more of her golden flesh exposed as the robe slid off her ravishingly sexy long legs.

Gina's smile was slow. "It's more that I want these moments to last. You delight and astonish me with your lovemaking, Cal, but you have never said *I love you*."

He rejoined her on the couch, handing back her glass. "Surely that applies to us both? I've never heard it from you. At least, of recent times."

She tongued a bead of champagne around the rim of the

flute into her mouth. Delicious! "Too much confusion. Too much pain. I thought the love you once had for me—or I thought you once had for me—had disappeared."

He leaned forwards to brush his mouth over hers, tasting the delicate yet intense fruity flavours on her luscious lips. He would never, never, never find another woman like Gina. "Where could the love go?" he asked. "It was always there. All locked up inside me." He drew his head back, murmuring, "You really do look like a goddess."

His desiring gaze enveloped her in flame. "A goddess?" She laughed shakily. "Not at all. I'm just a woman."

"If you were only *just* a woman I might have found it easier to forget you." When he spoke again his voice was edged with agitation. "I never got to be with you when our son was born."

She quickly set down her glass; cradled his beloved dark head. "And how I missed you! I cried out your name, not once but many times. Everyone in that delivery room knew the first name of my child's father if they were not to know the last."

He drew back, staring into her huge velvety eyes, brilliant with the glaze of tears. "I should have been there." His voice carried a mixture of great conviction and pain.

"You'll be there next time," she whispered, afraid she was going to break down.

"I couldn't forget you, Gina." His voice cracked with strong emotion.

"No more than I could forget you." She tried to encircle him with her arms, leaning into him to kiss his mouth. "Do you believe in Destiny?"

"I do now!" Cal's hands moved to her shoulders, peeling back her robe, then he dropped to his knees in front of her, his open mouth brushing against her throat, moving down lingeringly to the fragrant slopes of her full breasts. His strong hands were drawing her in nearer and nearer. Finally he eased the robe off her naked body cradling her back with his spread hand. "You're mine and I'm yours!"

Womanlike, she teased him, shaking her tumbled head. "I want you to prove it."

He didn't answer. He only smiled, picking her up and carrying her to the huge four-poster bed where he laid her down and slowly began to practise his magic on her.

"I truly, truly love you," he softly whispered.

"I truly, truly, love you."

"And I will to my last breath."

That night they made love not only with their bodies, but to the depths of their souls.

Days later Cal announced he was going to fly a blissfully happy Gina to Broome to buy her some pearls. "My wedding present to her. We'll only be gone a day or two."

Immediately Robbie piped up. "Can I come, too, Daddy?"

Cal placed his hand gently on his son's head. "Not this time, Robert, but I'll have a big surprise for you when we get home."

Robbie caught his mother's eye. "What *is* it?" he asked in a loud stage whisper.

"A surprise is a surprise, my darling," she told him, her mind already on giving him a little brother or sister to love. "But you're going to absolutely *love* it!" she promised.

Robbie gazed back at her steadily for a moment then he cried out in an ecstasy of excitement. "It's the pony!"

"Careful now, Robbie, you'll tip over your chair." Ewan reached out to steady it, looked at the child fondly. What a great little chap he was! Of course it was the pony. Every McKendrick had his own pony by Robert's age.

"Don't worry about Robbie, you two," Jocelyn said, flashing her grandson a big conspiratorial smile. "He'll be fine with me!" She couldn't help but hope that her rival for Robbie's affections, the flamboyant Rosa, would soon move off and take the besotted Ed with her. "I adore pearls as you all know. They'll suit you beautifully, Gina, with your lovely skin. Our South Sea Pearls are recognised all over the world as the finest of all white pearls. 'The Queen of Gems', they're called."

The multi-cultural city of Broome, with a vast red desert behind it and the azure-blue Indian Ocean in front of it, was a fascinating melting pot of nationalities, Gina found. European, Chinese, Japanese, Malay, Koepanger and Aboriginal cultures were all represented. Broome had quite a history going back to its founding as a pearling port. It was the English seaman and pirate William Dampier who was credited with having discovered Western Australia's fabulous Kimberley region for which Broome was the port. That was way back in 1688, when Dampier first visited "New Holland", bringing Britain's attention to the area's rich pearl-shell beds.

Gina actually owned little jewellery outside the costume variety so the afternoon's shopping expedition was very exciting, especially when the sky seemed to be the limit. The pearls that were put on display for them took her breath away. At first she didn't know what size she should be looking at. Even strands of smallish pearls were worth thousands. The boutique assistant steered them towards another showcase.

More strands were laid out for her. They were all so beautiful she stood staring down at them not sure what she should pick. No price was being mentioned. The assistant must have taken her silence for some tiny sign of dissatisfaction because she turned away and came back with a shorter strand, a *necklet* of magnificent, large pearls.

"That's it!" Cal proclaimed immediately. "That's what we want. You should have shown us these first," he said, softening the remark with one of his smiles. "Turn around, darling, so I can put them on. We'll need earrings to match. Pendant earrings, maybe a little channel of diamonds above the pearl?"

The assistant returned the smile warmly. It was a long time since she had seen such a *gorgeous* couple. And they were so very much in love! She loved it when couples like that came in.

It was the grandest day, full of happiness and excitement, and the day wasn't over.

Gina was finishing dressing for dinner—they had taken a suite—when Cal entered the bedroom. "I have someone in the sitting room I'm sure you'll want to meet," he announced casually.

She looked up quickly. That peculiar little tingle had started up at her nape. It didn't simply touch her, either. It actually began to *tap* away. "Okay. Do I look all right?" She presented herself for his inspection. She was wearing a new silk halter dress, very sophisticated, with a plunging neckline. Too plunging?

Cal didn't look like he minded. In fact, his eyes glittered with pure desire. "Yes, yes and *yes!*" he exclaimed, bending to kiss her on her luscious mouth. "But you must come along now."

"Who is it?" Her voice had turned quavery. "Or aren't I allowed to ask?"

"Oh, it's someone you know." He gave her a reassuring smile.

The tapping grew stronger.

"Are you going to ask them to join us at dinner?" Was it a man, or a woman? she briefly speculated.

A man, the voice inside her head said.

She felt like she was travelling on some new stretch of road. Cal took her trembling hand in his, drawing her into the sitting room. "Gina, my darling, he might have been a very hard man to find but I'm sure you're happy to see him!"

Shock and triumph folded into one another. Gina stood speechless for a moment then she cried: *"Sandro!"* It was a cry that came from the depths of her heart. "*My* Sandro! Oh, Cal, will I *ever* be able to thank you? This is wonderful, wonderful!" One brilliant upwards glance at the man soon to be her husband, then Gina rushed towards her long-lost brother who stood there with tears unashamedly coursing down his sculpted cheeks.

"How could you? How could you, Sandro?" Gina beat her fists against her brother's chest. "There's not a day I haven't missed you!"

"Forgive me," he begged. "I have so missed you, but I never knew Papa was dead. You know with him alive I could never go back."

"Well, you're not going to leave us again." Gina shook a warning head. "I won't let you."

Sandro, dark and handsome, perfectly beautiful to his sister's eyes, opened his arms wide.

Cal stood back watching with satisfaction their highly emotional reunion. He felt justifiably pleased with himself. "Back in fifteen minutes," he announced, moving smoothly to the door. Brother and sister could do with some time together before they all went down to dinner.

His determination to find Gina's brother had paid off. It had taken weeks for his agents to find him, finally tracking him to Broome, of all places. Sandro had changed his name without going to a whole lot of bother. He was now

Alec Sanders, a valued employee of the largest pearling outfit in the region.

Nothing is going to part those two again, Cal thought, happy to bring Gina's Sandro into the family. Broome, after all, was on their doorstep. From now on they all were to look to the future.

EPILOGUE

The McKendrick-Romano Wedding
Zoe Caldwell
Aurora Magazine.

I DO, I do, I do!
You all know the words! But do you know just how much excitement a girl can cram into a week-end? I'll tell you, a thrill a minute. Not the end of story. There was hardly a dry eye at the fabulous McKendrick pad, a vast cattle station in the Northern Territory, after the most moving wedding ceremony held in a flower-decked folly erected in the extravagantly beautiful tropical grounds of the homestead where this lucky social editor was privileged to stay. These cattle barons sure know how to live! Bride and groom had opted for a small private affair (not the rumoured *huge* affair coming up for the McKendrick heiress, Meredith, in a couple of months' time) but all the more intimate because of that. The bride looked a goddess come down to earth in a strapless white sheath dress with gold detailing, and an exquisite gold headdress. A fortune in pearls adorned her neck and swung from her earlobes. She was attended by her matron of honour, Mrs Tanya Fielding, in a divine, strapless, yellow silk chiffon gown, and her sister-in-law, Meredith McKendrick, breathtaking in a matching strapless gown of a wonder-

ful, harmonising shade of iris-blue. Last but not least, there was the little page boy, the couple's adorable three-year-old son, Master Robert McKendrick, who behaved perfectly throughout, or all the time I had my eye on him anyway! The bridegroom was attended by best man Ross Sunderland, of North Star Station, another trillion-square-miles Territory spread, and his soon-to-be brother-in-law, Steven Lancaster, of the Queensland Channel Country's Euroka Station. Quite a turnout of the dashing cattle barons! The bride was given away by her stunningly handsome brother. The bride's mother, Lucia—boy, the stars were in attendance when they handed out *that* family's looks!—and Dutch-born stepfather, Kort Walstrum, travelled from their coffee plantation in New Guinea to join in the celebrations, confessing themselves thrilled to be there.

The McKendricks will honeymoon in Dubai, returning through Hong Kong and Bangkok. It's understood the McKendricks Senior, now their son and heir is married, will be spending a lot of time at their luxury Sydney Harbour front apartment, with frequent visits to the legendary station. A little birdie whistled in my ear we're not looking at two McKendrick weddings, but *three*! Mr Edward McKendrick, the bridegroom's uncle, is said to be planning to marry the bride's glamorous godmother, Rosa Gambaro!

So get up to the Territory, girls, if you're looking for romance. It's contagious! Hire a Lear jet if you have to! I can't remember the last time I had so much fun!

* * * * *

CLASSIC

You can find more information on upcoming Harlequin®
titles, free excerpts and more at www.Harlequin.com.

HRCNM0512

REQUEST YOUR FREE BOOKS!
2 FREE NOVELS PLUS 2 FREE GIFTS!

❧Harlequin®

Romance

From the Heart, For the Heart

YES! Please send me 2 FREE Harlequin® Romance novels and my 2 FREE gifts (gifts are worth about $10). After receiving them, if I don't wish to receive any more books, I can return the shipping statement marked "cancel." If I don't cancel, I will receive 6 brand-new novels every month and be billed just $4.09 per book in the U.S. or $4.49 per book in Canada. That's a savings of at least 14% off the cover price! It's quite a bargain! Shipping and handling is just 50¢ per book in the U.S. and 75¢ per book in Canada.* I understand that accepting the 2 free books and gifts places me under no obligation to buy anything. I can always return a shipment and cancel at any time. Even if I never buy another book, the two free books and gifts are mine to keep forever.

116/316 HDN FESE

Name _____ (PLEASE PRINT) _____

Address _____ Apt. # _____

City _____ State/Prov. _____ Zip/Postal Code _____

Signature (if under 18, a parent or guardian must sign)

Mail to the **Reader Service:**
IN U.S.A.: P.O. Box 1867, Buffalo, NY 14240-1867
IN CANADA: P.O. Box 609, Fort Erie, Ontario L2A 5X3

Not valid for current subscribers to Harlequin Romance books.

**Are you a subscriber to Harlequin Romance books and want to receive the larger-print edition?
Call 1-800-873-8635 or visit www.ReaderService.com.**

* Terms and prices subject to change without notice. Prices do not include applicable taxes. Sales tax applicable in N.Y. Canadian residents will be charged applicable taxes. Offer not valid in Quebec. This offer is limited to one order per household. All orders subject to credit approval. Credit or debit balances in a customer's account(s) may be offset by any other outstanding balance owed by or to the customer. Please allow 4 to 6 weeks for delivery. Offer available while quantities last.

Your Privacy—The Reader Service is committed to protecting your privacy. Our Privacy Policy is available online at www.ReaderService.com or upon request from the Reader Service.

We make a portion of our mailing list available to reputable third parties that offer products we believe may interest you. If you prefer that we not exchange your name with third parties, or if you wish to clarify or modify your communication preferences, please visit us at www.ReaderService.com/consumerschoice or write to us at Reader Service Preference Service, P.O. Box 9062, Buffalo, NY 14269. Include your complete name and address.

HR11B

Harlequin® Romance

A touching new duet from fan-favorite author

SUSAN MEIER

First Time
D**A**DS!

When millionaire CEO Max Montgomery spots
Kate Hunter-Montgomery—the wife he's never forgotten—
back in town with a daughter who looks just like him, he's
determined to win her back. But can this savvy business tycoon
convince Kate to trust him a second time with her heart?

Find out this June in

THE TYCOON'S SECRET DAUGHTER

And look for book 2 coming this August!

NANNY FOR THE
MILLIONAIRE'S TWINS

Saddle up with Harlequin® series books this summer
and find a cowboy for every mood!

www.Harlequin.com

HRI7811

*The legacy of the powerful
Sicilian Ferrara dynasty continues in
THE FORBIDDEN FERRARA
by* USA TODAY *bestselling author Sarah Morgan.*

Enjoy this sneak peek!

A Ferrara would never sit down at a Baracchi table for fear of being poisoned.

Fia had no idea why Santo was here. He didn't know.

He *couldn't* know.

"*Buona sera,* Fia."

A deep male voice came from the doorway, and she turned. The crazy thing was, she didn't know his voice. But she knew his eyes and they were looking at her now—two dark pools of dangerous black. They gleamed bright with intelligence and hard with ruthless purpose. They were the eyes of a man who thrived in a cutthroat business environment. A man who knew what he wanted and wasn't afraid to go after it. They were the same eyes that had glittered into hers in the darkness three years before as they'd ripped each other's clothes and slaked a fierce hunger.

He was exactly the same. Still the same "born to rule" Ferrara self-confidence; the same innate sophistication, polished until it shone bright as the paintwork of his Lamborghini.

She wanted him to go to hell and stay there.

He was her biggest mistake.

And judging from the cold, cynical glint in his eye, he considered her to be his.

"Well, this is a surprise. The Ferrara brothers don't usually step down from their ivory tower to mingle with us mortals. Checking out the competition?" She adopted her most businesslike tone, while all the time her anxiety was rising and the questions were pounding through her head.

Did he know?

Had he found out?

A faint smile touched his mouth and the movement distracted her. There was an almost deadly beauty in the sensual curve of those lips. Everything about the man was dark and sexual, as if he'd been designed for the express purpose of drawing women to their doom. If rumor were correct, he did that with appalling frequency.

Fia wasn't fooled by his apparently relaxed pose or his deceptively mild tone.

Santo Ferrara was the most dangerous man she'd ever met.

Will Santo discover Fia's secret?

Find out in THE FORBIDDEN FERRARA
by USA TODAY bestselling author Sarah Morgan,
available this June from Harlequin Presents®!

Copyright © 2012 by Sarah Morgan